29c 7/97

THE
DEATH
OF
LOVE

Also by Bartholomew Gill

Library of Congress Cataloging-in-Publication Data

Gill, Bartholomew, 1943–
    The death of love : a Peter McGarr Mystery / by Bartholomew Gill.
      p. cm.
    ISBN 0-688-08715-9
    I. Title.
    PS3563.A296D44   1992
    813'.54—dc20
                                               91-27573
                                                  CIP

Printed in the United States of America

First Edition

1 2 3 4 5 6 7 8 9 10

THE
DEATH
OF
LOVE

A Peter McGarr Mystery

BARTHOLOMEW
GILL

William Morrow and Company, Inc.
New York

THE
DEATH
OF
LOVE

PROLOGUE

Mortality: A Personal View

"YOU'RE IN GREAT form altogether, Paddy. Simply brilliant. I've never seen you looking so fit," said the last guest to leave the hotel suite.

Perhaps Power was *looking* fit, but he was not feeling at all well. His heart was racing, and he did not have to glance in the mirror to know that his brow was beaded with a cold and sickly sweat. His legs were quaking, and he was aware of a vague feeling of unease. If he did not act fast, the sensation would soon plummet from anxiety through downright dread to a scarifying, wild panic that might land him in hospital. Power began to close the door.

"Are you still taking that potion for your ticker after all these years?"

Power nodded, but he added nothing. Nobody should know the precariousness of his condition, especially now, when he was about to step back into public life. Monday week—he now promised himself—he would visit the surgery of the cardiologist in Mayfair who had recommended a pacemaker.

"It always amazed me," the guest went on, "how punctual you were about taking the stuff. Middle of a meeting, middle of the night, middle of sex, for Jesus' sake, you'd pull yourself away and, damn all, take your medicine. Remember that time we were on a toot in

7

Paris? Any excuse—the telephone, a drink of water, the cat. You were always so secretive about the thing. What is it again? Quinine?''

Were he feeling better, Power would have objected; he had never allowed the condition to intrude on his life. Power could not abide people who were always running on about their aches and pains. ''Quinidine,'' he said, pushing the door a foot closer to the jamb.

In fact, when taking a pill in the toilet only fifteen minutes earlier, he had even considered removing his supplies from the cabinet there, so no inquisitive guest could pry. In order to sell his proposal to the conference, Power would have to sell himself as well, and the fewer doubts, the better.

''You should mind what else you swallow. Apart from the quinidine, of course.''

What was that supposed to mean? Power surveyed the tall figure, who was now standing in the middle of the hall, regarding him. Then again, most people seemed tall to Power. He himself was a short, wide man with a ruddy but handsome face that was usually lit by a pleasant smile.

''Really, I must say good night.'' He was trembling, and a wave of nausea rolled up from his stomach, crested through his chest, and broke in his throat. He choked it back down. ''Tomorrow is a big day, and I'm feeling a bit peakèd.''

''I'm sure you are.''

Power did not know how to interpret that remark either, nor did he care.

''Adieu, Paddy.''

''Bonsoir.''

Power managed a thin smile and closed the door, turning the dead bolt and fitting the night latch into its brass slide. Power was afflicted with Wolff-Parkinson-White syndrome, and he had weathered attacks of paroxysmal supraventricular tachycardia before. It was not usually a medical emergency, and he knew just what to do.

Turning from the door, he reeled into the reception room. His legs felt so weak, cold, and clammy, he thought his socks were wet. At the door to the toilet he steadied himself on the jamb, but, when he let go, he pitched, like a drunk, toward the basin. He tried to break his fall with his hands on the sink, but the porcelain was slippery, and his forehead dunted the mirror, shattering the glass.

When he looked up, he saw a bright wheel of spangled yellow light with his face shattered into mirrored planes. Like a Cubist painting, he thought, and he almost paused to admire the effect, until he noticed the blood.

"Oh, Jesus. Oh, Christ!" he now said aloud, talking to himself as he often did in his native Kerry tones, which, in spite of decades passed in Dublin, London, and New York, he had not lost. "You'll need a bandage plaster for that, so you will. And more, some right excuse tomorrow. The others'll think you've gone back on the booze," which Power had once imbibed in epic proportions but had given up since the diagnosis of arrythmia five years earlier.

His heart rate, he could tell, was well over a hundred beats per minute, each stroke of which now began coinciding with something new: a sharp, stabbing pain in his chest, the left side of his neck, and his left arm. Never, *ever*, had he felt anginal pain during an attack, and Power tried not to panic. "Yip, yip, yip," he said with each prick of pain. "That smarts, you bastard. I'll tackle you with high tech Monday week, just you see."

But all that he had read about cardiac arrhythmias—every book, periodical, and paper that he could find in the British Museum—came flooding back to him, especially the gruesome, horrifying details of ventricle fibrillation, which forced a person to witness his own death.

He tugged open the medical cabinet behind the mirror. His breathing was labored now, and his head felt as if it were made of stone. It lolled on his shoulders. Blood from the wound on his forehead now began trickling into his eyes. He tried to laugh and pretend it was all just a game, a practical joke that his body was playing on him, but the blood splatted on the porcelain by his hands, and he realized he would need every last ounce of strength and will to overcome the crisis alone. Without phoning for help.

By an act of sheer determination Power reached up and carefully removed the digitoxin bottle. Once it was in hand, however, he again staggered and careened into the steam rail with its hot towels. "Yah shite, you. Not now. It can't be now, not when everything I've worked for is about to come to a head," he bellowed. "I'll settle you, I will. I'm fed up with your carry-on." His right arm shot out, buoying him momentarily on the wall, the door, and the back of a stuffed chair as he wheeled into the bedroom.

But there he fell to one knee and collapsed on the carpet. Uttering another sharp cry at the pain, at the duplicity of his body, and at the intransigence of the security lock on the bottle, he managed to twist off the cap and spill out the tiny yellow pills. He placed one on his tongue. "There now. There. That's jam," he said. And in spite of the anginal pain, which continued unabated, in spite of his shortness of breath and the soreness in every unoxygenated muscle of his weak body, Power managed to crab himself up onto the soft bed.

"Now, my good man—we never died a winter yet," he said, lying back in the pillows relieved, believing he would soon be better. With the tips of his fingers he surveyed the extent of the gash on his forehead, saying, "But don't we be the talk of Parknasilla." He'd need some excuse, some way of explaining away the bloody gash and the shattered mirror.

The tiles, that's it. He'd say he slipped on the wet tiles in the toilet; with the mirror destroyed, the hotel staff would corroborate the story. Now he stanched his bleeding forehead with a pillow and waited for the digitoxin to take effect.

His chest was still heaving, and the bed was swaying with his effort. Were he not so physically fit, Power told himself, he would most probably now be dead from a myocardial infarction. He had suffered through other, longer attacks before, when he had been away from his medicine, but never one so severe. And the pain was odd—persistent and stabbing. In twenty minutes when the potion took effect, the pain would ease, he was certain.

But it didn't. Power kept raising his wrist to read the dial on his watch, and after thirty-eight excruciating minutes, his heart, if anything, was beating faster still. Yet in spite of the exertion he was cold, freezing, chilled to the bone, and he was feeling the same awful dread that *preceded* an attack. Why now, *during* one?

Power's head swung toward the toilet, and he squinted at the medical cabinet that was open. In his panic with blood in his eyes could he have chosen wrong? No—the shapes of the bottles were purposely different, and the bottles of quinidine and digoxin were still there.

Could there have been some mistake in the preparation of the digitoxin? Power did not think so. He had been taking pills from the quinidine bottle for days, and he had also taken from the digitoxin bottle before. He tried to remember when—only last week.

"Am I dying?" Power asked aloud. "Is it poisoned I am?" Power tried to pull himself up to see the lower shelves of the medical cabinet, but he was too weak and fell back into the pillows.

The phone. No time for private suffering now. The pain in his chest was excruciating, and his heart felt as though it would burst.

Power's right hand lunged for but missed the phone, and instead blundered through the small stack of note cards that he had written since he had arrived at the hotel and had not yet added to his file. He knocked them to the floor. He tried again, but he had moved himself so close to the edge of the bed that he toppled onto the carpet.

It struck then, the fibrillation. The stop.

It hit him a like roaring hammer blow in the sternum. His entire body spasmed once, lifting him off the carpet, then twitched; and things—the room, his thoughts, the note cards by the side of his face—began to grow grainy, dim, and distant. He was dying.

Frantically he reached out for the file box of note cards that he had placed on the lower shelf of the table beside the bed. The name of the final guest, the one who had as much as sentenced him to death, was contained among them in a separate listing, an entire subsection; but the box was empty. Missing. Gone.

Power had time only to seize one of the fallen cards by his face before suddenly, miraculously, the pain ceased, and a blinding magnesium light, just as he'd once been told by a nun he'd see, filled his mind. My God, he thought, she had been right about it all along. How had she known?

Power began laughing, or at least he thought he did. It was a great, hearty, orotund, silent laugh during which he relived in an instant every sweet moment of his life. He saw himself as a baby sitting in the sun by the side of his father's farm. There—he could see them—were the stony green fields sweeping up along rock walls to the top of the mountain where the heavens lay crystalline and glorious, filled with mansions of brilliant dream clouds.

And somehow he felt in a twinkling all the care, love, and affection his family had lavished on him in that packed, dirt-floor kitchen, and the joy they had taken in his every step and, later, his great progress in the world. It had been their love and support that had allowed him to go forward, nothing else.

In such rapture Power then witnessed his own ascension, the leave-taking of his spirit from his dead body.

As if from increasing height, growing small and smaller still, he left himself there on the carpet in the bedroom of the suite in Parknasilla, in Sneem, in his native Kerry, in Ireland.

Until he saw no more.

MONDAY

"To kill a man there is required a bright, shining, and clear light."

Montaigne

CHAPTER 1

A Dawning Predicament

WHAT WAS DESCRIBED for a while as the "untimely death" of Paddy B. "Buck" Power began for Peter McGarr in the wee hours of the next morning. His infant daughter, Madeleine, either did not yet quite sleep through the night or had inherited from McGarr his penchant for early rising. Mark that *earlier* rising.

For when her plaintive cry went up from the nursery across the hall from their bedroom in Rathmines, a neighborhood of Dublin, McGarr's eyes snapped open. It was a call etched so deeply into his mind that he believed he had been listening for it the night long. Yet he quickly glanced at the bedside clock, which read 5:00 to the digit, and closed them again.

He then feigned a deep, not overly sonorous, masculine sleep, which, as everybody knows, is deeper and far less perturbable than feminine sleep, especially with a baby in the house. In such a pose he listened to his wife pull her thirty-year-old body out of bed and shuffle sleepily toward the hubbub that was now in full, wailing spate.

McGarr's concern for the noise level of his snores was an obeisance to the fact that Noreen, when fully awake, had a keen appreciation for detail. Also the—compact was not quite the word—they had made in regard to the baby's care called for equal attention to every reasonable need by *both* parents. "That includes nightly feedings, nappy changes, baths—the lot,'' she had told McGarr when announcing her pregnancy.

"This is *not* going to be your typical Irish parenting arrangement, Peter McGarr. When I think of how my mother's career practically disappeared in my wake, and how my father always seemed to be out after a horse or a painting or at some convenient wet or other . . . And your *own* mother! My God, how did she deal with *nine* children with your father a veritable wraith between the job, the pub, and the lads?''

Which was, McGarr had thought, a rather neat explanation of their essential difference: she the only child of landed Protestant gentry who concerned themselves with horses, fine art, and the conservation of principal; he the fifth son of a Catholic Guinness Brewery worker who still lived, please God, a rather full life almost exclusively in the present. True, McGarr's mother was now dead, but he knew many another woman who had borne as sizable a burden and was still totting messages back for her man. A quick study, however, McGarr had said not a word. Instead he had taken himself down to his local to savor the advantages of patrimony in either persuasion.

McGarr was chief superintendent of the Murder Squad of the Garda Siochana, the Irish police. He was also by the sworn testimony of many a hard man an even harder man himself. But listening now, as Noreen soothed and changed Madeleine, then—singing to her lightly—carried the child into their bed, made him feel shabby indeed. Truly he desired to adhere at least to the spirit of sharing, but at fifty-one and after a life of studiously practiced, if judicious, abuse, his flesh was just not up to 5:00 A.M. baby service. McGarr smoked, he drank, he ate whatever tasted good, and it was well known to his staff that it sometimes took him whole hours in the morning to gather enough bonhomie to make polite conversation, and *never* without an eye-opener.

"Over. Push, push, push it, you lummox,'' Noreen now said to him, jabbing his shoulder with a hand. "Yah can't cod me. I know you're fakin' and awake.'' Not for the first time, McGarr noted how his wife's usual Ascendant tone muted during early morning feedings and made her sound like a hake-monger in Moore Street. But ever discreet in regard to her Anglo-Irish temper, he again held his guilty tongue and rearranged himself near the edge of the bed where, ten or so minutes later, he could watch them sleeping.

There was something about the picture of his child having been nursed asleep in the arms of his wife that McGarr found endlessly appealing. Like himself, both were redheads: Noreen, an auburn-haired woman with regular, if somewhat sharp, good looks; Madeleine, a study in pink with fresh cheeks and wavy strawberry-blond hair. Still half-awake, she was twining her cherub-pudgy legs and flexing her toes, like tiny fingers, in a kind of recumbent dance that McGarr had dubbed foot language.

At such moments she seemed to him more than just another person or another life or, you know, *his* child; she was also an opportunity, the chance for Noreen and him to provide her all the good, sustaining experiences that they had enjoyed in their own childhoods and to eliminate those that they now knew had been bad.

So precarious, precious, and transient seemed the life of *his* daughter that it was as though McGarr had been tendered with her birth a list of priorities, which supervened all else, and he would warden with ferocious love. In his billfold he would carry no photos for ready viewing, nor would he tell cute stories to others who had been children themselves. But he would always carry in his heart that first fierce affection for this little person, who had now thrown both arms back on her mother's chest and was sleeping with blissful, guileless abandon.

In such a way McGarr saw in Madeleine the possibility of making the world better. For a man who for over thirty years had daily involved himself with the details of destructive behavior and violent death, such a renewal of hopeful spirit had struck him like a revelation, and in that way he had himself been reborn.

In the tiny toilet under the stairs fifteen minutes later McGarr stared at himself appraisingly in the long mirror on the back of the door. He did not like what he saw: a stocky, bald, middle-aged man with a long face, morning-murky gray eyes, and an aquiline nose that had been knocked off-center more than once and now looked a bit flattened. The want of a shave made his shadowed chins look doubled or trebled, and the sorriest truth was that his formerly well-muscled body was running to fat. He looked . . . beaten wasn't quite the term, but battered sprang immediately to mind. His throat would be the death of him yet, so it would.

Or could it be mainly his posture, he hoped. Throwing back his shoulders, he snapped up his muscles into a strong-man pose. With his body tensed like that, he looked not half-bad, and he wondered if somehow he could initiate a course of bodybuilding—weights, Nauti-luses, tensioners, and the like—someplace out-of-the-way where no-body at Dublin Castle, where he worked, would know. A bit of a tan would also help to convey a younger image. Perhaps with sunlamps and ointments and so forth he could coax some color into his pale flesh and give out the story it was from gardening.

But cautiously, gradually, discreetly over time, for McGarr was nothing if not a private man, and it would not do to have anybody in the Garda Siochana thinking he was worried about his age or fitness. McGarr was two posts from commissioner—a political appointment that before Madeleine's birth he had decided he did not want—but that he could now see himself "retiring" from to some consultancy or private security firm with the enhancement of a commissioner's pension. One could serve the public only so long without becoming jaded, which he sometimes suspected was the cause of his long periods of silence. Plainly he had seen too much.

It also occurred to him that he could cut back on what—or at least how much—he ate, drank, and smoked, but at that moment he heard the kettle piping, and he wondered if hunger alone could have prompted this dire assessment of himself. He had worked late the night before and not had his tea, and from the light aroma that still lingered in the kitchen he could tell Noreen had baked scones last evening for the morning's breakfast.

He would look into a regimen of *moderate* exercise, he decided. Some fine Saturday morning when he was out with Madeleine, he would wheel her down to the public library on Rathmines Road and investigate what they had in the way of fitness books, you know: presses, sit-ups, exercises that could be practiced over the winter in the privacy of one's cellar. He might even buy himself a set of weights to throw around down there. Noreen herself had a video that she played through the telly to help her tone up after the delivery.

In the meantime—he opened the oven—there were the scones, which would toast up nicely under the gas ring while he fetched butter from the press and the jar of gooseberry preserves an uncle had sent from the hills of Monaghan. He would sit himself down at the kitchen table and rouse his sorry heap of past-prime flesh with a caffeine-rich pot of dark-roast coffee and look out at his back garden, which was his hobby. Now, in early October, the raised beds were fuzzed with the new green of winter "wheat." All else in the way of work had been retired until early spring.

McGarr had always enjoyed the crisp days of fall, especially when they were bright, like now, and the weather was holding. He had burned anthracite in the Aga for three nights running, and its pleasant, quiet heat pervaded the kitchen. With cup in hand while waiting for the scones, he glanced over the eaves of his neighbor's house at the dawning sky.

Lit by a pale sun, it was an oval of old blue porcelain that was greening at the edges and chipped here and there with hyphens of coded cloud. He had opened the window a bit, and his nose now caught a slight sour stench from the canals, the rivers, and Dublin Bay, which were purging in the cool autumn air. Tomorrow it would storm without fail; winter was a day away.

The phone rang, startling him, and he rushed to pick it up, lest the sound wake the baby.

"Up early, McGarr?" It was Fergus Farrell, the commissioner of the Garda Siochana.

"I am that, given my present . . . er, predicament."

"That's right. How *is* Madeleine?"

Hearing some movement in the hall behind him, McGarr turned to find Noreen holding the still-sleepy child, who raised her arm to him in praetorian salute. "Just fine, presently. Quiet and, I should imagine, hungry." He pointed to the scones and mouthed "hot" to Noreen.

Passing him, she muttered, "Predicament, eh? It better be good." She meant the reason for such an early morning phone call.

But it wasn't in any way. "I hate to disturb you at such an early hour, Peter, but we've had some bad news. Paddy B. "Buck" Power has died."

McGarr's head went back. Paddy Power was an important person in Irish public life whose career had been followed closely by the Irish press. Power had advised successive Irish governments on finance, founded his own commercial bank, which prospered, and then moved on to New York, where he seemed to profit from every vicissitude in world markets. But mostly Paddy was a philanthropist.

Monthly, it seemed, Power's odd face, beaming an impish, off-center smile, had appeared in Irish publications, photographed with bigwigs at some prestigious event. To McGarr's way of thinking, he was one of the handful of Irish emigrés who, having achieved celebrity status in world circles, had become necessary bragging points for a country that, because of her checkered history and present sorry state of affairs, wished at least to be loved.

Two, maybe three, years ago, McGarr now remembered, Power had returned to Ireland, and through his Paddy Power Fund had engaged in a broad range of philanthropic activities. Rumor had it that Power was about to enter the political arena and had even been mentioned as a candidate for president, which under the Irish Constitution was a largely ceremonial but high-visibility post.

"And now you're calling me?" McGarr asked.

There was a pause before Farrell said, "Well—I'm not certain I should. It appears to have been a natural death, some sort of heart seizure. But another man is crying foul, and we wouldn't want anybody to think we're not on the job."

We, McGarr thought. As far as he was concerned, Farrell was never on the job. He was a political animal (as was now said), who spent most of his time nosing about with politicians and party hacks. And how was it that a claim of wrongful death had been phoned to him and not to the Murder Squad? According to procedure, McGarr's staff should have been called first, and he would have known of it immediately.

"Dr. Maurice J. Gladden."

"Mossie Gladden?" McGarr asked. "The politician?"

Out in the kitchen Noreen straightened up from the range and turned to him. Although a backbencher for his entire career in the Dail, Gladden had been a character and was well known to most Irish voters.

"*Former* politician, I seem to remember. He was Paddy's doctor and, you know, friend." Farrell paused, as though dwelling on the last word. "It was common knowledge Paddy had a heart condition, which Gladden himself had treated him for. But now he's claiming it was murder, and working himself up into a . . . state."

Common knowledge to whom? McGarr wondered. Certainly not to him, and he had followed "Buck" Power's brilliant career with no little interest.

"Paddy and Mossie grew up together there in Kerry. As luck would have it, Mossie answered the emergency call. Now he's ranting and raving, threatening to go to the press if the *murderer* is not apprehended immediately."

McGarr waited. They had come to the important part—what Farrell thought he could ask of him.

"I want you to go down there, Peter, and find out what you can. If Paddy *was* murdered, as Gladden claims, I want you to do your duty as you have lo these many years. If he wasn't, all the better. But, Peter"—again McGarr listened to the buzz of the phone line, while Farrell chose his words—"I've phoned you this morning because over the years you've exercised rare discretion in situations that might have become inflated.

"I don't know what your politics are, nor do I care. But given all the problems the country has now—the debt, unemployment, emigration, the lot—we don't need any more bad news. If an investigation is warranted, so be it, but I want you to proceed, at least for the moment, on the assumption that he died by the natural cause of heart failure."

McGarr looked away, his eyes suddenly wary. Farrell might be commissioner, but he was not a pathologist, who was the only expert qualified to determine the cause of Paddy Power's death. Finally there was the rhetorical *we* again, which McGarr liked least of all.

"Where did this happen?"

"Parknasilla."

"The hotel?"

"In Sneem in Kerry."

"Wasn't that where Power lived?"

"Well—born and raised. Since his divorce I don't think he maintained a house there. Or anywhere else that I know of."

McGarr blinked. He had read that Power preferred hotel living, but it was rather late in the season for Parknasilla, which was a resort that Noreen's parents frequented. McGarr could remember them saying that it closed at the end of September.

"Family was grown and gone. And you know Paddy—"

McGarr wished he had.

"Billionaire monk," Farrell concluded sourly.

He meant that Power had lived simply, preferring to devote his time and money to the less fortunate. AIDS and drug-addicted babies, the homeless, alcoholics, the crippled and blind, had benefited from Power's largess, as had hospitals, libraries, schools, colleges, and universities. Quite apart from his prestige at being a self-made man, Power had enjoyed enormous moral authority, which in Ireland could easily have turned into political clout.

"The man to see down there is Shane Frost. He was Paddy's partner in Eire Bank, and they go way back. Both were born there in Sneem and came to Dublin together. You know, years ago."

Along with Mossie Gladden, McGarr thought. Three men from one village who had gone on to become national and—in Power's case—international figures.

"Be sure to look him up first thing."

If he saw him, McGarr thought. If not, all the better. He did not need instruction from a banker on how to conduct the investigation of a death. "What was Power doing at Parknasilla at this time of year?"

"Some sort of conference, I believe."

"About what?"

"No idea."

"Who are the other guests?"

"Nor that either."

Too fast. Farrell knew, but he wasn't telling. Why?

"What about the"—McGarr rejected the word "crime"— "scene? Has it been . . . ?"

"I understand he's just as he was found. The Guards there are waiting for you. Nobody has left the hotel. Nobody else knows."

"And the press?" It would be the biggest story of the year, *especially* if Power had been murdered.

"None yet. The officer in command, one—"

McGarr heard a paper rattle.

"—Superintendent Butler of the Kenmare Barracks has secured the area and cut off communications with the outside. The point is to minimize all the . . . speculation before it can get out of hand, which is why I'm calling."

And now for *the* question: "Why you and not my office?"

"*McGarr*," Farrell said in a tone of petulant exasperation. "Let's just say a 'source,' and leave it at that. I'm just trying to prepare you for what might possibly be a major investigation. As far as we're concerned, this conversation never took place. Your office is probably trying to get on to you as we speak.

"Be sure to check in with me the moment you get there. I want to be kept informed, hour by hour if necessary."

Then why not take over the investigation yourself, McGarr was about to suggest when Farrell hung up. McGarr had no sooner placed the receiver in its yoke than the phone began ringing again. It was his office with nothing new to add.

Noreen came next.

"Ah, no—not Paddy Power?" she said, her eyes brimming with tears. She sat at the kitchen table, Madeleine in her lap. After a while she went on, "He was so special. He radiated so much . . . hope, which, Lord knows, we need now."

McGarr supposed she meant the continuing economic slump. With unemployment over 20 percent, young people—especially graduates from Ireland's several, fine universities—had to emigrate to find work. Over thirty thousand had left in the last year.

"But *murdered*?"

McGarr told her what Farrell had said, then went upstairs to dress. When he got back down to the door, she was in the sitting room with both a radio and the television on. "Nothing yet."

At least that was something.

She shook her head. "You know, Paddy Power was a crony of my father's."

McGarr stopped in the process of patting his pockets, making sure he had everything necessary for a day or two. He had also packed a small bag.

"They met years ago, way back when Paddy was in government, before Eire Bank and New York and all his success. But they kept in touch. I can remember later, when I was in university, Paddy spending a Christmas with us, and he was so *alive* and irrepressible and brilliant. He had"—she thought for a moment—"wit without malice, obviously a keen intelligence, and he loved the small, fine details that make life interesting. You know, the sort of person you could point to with pride and say, Now *he*'s Irish."

McGarr leaned against the jamb. He had no idea that her parents had been close to Power, but then, with a large town house in Fitzwilliam Square and a horse farm in the country, her parents as much as inhabited another world—one of money, privilege, and leisure.

"There was some talk of Paddy having problems with his marriage, and, of course, he had no place to stay in Dublin but some hotel. So out of the blue he just rang Daddy up, and there he was—one of the world's richest and most successful men—with us for Christmas. And with no limousine or servants or profusion of gifts. Just Paddy stepping out of a cab with a single bag and the rumpled suit he had flown in with. It was the first time I heard that odd definition of a snob"—she turned to McGarr, and he saw that her face was streaming with tears—"you know, a person who is at home everywhere, but has no home of his own.

"One night when we had some people in, he regaled us with one delightful story after another about New York and London. He was able to appropriate dialects flawlessly, and he included all the quirks and curiosities of the Americans and Brits, whom my parents' circle of friends look down upon as only partially civilized yahoos on the one hand and"—she hunched her shoulders—"uncivilizable, inhuman elitists on the other.

"It's jealousy, I know—" Noreen paused to blow her nose.

That those two peoples, whose shortcomings were reported daily in the Irish press, perpetually seemed to enjoy a disproportionate share of the world's goods and resources, McGarr concluded.

"But what good is it being Irish, if you can't make fun of the little you allow yourself to know of the rest of the world."

McGarr almost smiled; it had been his thought exactly. Noreen and he were like two halves of the same brain.

"When somebody asked Paddy where he planned to live when he 'grew up,' he said Ireland, of course—'Who else would have me?' He also said that he planned to go into 'public service,' were his words. And now this . . . *before* he even got going." Again she stanched her tears. "I wonder, is it the sort of thing a country ever gets over?"

The death of a potential leader? McGarr didn't know if the question was rhetorical or if he should try to frame an answer. Instead he glanced at his watch.

"I'm thinking of Larkin and Collins here, or King and the Kennedys in America."

It was his turn to hunch his shoulders. Hadn't America survived its assassinations? And who was saying Power's death was that, though it was what some people would think.

"Peter"—she waited until his eyes met hers—"one way or the other, there'll be a hell of a stink when this gets out. Just watch yourself, please. Farrell, O'Duffy, and that crowd are a slippery lot, and will sacrifice anybody who gets in their way."

"Speaking of money—do you have any? After the weekend, I'm out."

"Try my purse, but I think you'll have to stop at the bank. I spent my readies on the pram."

The Irish were among the most heavily taxed people in the world, and with their combined income currently taxed at 70 percent, the McGarrs were always short of cash. He found two crumpled punt notes and a handful of change, which made seven-odd quid for the pocket of a senior civil servant. Not much in case of an emergency. But at least down in Parknasilla he'd be on the government's tab and would get back some pittance of the enormity that was relieved from his pay packet every month.

There was no time for a kiss. "Toodle-oo," he said.

"Toodle-ah." Out of the corner of his eye he saw Noreen reach down and draw Maddie to her, saying, "Darlin' girl, I love you so much. I don't know what I'd do if anything ever happened to you."

Nor did McGarr. To either or both of them.

CHAPTER 2

On Casting a Cold Eye

SMALL, WIDE, AND quick, like himself, McGarr's private car was a forest-green Mini-Cooper. Now nearly thirty years old, it was a much-pampered antique that clung tenaciously to any surface but was at its best dodging through Dublin traffic and on the narrow back roads of Ireland. On straightaways, like the N-7 down which McGarr now plunged on a southwest slant to Kerry, it also cruised handily, if not comfortably; and except while jinking through major Midlands cities like Naas, Portlaoighise, Nenagh, and Limerick, McGarr kept the needle above 100 mph.

Three-and-a-half hours later, he arrived at Parknasilla, which means "Field of Willows" in Irish and enjoys the distinction of being one of the few houses in Ireland to appear on maps. McGarr had never seen the resort and was surprised when an avenue of trees, leading from stone gates to the hotel, parted suddenly and presented a dramatic view of the Kenmare River, a long, deep marine bay dotted here and there with small, uninhabited islands. Caught in shafts of brilliant afternoon sunlight, they looked wind-racked and besieged in a brimming turquoise sea. Farther still lay the dark, perilous Atlantic, brooding after some ocean storm.

McGarr drifted through a car park filled mostly with automobiles that bore the logos of Shannon Airport rental agencies. Many of the

25

Irish cars were large and pricey—Mercs, Jags, and BMWs—which caused McGarr to think of the conference that Power had been attending and of which Farrell had claimed no knowledge. Had he seen something about it in the papers? No again, which was curious.

Since Power's return to Ireland three or so years earlier, the most sensational of the Dublin newspapers had been featuring stories about the "eccentric humanitarian billionaire," was the phrase he remembered—with headlines like, POWER WATCH, when Power was photographed raising binoculars to his eyes at a race meeting. POWER SURGE showed the man striding up the rocky face of a mountain. McGarr would have thought POWER MEETING a natural, especially in a setting, like Parknasilla, that was more usual to billionaires. But then he was not—thank Saint Mark, patron saint of scribblers and other idlers—a journalist.

Stepping out of the Cooper, McGarr had to snatch at the brim of his fedora. The tempest was enough to stagger him, and the small car rocked in its blast. Overhead as out of a cannon, a flock of teal—driven on the wind—shot in a complex weave of body and wing that looked suicidal. In a flash of white, bottle green, and dove gray, the formation bolted quickly toward a wall of dense trees where the birds separated suddenly and disappeared.

Pivoting, McGarr gathered his mac around his waist and propelled himself at the main building of the resort, which was both more and less than he had expected. Doubtless because of his in-laws' stories, he had thought the three-story Victorian structure castlelike and immense; instead he found it a graceful gray stone building with large, airy windows and gabled roofs.

A porter in white tie and tails met McGarr at the door and conveyed him to the office of the manager, one Jim Feeney. "Ah, yes. We were expecting you. You've had several calls." Tall, well tailored, and youthful in appearance, Feeney handed McGarr two phone memos, both instructing him to ring up the callers immediately. One was from Farrell, the other from Farrell's boss, Minister for Justice Harney, "ASAP." When McGarr slipped both in a pocket, Feeney conducted him to the third floor where Garda Superintendent Butler was waiting.

Paddy Power's face was the color of an old bruise. The jaw was dropped open, and the eyes were bulging. Lying on his back on the carpet with his arms thrown over his head, he looked as if he had died while issuing a final commentary upon life.

His smile was ghastly, like a kind of macabre guffaw, and the split in the skin on his forehead had added blacker streaks of bloody war paint that only elaborated the impression of wild, riotous, savage laughter. A single white card was clasped in a hand like a winning tote ticket at a race meeting. It was as though Power were saying, I know something you don't. This *is* the prize. There is none other.

McGarr wrenched his eyes away. It was a smile he would not soon forget. Also on the floor on the side of the bed closest to the toilet was a brown bottle from which small yellow pills had spilled.

McGarr turned his head and looked back into the sitting room at the large, paneled door that had been removed from its hinges with such care that the night latch was still snugged in its clasp. The door itself was leaning against the molding of the jamb.

McGarr glanced at Feeney, wishing him to explain. At six-three or -four, the young manager towered over McGarr. Bending slightly at the waist, he advised in a low voice, "Nothing has been disturbed. It's a heavy door, quality construction. The night latch had been thrown, and we found it quicker and easier to slip the pins and pull the door away.

"Mr. Power had asked for a wake-up call at six this morning. He's usually . . . he *was* usually an early riser whenever he stayed with us, which was at least twice a year when he came to visit the graves of his mother and father. And, of course, today his conference was to begin."

"Conference?" McGarr asked.

"Yes, and *has* begun, might I add, according to instructions from Minister for Finance Quinn in Dublin. We've made the excuse that Mr. Power is indisposed. So far, I believe, his death is not general knowledge."

McGarr blinked. So, to Commissioner Farrell and Minister for Justice Harney he now added Minister for Finance Quinn, who had been in touch with Parknasilla. Quinn was even now giving the orders about Power's conference.

Feeney went on, "As I was saying, I arrived at the door just around seven. I too knocked insistently. Receiving no answer, I ordered the carpenter to remove the door. It was plain the poor man was already dead, but I phoned the doctor all the same. And, of course, a priest." He paused for a moment before continuing.

"Dr. Gladden speculated that Mr. Power had died some time before, most probably in the early evening, and after examining the body and . . . the premises''—Feeney's eyes moved toward the medical cabinet that could be seen through the doorway to the toilet—''he insisted I phone the Civic Guards.''

''And a damn fool thing to do,'' said a voice behind them.

The men in the room turned to find a fourth man, who was as tall as Feeney but older, standing immediately in back of them, his hands clasped behind his back. He had a long, handsome face and gray hair that was thin on top but swept to a rich cascade of silver curls. He was wearing a black vicuña overcoat and a light-gray business suit set off by a pearl-gray silk tie.

His shoes were gray as well—capped bluchers with blond laminated heels—all polished to a mirror sheen. A lubricious ruff of silk scarf, which matched the tie, traced the line of his lapels. The man needed only a black bowler and rolled umbrella to complete the archetype, thought McGarr, and a different venue. In all he seemed better suited to the confines of financial Dublin than to the chambers of a quiet hotel on the coast of Kerry.

''I'm Shane Frost.''

McGarr had expected so. He was the man Commissioner Farrell had instructed McGarr to look up. First thing. Frost had been Power's partner in Eire Bank, and whereas that institution had thrived under Power's hand, under Frost's it was now petitioning the government for assistance in meeting its obligations. Or so the papers had been saying for the last several months.

''You McGarr?''

''Sorry,'' Feeney began to say. ''I assumed you knew each other. Chief Superintendent McGarr, this is—''

But Frost spoke over the hotel manager. ''Weren't you supposed to report to me?''

McGarr surveyed the bunched furrows on Frost's forehead, the raised eyebrow, his clear blue and accusatory eyes, the muscle that was twitching on the side of his cheek. He wondered if a commanding presence, so to speak, was usual to Frost, or had some other concern—perhaps sorrow at the death of an old friend and colleague—precipitated his imperious mien. As Farrell had said, Frost was also from this part of Kerry, and had been with Power ''all the way.''

''Before you listen to this gombeen-man and his self-serving prattle,'' boomed another voice from the doorway ''would you hear me, who was Paddy's doctor and, as it turns out, only real friend?''

McGarr turned to the man who now entered the bedroom and was struck by the contrast. Like Frost, Dr. Maurice "Call Me Mossie" Gladden was a tall man, but he was wide and stooped with bandy legs that gave him a busy, shuffling gait like a boxer angling for a kill: as now in moving toward the toilet, where McGarr could see a shattered mirror on the front of a medical cabinet above the sink.

Gladden gestured with a large hand for McGarr to follow, then turned to him an oddly configured face and clear hazel eyes that seemed to see best in sidelong glance. His skin was wind-scoured and red. It only added to the impression of combativeness that Gladden had developed over his nearly three decades in public office. Nor had his clothes been selected with an eye to please.

Gladden was wearing a farmer's heavy black coat with leather patches on the shoulders and an old belt cinched about the waist. His trousers were made of some coarse green material and had been stuffed into a pair of rolled-down Wellies. In his public career Gladden had played the wide-eyed-but-crafty Kerry gorsoon, even to the extent of larding his speech with country expressions given out in a thick Kerry brogue.

But his hand, which McGarr now took, had felt like flint, and he guessed that Gladden had spent the intervening years practicing the occupation for which he was dressed. Not doctoring, though the mantle was not fully off. McGarr tried to recollect what he knew of the man.

Although returned as T.D. (tachta Dail, a member of the Irish parliament) in election after election from a constituency in the South Kerry mountains, Gladden had resigned, when Sean Dermot O'Duffy was named taosieach (leader of the majority party) for a fourth time. In a press conference he condemned O'Duffy for confounding the economic potential of the country and running the Irish people into the "workhouses of foreign interests for his own personal gain." When asked if he had proof, Gladden had said not yet, but he would get it.

From what McGarr knew about the laws of libel, O'Duffy might have brought Gladden to court. Instead he only smiled and said, "Mossie Gladden is his own self entirely. He has served this country vociferously and in one particular instance with profound charity. He remains living proof that, although sometimes misguided, we Irish are a democratic and indeed a tolerant people." Of course O'Duffy was asked when the instance had been. "His final utterance, which we can only hope was sincere. His resignation."

It was a squelch that was repeated in all the media, in pubs, trains, buses, cars, and kitchens the country over, and proved effective. Three years had now elapsed, and McGarr could not remember another mention of or from the contentious Gladden, who at one time had been the darling of the more sensational radio-talk and late-night television shows.

"Look you now at this bottle here." Gladden pointed to the brown pill bottle on the floor. "And these other ones, here in the cabinet. Tell me, d'ye know their purpose?"

McGarr glanced down at the bottle on the floor, the label of which said:

M.J.P. Frost, Chemist
Sneem, Co. Kerry

From: Dr. Maurice T. Gladden
For: Mr. Padraic B. Power
Rx: Digitoxin: 1.0 mg. Max. dose 2 tablets

The pills were sprayed, like yellow dots, over the blood-red carpet.

Carefully McGarr stepped into the toilet, trying to avoid the shattered glass. Slivers crunched under his feet. The medicine cabinet, which was open, had a larger bottle on its top shelf that was also from M.J.P. Frost, Chemist. The label said it was quinidine in 0.2 gm units to be taken T.I.D., which—McGarr remembered from a bout of flu he once had—meant three times a day.

Said Gladden, "I don't actively solicit patients anymore, I only deal with them I had and them what come to me in need. Like Paddy, when he was here. Over in London he saw a pricey Mayfair cardiologist who never spoke him a word different from mine. I was his family doctor and good friend." His hazel eyes snapped to the door where Frost was standing. "The best, as it turns out."

Gladden waited, but Frost said nothing, and he continued, "Paddy had Wolff-Parkinson-White Syndrome. It's not a disease but something Paddy inherited. A kind of short circuit in the heart. The nerve signal is too quick and arrives early in one ventricle but on time in the other. The patient shows no real symptoms, unless he notices a"—Gladden waved his large, callused hand before his chest—"fluttery feeling. It can lead to atrial fibrillation, which is not a life-threatening condition unless the other ventricle becomes involved, and here did. I'd stake my farm on it."

McGarr canted his head to signal that he wished a further explanation of the medical terms.

Said Frost from behind them, "A fibrillation is a sudden acceleration of the heart. If it beats fast enough, it can seize."

McGarr kept his eyes on Gladden, who said, "Why t'ank you, *Chairman* Frost. Or is it *Dr.* Frost? For a jumped-up banker, costume and all, you're wonderful acquainted with cardiac arrythmias."

"I was with Paddy's. He was my friend too."

"Which remains only to be disproven," Gladden said, with a knowing glance at McGarr. When sitting in the Dail, Gladden had vanquished many a skilled parliamentarian with his quick and acerbic country wit. "And tell us then, *Dr.* Frost who knows so much, what are the causes of a ventricular fibrillation?"

McGarr turned to Frost.

"Well, since you ask—they can be several. Some coronary occlusion, or an overdosage of medication."

"Like digitalis?"

Frost nodded and pointed toward the medicine cabinet. "Or quinidine. There's also procainamide, potassium chloride, barium chloride, or a combination of those substances."

"You're taking all this in, sir?" Gladden asked McGarr, who neither nodded nor blinked. There was an antagonism between the two men that was deep and pointed, and he wondered at its cause. He also asked himself what he was hearing here and from which man. An accusation, perhaps? Or a confession? McGarr too had friends with heart conditions, but in what specific way he knew not.

"And Paddy, now—which misadventure befell him?" Gladden asked Frost.

Frost's eyes, which were nearly the color of his silver hair, surveyed the shattered glass on the floor, the open medical cabinet, the dried blood in the sink, on the tiles of the floor, and the wall near the steam rail, which was bent off center as though having been fallen on. He then glanced into the bedroom at the pills on the floor. Power's corpse was across the room, concealed by the bed. "I have no idea and, which is more, nor do you."

"Think you not? We're not all *amadans* here in the Kerry you turned your back on thirty years ago and would with O'Duffy and his tribe as soon forget. How convenient is it for you to be rid of Paddy Power on the eve of the week in which he would declare himself politically and expose you for what you are?"

Frost's features had glowered. But he now sighed and, muttering something that McGarr heard as "... your own self entirely," turned on Gladden a look of encouraging amusement. "Something tells me you won't be long in telling us what that is." Frost's eyes moved to McGarr's, as if to say, You're in for an earful now.

"I won't, Chairman Frost. I won't, to be sure." Lowering a shoulder the better to fix Frost with wide-eyed and deliberate accusation, Gladden summoned himself and said, "You and your bloated sow of an Eire Bank. You and O'Duffy and your pack of slavish jackals are thieves, every last one of you. You stole the wealth of this country and its future right out from under the nose of the poor, hardworking common man, and you'll do anything, even commit murder, to keep it in your grip.

"Paddy, lying dead out there on the floor, had been part of all that. But *he* was a good man and had second thoughts. He knew how it had happened and why, and he had devised a plan to place this country on a sound and independent financial footing, and then return it to its rightful owners." With the flat of his hand Gladden smote his own breast.

Trying to suppress a smile, Frost nodded. "In whose place you have always stood. Stolidly. But go on. Work away. It matters not that I encouraged Paddy and am one of the main architects of his plan. How did *we* slavish jackals accomplish Paddy's death? But watch yourself."

As though expecting some threat, Gladden braced himself yet more.

"Mention the phrase 'running dogs' and, sure, you'll reveal yourself altogether."

Gladden's body rocked and his nostrils flared, but like a gladiator or pugilist, he rolled his broad shoulders forward, saying, "With digitalis, as you outlined so knowledgeably earlier. And don't think for a moment Paddy was hoodwinked by you, who, like your chemist father before you, wouldn't give a man the heat off your water. He'd copped on to your greed years ago, Shane Frost, and knew what you were about with your carry-on of help and aid and suggestions. He knew and he told me, so he did, but, it seems, *I* failed."

Frost waited.

"A cock-up you were planning. Some way of confounding his scheme, and how better than knowing its provisions in detail beforehand. I argued against you, but not strongly enough. He wouldn't hear me. He said, 'It doesn't matter what Shane and his wrecking crew know, this way or that. The terms of my plan are inevitable and necessary, and they'll resist them at their political peril, I'll see to that.'"

"Paddy confided to *you* the terms of his plan?" Frost now asked with humorous skepticism.

"Indeed he did, and who else? Who else in this country has my moral authority? And *consistency*, might I add, from the day I first set foot in the Dail, till the day I denounced O'Duffy and your kind to the populace."

Smiling fully now, Frost said, "I'll allow you've been that, Mossie." Frost worked the fingers of one hand, as though feeling something. "Consistent."

Again Gladden flushed. "About you yourself, do you know what Paddy said?"

"I'm certain you can't resist telling us."

"He said, 'Shane is made for their crowd. We've been friends and are still partners, but experience has taught me what he is. Just another craven corner boy. Apart from O'Duffy, there isn't a man among them. When blood is drawn, you'll see, they'll scatter, and Shane will be the first out. He'll land on his feet, and Eire Bank will survive.' "

Frost's smile had fallen somewhat, but he only shook his head.

"Good man that he was, he didn't understand that surviving isn't good enough for you anymore. Nor is the welfare and future of the country even a consideration. You, O'Duffy, those bastard Harneys, and your confederates have supped at the trough of avarice too long, and now nothing, not even the murder of your oldest friend, is beyond you."

As though speaking of an absent party or a small child, Frost said to McGarr, "Pity that Mossie stepped down from the Dail. Three years of farming haven't hurt him a bit. His purple passages are still too good to be true."

A color that *was* close to purple rose to Gladden's face. He opened his mouth and closed it, as though having to summon his control. He then turned to McGarr and in a small, tight voice that was trembling with anger said, "To regulate the arrythmia in Paddy's heart and keep him from having an attack, I had put him on a strict regimen of quinidine tablets that he took religiously three times a day: when he awoke and then at four in the afternoon and at midnight. Last night at the reception that he gave for his arriving guests, somebody, who was well acquainted with his condition, slipped in here and substituted digitoxin or some digitalis-based substance for the quinidine.

"Paddy had been tramping about the mountains. He had even called in on me, wishing to use the telephone so he could ring up the Parknasilla staff to say he'd be late. But I have none. Instead I offered him a lift back, but he declined, saying his heart had been giving him trouble and he needed more exercise to smooth it out. He always felt better after a long walk. We had tea—noncaffeine for him—and our usual talk, and he invited me round to the reception later in the afternoon. I declined, but then I got to worrying about him, and so I jumped in the car and drove down here.

"I arrived about six. The reception had begun at four, and Paddy had got back at five. Since he was an hour late in taking his pills, I should imagine he came in here straightaway and reached for the quinidine." Gladden pointed to the largest bottle on the topmost shelf. "Of course, he had his guests to look after, and he would have taken the pill and gone right back out through the bedroom to the sitting room and, you know, mixed."

And how had Gladden arrived? In his farmer's storm coat with its old belt and rolled-down Wellies? Or in some more formal, suitable costume?

"By the time I got here—like I said, six—I took one look at him and already I could see something was wrong, though he wasn't letting on. His skin was gray and flaccid, the whites of his eyes had begun to yellow. There was a bead of perspiration on his forehead, but he looked like he was cold. Chilled.

"I was worried at first that the pressure of the conference and all had gotten to him, and he was off on some sort of *shaughrawn*." Gladden's eyes rolled to McGarr. "Paddy, you see, had been a bit of a bounder and aptly named." He meant that both Paddy and Power were names of Irish whiskeys. "In his time, sure, he'd guzzled enough whiskey to corrupt his kidneys and liver, and—story was—when inee-bri-*a*-ted, he'd go up on a midge. And there he stood, tumbler in hand, chatting up the few women about the place. Gretta, of course, his . . . assistant or whatever. And then the wives who'd been brought along on the junket by some of his guests.

"But wasn't the drink in his hand Ballygowan Spring Water and his conversation listless. Paddy was usually wheedlin' and needlin' the women, and he could coax a laugh from a crumpet. But all I heard from him was a yes or a no, and him breathing through his mouth. Beset. Going through the motions. With nothing lively, like, about him. Nothing whatsoever.

" 'What happened to you at all, Paddy, my dear man?' says I to him. 'Have you knocked back your tablet?' He turned to me, and it was then I saw his eyes. 'Janie,' says I, ''tis the digitalis.' 'Is it that you've taken? By mistake maybe?' Digitalis poisoning, you know, can kill. But somebody like Paddy, it *would* kill. And *did*.

"Paddy shook his head and, speaking low so only I would hear, said, 'The usual,' by which he meant his usual maintenance dose of quinidine. 'You sure?' He nodded, his poor sick eyes imploring me not to make too much of it there in front of his guests, and he virtually staggered away from me."

McGarr could imagine the difficult Dr. Mossie Gladden being just the sort of party guest who would keep others, even a host, stirring; the invitation to Gladden had most probably been perfunctory, Power never dreaming that Gladden would actually show up.

"The conference—which, he knew, some others would try to stop or disrupt—meant so much to Paddy Power that he was willing to risk his very life for its success."

Frost's nostrils flared. His eyes jumped to the translucent panes of the bathroom window, which was now filled with dun, stormy light.

"But *I* was not put off that easily, sorrh. Not me," Gladden went on, his head rising and chest inflating with what McGarr could only assume was mock-heroic exaggeration.

Was the man entirely right? And, speaking of eyes—how had he managed to keep his own so pellucid and sparkling? Like brilliant stones polished on a winter beach, they maintained their gleaming hazel fix without blink or waver.

"I traipsed right in here, opened this medical cabinet, and examined the contents of this very same bottle "—he pointed to the largest on the topmost shelf—"to ascertain, as well as I was able without lab analysis, that it contained quinidine, which it did. And does, I'm certain.

"For it was only this early morning when I arrived and found Paddy murdered that it occurred to me the base tactic those vile wretches"—on the squeak of a rubber heel, Gladden spun around, a finger pointed at Frost—"had wreaked upon our guileless Paddy who had opened his trust, his hospitality, and even, as it turns out, his heart to them the eventide earlier.

"Before—mind you, *before*—Paddy had even gotten back here yesterday afternoon, *somebody*, knowing Paddy's medicinal needs, his schedule, and even his sensitivity to digitalis, had slipped in here to this toilet ostensibly on nature's call and with low cunning placed a bottle of pills that looked similar to but were different from this bottle of quinidine here.

"Paddy—unknowing, already late, anxious to get back to his guests—simply gulped one down. Thinking it quinidine, he returned to the reception room, only to feel a half hour later the first effects of digitalis poisoning. A quick, sharp headache and abdominal pain. An hour later, when I first saw him, his symptoms had escalated to nauseousness and a general feeling of total, systemic muscular weakness. His pupils were, as I had also noticed, contracted, and thus his vision had to have been distorted. But mainly he was feeling precordial distress in the form of a rapid and violent heartbeat.

"But thinking to himself that he'd only just taken the quinidine, he must have decided that he was feeling the onset of atrial fibrillation, and if he could just hold out until his guests departed, he had the remedy for that too in the medical cabinet. The dinner hour was fast approaching, and already some of his guests had begun to leave. In the meantime the villain"—Gladden paused—"or villains had returned to the toilet and replaced the 'doctored' bottle with the real bottle, that one there."

Said Frost, "*He* said it, not me. I wonder, Mossie, can you type? Your explanation would make a hell of a mystery."

But Gladden ignored him. "When finally the last guest had gone, Paddy threw the night latch and, summoning his last ounce of strength, staggered—I can only imagine—through the sitting room, the bedroom there, and into the toilet here, where he fell against the sink. It was wet from his guests. His hands slipped off the porcelain, and his head dashed against the mirror." Gladden pointed at the shattered glass.

"He managed, though, to snatch down the bottle, but the effort was too great for him, and he fell that way"—the callused maw of Gladden's large hand moved toward the steam rail, which was bent and spattered with blood—"but didn't go down. No. Instead he pushed himself toward the bedroom, where finally he fell." Gladden lurched around and stepped toward the door in which stood Frost, who did not move.

They were about the same height, but Gladden, because of his stoop and his odd way of peering, had to look up at Frost. "Sorry," he said, by which he meant, Excuse me.

"I wonder if you are," said Frost. "It would appear to me you're delighting in all these details and what they might mean, say, to the press. Tell me, Mossie—have you something up your sleeve?"

"Sure, the fella without guilt has an easy pillow."

"Or a sheep on the mountain," Frost supplied. It was an old country saying and the basis of what Gladden had said: The fellow without a sheep on the mountain has an easy pillow.

"But don't I have plenty of *real* sheep on my mountain, which I own without lease or favor, ridge to ridge. No bonds, no stock, no usurer's mortgage, nor no bailout subsidies from a collusive government. Now, stand out of the doorway. I'll have no gombeen-man blocking my path."

Frost's ears pulled back. He was a big man who looked as though he had kept himself fit. His hands came up, and McGarr stepped forward.

Said Gladden, "Try that caper and I'll put you on the flat of your soft back."

Butler, the superintendent from the Kenmare Barracks, had moved toward them too.

Gladden pushed past Frost, and in the bedroom went on with undiminished alacrity. "As I was saying, Superintendent, Paddy fell here and managed somehow to get the cap off the bottle and one in his mouth and little else." He pointed to the spray of small yellow pills on the carpet. "The problem is that the remedy for the tachycardia he thought he was experiencing is digitoxin, and by taking that pill he as much killed himself as the person who switched bottles on him committed murder. But, of course, they—or, rather, *he*, the murderer—knew that." Again with the exaggeration worthy of a character in an *opéra bouffe* Gladden turned and eyed Frost.

"In some torturous way, I'm sure, Paddy got himself up on the bed," the covers of which were wrinkled and still bore the imprint of Power's small, squat body. "And there our poor Paddy must have tossed and turned, lying in agony as his heart beat faster and faster still. Finally the disorganization of impulses became so complete it involved the entire heart, which *locked*"—Gladden snapped his fist up into a tight, white ball—"in a complete, quivering, mechanical paralysis.

"This, this"—he shook the fist, searching for a term—"*heart cramp* hit him with such force and produced such pain that he was literally knocked from the bed." With his odd, pigeon-toed gait the large man shambled around the bed. "And he landed here." Gladden pointed down at the black face of the corpse that was grinning up at him with a hilarity that seemed no less real and therefore appropriate to the bathetic dithyramb.

"His final, desperate act was to reach for his note cards, the ones Paddy used to jot down matters of import to him. The ones he was assembling—he told me—for a memoir, and he kept under lock and key there in that case. But there again, the murderer had taken advantage of his trusting, kindly nature and had used his hospitality foully. The case was empty, the lock—see there—had been forced and the contents stolen sometime earlier in the day or afternoon.

"Paddy had time only to snatch up one of the recent cards that bears the date of Friday, when he flew in from London." Bending at the waist, Gladden twisted his head so he could read the handwriting on the card. "Apart from Paddy's opinion of Chairman Frost, it's worthless really, just some observations about life in Kerry and Ireland. This one describes how I shoot the wild jackals that prey on my sheep. Travelogue and literary stuff. Paddy always fancied becoming a writer one day when he got the time."

Gladden straightened up. "The others"—he pointed to the other cards scattered over the carpet and the only remaining card on the nightstand—"are mostly the same. Maybe if you conducted a search of the rooms in the hotel, Inspector, you might come up with the rest of them." Gladden obviously meant Frost's room. He stepped back from the corpse and folded his hands in front of him like two tanned spades.

McGarr concluded he was finished.

CHAPTER 3

Sympathy

IT WAS A demotion of several complete ranks—chief superintendent to inspector—and revealed Gladden's opinion of McGarr's abilities or his importance in the matter.

McGarr glanced from the toilet to the bottle of pills that had been scattered on the floor, to the rumpled bed, to the ghastly corpse, and asked himself what he was seeing. Was it a death by natural cause, as Commissioner Farrell, Shane Frost, and (McGarr assumed) the O'Duffy government would have it? Or was it, as Gladden was charging, a classic locked-door murder with the difference that, even if unknowing, Power had died by his own hand, which made it more cunning still?

Certainly the postmortem would substantiate or deny Gladden's analysis, from the particles of glass in the wound on Power's forehead to the amount and type of digitalis in his blood. A complete absence of quinidine might further support Gladden's contention, but what was there to suggest that the man's death was anything more tragic than the simple misadventure of his having chosen the wrong medicine bottle?

The theft of the note cards?

Perhaps, if in fact they had been stolen. Power might have lost the key and forced the lock himself. He might have stored the cards in some other place or have decided to abandon his memoir project and destroyed them himself. Also the theft, if that, could have been an act separate from and unrelated to the would-be murder.

McGarr turned to Gladden. "You touched the bottle in the toilet?"

For the first time that McGarr had noticed, Gladden's conspicuous hazel eyes blinked.

"Did you also touch the notecase?"

Again.

"What about these cards here? Did you touch those as well?"

With wide-eyed wonderment Gladden snorted dismay. "Don't I be the shame of the South Kerry Mountains. You mean to say I might have destroyed the, like, fingerprints of whoever—"

And added his own, perhaps all too conveniently, thought McGarr.

"I had to pick the thing up and turn it over in me hands to see it was empty. Same with the bottle and the cards. I held them to the light, the better to see. Murth-er was the furthest thing from my mind until it, like, struck me. The pieces, don't you know. And the whole"—he swirled a hand—"scene. Exactly. Surely you're the man who has experienced *that*, Inspector. The bolt of recognition."

But of what? McGarr wondered. Of opportunity? And "murther"—if "murther" indeed—was by no means exact, even were the autopsy to corroborate Gladden's suspicions.

Superintendent Butler cleared his throat. "May I say something, Chief Superintendent? If that happened, if Dr. Gladden touched anything here, it did not occur while I—"

But McGarr raised a hand, quelling him. Catching sight of Jim Feeney, the Parknasilla manager, who had discreetly taken himself into the sitting room, McGarr motioned that he should join them. "Were you here when Dr. Gladden examined these objects?"

Feeney nodded.

"How is it that news of Mr. Power's death reached Leinster House before the Garda was notified? *Was* the Garda *ever* notified?" By "Leinster House" McGarr meant Taosieach O'Duffy.

Feeney turned his head to Shane Frost.

Said Frost, "Paddy had asked me to meet him at seven in the dining room for breakfast. He wanted to review our strategy for presenting his plan to the conference, step by step."

"Bullshit, mister, and you know it," Gladden interrupted. "Paddy wouldn't have discussed the details of his conference with *you*!"

Yet again Frost ignored him. "When by seven he hadn't arrived, I decided to come up here and see what was keeping him. On the stairs I could hear Mossie here"—he nodded at Gladden—"literally raving bloody murder. I decided that in the interests of the conference, the hotel, and Paddy's friends and relatives, I'd try to keep a lid on speculation."

"Will you listen to him? Shpeck-oo-*lay*-tion," Gladden said in a thick brogue. "If to anybody other than me, Paddy would have revealed his plan to Gretta, and Gretta only."

Frost sighed. "Honestly, Mossie, you have me on the wrong foot, so you do. I have an idea what you're up to here, and let me say this. Two years ago or five or fifteen, this country could afford to indulge you and your quaint, peculiar bombast. Not now. This is a serious business Paddy and I were . . . *are* engaged in, where posturing and ego count for naught. 'Tis the future that's at stake, and nowhere in it does your Twilight socialism have a place." Frost meant the Celtic Twilight, which was a late-nineteenth-and early-twentieth-century movement that advocated returning Ireland to an idealized notion of its ancient past.

To McGarr, Frost said, "Gretta was there too at breakfast. I'm sure she'll corroborate everything I've said."

"Look who's speaking for the country now," Gladden said. "And what country? Drogheda to Naas to Wicklow Town. Behold the Pale rider." Gladden pointed at Frost's silver hair and expelled a mouthful of air in a kind of sardonic laugh. The Pale had been an area around Dublin where had lived the most obdurate of early English invaders.

"And the Guards?" McGarr prompted. "Why weren't the police called?"

Frost's eyes met McGarr's with cold, clear purpose. "It could be I acted hastily to protect a whole host of things—Paddy's memory, his family, the conference, maybe even Ireland itself—but I think not. If *his* story gets out, the cry of (I hardly dare breathe the word) *assassination* might be raised, and word of that sort never heals, most especially in this country with its love of martyrs. *That's* what I was trying to avoid by phoning Leinster House first. And that only."

"I understand you've been placed on notice. I'd take it seriously, were I you. You're to keep a low profile here. The lowest." Frost turned, as though he would leave the room.

Threat number three, or was it four? O'Duffy, Quinn, Harney, Frost, and company evidently had much to lose. What could Paddy

Power have been about to propose that they viewed as such a threat? "Not so fast, Mr. Frost," McGarr said. "I have a few more questions."

Frost kept walking.

"Unless you'd prefer me to ask them at dinner or in the bar."

Frost stopped. He turned his aquiline profile to them.

Again McGarr could picture Frost stalking the monumental granite lobby of the new-scheme financial center that Eire Bank had erected in Dublin.

"I'd mind your tongue, man. Dublin will hear of this."

McGarr hoped exactly, word for word.

"The note cards. Do you know about them?"

"Is the raven acquainted with the worm?" Gladden chimed in. "Of course he is. Tip to tail."

McGarr turned to Gladden. "Thank you, Doctor. You've been most helpful. Good day." He nodded to Butler, who moved forward to escort Gladden from the room.

"More Dublin, have we? Pity, reptile that he is, O'Duffy couldn't find the backbone to call round himself. He could have wrapped our poor murdered Paddy and his stillborn conference in a serpent's caul, sealed them off from the light of a new day."

Frost turned to him. "Why—haven't you heard, Mossie? Is there no wireless in your mountain aerie? Oh, that's right you've eschewed materialism and the accoutrements of your former life, as well as given your back to your old friends and colleagues. Taoiseach O'Duffy *will* meet with the conferees Thursday. It's been all the news this morning."

"*Now* that he can be assured of its result," Gladden said through the doorway, "we'll see about that." Butler pulled him toward the sitting room.

McGarr turned to Frost. "This conference—what is it about?"

"The national debt."

McGarr waited for him to say more. "The *Irish* national debt?"

"I don't think Paddy was much interested in any other."

McGarr wondered if Frost was leading him on. He tried to imagine what about the national debt—beyond its size, which he knew was substantial—could possibly be of such moment that Paddy Power would use it as an issue from which to launch a political campaign, if Mossie Gladden could be believed. Or would warrant the continuance of a conference in spite of the death of the man who had set it up? Or, now, the visit of a taoiseach? "*What* about the national debt?"

"Everything. Its structure, its longevity, its retirement. Paddy was nothing if not a creative banker. He had a little theory about lending being like love."

McGarr waited.

"You know, people have to love you or at least love your prospects to invest in you. All the more so on the state level. In spite of Ireland's indebtedness, banks, financial consortiums, and wealthy countries still seem to love Ireland, and Paddy thought he might turn that affection to our advantage."

McGarr blinked. He knew nothing about state financing. "How will the conference continue without him?" And why?

"Tell me the debt passed away with him and I'll call it off this instant. Paddy would have wanted his work to continue, and I'll make sure it does."

"But what will you say to the"—what was the word Frost had used earlier?—"conferees?"

"That Paddy was lucky even in death, and what will happen to us all happened to him in his sleep."

Death by the natural cause of heart failure, McGarr thought. "Who are the other participants?"

"Bank chairmen, senior investment officers, executives from the World Bank, the International Monetary Fund, and significant Irish debt holders—German, French, Dutch, Belgian, Italian, Irish. Some Yanks. Some Japs."

"All assembled at the behest of Paddy Power?"

Frost nodded. "Paddy made most of them a great deal of money at one time or another. He had . . . *clout*."

"And what did he wish them to do?"

Frost shook his head. "You'll have to get that from Gretta, if she'll tell you. I wouldn't want her to think I was the source of any leaks." His slight smile bared a row of even teeth and was not pleasant.

"Gretta who?"

"Osbourne. His"—Frost also seemed to have trouble nominating her position in Power's life—"colleague."

"Did Mr. Power have any next of kin?"

"Five children. The eldest lives in Los Angeles. The others—they rather sided with the mother in Paddy's divorce. I'd say speak to Gretta about that too, but, you know, it's not as though they care much for her either."

McGarr had his notebook out now. "The son in Los Angeles—do you have his full name and address?"

"His name is Sean Dermot. The address you'll have to get yourself."

McGarr looked up. "Named after Sean Dermot O'Duffy?"

"They go way back, the taosieach and Paddy. If the truth be known, they were the best of friends."

Not according to Gladden or the press; on more than a few occasions Power had condemned O'Duffy—a man ". . . sensitive to the needs of only the rich and powerful," was the phrase, McGarr seemed to remember.

He again glanced down at the note cards, on which—it now seemed—so much depended. "What can you tell me about these?"

Frost moved toward the corpse but cautiously, his step hesitant; he turned his head slightly, as though trying to read the few on the floor. "Paddy began the cards after the first crisis with his heart. It wasn't actually a coronary, just a—how was it phrased?—an 'event.' But it was then that his condition was diagnosed, and he went on the quinidine and digitoxin and so forth. Formerly he had used the cards for sums. You know"—he glanced up at McGarr—"loan rates, hedges, options, futures, and the like. It was before computers. Paddy was a wizard with figures, which was part of why he did so well in finance.

"But, you know, he kept the key to that box on his key ring." Frost pointed to a bulge in the right pocket of Power's trousers. "Had he the key, there would be no reason for him to have damaged the lock."

McGarr stepped around Frost and bent to the corpse. He had to tug to pull the key ring from the pocket, and the stiff body with its arms thrown back rocked like a gruesome Halloween effigy.

Frost moved back.

"Can you tell me which key?" McGarr fanned them on his palm, and Frost pointed to the smallest, which would have fit the lock. McGarr did not try. Perhaps Gladden had not touched the case everywhere, although, if it was murder, it had been a clever murder indeed, and he doubted the murderer would have left prints.

"Frost, the chemist in Sneem. He's your—"

"My aged father." Yet again Frost shook his head. "Jesus, McGarr. I don't know, maybe I began wrong with you. I've threatened you, I've asked you, and now I'm *begging* you not to stir things up. Parknasilla is served by people from Sneem. Sneem is a small town in a small country in a small country filled with people who, like Mossie Gladden, have small minds and little better to do than stir things up.

We—you and me—serve them at our peril. Don't add to the burden.''
He left.

McGarr lit a cigarette. Even as chief superintendent of the Murder
Squad, his own opinion of the people of Ireland was better than banker
Frost's. If nothing else before he left Parknasilla, McGarr wished to
know in detail how Frost thought he *served* the people of Ireland, apart
from the usual capitalist rhetoric that bankers gave out to justify double-
digit interest rates. McGarr too had a mortgage, which monthly reminded him of who to the exact penny was serving whom. As far as
he was concerned, there was no love between them, either way. It was
business, strict and uncompromising.

McGarr slipped Power's key chain into his own coat pocket and
squatted down beside the corpse. Had he missed anything? The Tech
Squad would go over the details of the suite with a thoroughness that
he could not hope to emulate, but they ignored all else: correlations,
feelings, atmospheres, sympathy. McGarr noticed for the first time that
Power's hands had been burned some time in the past. The palms and
fingers were disfigured with plated scarring. Tabs of flesh had been
gathered into rough ridge lines.

Also, his knees had begun to pull in as his stomach bloated, and
in all—flat on his back with arms and legs raised and his blood-
darkened face—looked like a large, unexpected road kill, a kind of
giant, clothed badger or marmot.

So much for sympathy, which made McGarr realize how little he
was affected by dead bodies. Here was a man whose career he had
followed in the papers, whose return to Ireland and possible entry into
politics he had looked forward to with no little anticipation and hope,
and yet Power's . . . remains, as it were, represented no more to
McGarr than potential evidence.

Yes, he was saddened by Power's death. And, yes, he would be
angry if it proved to be murder. But what had mattered about Paddy
Power alive was not what McGarr was viewing on the carpet in front
of him, but rather the spirit that had resided in Paddy Power while he
still had life. And while alive, Power—a man who had spurned the
selfish possibilities of his own vast wealth—had seemed to know that
himself. It was that generosity *of the spirit* that had died with the man.

And as usual when viewing a victim now since his daughter,
Maddie's, birth, McGarr reminded himself that Paddy Power had once
been somebody's baby. Two people, themselves now most probably
dead, had once gazed down on his tiny new body with love and hope,

and had then—if McGarr knew anything about life in Kerry—sacrificed the best remaining hours of their own lives to fulfill their aspirations for him. And to good point in the instance of Power. Much of the world and an entire nation had known of and respected the man he grew to be, to say nothing of thousands, perhaps millions, whom he had aided through his philanthropic and other *pro bono* work.

And now some other, mostly less well known and less well respected, men wished to have the circumstances surrounding his untimely death ignored. To further Power's work, they claimed.

McGarr reached out and shoved the knee of Power's corpse so that it began its grotesque rocking motion again, the mouth gasping, the eyes bulging in a wild, savage smile, and the note card raised over the head. "I've got it here!" it said to McGarr. "The prize. The winnings in life. And you won't *believe* what it is."

Pity that knowledge died with him, McGarr thought. And his prospects. Who knew what Power could have meant to the country? Now.

Before leaving the room, McGarr picked up one of the small yellow pills that were scattered over the carpet and slipped it in a pocket.

CHAPTER 4

Inexhaustible, Ineffable Sources

WETTING HIS LIPS on a drink a half hour later in the hotel bar, McGarr was approached by a Tech Squad sergeant who handed him a note card. "This is the one that was clutched in Mr. Power's hand. These," he placed the others on the cocktail table by McGarr's glass, "were on the floor. Only his prints and those of one other person are on them."

Gladden's, McGarr thought. "What are you having?"

The sergeant glanced from McGarr's glass to the remarkably well-dressed crowd who were conversing volubly at the bar. "Don't feel much like celebrating myself." There was a hard glint in his eyes. "But t'anks, Chief." He walked off.

And with all the mahogany, gleaming crystal, and barmen in tuxedos behind them, the bankers and their women looked like an outtake from *Lifestyles of the Rich and Famous*. Well, rich-looking and notable outside of Ireland, McGarr decided, scanning the sixty or so names on the guest list before him. He recognized only names of Irish people whose lives were unremarkable save for their attendance at select social events, race meetings, and—he suspected—conferences such as this.

Quiet money. He thought of what Gladden had contended apart from his charge of murder: who now owned the country and how that ownership had been derived. Paddy Power had been privy to all of that. He had profited and made "a great deal of money" (Frost's words) for others. Recently, however, he had had second thoughts, again according to Gladden.

On the table McGarr spread Power's note cards, which he arranged according to date and time. They seemed like a kind of log of Power's observations from the time he had arrived in Shannon Airport on Friday morning until he returned to Parknasilla after his walk on Sunday evening. Each was written in a neat, if crabbed, hand, the characters of which placed Paddy Power as an Irishman as surely as if he were speaking to McGarr. It was the peculiar system that was still taught only in secondary schools of the Republic of Ireland.

Each card was also dated and marked with the time in the upper-left corner. There was another heading in the upper-right corner that looked like a filing entry. With a pen McGarr marked the lower-right corner of the card that had been taken from Power's dead hand, but he began with the earliest entry:

> *Friday, 11:00 AM.*   *Kerry*
> *Well—this is it, the first step in my attempt to right the major wrong of my youth when, like the rest of them, I succumbed to raw greed. My public amend, it will be, which might take me the rest of my life.*

McGarr touched the glass to his lips and let the peat-smoky liquor seep under his tongue; little had Power known.

> *Here I sit in the back of a large car, passing through ragged, diesel-dusty towns that cower on the flanks of inhospitable, glorious mountains. The equally unforgiving beauty of the sea lies to my right, with an occasional habitation picketing, like a white stone bunker, the narrow chartreuse strand.*
> *Buses packed with garish tourists and other holidaymakers in rental cars sweep by most often without pause. When they do stop and get out, they look stunned or amazed to see how we live—offering in cramped, dingy rooms stale sweets, soft fruit, days-old bread and impedimenta of our ancient culture that has all but vanished.*
> *Like alms, they pay whatever we charge, which is al-*

ways too much, and they leave feeling—knowing—they've been cheated but wishing to come back. They have seen something, but they know not what.

It is what invites but will not submit to description in simple words—the cold, wild beauty of Ireland and the miracle of how we can continue to endure her barren caress. And why, when she can be made to change.

Friday, 1:30 P.M.   *Sneem*
Apart from a proud farmer's cottage, the only structures that invite a second glance are the relics of the age of villeinage that is now looked back on with bitter nostalgia, especially by those of my Irish colleagues who have donned the princely political mantle with its means of making money.

Of the Irish I've got only Gretta solidly with me. Some others I will sway, but my main hope is with the foreigners, who hold 60 percent of the debt.

Friday: 1:15 P.M.   Parknasilla: debt conference
Gretta is on the sun deck, waiting for me. What do you say about a person with whom you've shared a great passion, which has withered and died, but who remains staunchly by your side to fight the good fight with no mention of our former condition? Reward her amply? I've done that and doubly, since she'll outlive me. I only hope it is enough.

I've not been in the best form lately, and she's arranged for Mossie to come by for a checkup tomorrow morning. I trust it's only the same old thing. And not enough real rest. I want to hit the ground running. Sean Dermot and his henchman have already arrayed themselves against me, and I must catch them off-guard, lest they make a "Mossie" of me as well.

Friday, 2:15 P.M.   Parknasilla: debt conference
Shane Frost has arrived, and I am dismayed by his duplicity. Here he has the chance to act selflessly for once and aid the nation, admittedly at some immediate cost to himself. Instead he is shameless in carrying messages from Sean Dermot: a "final" plea, O'Duffy calls it, to bury my proposal and my candidacy. "They're offering you the presi-

dency. *They'll back you a thousand percent.* Guaranteed,''
says Shane. ''*What more could any man want? Prestige,
influence, respect on top of your fortune.''* What I want is
better *for Ireland, which requires* real *(as opposed to the
illusion of) power. The presidency is merely a ceremonial
post. But I've already told him that.*

*Shane can be a grand fellow, but he's just not up to his
destiny. Taking me into the bar, which he sees far too much
of these days, says he, ''It's important now to know where
O'Duffy stands.'' Says I to myself, '''Tis more important to
know who stands with him.'' Then he's up suddenly to make
a phone call. ''Options,'' says he. Put or call, think I.*

    Saturday, 7:00 A.M. *Parknasilla: debt conference*
*Still not feeling tip-top, in spite of the medicine Mossie
gave me. The flutters again. Walked into Sneem and had a
bit of a morning session with the local lads in Sneem House.
Lemon soda for me. When I got back I had to lie down for
a wee nap—until dinner! The sedatives Mossie gave me are
potent.*

    Sunday morning   Parknasilla: debt conference
*Arrivals better than expected so far. Many Yanks whose
view of Ireland's future is not as sanguine as O'Duffy's.
Spent the noon hour ''schmoozing,'' as they say—with them
and the Krauts. They are so much alike, the Americans and
Germans, that sometimes I believe they are separated from
each other by language alone. Both brash, materialistic,
aggressive, gregarious people.*

    *Tried to borrow Gretta's car to drive up into the moun-
tains and walk it off. She gave me the keys, but I could not
find it in the car park.*

McGarr glanced at the bar where now he could hear only English
being spoken, and he tried to pick out nationalities but could not.
Usually shoes and eyeglasses were tip-offs, but these people all seemed
to patronize the same set of conservative clothiers from Savile Row.
As far as their accents were concerned, apart from the obvious Texan,
the rest seemed to have been born and bred on the Queen Elizabeth or
the Concorde, then schooled by Berlitz.

Palpitations again and serious. I'll have to make apologies to Shane. He wanted me to meet with a group of Jap bankers to discuss the possibility of the Eire Bank matter, which he so much wants and I oppose, at least until we know more of how I will fare as a candidate. Eire Bank is at least a power base of sorts, and it was my first venture and is therefore most loved. Perhaps I could make it strong again.

I will take that hike I promised myself. Gretta's car is back. I can see it from my window here.

Sunday, 1:30 P.M.   Parknasilla: debt conference
Have paused on the pinnacle of Mullaghanattin, which is spectacular in its desolated beauty. From here I can see Kenmare to the southeast and Dingle Bay to the north. Below me I can also see Mossie Gladden's stony mountain farm, snugged into a lee ledge of the topographical curiosity that is called "The Pocket."

The pocket is a sudden, nearly circular declivity in the mountains that is watered by the two cascading sources of the Blackwater River. It is protected by a moat of sheer cliff that one can breach from above only if he knows the way; and Mossie's fastness sits there like a forlorn mountain island. In all, Mossie's property is testament to the ability of man to eke out a living from even the most barren pitch.

Mossie, of course, has his doctoring and his government pension, but if I had the time and inclination, I could count the white specks in the green between the rock formations that are his sheep. He must have several hundred head. Near the house he keeps two small fields in potatoes.

Card 2 of that entry went on.

I can see a figure, obviously Mossie, walking from the Land Rover that has just pulled in over the rough road he has cut to his perch. It'll take me an hour to get down there, and I hope he doesn't leave on some other message before I arrive. I could use some tea and and a bit of a rest. His chat, however, is something else.

Mossie contends that the country as a whole is a wasteland as definitive as that which I now see before me. We're

*cut off, he says, from the succor of our religions, which are
not relevant to the modern experience, and from the means
of bettering our daily lives by a government which serves
only itself. With this last I agree.*

*His approach, however, is to withdraw here and try to
reestablish touch with the ancient modes of who we were as
a people and who we can be. With the "Living Waters," he
calls it, pointing to the clefts in the rocks from which the
Blackwater springs, "of inexhaustible, ineffable Source."*

*All well and good, after the likes of O'Duffy are tackled
and brought to ground. With that Mossie concurs, but when
I told him about my plan for the national debt he flew into a
rage and asked me why I don't just go after O'Duffy with my
knowledge of what went on during the years that I served
in his governments. He's fixated on the man and doesn't
understand that politics of confrontation always boomerang.
What goes around, comes around. Better to propose doable
alternatives and remain aloof from naming-calling. I sometimes worry he's gone round the bend.*

The penultimate card, the one with McGarr's penned mark in the
corner, read simply:

Sunday, 3:30   Parknasilla: debt conference:
*Have stopped again to catch my breath before descend-
ing the narrow path through the cliff face. From time to time
the sharp report of Mossie's high-powered rifle comes to me
and then howls through the mountains. Target practice, he's
told me, for the dogs that summer people leave when returning to the city. Jackals, he calls them. The wily and
strong have survived to reproduce, preying on Mossie's
sheep. For a time he took to trapping the dogs, but with no
takers even for the pups of such animals, the local dog
warden only had to put them down.*
Now he uses the rifle.

The final card said:

Sunday, 4:30   Parknasilla: debt conference:
*Tom, the head porter, tells me Big Nell stopped by. Not
knowing where I was, he directed her to my room and let her*

in. What in the name of God can that troublesome, avaricious woman want with me after all we've been through? I hope she isn't up to staging another of her rows. Not here, not now when I'm about to step into the political arena.

McGarr glanced up. He needed another drink, and he now caught sight of Shane Frost, standing tall among a clutch of bankers at the bar.

"Still with us, McGarr?" Frost asked, assessing him from his eminence as he would, say, a servant.

McGarr only nodded. "Might I have a word." When they stepped away from the group, he handed Frost the final note card. "Who's Big Nell?"

Frost looked down. "Paddy's wife, of course. Or, rather, his ex-wife. They're divorced, you know."

McGarr remembered having read a report of it but years ago. "London, wasn't it?"

Frost nodded.

Divorce was still illegal in Ireland, and very much a political liability that only a Paddy Power, who had done so much good for others, might overcome. But then, of course, there was the Catholic Church, which O'Duffy had been courting for decades and was very much in his corner. McGarr could imagine an aggrieved, divorced wife, conspicuously on the scene, making a debacle of Power's "first step" into politics.

"Helen?" McGarr asked.

Frost nodded.

"Helen Power?"

Frost shook his head. "I'm not sure if she resumed her maiden name."

"Which was?"

"Nash. They were an old family in these parts."

"Does she live around here still?"

"I don't know. I'm not sure. I don't see much of her anymore. The parents' place was left to an older brother in England who sold the property. The house went to ruin and was knocked down."

"Could she be staying in the area now?"

The possibility seemed to worry Frost. "I don't think so. At least I hope not. Apart from the conference, the hotel is closed. The season over. You'll have to check. Nell is . . . contentious, and the thing with Gretta and then the divorce seemed to set her off. I'm not certain she's over it yet."

"What *thing* with Gretta?"

"Ah"—Frost looked away—"she blames Gretta for breaking up their marriage, but, you know, Paddy didn't marry Gretta. "What happens if you decide to investigate Paddy's death?" After tomorrow, he meant.

McGarr shook his head, not wanting to speculate.

"Promise me you won't flood this place with Guards."

McGarr turned and walked away. He tried never to make promises, especially to somebody like Frost, who seemed concerned only with appearances.

In the sun room Jim Feeney, the hotel manager, assured McGarr that Nell Power née Nash was not staying at Parknasilla.

"Why would your head porter have conducted her to Mr. Power's room?"

"Did he?"

McGarr nodded.

"Well, being from Sneem, Mrs. Power is known to all the staff. And then she's been coming here for years. *With* Mr. Power."

Tom, the head porter, was a short, square man who was nattily attired in tuxedo and tails.

"Did you see Mrs. Power depart?"

"I did, sir."

"And when was that?"

"Just about the time that Mr. Power's guests began assembling in his rooms for the reception yesterday afternoon. I believe she spoke to Miss Gretta Osbourne, a guest here, who was helping Mr. Power with the conference. After that, she left."

"Did she have anything in her hands?" The note cards, McGarr was thinking; given the size of the case, their bulk would have been too great for a purse.

He paused, trying to remember. "I can't say for certain, now, but had she anything sizable, like, I would have taken it from her and carried it to her car. So, I'd say she hadn't."

"Did you realize they were divorced when you let her into Mr. Power's room?"

"I'd heard that, but not from herself. Or himself, for that matter."

McGarr again asked to use the phone. When he finally located Superintendent Butler at home, he asked him to canvass the area for one Helen Power. "She might also be using the name Nash."

"The wife."

So, she was known to him too. Ringing off, McGarr drew on a

cigarette and eased his back into the cushions of the manager's desk chair. What did he have?

Until the postmortem report, which would not be available until tomorrow morning, nothing but Gladden's allegation and the missing note cards. Even if they had been stolen, what would that prove or even imply? Certainly not murder, which was McGarr's only concern.

Still, it irked him, the strategy Farrell had employed by means of his early morning phone calls: to bind him tight in the shackles of administrative guilt. If Paddy Power had not been murdered but Dr. Mossie Gladden insisted he had and rumor got out, McGarr would be guilty of a lapse in "discretion." If Paddy Power had been murdered, McGarr would be guiltier still, doubtless in equal measure with the murderer, of the failure to conclude—as had Farrell and Frost, who were expert in the matters of mortality—that Power had died a natural death.

McGarr tried to think of a way to keep Gladden from broadcasting his theory. As part of the investigation he could ask Gladden to "help the police," was the phrase, and hold him incommunicado for forty-eight hours. But that might only extend a claim of official complicity to the Garda itself. And as Taosieach O'Duffy himself had said and Frost had reiterated only minutes before, Gladden was his own self entirely. Gladden would do what Gladden would do, and there was no stopping him.

The most McGarr could do was to cover his arse and maintain a studious neutrality. What would he need? Witnesses who were sure to be friendly, if his own actions were ever questioned.

Again reaching for the phone, he seemed to remember that Ruth Bresnahan, a new inspector on his staff, hailed from Sneem and would at least know of most of the major figures in the case—Power, Gladden, Frost, and their families. He would place her among the guests where she could nose about and ask questions, perhaps even stir things up. He would need to equip her with, say, a large new rental car and some attractive, pricey clothes paid for out of the squad's "extraordinary expenses fund."

McKeon and O'Shaughnessy, the squad's two most experienced hands, he would place as delegates from two Irish banks where he had contacts. And finally he would put Detective Sergeant Hughie Ward in the bar.

He spoke to each of them in turn, requesting their confidentiality. "Have you phoned home?" Ward asked, when McGarr had finished.

"Not yet."

"You should—your wife has been on to us twice that I've answered."

"Has Madeleine et yet?" McGarr asked, when Noreen picked up.

"Of course she's et. A half hour ago. How's it going? Is it what they called you in for?"

"Care to dine out?" It was a cheap ploy; any invitation that included the word "out" was now irresistible to Noreen.

"Where?"

"Here, of course. Parknasilla."

There was only the slightest pause. Any *normal* person would have challenged him on the fact that the hotel was at least a five-hour hard drive from Dublin. This was a time, however, to try a recently parturated, young professional mother's soul, McGarr suspicioned, and Madeleine slept like a rock in their second car. It was a large, comfortable Rover that had been handed down by Noreen's well-off parents, who changed cars every few years.

"You haven't answered my question."

"And I won't."

She understood what that meant: It was a long-distance call that might well be monitored by an operator, and they discussed McGarr's work only in private.

"Well, when I arrive, how will I get *my* dinner?"

McGarr smiled, having led her to the magic phrase. "Room service."

There was another pause in which he guessed she was imagining all the delightfully restful ramifications of hotel living. "And you'll be up when I arrive?"

"Count on it."

"How long will we be there?"

"This week until Sunday."

"But how will we pay? Parknasilla costs a bloody bomb."

"It's official."

Noreen made a sound in the back of her throat that McGarr interpreted as delight.

TUESDAY

"The relations between sovereign borrowers and their creditors is like that of partners in a threelegged race; they can run, limp, or fall together, but they cannot part company."
World Debt Tables, 1983–84

CHAPTER 5

Scald / Squelch / Scorch

NOREEN MCGARR AWOKE with a start Tuesday morning. Blinding her was a burst of golden light made all the brighter by starched linen drape liners, in the gauzy mesh of which the new sun now caught. It was scouring a storm-washed sky. She blinked, trying to clear her vision, but the dazzling, shimmering film punished her eyes, and she turned her head to the wall.

Panic struck. Where was she? More—where was her *baby*?

She snapped her head to the other side and saw another large, but empty, unmade bed, a tasteful early-nineteenth-century chiffonier reproduction, and a stuffed oval-back love seat on a royal-blue carpet. Raising a hand to her eyes, she again tried to look out the two windows, which seemed to fill the wall of the room that had eighteen-foot ceilings.

There she saw sparkling green islands in a running jade sea. Closer was the corner of a terrace with white cast-iron furniture and a white iron rail. To one side was a boxwood maze patterning a lawn that swept down to a beach where the water was just the turquoise color of her eyes.

Parknasilla.

Noreen fell back into the pillows. Her hand reached out and lifted the receiver from the telephone. When a voice came on, she ordered

59

scones and butter. "And scalded coffee with scalded milk. I don't know if you still do that, but there was a time—" A small voice on the other end assured her that she could have her wish. "And I wonder, have you seen my husband. I'm Noreen—"

"Oh, yes. I can see him presently. He's with the other babies in the sun room, reading the papers."

Noreen stifled a laugh and thanked the woman.

"You're welcome, Miss Frenche."

The woman began phrasing her correction, but Noreen said there was no need. After all those years—how many? Five, seven? No, longer. It had been *nine full years* since she had last been here, and somebody on the staff had remembered that she—or perhaps rather *all* of the Frenches—ordered scalded coffee with scalded milk. She would have to tell her mother and father. It was the sort of thing they appreciated, and provided the illusion that, in spite of being a tiny minority in an often exasperating country, they still belonged to the *right* things, some of which endured.

And yet, ringing off, she felt glum. Here she was in one of Ireland's premier resorts, which her parents had visited for whole weeks at a time but she herself could afford only on a government freebie. Barring some windfall, Maddie would never get to know the little bridges and lovely shadowed walks through the groves of island willows, the small, hilly, difficult golf course, the great green bay that she could now see in front of the hotel.

Times had changed, and whereas she and McGarr enjoyed a combined income that on paper would have classed them as wealthy—no, *rich*—twenty or thirty years ago, they in reality had been caught in a kind of financial vise. Taxes on everything—income, property, gasoline, the V.A.T.—just seemed to go up and up, while inflation made what little money they had to spend worth less and less. At the same time property values had plummeted in the nine years since they had bought their house, which meant that they had lost money on their only real investment.

Well, maybe somebody or something would bail the country out, she thought, but in the meantime she would enjoy the place while she was here. Noreen was about to palm a pillow over her eyes, when she heard some rustling and looked out through the sitting room to see a large buff envelope being eased under the door. On it was an official seal and stamp, and her languor was immediately dispelled. Paddy Power had died, her husband had been called in, and the envelope might tell her why.

A thin, quick woman, she hopped from the bed and was soon back under the covers with the seal broken, the envelope open, and what proved to be Power's autopsy in her hands. Tears came to her eyes, which she had to blot with the sheet, before she read, "Padraic Benedict Power, Age 58, Final Diagnosis." A summation on the title page said Power had died of a ventricular fibrillation brought on by acute digitalis poisoning. It then listed the effects of the fibrillation on his heart and body, along with signs of aging that were also discovered during the postmortem: a hernia, some arteriosclerosis of the coronary arteries, scarring in his kidneys, liver, and pancreas.

He had a gash on his forehead and bruises on other parts of his body, evidently the result of a fall. There was evidence of burn scarring from some prior accident on both hands. The digitalis in his system was ". . . far in excess of what might be expected from the administration of the maximum dose of two 1 mg. tablets, as prescribed as a remedy for an attack of tachycardia," the report concluded.

Digitalis poisoning—was it unusual? Why else would her husband have been called in?

Noreen was now wide awake. The details of McGarr's investigations were a kind of leitmotiv in her life: a constantly unfolding, complex subplot, the installments of which she wheedled from him over breakfast in the morning, over drinks before dinner, and sometimes, when she couldn't sleep and had nothing good to read, late at night. A native Dubliner, she could not resist the least bit of information concerning anybody she even vaguely knew, much less an investigation surrounding the death of a person of Paddy Power's caliber and . . . potential. Again tears rose to her eyes.

But when the news got out, she now realized, Parknasilla would be besieged by journalists. When she had arrived last night, she had found only a team of Gardai at the gates. She wondered how long Power's death could be kept a secret. Or his *murder*. My God, what a story, and there she was in the thick of it. She almost wished she were back in Dublin where she could make "insider's capital" of what she knew.

Noreen tossed back the covers to swing her legs out of bed when the phone rang.

Said McGarr, "We're having breakfast in the dining room in ten minutes. Maddie, me, and Ruth Bresnahan."

"But I've just ordered coffee."

"You don't drink coffee."

"I do here."

"I'll have it brought to the table instead."

"Ah, Peter. We've just got here, and I'm shattered from the drive and all. I thought we might have a simple breakfast, just you, me, and Maddie."

There was a pause, and McGarr said, "So—the postmortem arrived."

"It did, sure, but I'd just like to be brought up to speed on the matter."

"So you will. Over breakfast. Unless, of course, you prefer to sit this dance out."

Hanging up the phone, Noreen heard a noise and turned her head to see another envelope—small and white—being fitted under the door. The official Garda seal did not deter her. It was from Superintendent Butler of the Kenmare Barracks, saying that Nell Power was presently registered at the Waterville Lake Hotel, another resort that was only twenty-five or thirty miles away.

Noreen showered and dressed quickly, and soon found herself on the carpeted stairs where she tripped past Detective Sergeant Hughie Ward without recognizing him.

Little wonder, Ward thought, glancing at himself in a mirror. He looked like a character out of Dickens, he decided. A reverse Copperfield who had been snatched from the comfort of his familiar urban surroundings and thrust headlong into rural domestic service.

A former international boxer in the seventy-kilo weight class, Ward was a small, dark, handsome man who took pains with his appearance. Thrice weekly he toned up his well-muscled body by jogging, bag work, and sparring at Dublin's newest sports facility, and every month without question his largest personal expense was on clothes. Ward was nothing if not dapper. Undercover here, literally, in a servant's swallowtail tuxedo that was a size too large, he looked bereft and juvenile.

Stopping his work of washing glasses for a fifth time to scan the hall, Ward at last caught sight of Bresnahan, who was standing at the reception desk, speaking with the manager of the hotel, who was yet another large person.

Christ, he thought—making sure Sonnie, the tall beverage manager, was nowhere in attendance—his situation had changed from Dickens to Swift—that is, bad to worse. He was surrounded by a hotel of Brobdingnagians, and his only hope was that its womankind would treat his Gulliver as immodestly.

It was a sleazy, macho, sexist thought, but Ward, who had long ago learned how sexually expedient it could be to sublimate the macho elements of his personality, was not feeling very good about himself today. And Bresnahan looked smashing—there was no other word for her—in a new outfit, the brilliant colors of which made a point of her stature and angularity.

A tall, shapely young woman with stormy gray eyes and waves of bright red hair, Bresnahan was today wearing a speckled—was it cashmere?—three-piece suit with white arabesques flowing across the front of a tight crewneck top. The graceful designs were repeated on a midthigh-length cardigan jacket. This last had blousey sleeves and on most women would have required padding in the shoulders, which were cut wide. The color was cobalt blue, as were her shoes, the silk scarf around her neck, and her knitted cashmere gloves, which suggested that she had just come in from outside.

Her long, shapely legs, set in ballet's first position as she conversed with the manager, were attracting the darted stares of passing men. Wrapped in longitudinally ribbed bright orange hose that was the same color as her hair and, in fact, a nearby tangerine banquette, they made her look like a stunning ornament of the sumptuous lobby. In all, she was a match for the tall, coolly striking models who graced the pages of slick women's fashion magazines that Ward considered more tantalizing by far that the graphic nude glossies some of his friends perused. All this Ward's eyes took in at a glance.

And to think, he thought, that of all the rich and powerful men presently resident in Parknasilla—heads of international banks and lending institutions, finance ministers of various countries, from what Sonnie had told him—only poor he (amateur pugilist, detective sergeant, barman) knew her intimately. It was an even sleazier thought, but Ward believed he had never desired Bresnahan more, and his mind flooded with the potential for quick, secret, occupationally illicit sex that the hotel might afford.

Bresnahan would be given a room, or so he assumed; and he, inconspicuous servant that he was, had access to *all* parts. After all, in spite of her recent cosmopolitan pretensions, she was merely a farm girl from one of the hills he could now see outside the windows. And in Ward's precociously bountiful experience with farm girls, he had noted a singular approach to the male of the species. They treated men like cattle, namely, the Bull; often Ward had found such a stance availing.

But another disturbing thought struck him as well. *Where* had she gotten that suit, and *how much* had she spent? Ward knew the price of clothes, and, if her suit was woven of cashmere, as it appeared, she had either happened upon the buy of the decade or—his ears pulled back—she had been given the brilliant blue suit as a present by another admirer. It had to have cost the sort of packet that no detective inspector in her right mind could splash out.

Seeing her now approach him down the long, carpeted hall, Ward moved to the shadows of an alcove. "Psst—Rut'ie," he whispered, as she powered her orange legs and cobalt-blue heels past him. "Rut'ie—here. C'mere a minute."

Bresnahan looked both ways before joining him. She smiled. "What do we have here, an apprentice barman? Should I be speaking to you? May I congratulate you on your humility, if not your appearance. I must get a camera."

Ward waved a hand to mean he was unfazed and it was all in a day's work. "God, you look brilliant this morning. Really. Where did you get that dress?" He reached out and touched her elbows.

It *was* cashmere, but she only smiled at him. She was not telling.

"Turn around now, so I can appreciate you in all your exquisite totality." Ward was a great man for compliments, which cost nothing, and his hand lingered on the significant curve of her hip. They had been "dating" now for nearly a year. Discreetly. Apart from eye contact, they had made no acknowledgment of their liaison while at work, lest one of them be transferred to some other squad. "Grand, really. Glorious. To be sure, you're the best-looking woman on the ground floor of Parknasilla—foyer section, bar part." His hand slipped farther. "Look—do y'have your room yet?"

She nodded.

"What's the number?"

"Why?"

Ward's head moved back dramatically, and he regarded her with quizzical dismay. "Well, you know, I thought—"

Bresnahan's smile muted. It became brittle, pouting her cheeks and making her eyes seem overbright. Ward's hopes plummeted. He had seen that smile before; it was the smile that said no.

"You thought wrong, and I think you know it. Not only are we on duty, we're on my turf now, and I'll not have a word said of me that isn't already in circulation."

Ward opened his mouth to object, but she placed a finger on his lips. "Listen to me now while I tell you, and don't take offense." She waited until he looked at her, and he fell into the limpid pools of her slate-gray eyes in which he would have—and sometimes feared he already had—happily died.

Ward was put in mind of a deer startled in a field. The impression was of abundant and even *animal* good health. One perfect nostril, arced like a cashew, flared as she drew in a large chestful of charged, serious air.

"You might think you know about country places like this, but you don't. A city fella like you *couldn't* without having lived here yourself, and maybe not even then.

"Parknasilla, this hotel, is in Sneem, and Sneem is my village. There's not a person who works in this hotel, including Sonnie, your boss, who doesn't know every public detail about my family, high points and low, within memory." She pointed down the hall where they now saw the head barman standing, hands on hips, his head turning this way and that, looking for Ward.

"There're good points and bad to that, but I can't let anybody cop on or even sense the drift of you and me, who are not married, you see. You *do* see, don't you?"

Ward thought he did, but he was not about to let on.

"As it is, my parents are over the moon because of the account they think I've made of myself in Dublin. You and I know it's nothing, but they look at me, see a detective inspector in the Murder Squad, and they can hardly believe their eyes. To them and everybody else they can tell, I'm pure gold. It's helped them get over my decision that I won't be returning one day to take over the farm they've worked to build into the best single holding in the district. As you know, I'm their only child."

She paused for a moment, as though considering the enormity of her mistake. "Above all else they would have preferred I married some young country buck with his own property, and popped out a brawny brood to work the acres and add still more in their time. It's the farmer's dream of immortality, don't you know."

Ward did not and he *would* not. Profoundly citified, Ward scarcely credited the possibility of meaningful life beyond the Pale of Dublin.

"You?" She looked down the five feet eight-and-a-half inches of Ward fondly. "You'll just have to grow on them, I'm afraid."

At thirty, how realistic was that, he wanted to say, if only to deflate the serious finality of her message. Sex wasn't serious, it was fun. Well, fun if it happened, serious if it did not.

"And since we're both here in Sneem, now's as good a time as any, I suppose. For them to take their first bite."

Which was Swift enough for any close reader, Ward thought. "But the place here. Parknasilla. The hotel. It's *immense*. Floors and floors with dark hallways, all carpeted. Who's to know?"

She shook her head. "In spite of what you might think about Kerrymen and culchies, thick they are not. They'll take one glance at you and one at me, and if there's so much as a long look or a lingering touch, we're chat that will nestle—count on it—in my father's ear. And you"—again she regarded Ward—"you don't want that."

"So!" another voice boomed. "Here you are." It was Sonnie, who had treacherously misused the potential for stealth that Ward had assayed in the carpeted hall. "Come with me. I'd like a word with you." And to Bresnahan, "Has he been bothering you, miss?" It was only then that he recognized her. "Why—Ruth Honora Ann Bresnahan, is it you?"

Apart from her name, Ward heard only a kind of warble that ended in ". . . ooo?"

"'Tis, and who else would I be, I wonder? How're yah, Sonnie?" She held out her hand, which the tall man, who was only a bit taller than she, took. A full smile had transformed his features, and he looked her up and down. "It's just that you look *different*."

"And I will, to be sure, if I don't run." She turned her head toward the ladies' room.

"And lovely. Lovely! God, how you've grown. Are you staying with us now?" He meant in the hotel.

Bresnahan nodded.

"Wait till I tell your father, won't he be proud. Tell me now"—without having released her hand, Sonnie stepped closer to her and in a near whisper asked—"is it official business that brings you here?"

She moved her head from side to side. "Yes and no." Apart from McGarr himself, Bresnahan was the only other squad staffer instructed so to admit.

"You mean Paddy Power? Could it be . . . ?" Sonnie continued, encouragingly.

"Ah, nothing of the sort. A mere formality, really, the government being overcautious, as you can understand. But, if it provides me with a bit of a buswoman's holiday, well—who's to complain? I've been here under other circumstances, don't you know." She meant as scullery maid, a job she had taken happily during a summer holiday from school.

"I do, but—Janie—the *difference*!"

"Which reminds me. I've got to run." Bresnahan broke away from him and moved toward the open door of the passageway in which they were standing.

"And *you*." Sonnie turned and looked down on Ward. "I'll say this once and once only. Somehow, through one of your Dublin connections, I don't doubt, you were jumped over many a good local lad who would have *worked* this job gladly. And gurrier or no, you *will*, or you won't work here long. *That*'s a promise." He waited until Ward nodded.

"First rule—you're here to serve patrons, not socialize with them. Second—never leave the bar without permission. Now, get in there. You've got the glasses and the stocking to do. The keg of Guinness needs changing as well."

Ward paused.

"You *do* know how to change a keg, don't you?"

Ward did not have a clue. "Years ago," he lied.

"Doubtless time out of mind."

CHAPTER 6

On Full Faith, Credit, and Giving the Other Side

MCGARR EXPLAINED TO Noreen that he did not want to be encumbered by wife and child, that the Power case was not just another investigation, and that she could best serve him by remaining in the hotel and keeping her eyes and ears open. "Also there's the press conference at eleven when Shane Frost will announce Paddy Power's death. Surely that'll be more interesting than interviewing a dead man's ex-wife. The press are out at the gate now, fighting to get in."

"That settles it. I'm coming with you," said Noreen, who usually wanted to be in the center of things. And the reason? "I'm tired of being confined." Which McGarr thought the better of questioning.

At the gates they discovered a cordon of Gardai who were holding back what seemed like a motorized brigade of cars and media vans. McGarr pulled the brim of his hat over his eyes and waited until a path was cleared before he ran the gauntlet, then sped toward the village.

Overnight a keen edge had been added to the wind, and a rime of frost had hoared the fields. Yet the day was brilliant, and Sneem sparkled in a thin, fresh sun. Each house on the two main squares had been painted a different, bright color, and immense tour buses were parked across from woolen and "traditional" Irish goods shops, which seemed to be doing banner business.

"We should stop and get Maddie a little knitted jumper and knitted tam," Noreen suggested.

McGarr only eyed her in the rearview mirror.

"Well, later maybe. On the way back."

Beyond the village, blue plumes of peat smoke were rising from the chimneys of farmhouses. Like neat cubes, the buildings were spaced out at generous intervals along the flanks of a vast sweep of gray-green mountain to the northwest. "Smoke," he said to Maddie, who had insisted on sitting beside him and was locked into her crash seat to his left. He pointed to an azure billow that was passing across the road from a nearby farmhouse. "Smoke," he repeated.

With her own pointed finger she followed his hand, then lowered it to the cigarette he was holding. " 'Moke."

"Very good, Miss Maddie. *Very* good," he said, and she squealed her delight in his praise. "Now, where's the smoke?" Again she pointed out the window and then to the cigarette, and McGarr repeated his acclaim.

From the backseat, Noreen said, "You know—she never does any of that for me. Sometimes I feel—" But she held off. McGarr knew the plaint, having heard it now and then since Maddie was born. "Sometimes I feel like Maddie doesn't even *like* me," Noreen had once told him. "She takes me for granted. But you she responds to. For you she's always got a big, sunny smile or a laugh or a warble. Her mannerisms and gestures are *yours*, for Jesus' sake, not mine, and she even *looks* like you."

McGarr certainly hoped not.

Another time Noreen had come up with, "I guess I expected too much from you two. You're both working-class Turks, hard as nails, like your people before you." When McGarr had attempted to sound her out, she had added, "I just want somebody who likes, wants, me, needs me for myself. But if that's all you have to give, well—I guess I've got no choice but to live with it."

Or with you two Turks.

On the most extreme occasion McGarr had arrived home one evening to find Maddie playing with her nanny, and Noreen out in the back garden pacing, her eyes flashing up at the house. "I know it's my hormones," she had said in a tight, wild voice. "But that doesn't keep you from being a heartless, miserable, selfish son of bitch and the ruination of my life. Body *and* soul!"

It happened to some women after giving birth and when nursing, a doctor friend had told McGarr, and was only somewhat less disturbing than what did *not* seem to happen anymore: *ess, eee, ex*. The McGarrs had not had a satisfying "session," as it were, for longer than McGarr cared to remember. "Who's counting?" Noreen had said. "Counting makes everything rather petty, wouldn't you say? Or would you prefer charity or duty? For me there has to be a certain . . . magic."

Rather less petty than no count at all. Or, to speak of magic, "ledger nodame," though McGarr had wisely kept the smart, working-class-Turk remark to himself.

At Rathfield the road began its winding, switchback climb over rugged, towering mountains. It was narrow and bounded on the cliff side by a low rock wall that bore the impress of tour-bus bumpers or was gapped here and there the width of a car.

"Do you suppose . . . ?" Noreen asked him.

He did not. The wall had simply fallen in on itself, although plunging out into the ether in such a picturesque spot would be a way to go better than some that he knew of.

Twice at step-asides they pulled in, "So Maddie can appreciate the singular beauty of her country," Noreen enthused. But it was she who got out to stand with hands on hips, eyes narrowed in smile, and the waves of her auburn hair snapping in the cold, sea-tangy blast.

There below them lay miles of wall-ribbed chartreuse fields that more than a millennium of toil had won from the rough mountains; today they were being menaced by the wild Atlantic. The surge from the storm of the night before was pounding the cliffs and beaches, sending up clouds of spray that fringed the green fields with rainbow lace.

Farther still were Scariff and Deenish Islands—two dots of grass-tufted rock that appeared to be foundering in the giddy, foam-silvery sea. Every so often gannets, plying the wrack, flashed like far-off bits of mirror. Geysers of spray from a rocky hazard in Waterville Harbor, which they reached ten minutes later, seemed to be carrying hundreds of yards over the chop, and tourists had gathered along the seawall to watch its plume.

McGarr wondered how it would be to live out here—on the edge of the continent, in the middle of the ocean, on the lee shore of the Gulf Stream—surrounded by the ever-unfolding high drama of nature? Great for the soul, he imagined, watching the tourists. Seemingly lost in their thoughts, they now began returning to the bus.

Having *seen something*—McGarr remembered from Paddy Power's note cards—*but they know not what.*

It is what invites but will not submit to description in simple words—the cold, wild beauty of Ireland . . . and the miracle of how we can continue to endure her barren caress. And why, when she can be made to change.

How, McGarr wanted to know.

The Waterville Lake Hotel is modern and Promethean. With views out over Lough Currane in one direction and Ballinskelligs Bay in the other, its setting is enviable.

At the desk in its spacious lobby McGarr inquired after Helen N. Power.

"Has Nell returned from her round of golf?" one young woman asked another without looking up from the papers she was sorting through.

"Just. I'm only after seeing her coming in."

"Room four-eleven."

There McGarr knocked, and without so much as a "Who is it?" the door was opened.

In it stood a short, older woman with wide shoulders that were marked out by the sheen of a stylish golfing jacket. The collar was raised. Thin-hipped, she was wearing slacks of the same tan material and athletic shoes that were new and white.

Her hair, which was dark and wavy, had been cut short, and a deep tan made her look younger than her fifty-five or so years. With smooth, regular features and a definite chin, she was still what McGarr thought of as fetching. Her eyes were two black buttons that regarded him, then glanced at Noreen and Maddie.

McGarr had reached for his identification case, but before he could introduce himself, Nell Power asked Noreen, "Don't I know you? You're—"

"Noreen Frenche."

"Of course. Fitzhugh and Nuala's girl. You're married to—" Her eyes then returned to McGarr, who now raised his laminated picture I.D. into the light.

"Peter McGarr. I'm with the—"

"Yes, quite. I know who you are. Don't stand out there all day now. Come in, come in." She glanced up the hall before closing the door, and McGarr let his eyes sweep the sitting room of what looked like a three-room suite.

The furniture had been moved back against two walls to make room for a portable putting green made of some green synthetic material. Beside it was a practice tee wired to a small electronic machine that, McGarr assumed, informed the golfer about the precision of his or *her* shot. There were golf balls, golf clubs, golf bags, and golf shoes stored neatly against the furniture in one corner. In another was a stack of magazines, the top cover of which showed a woman spraying sand and the white dot of a golf ball from a trap. Grim determination creased her face.

McGarr turned his head to the wide modern windows that ran the length of the room. There a long table was covered with photocopies of note cards in handwriting no different from those he had found with Paddy Power's corpse.

Said Power's ex-wife, moving into the room after them, "Please pardon the shambles. I'm in training, don't you know."

Noreen turned to her, awaiting a further explanation, while McGarr stepped closer to the table.

"I'm thinking of entering the senior women's tour. You know, the one for old cows over in the States. At one time I regularly shot men's par, and I was thinking that if I could again here, I'd give it a go. As you probably know, the Waterville course is the most challenging in Ireland. And probably the best.

"So, tell me about your parents. How are they keeping? And who is this little one in your arms with the face of her mother and the eyes of her father?"

Whose own were now scanning the neat, crabbed hand of Paddy Power. Photocopies of his note cards had been arranged according to subject heading. There was a grouping for Shane Frost, another for Gretta Osbourne, yet another for Eire Bank. O'Duffy, and "The Debt," were some other arrangements. In the shadows beneath the table was a large, plasticized courtesy sack printed with the name of "M.J.P. Frost, Chemist, Sneem."

McGarr picked up the pile that was titled "O'Duffy" and fanned through the sheets. There were six cards arranged neatly and photographed on each page. Subheadings said "Political Roots," "Political Debts," "Economic Policy," "Favors Owed," "Election Financing," "I, Bagman," "Dirty Tricks." McGarr replaced the grouping.

Noreen introduced Maddie, and while Nell Power was making a fuss over her, he stepped into one of the other two rooms, which turned out to be a newly made-up bedroom. A rather complete wardrobe for a mere golfing outing hung in the closets, and the storage areas of the toilet suggested that Nell Power had been there for a while. There were many and different types of cosmetics, placed on all the shelves and not just the lower ones that would be handiest for a person of her height. The only medicine he could find was aspirin.

The women were still talking when McGarr stepped back into the sitting room. Passing to the other side of the table, he entered the third and final room of the suite.

It was a kind of study that contained a writing desk positioned before another floor-to-ceiling swath of glass, and several comfortable reading chairs. On the desk was an addressed envelope and a partially written letter to a daughter in Washington, D.C. It described in detail Nell's attempts to ''groove'' her swing and how she had to remind herself constantly to keep her hands loose. With the golf club in them, McGarr supposed. The daughter was evidently arranging the Stateside aspects of the woman's attempt to get onto the senior women's golf tour, and much of the letter was devoted to that.

Paddy Power was mentioned only once.

> *Your father is presently in Parknasilla. I don't know if he has told you or not, but he's out to save the world, or at least the Irish part of it. And not simply by enriching every wastrel, layabout, and tinker with that giveaway Fund of his. He's planning to run for office, and he has his cap set for no less an office than taosieach. His thinking, I've been told, is that no party will be able to resist taking him in. Given his popularity, he well may be right. Worse still, he has a drastic, harebrained scheme to restructure the Irish debt at our expense. It includes a* write-down. *Everybody from Sean O'Duffy to Shane is against it, but you know your father. That blessed perfectionist woman, whose idea it probably is, is behind him all the way. They've been working on nothing else for the past six months, and they just might get it done, says Shane.*

Gretta Osbourne, McGarr supposed, was the ''blessed perfectionist woman.''

In an open briefcase beside the desk McGarr found two of three quarterly reports of Eire Bank for the present year, and the full annual reports for each year since its inception some fourteen years earlier.

He opened the report for the last fiscal year to learn that "Eire Bank is a privately held fiduciary trust with some eleven owners of record to date." None was named. He could not tell—and understood that it would probably take somebody skilled at financial reporting to know—if Eire Bank had made a profit in that year, though some £15 million had been claimed.

If Eire Bank was private, why the elaborate annual report with full-color pictures of the new banking complex in Dublin? His eye caught on a sentence in Chairman Shane Frost's opening statement: "Eire Bank continues to enjoy the full faith, credit, and support of the government of the Republic of Ireland."

In the most recent quarterly report Frost also said, "Given the current international banking environment, Eire Bank has informed the government of its willingness to explore the possibility of extranational merger and/or acquisition."

He closed the report, replaced the several documents in the briefcase, and stepped out into the sitting room.

Nell Power waited until her conversation with Noreen had drawn to a close before she turned to McGarr and in the same pleasant voice, asked, "Well, sir, now that you've gone through my belongings, may I ask the purpose of your visit? Or is it just habit, after all your time with the Guards?"

Flourishing his hand, McGarr offered it to the woman. "Now that's what I like—a compliant woman with a sense of humor. I must confess to the latter. Noreen here will tell you, I'm a born snoop, and wasn't I wondering just what a soon-to-be professional athlete—and woman at that—would choose to have about her person while training."

Nell Power had a small hand but a firm grip.

McGarr avoided looking directly at Noreen, whose practiced, in-company smile had been replaced by a look of acute social pain. From the easy manner in which Nell Power had greeted them, she was obviously good company. Of greater concern to Noreen was the fact that Nell Power, as the former wife of Paddy Power, was an acceptable person, both here and back in Dublin among Noreen's parents' set, who included—by their own estimation—the best people in the country.

What bothered her most, however, was McGarr's deceit. It would later be told by Nell Power that McGarr had waited until he had extracted the last bit of information before breaking the news of her ex-husband's death.

"May I ask you something?"

She swung her head to one side and smiled. "Why not?"

"Where'd you get these?" McGarr pointed to the photocopies of the note cards on the table.

Her head moved to the other side. She had opened the golfing jacket, and the reason for the appellation "Big Nell" was now apparent. Her jumper was made of some sheer material beneath, and McGarr could see the lacy array of some substantial support. "So, is that what this is all about? Curious—I thought you were homicides, or are you another one of Paddy's 'friends'?"

McGarr only waited.

Holding Maddie in her arms, Noreen shifted from foot to foot. Her green eyes wheeled toward the door. It was one thing to dissect the fine points of an enquiry over tea, quite another experience gathering facts firsthand.

Nell Power moved toward the table, her thin-hipped stride lithe for a woman of her age. "Those are my erstwhile husband's notes on his life. He's assembling them for a memoir, so. It's common practice among great and near-great men, I believe. Do you think you'll ever be bitten yourself, Peter?"

"You're helping him with the work?"

She paused, as if playing the sentence over in her mind, then smiled again, liking the thought. "I guess you could say that. Yes, or at least I've *tried* to help him."

Again McGarr waited.

"Listen," said Noreen, "I think I'll—"

But Nell Power began speaking again. "What I mean is, I've taken the time and summoned the . . . strength to read them all. I then tried to reach Paddy to give him my opinion, contrary as it is. But he was out when I called round."

By "called" she meant "visited." "At Parknasilla?"

She turned and smiled at him, her dark eyes glittering with evident anger. "The very place."

"When?"

"Sunday afternoon."

"He was expecting you?"

She laughed once. "Not likely. His debt conference was about to begin, and I met his chargé d'affaires on the stairs. D'you know *her*, Peter?"

"Gretta Osbourne."

"So, you do. We had words, as usual, and I thought it best to depart. Life's too short for that, and, when he knows that I'm now privy to these immortal thoughts''—her hand swept the table—''he'll be by.''

"Did you tell Gretta Osbourne you had them? Copies of the note cards.''

"What's this all about?''

"Ah, Nell—'' Noreen began to say, but McGarr, stuffing one hand at the floor, stopped her.

"Well?'' Nell Power demanded, now seeming to sense that some purpose larger than the note cards had propelled the McGarrs at her door.

"You first. The note cards. Gretta Osbourne. Did you tell her you had copies of them?''

"I didn't have to. Wasn't it she herself sent them to me?''

"Do you know that?''

"No—but who else could it have been?''

"When were they delivered?''

"That morning. Sunday morning. There was a knock on the door, and a porter was holding that sack''—she leaned back and pointed to the ''M.J.P. Frost, Chemist'' sack in the shadows beneath the table—''filled with the photocopies. I read my own first, or, rather, Paddy's poor opinion of me, his children, and the life we'd passed together for nearly fifty years, counting our childhood in Sneem. I then set off to see him, to give him the other side, don't you know. It's like''—she regarded the stacks of note cards and shook her head— ''two people, one life, but reading those cards, you'd think he'd spent it with somebody else.''

"How do you know Gretta Osbourne sent them?''

"I just *know*,'' she snapped. "Who else could it have been? Who else has access to Paddy but her? Or the spite.''

"Did the porter mention her name?''

"No, but I know.''

McGarr waited, and when she offered nothing more, he asked, "Eire Bank. You're a shareholder?''

She nodded. ''Isn't it about time you told me what you're about here?''

"*Yes*, Peter,'' Noreen echoed.

"Because of your divorce.''

Nell Power nodded.

"You *are* divorced?''

Again. "'Tis a wonderful lot of questions over some photocopies of some note cards?"

"Who else are shareholders in Eire Bank?"

Nell Power only regarded him.

"You, your former husband, Shane Frost," he prompted. "Gretta Osbourne?"

Still she said nothing.

"The Irish government—how much aid have they given Eire Bank?"

"What happened to Paddy?" she asked.

McGarr drew in a breath and let it out slowly. "He's dead."

Nothing about her changed: not her stance, her facial expression, not even a blink. "When?"

"Sunday evening."

"His heart?" she asked.

"Did you know about his condition?"

"Wasn't I his wife for thirty-plus years? How is it you're telling me of it now and like this?

"Who knew you were here?" *With* the bulk of the note cards, McGarr thought.

"My daughters, my sons."

"We've been trying to get in touch with your son Sean Dermot in Palo Alto. Perhaps you can do that for us now." McGarr reached for the plastic sack. "What had you planned for the note cards?" He looked around for another container to hold the cards.

As though lost in her thoughts, it took some time for Nell Power to reply. "I don't know. I had thought of destroying the lot."

"Looks like years of work." Seeing an empty waste bin, McGarr reached for it.

"Malevolence, I'd call it." There was a pause, and then: "Pity a life should come to that."

McGarr began placing the stacks as neatly as he could in the bin.

"Hold on—I'll get you another plastic sack. I have a bunch of them." Nell Power had nearly reached the study doorway when she stopped. "Why . . . *you* and not—" A priest, she meant. "Was Paddy murdered?"

"Commissioner Farrell asked me to look into the matter. Tell me about the medicines Paddy was taking for his heart," he went on, drawing the groupings together and trying to arrange the subject headings in some rough alphabetical order.

"I have no idea. Shortly after he began taking them, he left me, saying he didn't have much life left, and he wasn't going to waste it 'for the sake of the children.' No mention of me or us, which he *said* he didn't remember. Apart from my bad opinion of him."

Again she began turning away before she asked, "Will you read them?"

"Yes."

"Then I want you to remember one thing and one thing only. Anytime I asserted myself, Paddy felt threatened. He got me to quit golf. He got me to quit my little business. He got me to quit this, that, and the other thing until he had me all to himself, body and soul, which is when *he* quit *me*."

When she returned with a small valise, she asked, "Where is he now?"

McGarr explained that a postmortem had been performed and named the hospital.

"So, it *was* murder."

He snapped his eyes up to hers. "And if it was, whom would you suspect?"

"Gretta. The Osbourne woman, of course."

"Why?"

"Because he used and spurned her, like he used and spurned me. The difference being that at least we were married, which is what she had wanted and didn't get."

"He would have had a will?" McGarr asked.

"Certainly. In matters financial, Paddy was most careful. With his own money."

McGarr recalled what he had seen in the desk in the study and her letter describing how Power's debt conference would cost Nell Power and her children money. "You mean he owned no part of Eire Bank."

She shook her head. "I didn't say that. As far as I know, he was still the largest shareholder by one percentage share. The children and I got nineteen percent in settlement of the divorce."

"And Shane Frost told you your husband was now proposing that Eire Bank 'write down' its share of the Irish debt? What exactly does that mean?"

"*Some* of its share. It means forgive, forget, expunge. Twenty percent, to be exact."

"Which means in pounds?"

She shook her head. "I have it somewhere, but not a *small* fortune by any means. Millions and millions of pounds."

"Can Eire Bank absorb such a loss?"

"Paddy can or . . . could, and what did he care about us?"

"Where will you be for the next several days?"

"Here."

McGarr waited.

"It's close to Sneem, where, I assume, Paddy's children will want him buried. And, you know, he taught me once before—*my* life will go on."

The porter, who had been working Sunday morning, said he had gotten the plastic sack bulging with photocopies from the front desk, along with the order to take it to room 411.

The desk clerk said it had been delivered by "A kind of country gorsoon. I fully expected him to have an ass rail of turf waiting for him outside."

"Small, tall, young, old?"

"Tall. Quite tall. And, er"—the young woman's eyes flitted over McGarr's bald head and then lighted on Noreen, who was about her age—"middle-aged, I'd say. A rough-looking fellow and hardly a word on him. He handed me a note, asking that the sack be taken to Nell."

"Do you have it still—the note?"

"I'm afraid not. That was two days ago, and our trash gets compacted daily."

"By middle-aged, you mean my age or her age?" He nodded his head toward Noreen.

"I beg your pardon—" Noreen began to say.

"More yours, sir." The desk attendant lowered her eyes to McGarr's photo I.D., which he had placed on the counter.

"Dark, red, gray, fair?"

"Fair and gray, what I could see of him for his hat. A shabby thing and wet, since it had been raining. Hanging before his eyes. A greatcoat."

"What color?"

"Black, of course."

"Leather shoulder patches? An old belt cinching the middle?"

A finger darted at McGarr's chest. "Precisely."

McGarr glanced at the clock and guessed he had time to phone

Parknasilla before the press conference at which Shane Frost and Gretta Osbourne would announce Paddy Power's death.

After filling in McKeon on what he had discovered at the Waterville Lake Hotel, McGarr asked if Mossie Gladden had arrived.

"Complete with solicitor. They've gotten as far as the foyer, and I can hear them now, arguing the point of whether Parknasilla is a public facility or a private accommodation at this time of year. The place is crawling with Great Southern Hotels security and the press, who Gladden has already attracted."

McGarr rang off. Given what he had seen of Paddy Power's "O'Duffy" file, where would Gladden have hidden the note cards? Certainly in no bank or other public place. Perhaps in his "mountain aerie," as described by Frost, which was remote, as described by Power. *If* Gladden had been the country gorsoon who had delivered the cards to the desk at the Waterville Lake Hotel.

Turning to Noreen, he said, "I'll take you two back to Parknasilla, unless you'd like to wait here."

"Why?"

McGarr attempted to summon a smile but failed. "Because I have something to do."

"Like interview Mossie Gladden?"

"Something on that order."

"Why can't I come along?"

"Well, it's not just you, is it? And it's a long ride and rough, from what I read in Power's note cards."

"But Maddie *sleeps* in cars, no matter how rough the road. And presently she's very tired."

CHAPTER 7

On Scratching the Good Life

QUONDAM DETECTIVE SERGEANT Bernard Quintus McKeon was suffering from just the condition that Nell Power had said Paddy Power had had in their marriage. McKeon was scarcely twelve hours on the job as undercover Allied Irish Bank's "empty suit," and he could barely remember his thirty-year career with the Guards. There he sat in the plush of a wing-back chair at—he checked his watch—10:32 of a Tuesday morning with nothing more disagreeable to do for the rest of the day than to keep his ears open and his mouth occupied. Even more agreeable still was his condition.

Already McKeon had one potent libation settling comfortably in the cavernous confines of his unslakable gullet and another on the way for him and O'Shaughnessy, who was also masquerading as bank executive and was sitting on the divan across from him. It was the first chance that the two senior squad staffers had had to speak in a day, and with the Shaw Lounge now packed with reporters, photographers, and even a mobile television crew, the few words they were exchanging would go unnoticed.

"Tell me, Liam—ascribe you to the 'great man' theory of history?" McKeon asked in the pancake accent that branded him unmistakably as a Dubliner.

Dialogue only served to make McKeon more loquacious, and

O'Shaughnessy's eyes rolled toward the door. His drink could not arrive too quickly.

"You know—the right man, in the right place, at the right time."

O'Shaughnessy thought McKeon would mention something further about Paddy Power, whom both already had agreed had been the right man to lead the country, when McKeon pointed to a tall, gray-haired man who had just entered the room. He was wearing a tuxedo with a little nameplate saying SONNIE on his lapel, and with a practiced snap of the wrist McKeon called him over.

"I told your helper there—Hughie, I believe his name is—that I *didn't* want another of these.' McKeon waggled his empty glass. "If I did, why sure he'd probably get caught taking drinks orders from all the bankers and reporters hereabouts, and you two would be doing a roaring trade. Fully ten minutes ago. I'm glad to see he took my advice. If he appears now, he'll probably get et—his tray, his obsequious smile, and his big brother's tuxedo, spiffy as it is."

With clenched fists Sonnie left the room, and in mere seconds, it seemed, Ward appeared in the doorway carrying a tray brimming with drinks.

"Will you look at yer mahn there. He's magic, isn't he? How long did it take for him to master that? The balance, the grace."

A walrus of a TV producer with a shoe-brush mustache and rolls of tanned flesh lobbed over his collar now stuck four fingers in Ward's face. "Four, count 'em. Four pints of Carlsberg. We're parched here, and if you get them to us double-quick, there's fifty pee in it for you, my good man." Ward only smiled and nodded and continued on his way.

"A day?" McKeon went on. "No—what am I saying? He learned his trade in a morning only, precocious lad that he is. Must be all that training in the ring."

Setting the brimming jar of alcohol in front of McKeon, Ward glanced up and thought McKeon looked, acted, and even sounded like the former Soviet premier Nikita Khrushchev, whose brutish visage Ward had gaped at as a child on his family's first television set. McKeon was small, wide, drunken, and sly, with quick, beady eyes and the effusive manner of a roistering proletarian. Who else would come to Parknasilla and order a Black-and-Tan, which was something dockworkers drank.

Granted it was fair play to take unfair advantage of another staffer's disadvantageous assignment, but how was Ward supposed to poke about and find out what was what when he spent his day running drinks for McKeon? And then to sic Sonnie on him was just plain low.

"Will that be all?" he asked, straightening up.

"For the moment," said McKeon. "We understand you have your hands filled. Chin up. Work away. Don't forget, there's fifty pee coming to you if you're double-quick. But don't expect anything from us. Like you, we're working." McKeon winked and raised his glass to O'Shaughnessy. "Cheers, my man."

Ward departed quickly, and McKeon eased himself into the cushions and considered the creamy buff head of his drink.

O'Shaughnessy managed to take a sip from his own before McKeon began again. "This is the life, is it not, Superintendent? Ever think of it for yourself? You know—buying a bit of land down here in the country, going on the dole? You could drink a few jars, put a few bob on a nag or two, and contemplate the whole bit out there"—McKeon cast a hand toward the window where beyond the terrace they could see surf rioting in the bay—"Mother Nature in all her incontinence."

It would take dynamite to get McKeon out of this or some other lounge, of which he was most definitely a lizard or some other cagey, profoundly urban creature, thought O'Shaughnessy. Cockroach, he decided.

"How much is the dole these days?"

"Sixty-odd pound."

"Per week?"

O'Shaughnessy nodded.

McKeon raised his glass. "You're good with figures, Liam. How many pints is that?"

"Thirty-seven and a swallow."

McKeon did, and long. When he had regained his voice, he concluded, "Well, scratch the good life. It's simply not affordable down here in the country."

It was eleven o'clock, and the room was packed. Shane Frost pushed through the door and, working the crowd of reporters with smiles and handshakes, made his way to the lectern. Tall, silver-haired, and distinguished-looking, he assembled his notes, and voices quieted. When the television lights snapped on, he raised his head, as though he would speak, but the doors opened and Bresnahan stepped into the room.

Frost glanced at her, looked down at his notes, then glanced back again. Even the television camera panned in her direction.

She was wearing the same cobalt-blue suit that McKeon suspicioned had been requisitioned from McGarr's slush fund, which was otherwise spent on a pre-Christmas slush, and he hated her for her profligacy. Eventually women got everything they wanted, one way or the other, which was often by some dramatic display.

Nevertheless, he wondered how he could have failed to appreciate Bresnahan's special beauty when she was still wearing uniform blues and was a diamond in the rough. Maybe he was improving with age and with twelve children was now beyond such considerations.

He took another long swallow and sincerely hoped so. A person only *thought* sex was fun when he was at it, tooth and . . . well, *not* nail. Sex was dangerous and could threaten every fiber of a man's corpus with all the penalties, expenses, and most recently even fatal conditions that could be laid on even a single slip into that treacherous vale of despond. McKeon tugged at his drink yet again.

Bresnahan blushed an apology, which only added more color to her bright appearance, and tripped gracefully for such a large person toward the reporters who were standing behind the divans. Eyes followed her every lovely lope. In her hands she held a notepad and pen.

"As many of you may have already heard, I am here to confirm tragic news that will sadden this conference, the Irish nation, and many others in the world. Yesterday Paddy Power passed away," Frost began.

Suddenly the room was so quiet that the only noticeable sound was the whirring of the television cameras.

"Paddy was only fifty-eight years old, but he had a heart condition and, as was his wont, had been working at a torrid pace both to prepare for this conference and to announce that he would soon enter politics and stand for the Dail from this very constituency here in the South Kerry Mountains. Paddy thought he could bring his expertise in finance and management to bear on the problems that Ireland now faces, and there were not a few of us who thought that Paddy might have made a difference."

From outside of the building on the terrace they now heard shouting. Turning his head, McKeon saw Mossie Gladden, waving his arms, his mouth working, even as two large young men approached him. Gone were the greatcoat, boots, and farmer's cap that McGarr had said he had been wearing the day before. Instead he was dressed in a TD's pinstriped suit covered by a dark, formal topcoat. A similarly dressed man beside him now began gesturing a hand while shouting at the approaching security guards.

"It is not for me to eulogize Paddy from this podium, nor could I, or anybody else, tell you of the countless thousands of lives he touched, always for the better. Paddy had brilliance, courage, tenacity, and a generosity—not of the spirit alone—that made him unique. How many people the world over are living better today because of Paddy? And for those of us who were fortunate to count Paddy as colleague and friend, his death comes as a special loss. He will be sorely missed.

"Funeral arrangements including a requiem high mass and burial here in Sneem, which was Paddy's birthplace, are scheduled for Thursday. Taosieach Sean Dermot O'Duffy will deliver the eulogy."

Murmurs arose from the reporters, but after a seemly pause Frost went on. "Paddy has been taken, but he would have wanted his work to go on, and it will. Paddy had intended this conference, which is presently taking place here in Parknasilla, to be the cornerstone of his entry into politics. I know of no more fitting memorial to him than to have us proceed with his wish. Gretta Osbourne, executive director of the Paddy Power Fund, will now chair the conference."

Elaborately Frost turned his head to a middle-aged woman with long silver-blond hair who was leaning back against the mantel of the fireplace. McKeon noted that she was yet another tall, well-built person whose good looks were marred by a rough complexion that much makeup only partially concealed. The lumps and streaks of whatever had ravaged her face were apparent even at a distance.

"Gretta helped Paddy draft his proposal and has worked with him throughout the past year to bring the conference about. I'm happy to say that Paddy's final project is in capable hands."

The woman only lowered her head, as though taken by grief or the magnitude of the challenge of filling Power's shoes.

"I also should announce that Taosieach O'Duffy is sending Finance Minister Patrick Quinn to take part in the proceedings."

Another murmur swept the crowd. ". . . now that he's dead!" McKeon heard somebody say.

Questions were then barked, but Frost, raising a palm, stayed them. "Eire Bank has prepared a bio of Paddy that will be distributed to any and all members of the media in the bar. If you have any other questions, I—"

As one, the reporters began speaking, and Frost had to single them out and call for quiet so he could hear their questions. They wished to know when exactly Power had died, the correct spelling of his heart dysfunction, why there had been a lapse between his death and this announcement of it. "We understood that Paddy was resting and did not wish to be disturbed."

Other questions had to do with Power's heirs—"I don't know. His family, I should think"—his exact political plans—"As I said, he would stand for office from this riding. If he had been successful, then . . . well. Who knows?"—the size of the estate, which was always of interest—"I don't know, nor do I know if it's the sort of question that we should be addressing ourselves to here. Yes, from the little I know, Paddy was quite rich, but what matters is how he lived his life, which was simply and in the service of others. From my understanding, the great bulk of his money will be devoted to charitable undertakings, as it was in his life."

Yes, you bastard—and doubtless devoted to whoever will now control his money, thought McKeon, who had long admired Paddy Power and had looked forward to his entry into politics. It would be hard to count the people who would benefit from his death, which McKeon assumed had been a class of sneaky, well-planned murder.

There were the political beneficiaries, like O'Duffy and his party, which Power would not have joined. Even Mossie Gladden might have benefited, were he planning a political comeback. Then there were the financial beneficiaries. With a fortune as large as the estimates of Power's—hundreds of millions of pounds—some lucky person or persons would now find themselves suddenly enriched, unless—McKeon smiled to think of it—Power had foxed them all and socked the whole bundle into his Fund.

Finally there were the aggrieved parties in Power's life, of whom McKeon knew only of the wife, Nell.

It was then Bresnahan spoke up. The questions had been entirely too general for her, too soft and sympathetic to the explanation that Frost had put forth. And there was something about him that got her hackles up. Maybe it was how sure Frost was both of himself and the cause of Power's death. She couldn't imagine the temerity it would take to stand up before television and the press and announce to the "world," as he had pointed out, his finding. Frost might look like some new-day Celtic hero with his high forehead, wavy silver mane, broad shoulders, and commanding presence, but he was in reality just another local, who in all probability had had to leave Sneem for work, as had she.

A big person herself, Bresnahan had a big voice. "Excuse me," she said in her best Southside Dublin drawl. "Excuse me—I have a question that I would like to ask."

Frost, who had been pointing to this reporter or that, now swung his finger to her. He smiled. "Yes, Miss—?"

Bresnahan would not give her name. "Who will run Eire Bank now that Chairman Power has died?"

Frost smiled condescendingly, as at her ignorance of the particulars of his life. "I will, of course, as I have now for several years. Paddy's position with Eire Bank was titular alone." Frost raised his hand, as though for a question from somebody else.

"Wait, please. I have a follow-up question," Bresnahan called out, her hands behind her back, one long tangerine leg set rakishly before her where she was moving that shoe on the pinion of a cobalt-blue heel. "Wasn't Mr. Power the largest individual shareholder in Eire Bank?"

Frost waited, his eyes watchful.

"Yet wasn't he now asking you to write down twenty percent of your stake in the debt? As part of his proposal to the debt conference."

Gretta Osbourne took a step toward Frost and was heard plainly to say, "Where did she get that?" Her expression was stern; her eyes were accusatory.

But Frost lost none of his aplomb. As though having heard something curious, he inclined his head, smiled wanly, and said in a be-mused tone, "We asked you here this morning to make public our unhappy news, *not* to discuss the debt conference, the details of which will have to wait until the end of the week, *after* Taosieach O'Duffy addresses the conference on Thursday."

"That's in addition to his eulogy on Thursday?" somebody else asked.

Frost nodded. "So I understand."

"Had that been planned *before* Power died?" yet another voice called out.

"I believe the taosieach is now concerned that Paddy's proposal might be obscured by his death. But, of course, I'm *not* speaking for the taosieach."

But you have been speaking *to* him, and at length, Bresnahan thought. Now Bresnahan's Irish was up; she had read Power's note cards, the ones that had been found with his corpse, and she knew Power's opinion of Frost. According to Power, Frost was a self-serving chameleon and toady. McGarr had told her to play devil's advocate, if necessary, and she called out, "Who was the attending physician when Mr. Power was taken?"

Sensing Bresnahan knew more than they and was onto something, the reporters in the room quieted.

Frost's ears pulled back, and McKeon, sitting directly in front of the podium, smiled to see the man's jaw firm. Frost's polish was beginning to wear thin, and his eyes shied toward the windows where Gladden and the man with him were still arguing with hotel security. "Dr. Maurice J. Gladden, who was Paddy's family physician here in Sneem."

"A postmortem of Mr. Power's remains was performed." It was not a question but rather a statement of fact to be denied at Frost's peril.

He nodded.

"What was the finding?"

"I don't know. I haven't read the report." Frost glanced up at Bresnahan, who let the silence carry the thought that he had already spoken of the cause of Power's death without having read the postmortem report.

"Is there any question of foul play?" another reporter jumped right in.

Frost only stared at him.

"Why was a postmortem ordered?" yet another put in.

"Has the Garda been called in?"

"Was that the reason for the delay in announcing Mr. Power's death?"

"Are there copies of the report available?"

Frost closed his eyes and turned his shoulders away from the lectern. "Please. Let us spare Paddy's family any undue agony. Their loss is great enough. Paddy was a brilliant, resourceful, involved man in the prime of his abilities. A potential leader. If the Garda were informed, it was merely as a formality. At the moment it's all that can be said. Try to keep yourselves from sullying his record accomplishment and humanitarianism." Frost stepped away from the lectern.

A barrage of other questions were shouted at him, but he only clasped his hands behind his back and maintained a polite, if grim, smile of resignation.

Gretta Osbourne had already left the room.

O'Shaughnessy nodded to McKeon, who rose to take a turn around the terrace where Gladden could still be seen. On his way out the door he heard one reporter ask another, "Who the hell is she?" meaning Bresnahan.

"Dunno."

Said the walrus with the shoe-brush mustache, "Canadian television. I saw her a number of times over there. Brilliant, isn't she? And—"

And, the others were thinking.

Frost was now surrounded by reporters, but he pushed through them and approached Bresnahan. "I'm Shane Frost. I don't believe we've met." He held out his hand. "You're—?"

"Ruth." She did not take his hand.

"May I buy you a drink?" He checked the glitter of his gold watch. "The sun is over the yardarm, as is said. Just. Two past twelve. What say?"

"If I can ask you some questions."

"And I you. I think you're somebody I should get to know."

"Here or in the bar?" she asked.

Frost turned his body, as though scanning the room or wishing her to study his distinguished profile.

"The bar," she decided. If Hughie could stay close enough, she would have a witness to Frost's remarks.

Out on the terrace, McKeon watched Gladden harangue a group of reporters, while another man distributed fliers. Thought McKeon, studying Gladden's wind-reddened features and his wild and unlikely glossy green eyes, now there stands some sly class of culchie madman who will do anything to get what he wants. The photocopied sheets announced a "different" press conference that Gladden would give at the bridge in Sneem on the morrow.

"The hypocrites!" Gladden roared. "They murdered Paddy. Now they'll mourn him. They scoffed at his proposal when he was alive, wouldn't even send a representative down to his conference here. By Friday—mark my words—it'll be their conference with their priorities and their agenda."

Several reporters attempted to sound him out, but Gladden would only say what was also printed on the fliers. "Tomorrow at noon I'll give you the facts on the murder of Paddy Power. The motive. Who benefits and why."

"What d'you mean by murder?"

"What proof do you have, Mossie, or is this another of your charges?"

"Give us some proof!"

When Gladden refused to offer any, the reporters began withdrawing to their cars. Gladden turned to the man with him and said, "I'm off now, straight home. I'll have the masters there in your office by four at the latest. That should give you plenty of time to make copies before the press conference."

"How many will we need?"

"At least enough for all the major papers, radio and television. Say, a dozen, to be safe."

His assistant looked away, as though it was a tall order.

"Do you have enough paper? We don't want to run out again."

"With that ream you bought, I should have enough."

Gladden then launched himself at his battered Land Rover, his odd, rolling gait making his shoulders pitch and heave. He grappled himself into the ancient vehicle that with a cough and a cloud of diesel smoke churned toward the gate.

McKeon fell in behind Gladden's helper, whose car was parked farther up the drive. "Fair day in spite of the chill," he remarked.

"'Tis, but we'll see frost again by sundown."

Count on it, thought McKeon. "Overheard you speaking to yer mahn." He meant Gladden. "You wouldn't happen to be a solicitor hereabouts, would yah now?"

A quick, suspicious gaze fell on him. The man was a tall, lean, tough-looking customer with a pocked complexion that the sharp wind made look red and blistered. "Are you with the press?"

McKeon closed his eyes and expelled some air, as though it was the last thing he'd be. "Not at all, at all. I'm a banker, here for the debt conference. But I've always been in love with Kerry, don't you know. And thinking about buying a bit of property in the area, now that I can. I've got a problem though, since I spend most of my time in Dublin, I had it in the back of me mind that a solicitor— Here." He reached into a pocket of his suit coat and drew out a card, the ink of which he hoped was dry. It said:

Bernard Quintus McKeon
Managing Director
Information Services
Allied Irish Banks

"Have you one of your own?"

The man did. "Of course. My office is on the square in Sneem.

On the laneway leading to the church. Anything I can do to be of service, just ring me up. Here, I'll include my home phone." He wrote that on the back.

As McKeon had suspected, Kieran Coyne was a solicitor with an accent no less unmistakably Dublin than his own. And hungry for any fees he could find in this godforsaken place. Or clients, like Gladden, whom he might charge for copying documents. Of what, McKeon could not guess.

The postmortem report? No, he decided, ambling back toward the lounge where, now that it was past noon and lunch would soon be served, McKeon could resume his enjoyable work in earnest. The postmortem of Paddy Power was now a matter of public record and would soon be in the possession of every reporter who had just left Parknasilla.

Some transcript of Power's proposal to the debt conference? Perhaps, given Gladden's promise to the press. Or Paddy Power's note cards, copies of which had been sent to Power's ex-wife and had been discovered by McGarr in her suite at the Waterville Lake Hotel?

No—that would be too much to hope for, since Gladden would be as much as implicating himself in Power's "murder," as he was calling it.

CHAPTER 8

O'Duffy's Man, Slane

FROM THE ROAD below, Mossie Gladden's farm looked like a green bite that had been nipped from the gray mountain. Contained in "The Pocket," which Paddy Power had called a "topographical curiosity," it looked more to Noreen like "the kind of pleasant, atavistic vision of the Ireland you see in travel brochures.

"You know, the independent farmer's small holding, complete with thatched roof, two-room cottage, and a neat row of outbuildings to the rear. And clear, cold streams—twins, no less—gushing from the cliff face of a mountain with a high, glorious sky beyond. Tell me I'm not counting four green fields, as in that old chestnut of a song the Abbey Tavern Singers forever abuse. It's a wonder Guinness or Harp or one of the other beer companies haven't snapped it for an advert."

McGarr thought they had, or at least it was a sight that he had dreamed or imagined before. What wasn't showing, however, was the labor it had taken to clear the fields of boulders and rocks, and how dark, musty, and cold that pretty cottage was in most weather, and how cramped on a brilliant autumn day such as this. McGarr could see no utility lines leading into the house. Gladden either had his own generator, or he had "eschewed"—Frost's word, when excoriating Gladden—that aspect of modern life as well.

Yet there was a wisp of turf smoke curling from the chimney, and, when McGarr parked the Rover in the turnaround on the drive and climbed out, he was struck by the near-silence of the place. All he could hear was the distant plashing of the twin streams and the occasional jingle from the bell of a far-off sheep.

As advertised, Maddie was asleep, and Noreen had rolled down the window. "Listen," she whispered. "The weeping cries. That's lapwing—you know, crested plover—which winters here in Kerry and then flies back to Norway in the spring." As if on cue, a small flock of birds appeared, wheeled overhead, and beat toward the mountain. "I think I've also heard thrush, lark, and linnet."

McGarr didn't know one from the other. He was a Dubliner born and bred; his parents had had no country house in Kildare, like hers, and the closest he got to nature was the carefully nurtured confines of his back garden.

"This place could be on Mars for all you can sense of the rest of the human world," she went on. "I wonder how long Gladden has had it?"

Or how long it would take him to return, thought McGarr, who wished to look around undisturbed. "Honk if you hear somebody coming." He then advanced upon the house, first checking around back to make sure Gladden had not returned from Parknasilla, and pulled his truck in where it could not be seen from the drive.

No dog, which was a blessing but curious for a farmer with sheep. Not in the sheds or in the house. McGarr knocked and called out to make sure, then pushed open the door, which was hung on goatskin tethers and clasped by a hand-carved wooden latch.

Inside was clean, neat, and warm, heated by a shiny Stanley number-eight range, the pipe of which had been inserted into the flue of the chimney. Near it an accordion rack held drying clothes. A large, similarly bright kettle on a trivet was jetting a funnel of steam.

To one side of the large, open room, which had once been divided in two, was a long, narrow pallet padded with eiderdown comforters where, McGarr assumed, Gladden slept. Nearby were an armoire that held Gladden's clothes, a comfortable reading chair with a spirit floor lamp behind, and a tall case of books.

After closing the armoire, McGarr checked the titles. Irish classics on the topmost shelves. All were well thumbed, especially Yeats's *Countess Cathleen*, which McGarr seemed to remember was a dreamy play about an Irish countess who sold her soul to save her people but got into heaven all the same. He replaced the book.

The lower, more accessible shelves were stocked with newer books, by the look of their bright dustcovers. Most seemed to deal with political and economic issues. McGarr switched off the lamp and turned around.

The length of a country kitchen table divided the room. On the other side was a kind of rough surgery with a raised hospital table of gleaming stainless steel, several medical cabinets nearby, and another collection of books, all medical. Overhead was a large lamp, again lit by alcohol, of the sort that McGarr had used before and that was equipped with a mechanical spark.

He pushed the red trigger. On the second snap the wick caught and burned with a blue flame that he turned up into a bright white light. The medical cabinets contained lotions, ointments, salves, gauze and plaster bandages, splints, and two neatly arranged drawers of medical instruments.

Of pills, tablets, and ampules, there were dozens of vials, bottles, and containers; McGarr tried to guess at the number and type of people whom such a remote surgery could possibly serve. Other than mountain farmers, such as Gladden had said he himself had become. But from where, some even more remote reach of the South Kerry Mountains? McGarr hadn't seen more than a dozen farms after they had left the main road beyond Sneem, but he remembered Bresnahan saying that Gladden would treat anybody and never turned a patient away.

McGarr was about to close the drawers when a device caught his eye. It was made of some strong, light metal, like aluminum, and was essentially a stationary arm with a lever that, when thrown, brought pressure to bear on a central point. There, small dies in different shapes and sizes could be inserted into yokes in each arm to produce, McGarr guessed, pills and tablets.

In the kitchen, which was no more than a cubby with a two-ring cook stove, a sink, and a single, cold-water tap, McGarr found a plastic sack. In it he placed the device and its dies. It all looked clean and gleaming, but the Tech Squad might find residues.

The small kitchen itself came next. Apart from a flitch of bacon, hanging from a rafter, it too was spartan. McGarr could discover only the wedge of cheddar cheese, the stale heel of barmbrack, and the tins of brislings that were a feature of bachelor digs the country over. Gladden obviously took most of his meals in some other place.

Behind a door he found a shotgun and a .306 bolt-action rifle with a telescopic sight, and some targets hanging from a peg. The top one pictured what looked like a wild dog with SEAN in Gaelic letters written below the head. McGarr remembered Power's note card, the one that had been clutched in his dead hand, describing how Gladden had been forced to begin shooting the wild dogs that were preying on his sheep. Sean was a euphemism, McGarr supposed; as in, having lost another sheep to—

Maddie had wakened, and McGarr could hear her complaining as he made his way across the haggard to the outbuildings. He chose the farthest shed first. The door was locked but yielded readily to one of the several picks on McGarr's key ring. Inside he found a half-dozen pieces of rusting half-inch steel plate. Three pieces had recently been cut with an acetylene torch and tank that sat on a dolly nearby. Farther in was a nearly new Ford Granada with number plates from Northern Ireland. Cupping a hand to cut the glare, he peeked at the odometer, which read just 367 miles, about what it would have taken to drive it from the North to Kerry.

McGarr replaced the cover. He closed the door, slipped the shackle through the swivel eye, and snapped it home.

In the next shed he found farm implements and various animal feeds. The next was a chicken coop with an alarmed brood that scolded him. Closest to the house was a kind of changing shed where Gladden kept the roughest of his farm work clothes and foul-weather gear. Beside them were a collection of dirt-encrusted slanes, a breensler, and spreading pikes, tools that were used for cutting peat. A heavy black coat, cinched by an old belt, was hanging from pegs there, but the side pockets of the coat yielded nothing but a physician's thermometer and a small pad for writing prescriptions. Gladden's name was printed on top.

In the large interior pocket that farmers sometimes used to warm a newborn lamb, McGarr's fingers felt something thick and soft, and he pulled out what looked like human hair. It was an ash-blond wig, the synthetic strands of which were at least two feet long. McGarr asked himself what Gladden could possibly want with that. Some disguise for hunting the wild dogs that were preying upon his sheep, since the pocket also rendered a handful of .306-caliber cartridges? Some other farm use—say, to warm wild-bird or duck eggs that Gladden discovered while tramping the mountains? Some . . . dramatic use for a play Gladden had been in? McGarr thought of the several play scripts in the case of books near the reading chair. Or perhaps some predilection of Gladden that was known only to himself.

McGarr replaced it and stepped farther into the outbuilding. There, he found saddlebags for a horse, and other leather satchels that could be hung on an ass rail, which was shielded by a tarp. All were empty.

McGarr was about to return to the house for a closer search, when his foot blundered into some old Wellies that lined a dry, shadowed corner of the shed. Two had fallen over, and in picking them up, McGarr found he could not get the soft rubber to remain in the former upright position. Somehow they were too worn or too heavy. He squatted down and tried again with no luck.

Only when he held the top of one boot to the light and looked in did he see the cause. Stacks of note cards had been stuffed into the rubber boot. He pulled a bunch out and saw the now-familiar neat, crabbed hand. He carried them over to the light; it was Paddy Power's writing.

They were Power's note cards, the originals. McGarr lifted them out and fanned through some, his eyes falling on the subheadings, "Political Roots," "Political Debts," "Economic Policy," "Favors Owed," "Election Financing," "Dirty Tricks"; the same categories that he had seen in the photocopies he had taken from Nell Power's suite at the Waterville Lake Hotel a few hours earlier.

The card material was slick, and in trying to group them, McGarr kept dropping one here and another there. Bending to gather them up, he saw a shadow dart across the front of the haggard, and before he could look up, a deep, enraged voice cried, "So—it's *you*, O'Duffy's man, messing about where you don't belong! Won't I give you a toompin' you'll never forget."

There stood Gladden, looming in the shed door, but for a moment only. Quick for a man of his age and size, he snatched up the handle of a slane and, taking two short steps, swung it with both hands at McGarr. The heavy, shiny blade clipped through a row of stacked flowerpots that exploded in McGarr's face. He had time only to turn his shoulders away, and the head of the slane caught him in the small of the back.

The force of the blow spun him around, and the note cards squirted from his grasp. The smashed flowerpots had sprayed into his eyes, and he could only hear and feel Gladden's footsteps on the loose floorboards of the outbuilding as he charged, blade lowered at McGarr's chest.

McGarr launched himself low and hard at Gladden's ankles, and the big man, carried forward by his own momentum, fell roughly over McGarr, who pushed himself up so that Gladden's tumble would throw his legs high. Gladden crashed hard into the back wall of the shed and took some time to get to his feet, but still McGarr could not clear his eyes. Whatever the pots had contained burned and stung. His back was now galling him, and he could see that Gladden had something else in his hand that looked like a breensler's pike.

Anything that McGarr could lay his hands on he now threw in front of Gladden—a chair that was kicked out of the way, some sawhorses, a wheelbarrow that Gladden shoved back into his shins—until McGarr backed into something solid. He threw out his hands. A wall. He began moving to what he could just see was light.

But Gladden had cleared his feet and took two quick steps to load his weight into his swing. The blow caught McGarr high on the shoulder and ripped across the base of his neck, his chest, and the hand of the other arm. And again across his thighs, the material of his suit shredding as the blade bit into his flesh.

Gladden had him pinned against the wall, and McGarr could feel the blood hot from his shoulders to his knees. He was about to push himself off the wall and charge, which was his only chance, when he heard:

"Drop that, you bastard, or I'll blow your head off."

There was a pause, and then the shed was filled with a noise louder than McGarr thought he had ever heard.

Because of Maddie's complaining, Noreen had not heard a car on the drive. Maddie had wanted to get out of her car seat, then get out of the Rover, then walk around to a field on the other side of a wall, where there were multicolored stones and the sun was bright.

Gladden, Noreen now suspected, had caught sight of the Rover from the crest of the neighboring hill. He had switched off his engine and coasted down the incline until he got near the house.

In any case—busy with Maddie in the field—Noreen had not seen Gladden until he was well beyond her and about to enter the final outbuilding, the door of which was open. She knew immediately from the stiff and truculent look of him that trouble would start, and instead of honking the horn, she lifted Maddie into her car seat, clamped it down, closed the door, and rushed around to the other side of the car. She reached under the driver's seat for the Walther that McGarr kept there.

The clips were concealed under the dash, and Noreen, whose sporting parents still hunted in three seasons, quickly armed the weapon and sprinted the hundred or so yards through to the door of the shed. Now she held the handgun in both fists, the barrel pointed at Gladden's heart. The first shot had passed within inches of his head. With the next she would kill him without remorse; she hoped he could read the purpose in her eyes.

Her husband was pinned against a wall, trying to look around. He looked as if he was stunned or . . . something. Shock? All of him from the shoulders down seemed bloodied, and there stood Mossie Gladden with a long, sharp pike in his hands.

"Noreen?"

"Yes."

"Get him out of here. Get me out into the light where I can see. And give me some time. Did he come alone?"

It wasn't shock; it was anger. And she knew what he wanted. "Ah, Peter," she pleaded, "are you sure—"

"Out! Get us out. And give me some time. I'm fed to the teeth with *shit* like this. Jesus." He tried to look down at his sliced and bruised body, but he could not see.

"Now, missus," Gladden began saying, "if you'll just give me that gun—"

When it went off again. The blast was stellar and left McGarr's ears ringing with crinkling sounds, like icicles falling.

"Out!" Noreen ordered. "Get out into the yard, and if you so much as move quickly or break, I'll put one of these in your hide. I'm a dab shot, and Paddy Power was a hearty of my father. Because of you I've got a husband half-destroyed and a baby scared to death. And not a witness within two leagues."

"What does Paddy Power have to do—"

"Out! Get out!"

McGarr was now seeing enough to watch Gladden move by them. Out in the sun of the yard McGarr doused his eyes in the rainwater of an animal trough that had filled during the storm of the night before. He then felt the depth of the slices below his neck and on the palm of his right hand, which were still bleeding. Both needed stitching, but not by Gladden.

"Take that thing out of here," he said to Noreen, meaning the gun. "Go back to Parknasilla and find Bernie in the lounge. Tell him what happened and to stay close to a phone."

Noreen began to object, but all McGarr had to add was, "Maddie," and she left to quiet her baby, who was now bawling.

"So, you were going to give me a 'toompin' I'd never forget,"
said McGarr, moving in on Gladden, who did not stir. "Can I tell you
what I'll never forget?" He had stopped in front of the larger man to
look up into his strange, polished-looking jade eyes. "That slane. And
the pike. No 'toompin' at all, you had weapons. Now I'll give you a
second chance. With your hands."

Gladden's punch, wheeling off the breadth of his shoulders, whis-
tled over McGarr's head. And a second, thrown with the other fist as
he rocked back and in at McGarr.

Injuries or not, it was McGarr's type of brawl altogether, and he
wondered how many actual fistfights the good doctor and former,
visionary TD, who had been born and raised in these barren hills, had
had in his time. Not more than a dozen, he was willing to bet. If that.

McGarr, on the other hand, had been born and raised in Dublin's
Inchicore, hard by the rail yard and gasworks. His first sport had been
the punch-up. Necessarily. Then, of course, there had been his work,
and he now took full advantage of the larger man's propinquity, butting
his head into his sternum and lashing out, once low and once high,
with his fists.

The first blow buckled Gladden's body, so that the second landed
squarely on the bridge of his long nose just as his head was jerking
forward. The cartilage folded under McGarr's knuckles, blood burst
over Gladden's face. His long, bent legs shot out, dumping him on his
backside in front of McGarr, who stepped quickly out of range of his
large hands.

McGarr knew what Gladden was now seeing. A great, bloody red
blotch of color that would molt into a rainbow of blinding pain. And
yet McGarr felt cheated that it was over so quickly. The big man now
turned aside, and his breakfast came up.

McGarr noticed a bucket, filled it with trough water, and dashed
it into Gladden's face. McGarr looked behind him to see Noreen's car
on the narrow drive, slowing to ease around Gladden's battered Land
Rover.

Gladden was trying to gain his feet. He slipped on the mud and
fell into his vomit. When he had gotten to hands and knees again,
McGarr put a shoe on his buttocks and sent him sprawling toward the
trough. There, like McGarr before him, he doused his head in the
water.

A jetliner, making for Shannon to the north, now passed silently
far above the pinnacle of the mountain, its great silver wings glinting

in the full sun. McGarr went into the shed and gathered up Paddy Power's note cards.

The whine of the descending jet now came to them. He waited until it had diminished before saying, "You stole these before you poisoned Paddy Power. That makes it premeditation, murder in the first degree."

"I didn't murder Paddy. Nor did I steal his note cards. I was *sent* them." Gladden again lowered his head to the cold water in the trough.

"By whom?"

"By Paddy."

"Why would he have wanted you to have them?"

"Because he knew they would try to kill him."

"They?"

"Frost and O'Duffy and their crowd."

"Where were they sent you? Here?"

But Gladden would say no more, and McGarr collected the rest of the cards.

Next he lifted the greatcoat off its peg. "Where's your felt hat?" he called out to Gladden, who was now sitting against the trough, both hands raised to his nose as though attempting to reset the cartilage. One hand came down and indicated the old Land Rover that was parked at some distance from the house.

McGarr made Gladden drive. "Take us to the Waterville Lake Hotel."

Gladden shook his head and looked away. Already the sockets of both eyes were bluing, and his puffed nose with its split nostril was canted off to one side. "I only hope you know what you're doing," he observed, turning the truck around. "There's a hell of a stink in this. Your career and a lawsuit to boot."

Or a *hell* of charge against a man who, as a doctor, had sworn to heal and protect life whenever he could: murder of his self-described best friend.

And the attempted murder of another man who had sworn to protect life and society whenever he could.

"Is there a doctor in Waterville?"

"I don't need one."

No, McGarr thought; Gladden would wear that nose like a badge of high culchie honor, having been set upon by "O'Duffy's man." The tough little police gurrier and gunman from Dublin.

But McGarr hadn't been thinking about Gladden's medical needs.

He had his own wounds to worry about, and whatever sepsis the crusted blade of that slane might create.

First, however, he would take Gladden to the desk of the Waterville Lake Hotel for an identification. Some country gorsoon had delivered Paddy Power's stolen note cards to his ex-wife, Nell Power, and McGarr was betting it had been Gladden.

CHAPTER 9

Debt Service

OVER BREAKFAST MCGARR had told Ruth Bresnahan, "This is not a murder investigation. It can't be, no matter how right Mossie Gladden was in predicting how Paddy Power had died," which was by digitalis poisoning. "We've got the locked door, the proper medications in the appropriately labeled bottles, and the obvious signs that Power had attempted to treat himself. If he was murdered, he was murdered by his own hand.

"That leaves Gladden's charge of murder, which means we must investigate the death. Even if it were outright murder, I'm not sure we would want to call it that, at least until we had proof." For the sake of the country, which would be mourning Power, he had meant.

"The most we can do is poke around, perhaps stir things up *gently*," he had emphasized, "if we can. But mainly we should listen and observe. There has to be some reason that we don't yet appreciate why the government in the form of Commissioner Farrell and Ministers Harney and Quinn are so concerned. Perhaps if we're patient, they'll let us know what it is."

Which had long been McGarr's approach to interviewing. On Bresnahan's first case McGarr had told Bresnahan, "If you can keep the person talking, sooner or later he will tell you what you wish to know."

And was Bresnahan's approach now, while sitting with Shane Frost in the bar at Parknasilla.

"Are you acquainted with the Irish debt?" Frost asked. "Is it an Irish accent I'm hearing?"

"Pretend I'm not," Bresnahan replied. "Fill me in."

Frost liked the sound of that. He smiled.

They had taken the last two seats at a corner of Parknasilla's small, tasteful public bar, which was now crowded before lunch. Bankers and the few reporters who had remained to follow up on the revelation of the press conference were sitting in tight groups or standing in clutches, their voices lowered so as not to carry in the gleaming chestnut and cut-glass confines of the narrow room. Paddy Power's death was on every lip.

"After the Second World War Ireland found itself a small agrarian nation with a stable population, no debt, much genteel poverty, and little future beyond whatever Britain, who were still our major trading partner, were willing to grant us. Historically that had been less than nothing, and after we decided to remain neutral during the war and winked at German submarines charging their batteries in our bays and harbors, well—we had to do something. Certainly Britain was not going to reward us for betting against them.

"Debt was the key. The idea was to prime our economic pump with borrowed money, get some industries going and Irish-made goods on the world market. When money began coming in, the whole mechanism would become self-sustaining. And there we'd be—a modern, productive *republic* for nothing more than the courage and foresight to risk debt." Frost raised a finger. Watching it descend, he pointed it at the long and gentle slope of Bresnahan's chest. "Mark that word."

"Republic," she said.

Frost nodded. "When tied to entry into the European Community and cheap petrodollars, it made great good sense. Some—Paddy was one—made the point that with worldwide inflation and low interest rates, it was foolish *not* to borrow as much as we could at what amounted to negative interest rates. Every underdeveloped country did.

"The second oil shortage and Reaganomics in the eighties ended all that. Interest rates soared instead of falling, and economic contraction set in. Suddenly new borrowing and the easy money of the seventies had to be paid back in hard currency, the *hardest* for a fledgling industrial nation with the largest debt in relation to gross national product in Western Europe.

"Still and all, we would have been great, had the bulk of the money been spent on the capital-producing aspects of the economy. But we Irish are an impatient people, and we desired to leap, all at one go, into the twentieth century. We demanded all the welfare benefits of a modern, progressive industrial society—a Denmark or Holland—before we possessed the means of paying for those privileges. Hadn't we the example of Northern Ireland with its British benefits just across the border?

"I don't much fancy politicians myself, but they found themselves snagged on the horns of a dilemma. They could oppose such spending and be voted out of office, or support it and be condemned for corrupting the economy at some later date. Of course they took the easy way out.

"And thus was born the villain of the piece, the Irish welfare state and not—"

"An Irish *republic*."

Frost smiled fully and let his light gray eyes mingle in hers. He had an apt, as well as a beautiful, pupil. "We also got ourselves debt. Big debt. It eats up sixty-five percent of the average unmarried urban worker's wages."

There he was referring to Bresnahan's pay packet exactly.

"Ninety percent of all income tax collected—some thirty percent of all annual government revenues—goes just to service its interest. Sixty percent of that money leaves the country." Frost turned his head down the bar. "Excuse me?"

Ward, who was washing glasses, looked their way.

"Could you come down here, please? We'd like something wet."

Undoubtedly, thought Ward, drying his hands.

"Whiskey?" Frost asked Bresnahan.

"Neat. Water on the side," she called down to Ward.

"Two. *Now*, please."

"And Mr. Power's proposal, the one he was going to ask this conference to consider?" And use as his first step into politics.

Frost tilted his head and smiled ruefully. "Brilliant, uncomplicated and . . . elegant, like most everything Paddy did. His purpose was to clear the debt in one swift act, insist upon a change in the Irish tax structure, and thereby position the country to deal with the challenges of the Single European Act of 1992, which will abolish trade tariffs in the European Community."

Ward set the drinks before them and allowed his eyes to flicker up at Bresnahan, who smiled. He moved a step or two away, as though busying himself with some bottles. At the other end of the bar Sonnie was dealing single-handedly with a brisk trade.

"Using Chile as a model, Paddy was planning to put before this conference the proposal of converting Irish debt into equity in Irish government enterprises. He had in mind privatizing all the wasteful state-run enterprises like the rail and bus systems, the phone network, the Peat Board, Radio Telefis Eireann. Those agencies are sitting on valuable resources but can't compete even now, when protected by government rules and regulations. Faced with foreign competition in 1992, they'll only become further burdens on the Treasury. Why not barter them away while we can, for debt relief? Retaining Irish control, of course."

But all the jobs that would be lost, Bresnahan thought. Private enterprise would never put up with the featherbedding and shenanigans that went on in most state-run organizations she knew of. And then there were "The unions," she thought aloud; Irish unions had to be either the best or the worst in the world, depending on your membership or lack thereof. Every third person either groused or practiced rabble-rousing as a matter of ethnic pride.

"Paddy had an answer for them as well, which would also solve one of the major challenges of 1992. What if all those union members who deserved to retain their posts under the new scheme suddenly discovered their pay packets taxed *not* at the current sixty-five percent, but rather in the neighborhood of twenty or twenty-five percent? How would that sit with most Irish voters? With no debt, income taxes could be more than halved. Immediately.

"Also, foreign firms—all those companies that we piled up our debt trying to attract to Ireland—would be less likely to pack up and leave in 1992. Because of our tax structure, foreign firms must now systematically double the salaries of the employees they send here. With trading advantages expunged in '92, many are likely to leave."

Frost reached for his glass.

Bresnahan thought for a moment. Like most bold new initiatives, the Power plan sounded marvelous, and she wondered why it had not been thought of before. But of course Frost had said it had. "Isn't Chile saddled by some atrocious dictatorship?"

Frost smiled and nodded, carefully setting the brimming glass before him. "It was, when the restructuring occurred. Which is the point. It's something that only a Paddy, who had no political 'debts,' as it were, could have gotten through. Somebody who was independent, new to politics, and enjoyed widespread popular support. And then not without a lot of help and by referendum.''

Bresnahan nodded. Although a *fait accompli*, the 1992 SEA was still being hotly debated all over the country. But, say he had gotten the Irish people to accept his program *and* it worked, Power would have been canonized. He would have solved the central problem that was causing so much hardship and emigration. ''What happens to the proposal now? Did it die with Power?''

Frost shook his head. ''Not in the least.'' His eyes snapped up at hers. ''Do you want Eire Bank's opinion, or my own?''

''Your own, surely. We're being candid here, are we not?''

Frost returned her smile, then raised his chin to look away, as though contemplating the future. He waited while she studied his severely handsome and chiseled features. ''That in this, as in other matters, Paddy was a genius. A kind of seer. It's undoubtedly an idea whose time has come and just might make the difference between Ireland's foundering on the rocks of 1992 or our sailing off into prosperity. Without debt we could respond to the challenges of the SEA. With it . . .'' Frost shook his head.

''And that Paddy Power dead is probably more valuable to the Irish people than Paddy Power alive.'' Frost glanced at Bresnahan to see if she was shocked. ''*In this situation*. Sure, Paddy had personal force and charisma. And *genius*, that much is history. But what is also established was his record as a''—Frost looked away, as though having to choose his words carefully—''do-gooder and . . . crank. It was not for nothing he called somebody like Mossie Gladden his doctor and friend. And the Power Fund!''

Frost returned his gaze to Bresnahan, and his eyes were suddenly glassy with contempt. ''All that house-building and giveaway to people who are too weak, meek, or ignorant to help themselves. Encouraging them to''—he searched for a term—''*procreate*, for Jesus' sake. He was just compounding our problem with them through further, innumerable generations. More good would have come had he taken the money out and burned it.

''No''—Frost shook his head once, as though deciding with finality—''Paddy might have sold the program to the nation, but its implementation would have been botched. Politics is a fine art that is not learned late in life.''

''And now?'' Bresnahan encouraged.

Frost's eyebrows danced once, and he even smiled slightly. "The future of Paddy's proposal?"

Bresnahan nodded.

"Why, it's bright, of course. Now that it is in more capable hands. Done right, I can see it becoming a kind of . . . memorial to him, who was so much loved for his simplicity and generosity. You know, a kind of national paean to Saint Paddy the Second. We Irish are such a contrary people. We love nobody more than a—"

"Martyr," she suggested.

"—and a man who—think of it—championed gross, unlimited debt, and then founded a bank to profit by the borrowing. Suddenly as rich as Croesus, he would have turned around and redistributed our money according to his own plan of how things should be. And for *that* he will be loved."

Which wasn't quite fair, thought Bresnahan, according to Power's history, which had been well documented in the press. Power had begun his fortune with Eire Bank, but made the lion's share of it abroad with the Yanks and the Japanese. And then there were plenty of rich people the world over who never gave other human beings a passing thought. Also, Power had donated his time and *worked* for the poor, often with pick and shovel for weeks on end.

"But who, then, if not Mr. Power?"

Heated on her tangerine legs that were crossed in front of her, Frost let his smile climb her body and settle on her lips. "Who else but the sanest and most deft of Irish politicians? Who is himself a self-made millionaire and throughout his career has been all for privatization and free enterprise. Who began his career with Paddy and after whom Paddy even named his first son."

"Sean Dermot O'Duffy," said Bresnahan. The man who through his toady Fergus Farrell had as much as named the way Power had died. Or had been murdered.

"Certain details, of course, would have to be changed."

"What about the write-down? Is that one of the details that will be changed?"

Frost's smile fell slightly, and he released her hand. "May I ask *you* something and expect a candid answer? Where did you get that?"

"Another shareholder in Eire Bank. How many are you, by the way? Is there a list of shareholders available?"

Frost said nothing, only regarded her.

"What share is yours?"

"Nell Power told you," he said.

"Will *she* inherit Mr. Power's share?"

"I don't believe you. Nell would never—"

"Ask her."

"She's *here*?" Frost's eyes strayed to the sun room that they could survey through French doors.

Bresnahan thought of another question that McGarr had asked her to put to Frost. "What about lending as love? Power's idea or yours?"

Elaborately Frost unbuttoned his suit coat and spread the lapels. Turning his body, he looked down at himself. "See anything you need the loan of?"

Bresnahan laughed. He *had* a sense of humor, which rather softened her hard opinion of him.

"My turn with the questions. What about dinner tonight? Away from here. I know a hotel in Kenmare with a three-star Michelin rating. Their other accommodations are more agreeable still."

Bresnahan tried to look flattered, but it was all too apparent from Frost's easy delivery that he was used to receiving a yes. "Why don't you start by asking my name."

"Ruth—"

"Bresnahan."

Frost said the name over to himself. "I know some Bresnahans. Grew up with a family by that name here in Sneem. There's Tom still hereabouts. He has a daughter with the—"

"Guards," she supplied. "Detective Inspector Ruth Bresnahan, actually. I'm helping Chief Superintendent McGarr."

Frost looked down at his drink, then pushed himself away from the bar. Suddenly his visage was somber. "Ruth—can you take a bit of advice? I've asked your boss, and I'm asking you now. Don't make too much of this. Paddy is dead, and all the country will want to know is that he died well. This conference can speed the process along. Don't get in its way, it'll mow you down."

At the reception desk of the Waterville Lake Hotel, McGarr seized Dr. Maurice J. ("Call me Mossie") Gladden by the arm of his greatcoat and pulled him around so he was facing the clerk. He then shoved him into the high counter. Gladden was also wearing his felt hat.

"Is this the man who dropped off the plastic sack for Nell Power?" McGarr demanded. The one that had been filled with photocopies of Paddy Power's note card, he meant.

The young woman's eyes surveyed Gladden's swollen and split nose, his blackened eyes. "It is not. Don't you think I would've told you it was Dr. Gladden, had it been him? Dr. Gladden is the most . . . notable man in the area.

"Did *he* do this to you?" she asked Gladden, who turned and looked down on McGarr with a predatory smile.

"Had he asked me, I could have told him as much. But he insisted on this." Gladden pointed to his nose. "A classic case of police brutality, I'd say. Might I have the use of your phone? I'd like to ring up my solicitor, Kieran Coyne. I believe I should have a word with him."

McGarr looked away. A bad investigation with government interference from the start was rapidly growing worse. He had hoped to cover any charge of police brutality with a thick patch of Gladden's guilt. "How was the man different?"

The clerk, bending to the phone, did not answer.

"Shorter, taller, smaller? Younger, older? Is the coat the same? You can answer my questions here or in Dublin." And McGarr was angry. If it hadn't been Gladden who had dropped off the sack of photocopies, then who?

The clerk turned her back to McGarr and spoke into the mouthpiece.

Somebody behind him said, "Phone up our own Guards. They'll sort that man out."

"Who is he, anyway?"

"Some pug, by the look of him."

McGarr's suit coat, shirt, and tie were caked with dried blood.

Said Gladden, "Doing anything tomorrow, Chief Superintendent? Say around eleven at the bridge in Sneem. It will be helpful, can you attend my press conference? I'd like to be able to point you out. You know, the 'government' man who did this to me. Or will I be holding my conference from a jail cell? It's all one to me."

McGarr's temper squalled, but there was little he could do. If he charged Gladden and put him away for the duration of the debt conference, it would only lend credence to Gladden's claim of a government cabal. Also, McGarr's only witness was his wife, and questions about what exactly she had been doing with him during the investigation of the murder of one of the country's premier citizens might prove embarrassing.

He turned and walked away.

CHAPTER 10

Debts Illuminated

MOTIVES ASIDE, THE case was really simple, reasoned Ruth Bresnahan as she stepped down a carpeted hall in Parknasilla toward the door of the room that Gretta Osbourne occupied.

If Paddy Power had been murdered but the evidence (a substitute pill bottle) had been removed, then there could only be three primary suspects, who were around Power at the time he was poisoned and knew enough about his heart condition to accomplish his death: Gladden himself, Shane Frost, and Gretta Osbourne.

Gladden's reason for killing his best friend might have been the desire to use the death to stage his own political comeback at the expense of Sean Dermot O'Duffy, whom he hated and Shane Frost courted assiduously.

Frost's motive might have been more direct—preventing a write-down of the national debt, which would cost Eire Bank money, while at the same time eliminating the political challenge to O'Duffy that Paddy Power had represented.

Finally there was Gretta Osbourne, at whose door Bresnahan now stopped. What did Bresnahan know about her? Only that Osbourne had been Power's trusted assistant and onetime lover. And that the woman had enjoyed Power's good opinion right up until the time of his death, as noted in the cards that had been found beside his body.

"What time is it?" asked Gretta Osbourne, offering Bresnahan her hand in a practiced manner. She ushered Bresnahan into a sitting room that was sealed now at night by pleated drapes in some pretty floral pattern.

"Nine o'clock."

"How long have you been trying to get ahold of me?"

"Since three."

"That proves it then—I *am* a busy woman. I only wish some of these foreigners had thought to bring translators. One Japanese man told me he speaks English. He does. Five words 'pé feć wy.' "

Bresnahan smiled and looked around the room. The carpet was mauve, the furniture Edwardian, except for one item. A long conference table and eight chairs filled the middle of the room. On it were stacks of computer printouts and what looked like a series of brochures. The other room appointments—a desk, some chairs, a small portable bar—had been placed against the walls.

"I hope you haven't grown impatient?"

The question was pleasant enough, thought Bresnahan, but the tone was probing, of the sort asked by an executive officer of a subordinate. Again she reminded herself of McGarr's technique of letting the interviewee talk, all the more in this case, which was not a murder investigation. Or at least not yet.

"I must tell you that I didn't like, but I admired, the way you dealt with Shane at the press conference this morning," Osbourne went on. "I can't remember—did you identify yourself as a Garda officer?"

Bresnahan allowed her eyes to sweep the rest of the room, noting the several telephones, one with a red call light blinking. A portable computer that opened like the shell of a sea clam was also activated and showing an amber bar graph. There were fax and photocopy machines, and what Bresnahan guessed was a paper shredder. In all, the place had the look and feel of an exclusive business office or command center.

"Do you have some now?"

"Some what?"

"Identification. I always like to know to whom I'm speaking. You as much as destroyed the possibility of this conference accomplishing anything with your irrelevant questions this morning."

Bresnahan handed her her photo I.D. "It would have come out sooner or later." The truth, which could hardly be irrelevant.

"Later would have been far, far better."

"With Dr. Gladden outside distributing leaflets calling Mr. Power's death murder?" Bresnahan could see one on the conference table; Gretta Osbourne was obviously a person who kept herself well informed.

"Who says it was murder apart from him?" Osbourne took a seat at the head of the table, where she began copying Bresnahan's name and identification number into a diary/journal. She used a large black fountain pen with a gold nib and wrote with her left hand.

Bresnahan looked over her shoulder. Except for six hours of sleep each night, most of the hour headings from Sunday through Saturday of the current week were filled in. "Nobody that I know of. But given Dr. Gladden's charges, would you not want his allegations investigated?"

"Your boss, McGarr?"

"Not that I know of."

"If he did think it was murder, to whom would that be reported?"

"The commissioner, in the daily report."

"Fergus," said Osbourne, meaning Fergus Farrell. "Would the press know what's in those reports?"

"Not unless you tell them."

Gretta Osbourne looked up at Bresnahan and smiled, as though having been waiting for her to assert herself. She handed back the I.D.

Osbourne had knotted her silver-blond hair at the back of her head; black half-glasses sat on the bridge of a long, thin nose. She was a handsome woman, Bresnahan decided, or at least sexy in the way that Bresnahan herself was.

There was an interesting tension between the breadth of her shoulders, the narrowness of her waist, and the graceful shape of her long legs. She was wearing a black silk dressing gown, which was slightly diaphanous and revealed in oblique light a gray silk liner that was slashed with silver chevrons. Between the plackets of the gown, Bresnahan could see the lacy fringe of a costly chemise. On her feet were black silk flats decorated with the same silver pattern; given the soft lighting in the room, which cast a few shadows across her rough complexion, Gretta Osbourne looked elegant and enticing. She was also wearing the same expensive scent that Bresnahan herself had bought a small quantity of specifically for this assignment.

Osbourne now pushed herself back into the chair and peered up over the frame of the half-glasses. "Yes—Shane told me you had him off a second time at noon. Smartly. Got him to speak his mind and only afterward told him who you were.

"Sit down, please. Coffee, tea? Or would you care for a drop of anything?" She waved a hand toward the portable bar.

Bresnahan only sat.

"You're a local girl, Shane tells me. It doesn't seem fair, does it? How so much talent, intelligence, ambition, and guile can have originated from one small, unlikely village in benighted Kerry. There was Paddy, and there is Shane. And now you. It must be the water. Or the air." There was a noticeable, sharp twinkle in Osbourne's clear gray eyes; she was enjoying herself. "That's a brilliant outfit you're wearing. Just perfect for here and the—is it?—undercover role you're playing."

Bresnahan kept asking herself what sort of accent she was hearing. Irish, like her own, *new* Dublin drawl. Or was it more an American drawl, something southern. She believed she had once heard somebody from South Carolina speak that way.

"Well—you're doing it again, I fear. Getting your target to talk. Tell me what Shane said to you. After the conference."

Why, Bresnahan thought, when Frost—carrying messages still—had doubtless told the woman in detail? "Does he work for you or you for him?"

"Sometimes we work together. At other times we agree to disagree and work apart."

"As now?"

Osbourne crossed her legs, and Bresnahan noticed that she was also wearing shimmering silver stockings. She wondered what else the gown might conceal and if, perchance, Osbourne had garbed herself for some other activity that had not been penciled into her diary. "Officially Shane is president of Eire Bank, and I am merely senior director, presently on leave of absence."

"To the Paddy Power Fund."

She nodded. "Come now, Ruth. Loosen up. Tell me what Shane said this afternoon. I'm bursting to know."

"Why?"

"Well"—she looked away—"call it professional curiosity or the fact that with Paddy's death everything is up for grabs." She sounded not a little cheered by the prospect, and certainly neither she nor Frost seemed to be grieving Paddy Power in any way, shape, or form. Unless the black gown and what it concealed were for mourning. "As a woman, I need every advantage I can muster. Certainly *you* of all people can appreciate that. I'm told you're the only woman in your agency with a group of men who are—how shall I put it tactfully?—unreconstructable."

How had she learned that? Bresnahan had not told Frost anything of the sort, and certainly McKeon or Ward, who were working with "beards," as it were, would have said nothing.

No. Bresnahan's eyes slid over the stacked computer printouts in front of her. Here was an informed *and* careful woman, who had used the delay of the meetings she had attended to do some checking of her own.

"Now, about Shane," she repeated.

Why not, Bresnahan thought. McGarr had also told her to stir things up, if she could, and she quickly recounted how Frost had blamed the debt on what he had called the Irish welfare state.

Osbourne's smile was contemptuous. "Ah, yes—Shane, the elitist. He blames the debt on Joe and Joan Soap, those two greedy freeloaders from Ballyrathdrum who are responsible for the shambles of the economy." Suddenly Osbourne was on her feet, and Bresnahan caught the complex scent of some exotic perfume.

"They insisted on free housing, free health care, free university educations for their layabout kids, who emigrated with their Irish degrees to cushy jobs in Frankfurt and New York. Now they're sending back tax-free remittances and the like that are fueling the underground economy.

"But not even that is enough for the grasping Soaps, who are also lazy, unproductive, and don't want to see themselves or the country go ahead. There's the dole for Joe, whenever he feels like a paid holiday, and finally some fat citizen's pension for both of them as a kind of reward for their having avoided work for fifty years."

Bresnahan smiled. To the list of Osbourne's other attractions, she now added passion and sarcasm, the last being of no little value in the country she was describing. If not to her heavily made-up cheeks, color had risen in Osbourne's long, smooth neck.

"What about Paddy's plan? My plan now, I suppose."

"He outlined it."

"And concluded?"

"That the proposal has a greater chance of being accepted with Mr. Power dead than alive."

"As, say, the 'Sean Dermot O'Duffy Proposal'? You know, a program of economic restructuring that will lead Ireland into the twenty-first century? Do you want my opinion of that?" Osbourne had stopped at the drinks cart and splashed some whiskey into two glasses. "Neat, isn't it? Water on the side?" She opened a bottle of Ballygowan Spring Water and clinked some ice into another glass.

Frost had left nothing out, Bresnahan observed. Not even her choice of drink.

Back at the table Osbourne placed the glasses in front of Bresnahan; when she sat, she leaned both elbows on the table and looked into Bresnahan's eyes. Hers were a curious gray color, lighter even than McGarr's or—Bresnahan now remembered—Shane Frost's. Close, like that, Bresnahan could see the ridges in Osbourne's face. Why hadn't modern reconstructive surgery, which doubtless she could afford, been able to help her? she wondered. Or had the woman chosen to keep her disfiguration? Why?

Osbourne reached for a whiskey glass and clinked it against the other. "To candor."

Bresnahan only regarded her appraisingly.

"The economic pump Shane mentioned? It required priming. Did he mention how much?"

Bresnahan shook her head.

"To date, twenty-seven billion Irish pounds. That works out to thirty-five billion U.S. dollars, which is the currency much of it will have to be paid back in.

"If the borrowed money had simply been divided equally and distributed, Joe and Joan Soap would probably have been better off, to say nothing of the Treasury, which at least would have been able to collect taxes on the money.

"There are three-point-five million souls in Ireland, which works out to some seventy-seven hundred pounds per man, woman, and child. A family of five would have had thirty-eight thousand pounds. A family with five *children*, which is not unusual, fifty-four thousand pounds. How many people do you know who have derived benefits anywhere near those figures?

"Even most of us who have gotten jobs because of our miraculous economic transformation haven't seen that value."

Bresnahan blinked. Her salary was close to twenty thousand pounds per year.

"Subtract what you would have made in the original economy, the incredible double-digit inflation of the late seventies and early eighties, and the sixty-five percent tax rate that comes right off the top of your salary and the eighty-two percent off mine. I won't be petty and mention the other taxes on gasoline, tobacco, automobiles, alcohol, appliances, and so forth that make us among the most heavily taxed people in the world and virtual workers for the state.

"And what have we got for it? A large number of low-pay jobs that might evaporate in 1992. A diaspora of new, shoddy housing estates that will soon be unsightly slums. Urban sprawl, traffic congestion, air pollution, crime, and drug abuse. All the sordid details attendant to an industrial society that you in the police see every day in Dublin or Cork or Limerick. Even sometimes out here, which twenty years ago was unthinkable.''

Like a nice, neat locked-door murder, perhaps committed by one or several of the best persons in the society. Or maybe even the government itself for motives political and economic, though Bresnahan hoped not. The police did not see *that* every day.

"Let me ask you something else. Do you know anybody who pays little or no direct taxes at all? Who, on the other hand, has benefited mightily from every sort of machinery grant, land consolidation, fuel support, and other government subvention?''

Farmers. Her own father was one.

"Then we have development grants, low-interest, government-guaranteed business loans, matching grants, government tax abatements and deferrals and suspensions.''

Developers, entrepreneurs, financiers, business owners large and small, had benefited from those, and they were Sean Dermot O'Duffy's staunchest supporters.

"What I'm saying—Shane's and O'Duffy's and all the other boomers' great gusher of a pump hasn't splashed everybody equally, and with twenty-seven billion pounds flowing, you didn't have to get too wet to get rich. Sure the Irish government has grown by leaps and bounds. Certainly a welfare state has been created. But the fact is that six percent of the people in this country now own eighty-five percent of our goods and resources. And now that they have political clout, they want somebody else to pay their debt. If that continues to happen, things for them will only get better. For all others, worse.

"That's what Paddy was trying to prevent with this conference. And now me.'' Osbourne waited until Bresnahan's eyes met hers. "Finding ourselves soon—sometime in the 1990s—a nation of young urban poor. Exploitable poor. You know, a ready pool of low-pay laborers. Those who remain and don't emigrate.''

"O'Duffy intends that?''

"Think of the advantages. Free trade with Europe. Transportation costs much less than to the Pacific Rim nations, which by then will find their cost of labor rising while ours is falling. Already we're the third-poorest-paid work force in Western Europe, after Spain and

Portugal, who have only recently entered the Market and whose people are nowhere near as well educated or trainable.''

Osbourne finished her drink and hunched a shoulder. The skin on her upper chest was fair and smooth and certainly looked younger than her—how old could she be?—thirty-five or forty years. ''Far be it from me to know what O'Duffy intends, but his actions have seldom failed to benefit those who support him. Why would that change? And with him and not Paddy in charge of the details of any debt-for-equity swap, I should imagine there could be smiles all around their small group.''

Bresnahan did not want to believe that the government might be involved in murder, but even if in some way it were, the act itself had to have been committed by a hand that would have had its own motive.

''Mr. Power was a wealthy man?''

Osbourne shook her head. ''No—Mr. Power was a *rich* man.''

''Billions?''

''I don't know. He didn't share that information with me. Or anyone.''

''Who inherits?''

''I don't know that either. The Power Fund, I should imagine. And his children.''

''The wife?''

''Again, I don't know, but I don't think so. Paddy had a bitter divorce. 'Highway robbery,' he called it, and I don't see him leaving Nell, who has already gotten her share, in his will. You should ask Shane, who was Paddy's solicitor.''

Bresnahan waited.

''Oh, yes—Shane's a lawyer too. He only became a banker on Paddy's insistence. You know, an offer too good to refuse.''

Bresnahan inclined her head, wishing to know more.

''The founding Eire Bank agreement was a seventy/twenty split with ten percent to various political and, you know, *establishment* insiders. Paddy's was the biggest part since, really, without him there would have been no Eire Bank. Paddy had all of the connections, all of the expertise, and much of the original money. Shane's portion of twenty percent was more like a gift. An incentive for him to remain with the bank as . . . figurehead, when Paddy moved on.

''But it was Eire Bank that became the bone of contention in his divorce. Paddy was partial to Eire Bank, since it was his first leap into finance and his only real commercial creation. The greater part of his money was made abroad in strict capitalist practice, buying and selling securities, financial vehicles, banks, savings institutions, and the like. Also, he wished to maintain a base here in Ireland so that, when he returned, people would know that he had shared their experience in good times and bad, and was not just another 'conquering blow-in,' was his phrase.

"Nell knew it, and out of grasping spite, I'd say, demanded a half share of everything he was worth, even though they had not lived as man and wife for nearly twenty years and *she* had left *him*, though she now tells everybody different. Their lawyers negotiated back and forth for more time than I care to remember. Finally she settled for an enormous sum of money, which was never revealed, and a nineteen percent stake in Eire Bank. Leaving Paddy a controlling interest of fifty-one percent."

"And a finger in his pie," Bresnahan thought aloud.

Osbourne nodded. "Which is just what she wanted. Given what she's now worth, it could not have been anything else."

"Sounds as if the woman was angry."

"With every right, really."

Bresnahan raised her glass and pretended to drink.

"Ultimately Paddy was a . . . vain, self-centered man, who was careless of his lovers, friends, and associates. Oh, I know"—Osbourne raised a palm—"what was said of him publicly. All the extolling of his brilliance and compassion, his generosity and humanitarianism. AIDS victims, battered women, abused children—Paddy was there first with the most. And I suppose he *demonstrated* concern for the people he dealt with daily, knowing the names of their spouses and children, where they went to school and university, their hobbies, their passions.

"And Paddy was entertaining and could have gone on the stage. Really. A one-man show. He could tell a story better than anybody I ever heard. But it was all so . . . *considered*, so much to purpose. Against the day when he would need something from you."

"But his philanthropy?" asked Bresnahan, drawing Osbourne out.

"Answer me this—at whom was it directed exclusively?"

Bresnahan hunched her wide shoulders; she knew only what she read in the papers, which was that Power had given enormous sums to a broad range of Irish funds, charities, and institutions.

"The Irish people," Osbourne said through a bitter smile. "Against the day when he would call in that debt too. In the voting booth."

"Where on Sunday afternoon did you see Nell Power?"

"In Paddy's room. I was delivering some of these for the cocktail reception." Osbourne reached for a fanfold brochure, which she placed in front of Bresnahan. "They had only just arrived from the printer."

"You had a key?"

"Yes, of course. As Paddy had a key to this room. We were a team."

"But no longer lovers."

The question made Osbourne's ears pull back. She pushed herself up in the chair. "I don't know if we ever were, as that term is currently used. Let's say that we were no longer *that* sort of team."

"Your choice or his?"

"Neither. Or both. I don't know. People change, life goes on."

"What about lending as love?"

"Did Shane mention that to you?"

Bresnahan blinked.

Osbourne laughed and shook her head. "Shane's the complete parasite, really. His mind has never been violated by an original idea. Lending as love was Paddy's notion. He used to say that you have to love a borrower's possibilities to lend him money, and he must value your good opinion of him to pay you back. But it was just the salesman in Paddy. You know, seeing things in clear, catchy, and simplistic ways. But it was revealing nonetheless. As I said, Paddy did nothing for nothing."

"And your opinion?"

"Of that? Well, love is love, and banking banking. And there's not enough of the pure kind of either activity in circulation these days."

You yourself being living proof, thought Bresnahan, who had yet to hear a sympathetic word about Paddy Power or anybody else from the woman. "Did you tell Mr. Power that his wife had somehow come into possession of photocopies of his note cards?"

Osbourne shook her head. "To tell you the truth, it slipped my mind, what with the cocktail reception, the guests who were arriving, the conference itself, and Paddy's looking so ill. Mossie Gladden called my attention to it. Paddy asked about Nell's visit, but he looked so . . . gray I decided to put it off until the morning, and I'm glad I did."

"Why would Dr. Gladden have been sent Mr. Power's note cards?"

Osbourne sat up. "*Really? Mossie* Gladden?" Her smile was playful and genuine, Bresnahan judged. "Isn't that interesting, what with all Paddy's insider information that the cards must contain. I should imagine Mossie's just the man to make the most of them. Have you seen that he's scheduled his own press conference for tomorrow at the bridge in Sneem?'' She stood.

''Mind if I take a sheet of paper from your photocopier?'' Bresnahan pointed to the machine by the wall. ''What happened to your face?'' It was another McGarr technique: the unexpected hard question at the end of an interview.

''Fire.''

Bresnahan wondered if Osbourne had scars on other parts of her body, but she could not bring herself to ask. ''Aren't you going to answer that call?'' She pointed at the phone and its red blinking light.

Osbourne only smiled, as though to say, Whenever you're gone.

''Well, I must be off now.'' Bresnahan offered her hand. When Osbourne took it, Bresnahan reached for the phone with her left, picking up the receiver and pressing down the blinking button.

Osbourne cried out, objecting, and reached for it, but Bresnahan held her away.

''Hah-loo, Gretta? Nell Power here. I'm sorry to pull you away from your conference, but shouldn't we have a chat, after what's happened?''

''About what?''

Osbourne said, ''It's not—'' before Bresnahan, applying pressure with her right hand, folded under Osbourne's knuckles and brought her to her knees.

''The bank, of course.''

''What about the bank?''

''With Paddy now gone, it changes *everything*, doesn't it? For you, for us. We must get Shane to reopen negotiations, since the Japs are here for the conference. We might even wrap it up before they have to return.''

''Why?''

There was a pause, and then, ''Hah-loo, is this Gretta Osbourne?''

''Hang on, I'll get her for you.'' Bresnahan smothered the mouthpiece of the phone on her chest and said to Osbourne, ''What about Mr. Power's death changes things at Eire Bank? For you and Nell Power.''

Osbourne, her face contorted in pain, shook her head. ''I don't know. I don't own a share. I only *worked* for Eire Bank.''

Bresnahan squeezed harder.

''I don't know. I don't *know*, I told you. I'm on leave to the Fund and not privy to anything there anymore.''

"What negotiations should Shane Frost reopen, now that Mr. Power is dead? With some Japanese."

"I have no idea."

"You're lying." Bresnahan loaded her shoulder into the grip she had on the woman's hand. Osbourne cried out again, and her head drooped toward the carpet.

"I'm not lying. I don't know. For a year now I've been working on the proposal for this conference. I've had nothing to do with Eire Bank."

Bresnahan released the hand. "Speak to this woman as though I'm not here." She reached the phone to her.

"Yes?" Osbourne said, when she had recovered herself. "Yes, it's Gretta, Nell. I don't know what you mean. She listened, said, "Fine. Tomorrow, lunch," then handed the phone back.

Bresnahan listened, but Nell Power had rung off.

"Never in my life have I felt so . . . *violated*," Osbourne began complaining.

Then you must have led a sheltered life, Bresnahan thought, in spite of your brilliant career. She advanced on the photocopy machine.

"Fergus Farrell will hear of this. And my solicitor."

"Could he be Shane Frost as well?"

"I'll ring Farrell up right now."

The machine was already on. Bresnahan pressed the button, and a sheet of paper was discharged from its maw.

Down in the business office of Parknasilla, she found another machine exactly like it and did the same. "Are there any other copying machines in the hotel?" she asked the assistant manager.

"One, which we've supplied to a guest for the duration of the conference."

"Gretta Osbourne?"

The woman nodded. "No others anywhere in the hotel?"

"Not that I know of."

Walking past the telephones, Bresnahan thought about ringing up her parents, who had most likely heard from the hotel staff that she was in residence at Parknasilla. They would be miffed that she had not contacted them immediately upon arriving, but she saw by the clock above the desk it was already quarter past ten, and, elderly now, both would have long since retired to bed. After all, they were farmers.

Also, she had something else on her mind. It was doubtless juvenile, but she wished to drive into Sneem to see if any of the "gang"—the people she grew up with—were about in the pubs. It was getting on now to closing hour, and perhaps a few might need a lift home in her glorious Merc that was a block long and looked like the staff car of a German industrialist. And some of them might have seen the country gorsoon who had dropped off Paddy Power's note cards at the Waterville Lake Hotel.

To be fair, Bresnahan did think about Hughie Ward, her . . . paramour who was lodged with other resident Parknasilla personnel in a drafty old house behind the hotel. But fleetingly, it must be admitted. She told herself that Ward, who was a physical-fitness fanatic, did not much care for bars, and it took even her whole minutes to "tune in" her ear, as it were, to the local dialect. And there had been a time when she had spoken as "pure Sneem" as they.

Which thought made her not a little wistful, as the Merc powered up the drive, giving off a muffled growl—like some large, angry cat—every time she so much as brushed a toe against its hair-trigger pedal. The car was so quiet she scarcely heard the whoosh of a government limousine, passing in the other direction.

Had she lost something essential in leaving Sneem? And gained only the superficial?

If so—she decided, examining her face in the brilliant display of the lighted vanity mirror on the flip side of the Merc's visor—it was a stunning superficiality, the full effect of which she would wield with authority for whatever little it was worth.

Like a long-exiled and returning queen, she swung her tangerine legs out of the car and strode toward the pub that she had not set foot in for three years nearly to the day. A day incidentally that she had struggled unsuccessfully to forget.

Tonight would help.

CHAPTER 11

Rot Beneath Heather

STEPPING AWAY FROM the Parknasilla main entrance where he had been standing, McGarr walked toward the dark limo with blackened one-way windows and government plates. He had been waiting now for over an hour, ever since he got the phone call from Commissioner Farrell. "You're to be at the door. I'll be by to pick you up directly."

"Mossie Gladden give you that?" Farrell now asked, when McGarr finally lowered himself into the spacious backseat and the door was closed. Farrell meant the bandages on McGarr's left hand and the others that could just be seen on his neck above the collar of a turtleneck sweater.

McGarr said nothing. He had spent most of the early evening in the surgery of a Kenmare doctor, getting the wounds cleaned, stitched, and bandaged, and he was trying to forget the . . . misadventure if he could.

"You should press charges." And relieve Taosieach O'Duffy of the prospect of Gladden's press conference on the bridge in Sneem tomorrow, he meant.

"So that Gladden can hold court from a jail cell?" McGarr replied. "How would that look?" For your government, he did not think he had to add.

Farrell blinked. Obviously he had not thought of the possibility. McGarr regarded the man's liverish complexion and watery eyes, which, framed by tortoiseshell glasses, made him appear puffed up and owlish. His cheeks were full, his forehead wide, his mouth small and pursed. He was wearing a pink blazer over a plum-colored sports shirt and looked as though he had just stepped off a beach.

There was a gold bracelet on one wrist that was balanced by a sizable ruby in a ring on the other hand. The car was Farrell's own, driver and all, and went with the town house in Dublin and breeding farm in Kildare. McGarr nearly smiled to think that in a time of economic crisis and gross public debt, Farrell had the charity to serve government sometimes at his own personal expense. But then government—its leaders, policies, and opportunities from which he might profit—had always been an interest of the man. Farrell might be stupid, but he was not dumb.

"Aren't you interested in where we're going?"

McGarr returned his gaze to the dark window. He already knew. They were following the river toward Kenmare. The sky was clear, and a waxing moon, three days from full, was stippling the car with achromatic semaphore, whenever they passed under trees. Somewhere out beyond the estuary that looked placid and eternal, like a soft green dreamscape in the moonlight, Taosieach Sean Dermot O'Duffy was waiting to hear the details of what McGarr had learned so far. He had a house in West Cork, McGarr seemed to remember, and otherwise Farrell would have asked for an update.

"Will you be having something?" Farrell opened the front of a small bar.

McGarr ignored the offer. He chose with whom he drank.

The house was unpretentious, a stage set where Sean Dermot O'Duffy was often seen by television audiences as living like one of them. A rambling bungalow, it was distinguished from neighboring structures only by the security squad at the gate, the electronics antennae on the roof, and the half-dozen costly cars in the drive.

Stepping out into a cold wind that was gusting from the west, McGarr again glanced up at the moon. It was crystalline in a limpid, starry sky. He would see it again at better times, he decided, but never more clearly, which he hoped was a sign.

A different kind of light greeted them when the door opened. It was warm, yellow, smoky, flatteringly dim, and laden with smells of costly foods, liquors, wines, and cigars. Dinner had evidently just finished; McGarr could hear sounds of water running, plates clacking, and women chattering away gaily from the kitchen at the back of the house. Another voice came to him from behind the sitting-room door. It was low, confidential, and sounded nearly like prayer.

Without knocking, Farrell opened the door, and McGarr stepped into a low, narrow, but long room, at the farther end of which three men were gathered in an inglenook. The younger two were sitting on one bench, Sean Dermot O'Duffy was alone on the other. Like the lumpy cracked eye of a Cyclops, a mound of peat was glowing in the hearth.

O'Duffy raised a hand in greeting to McGarr, but he continued his remarks to Harney and Quinn, his ministers for Justice and Finance respectively. O'Duffy was a pale, bald man with freckled skin and a soft, musical voice that revealed his beginnings here in the hills of West Cork. It was said he had never once been seen to lose his temper, which in Ireland was something of a wonder, and he had negotiated the treacherous fens of the Irish political scene with a buoyancy that had left his opponents in a kind of awe. He had been taosieach on and off for over two decades, and when times were tough, as they were now, his leadership was called for.

Having finished what he had been saying, O'Duffy now turned to McGarr and Farrell. Bloodshot hazel eyes that were pouched in deep folds regarded them, each in his turn. With a raked forehead and a bluff nose, his head had the shape of a medieval battle helmet. Tabs of shiny flesh—under the eyes, along the line of the jaw—glinted like sheered armor plate. There was even a dent along the temple where O'Duffy had been injured at one time or another. He looked ancient and scarred.

"How are you this evening, Peter?"

McGarr nodded a greeting. Ireland was a small country, and he had met O'Duffy on several occasions, mainly social.

"And the wife—"

"Noreen," McGarr supplied.

"Fitzhugh and Nuala's daughter." O'Duffy often saw the Frenches, who were prominent in social and cultural circles.

Again McGarr nodded.

"That's grand. I assume you know Des Harney and Pat Quinn—" O'Duffy motioned to the other men, who rose slightly, offering their hands.

"Sit you down here now and tell us what you've been up to today." O'Duffy patted the cushioned inglenook bench beside him. "Drink?"

McGarr shook his head; none of the other men had glasses. O'Duffy was smoking a pipe, Quinn a cigar, and Harney—the youngest of the three—had folded his hands across his sweatered chest and was regarding McGarr with pointed interest.

McGarr sat and reached for a cigarette.

"So you're not mistaken," O'Duffy began, "let me say that all here are deeply saddened by Paddy's death. He was unique, a kind of unlikely human being that the world could use more of. He was also my friend with whom I shared what I think of as my 'Young Turk' years, and he will be held forever dear in memory.

"On another level and for your ears alone—if Paddy had to die, he could not have picked a better time. For us and for the country, but I believe Shane Frost has already expressed that thought to your subordinate. The handsome young woman."

"Detective Inspector Bresnahan," McGarr supplied.

O'Duffy nodded. "Young Hughie Ward the pugilist's friend."

It was indeed a small country, McGarr thought while lighting the cigarette; Ward and Bresnahan had been discreet nearly to a fault, but here their liaison was known to the taosieach.

"Now, then—you've had a chance to look things over there at Parknasilla. I understand the postmortem has been completed, and that you've even had to grapple with the avatar of all that's rural and righteous, the fearless Mossie." O'Duffy flicked a finger at McGarr's bandaged hand. "What say you—was it murder, as Mossie claims? Or did Paddy die through some misadventure with his medicines? Or—even better for Paddy's family—did he just die?"

McGarr drew on his cigarette. He would not lie, but he wondered how much of the truth he could tell O'Duffy and still remain in charge of the investigation, which he thought of now as essential. He never wanted it said that he had succumbed to political pressure and covered up Paddy Power's murder. At the same time he wished to finish out his career as a policeman in the Guards, preferably in his present post as chief superintendent of the Serious Crimes Unit, which was the official title of the Murder Squad. He had a young daughter to raise and a family to feed. He also enjoyed the prominence of his position and the respect in which he was held in police circles and by the country as a whole.

Exhaling the smoke, he decided to take it slow and discover what O'Duffy already knew, which might easily be more than he. After all, the man had an entire government at his service, to say nothing of sycophants like Shane Frost and Commissioner Farrell.

"Unfortunately it's like Dr. Gladden wrote the script in every particular from the physical evidence, through the . . . situation in which we found Mr. Power's corpse, to the postmortem report." McGarr glanced up and noted the disappointment on the faces of the four other men.

"More troubling still," he went on, "is the fact that Mr. Power's note cards that he had assembled over the years to write a memoir are missing. They were contained in a large notecase. The clasp was broken, and all cards but those that he had recently written and were evidently on his person at the time of death are gone.

"It could be that the theft was incidental to Mr. Power's death, but it wasn't noticed until then, and Dr. Gladden is claiming—and will elaborate in his press conference tomorrow—that the cards are part of the reason that Mr. Power was," McGarr drew in a breath, "assassinated."

Several heads went back, but O'Duffy only smiled slightly. "And the other part of his *reasoning*?"

. "That there was need to remove Power from the political scene and to co-opt and control his plan for restructuring the national debt."

"My need?"

McGarr nodded.

"And my agent of necessity?"

McGarr hunched his shoulders. "Other than Dr. Gladden himself, the only other two people who had access to Mr. Power's medicine cabinet and who knew enough about his heart condition and his medications to accomplish the deed were Shane Frost and Gretta Osbourne. His ex-wife, Nell Power, did visit Mr. Power's room sometime that day. She might have had the opportunity to change his medications, but she would have had to have been present at the cocktail reception that Mr. Power threw for the arriving conferees on Sunday afternoon to remove the evidence and replace the proper bottle. If Dr. Gladden's scenario is accurate."

O'Duffy shook his head. "Is the man entirely right? I always knew Mossie was a bit cracked, but with this he's gone round the bend altogether."

McGarr pointedly looked down at his bandaged hand. "It would appear so."

"But *your* opinion, Peter. It's that which I called you down here tonight to learn. You're our expert. I'm interested in what *you* think."

As from the cracked red pile of burning peat in the hearth, McGarr could now feel the eyes of the other men upon him, and he imagined that the continuance of his career in public service hinged upon his response.

"If it was murder, then it was a rare and cunning act devised to look like a death by the misadventure of Mr. Power's having mistaken his medications. But in my experience murderers always try too hard—to provide themselves with alibis, to cover their tracks, to inculpate others."

"Here with the note cards," said O'Duffy.

Having come to the most perilous aspect of his report, McGarr nodded. If he admitted he had the note cards, O'Duffy might demand that they be turned in to Farrell before he had a chance to read them. If he did not admit to having them and Nell Power had already told O'Duffy about the photocopies, he might be accused of deceit. McGarr was betting, however, that Nell Power, who had complained of Power's poor opinion of her and their marriage, only wished to forget them.

"If the note cards hadn't been stolen," McGarr went on, "I might suspicion murder, but I wouldn't have enough cause to pursue it. The door to the suite was locked, all the proper pills, tablets, and ampules were either in their proper bottles or had been at the time Mr. Power was stricken. The digitalis that killed him was taken orally and therefore self-administered. But until we discover who stole the note cards and why, I'm afraid we can't dismiss Dr. Gladden's charge out of hand without risking—"

"The further charge of a cover-up," O'Duffy concluded before drawing on his pipe and exhaling stream after stream of blue aromatic smoke for what seemed to McGarr like an eternity. "It has to be Mossie," he finally said. "It can't be anybody but Mossie. Nobody but Mossie is so . . . daft to dream up such a scenario. But, you know"—the hazel eyes swung to McGarr—"I don't want it to be Mossie. Or anybody, for that matter. I want Paddy Power to have died of natural causes. For the country. For myself.

"The note cards, Peter. What's in them? What do they contain?"

Again McGarr shrugged. "I haven't read them. Dr. Gladden claims—and Gretta Osbourne has corroborated—that they deal with all aspects of Power's life, that they're particular as to detail and"—he paused, as though trying to choose the proper word—"revelatory."

"But have they told you what those revelations are *in the particular?*"

McGarr shook his head. "I brought along these, however, which were found by the corpse. I thought you might like to read them." From a pocket he removed the seven cards and passed them to O'Duffy. "I was hoping to discover some clue to the whole business, especially in this one that was grasped in Mr. Power's hand. But"—McGarr shook his head—"it's just the description of his last few days, some maunderings about Ireland, and his hopes for the conference. If somebody could take a photocopy of the lot, I'd appreciate it. I'll need them back."

O'Duffy held the cards toward the fire but obviously could not read Power's crabbed hand in the dim light. "Dessie—would you be good enough to make a copy, as the chief superintendent suggests. And enlarge it, if you can."

"Might I have one as well?" McGarr put in. "My eyes aren't what they once were."

"Why not," said Harney, a smooth young man whose developer father had contributed mightily to the coffers of O'Duffy's party and now controlled a new, successful newspaper in Dublin. "Anything to further the cause of justice."

Quinn too was now on his feet. "Drinks," he explained. "All around?"

"That would be grand," said O'Duffy. "And bring Peter a tot too, Pat. It's dry work, all this cloak-and-dagger."

Said Farrell, "I'll give you a hand," and suddenly McGarr found himself alone with the taosieach, who tapped his knee.

"Listen to me now, Peter, and harken to what I say," he said in the same confidential tone that he had been using with his two cohorts before McGarr had entered the room. "I would never ask you to do anything wrong, but I wish simply for you to keep me in mind as you perform your duty.

"Governing this country is like living in a small town in the West. Sneem itself, say. There behind closed doors a person can be anything he wants. He can gather powerful people from all over the world and plan and scheme and work for evil or—in the case of Paddy Power *and* this government—for good, so long as he breathes not a word of his intentions and presents a picture of rectitude.

"The cardinal rule, however, must be observed. Never reveal the confusion of the decision-making process or any disunity in the ranks. In politics, quick, sure strokes count for everything."

O'Duffy's fiery eyes regarded McGarr, who only held his gaze.

"Once you become fodder for public chat, once the populace is allowed to chew the honeyed cud of your indecision or, as in this case, to suspicion that you might be divided as to fact, your cause is lost. I'm at a crisis here, and how you handle this sad situation will as surely shape my future as any of the good things I've done in the past. I have confidence in you. I trust you. Don't do me wrong."

But the drinks now arrived, and Harney returned with the sheets on which the seven note cards had been photocopied.

"How long did it take you to make this page?" McGarr asked.

"Longer than you'd think. The first few times I put down the lid, the force of the air blew them off."

The cards were this way and that, whereas the photocopies of the cards that McGarr had found in Nell Power's room had been perfect, every last page of the thick sheaf.

"They're still a bit disarranged," Harney went on jocularly, "but then I hope I'm never forced to be a secretary."

So did McGarr, who might soon be looking for any work he could find.

Politics was a vast, unchartable moorland, McGarr mused as Farrell's limousine stole through the moonlit darkness a half hour later. For those who could smell rot beneath heather, he imagined it was a heady, bracing, and often profitable adventure; but for those many others who saw only bright flower and green petal, it was a dark, dangerous bog best avoided whenever possible.

How many civil servants had he seen slip into its perilous depths? Too many not to be wary of the—was it?—fair warning O'Duffy had tendered him.

How long did he have? Only until Frost or Farrell discovered that he was in possession of the note cards and had as much as lied to the taosieach.

Could Gladden have made himself another copy? He didn't think so. Gladden's reaction in attacking him had been too visceral.

McGarr ran his fingers over the slick surface of the photocopied page. The lenses of no two photocopy machines produced the exact same image, regardless of any other similarity. In the morning he would send to Dublin for analysis a page from Nell Power's photocopy of Power's notes along with sheets from all the copiers they had discovered so far—in Gretta Osbourne's room, the Parknasilla office, and now Taosieach O'Duffy's house.

The note cards had been stolen from Paddy Power's room in Parknasilla sometime between Power's arrival there on Friday and Sunday morning when Nell Power claimed—and the staff of the Waterville Lake Hotel confirmed—the photocopies were delivered. By the tall, rough-looking gorsoon who was *not* Mossie Gladden.

With literally thousands of cards, how long would it have taken to create the photocopy that McGarr discovered in the ex-wife's rooms? Six cards were reproduced on each page. Say it took Gladden or whoever photocopied them two minutes to place the cards on the machine, align them, and ease the top down so they weren't forced off by the compression. That group would then have to be removed from the machine and another added in sequence, left to right, working down the page.

Five hours per thousand. Even at one minute, a large block of time would have had to have been devoted to nothing else. And unlike the page that Harney had made, the cards in the photocopy were almost perfectly aligned on every sheet. Which took concentration and care. By the tall, rough-looking country gorsoon who was *not* Mossie Gladden, McGarr assumed.

Farrell interrupted his thoughts. "I hope you're not playing us false, McGarr."

Us, was it? There had been a time no less than a year or two ago when McGarr would have told Farrell where to get off. But now with Maddie to think of, he only reached for the side of the bar and helped himself. He would drink on the government—or at least a man who represented it—while he could.

WEDNESDAY

"The soul cannot exist in peace until it finds its other, and the other is always a you."

Carl Jung

CHAPTER 12

Appearance and Reality

RUTH BRESNAHAN GOT up early Wednesday morning, astounded at how refreshed she felt on only a few hours' sleep. It must be the assignment, she decided. Or the venue. Most of her work usually kept her in and around Dublin, but here she was on her own turf and centrally involved in the investigation of what the *Times* was calling ". . . the most troubling death of the decade." The newspaper had been slipped under her door.

She bathed, dressed in another of the eye-catching costumes paid for by McGarr's bountiful dispensation from the extraordinary-expenses fund, and picked up copies of the other morning papers on her way through the hotel lobby. It had rained sometime during the night, and there in the car park sat her gorgeous Merc, sparkling in the fresh sun like a wedge of black diamond.

Sipping from a container of coffee, she scanned the several journals as the digital report of the temperature of the "cabin"—a priceless choice of word—rose in the periphery of her vision.

Banner headlines studded black-bordered front pages. Mossie Gladden's broken nose and blackened eyes stared up at her from the *Independent*. The headline read:

POWER MURDERED
GLADDEN CLAIMS
BEATEN BY POLICE

135

The front page of another paper said:

POWER CUT DOWN
GARDAI ENQUIRY LAUNCHED
PUBLIC OUTCRY

And yet another:

ASSASSINATION CLAIMED IN PADDY POWER DEATH

The pages were filled with lengthy obituaries, eulogies, and retrospectives of Power's life, but it was the Shane Frost press conference and Mossie Gladden's allegations about the circumstances that dominated the lead stories. And the promise of Gladden's press conference scheduled for eleven o'clock on the bridge in Sneem.

Bresnahan reached for the stick shift, which she only now realized had a startling shape and feel, and the car pounced down the long avenue of hardwoods toward the gate. Bresnahan drove fast and liked the big, muscular, but agile feel of the powerful, luxurious car. God, she thought, running her finger over the soft kid-sheathed cap and glancing toward the barracks where Ward was housed—what she wouldn't give for one for herself. It was as though the Krauts had designed the seat, the wheel, the—she glanced down—everything just for her, and she promised herself that someday she would own such a glorious machine.

The gate and the road in both directions were packed with journalists and media vans, and she had to wait and sip her coffee while uniformed Guards cleared her a path. Even so, the Merc was besieged, and she had to dodge and swerve and gun the engine threateningly to clear herself a path.

Sneem itself was little better with cars lining every street, but after more waiting, Bresnahan finally found herself beyond the village where, not many minutes later, she pulled her rented Merc off the road and stopped. She had an hour and a half to kill before Gladden's press conference, and she would do some "probing" Sneem-style, which was mouth-to-ear.

Touching a button, she slid down the window and looked out over the sweep of field, upland pasture, and mountain—some 350 acres in all—which comprised the freehold of her father, who was a "strong farmer" in every sense.

Before her was the semicircular entrance gate, the pebble dashing of which was touched up with white paint at least once a season. The stubby columns were topped with redbrick and framed a long gravel drive, bordered by Lombardy poplars, that climbed the slope of the mountain to a nine-room house, all on one floor. It too was faced with white dashing and roofed with terra cotta tile.

To appease her mother's notions of gentility, there was a lawn, which her father cursed when having to mow, and a solid, drained barnyard of cut granite. Surrounding it were many substantial outbuildings, the roofs of which were either in perfect thatch or covered with slate. These last were guarded by a shelter belt of towering Norwegian spruce that keened in the slightest breeze and before pesticides had been home to eagle and osprey. Above the trees was the great bald crag of the mountain and then sky, washed by winds off the Gulf Stream that flowed off shore here on the southwest coast.

A wisp of peat smoke was curling from the kitchen chimney, and Bresnahan knew that the considered, dowdy interior of the house would be as clean and orderly as the exterior was spotless, which on a farm was a labor. Now at half-nine her mother would be beginning her long preparation for the midday meal, which was still called dinner and left one feeling stunned at the sheer volume of food laid on the table. How she managed the ritual day in and day out was a mystery that Bresnahan wished herself never to solve, and, suddenly saddened, she eased her head against the back of the leather seat and considered the place in its totality.

In the brilliant morning sun the entire compound looked verdant and fine and today all "stitched up," as her father said, for the coming winter and the Atlantic storms that raged over the cliffs a quarter-mile to the west. The winter wheat was already shin high, and dried hay bulged from the barns, the excess gathered in great cylindrical rolls that were bound in plastic and tied neatly with line. Also covered were reeks of cut and dried peat, "Hard as black diamond and heavy as lead," her father often bragged. "The best turf for burning in all of Kerry," out of which he hadn't set foot in twenty years. Profoundly a homebody, his farm was his life and his world, and he asked for little more.

There he was, she could see, standing tall in the farmyard with some other man, looking down toward the gate where she was parked. They would be speculating about who she was and what she wanted, and it occurred to Bresnahan not for the first time that no character as rude as Mossie Gladden or some other country gorsoon could travel from Parknasilla to the Waterville Lake Hotel without having been noticed and remembered by at least one man or woman who worked the land. Every sound and signal, natural or man-made, every local automobile, tractor, or bicyclist was known to them, and many of those, which were new, were remembered, especially now that tourist season had passed.

Slipping the Merc into gear and slowly moving up the drive, Bresnahan reminded herself that there would come a day in the not-too-distant future when she would either have to manage or in some other way dispose of these acres, and it would break her heart. In her father's younger days times had been tough, and he had had to wait to inherit the farm before marrying. Although still square and strong, he was now in his mid-seventies. His eyesight was failing, and within the last year his gait had grown stiff. Her last time home, Bresnahan had rounded a corner of the milking parlor to find him sitting on a cream can, having fallen asleep in the sun in midafternoon, something he had never done or admitted to before. Not even her humming or her startled cry had wakened him.

When she had mentioned it in the kitchen, tears had come to her mother's eyes. "Ah, well now—he's winding down, isn't he? And wouldn't we all be after his seventy blessed years of toil. How he keeps on, I'll never know. The place really is too much for him now." And for me, Bresnahan also heard. "But it's like he's waiting for something or . . . somebody." Before calling it quits, Bresnahan knew she meant. It was a further, fervent plea of the sort she had been hearing since childhood, but with her mother fully sixty-seven herself, its finality had never been more apparent. "I've been thinking that I'd like a bit of the city myself," she had said on another occasion. "You know, *after*. All I've known in my life is quiet."

Which Bresnahan now heard as she opened the door and swung her legs out onto the recently swept stones of the barnyard. To think that sometime soon she would arrive under different circumstances and not find her father standing there to greet her made Bresnahan turn her back to the two men, ostensibly to belt her new winter coat, which was the same color as her hair. But she also dabbed at her eyes with a hankie and pulled in a deep breath of the cold mountain air that she only now realized she had been missing so much. She then glanced up once more at the ever-changing, changeless sky above the peak and, forcing a bright, brittle smile to her face, turned to them.

"What?" Her father set the broom against the hitching rail, and all six feet six inches of him stepped forward. As always, he was wearing a wool cap, bib overalls, and a white shirt with the sleeves rolled to the elbows. "Is it our Ruthie?"

And her heart went out to him to see how he had to move within a few feet of her and cock his head to know who she was. He had slipped further in the—could it be?—seven months since she had last been here. His eyes were clear but looked starred, like shattered blue glass.

"It *is*! Amn't I after meeting Sonnie, the barman from Parknasilla, in town and him telling me you're staying there as a guest and hadn't so much as rung up your mother. And now Rory here from the next farm, you'll remember, 's come over to say didn't some friends of yours see you in the pub last night and were you here for a visit but not home?" He meant the young handsome man in back of him, who was as wide and only slightly shorter.

"I wonder now"—his strong hands, which were tight on her arms, now held her back so he could examine her, like a new colt or calf—"what's come over our little girl?"

Bresnahan waited while he turned her this way and that, then without releasing her arms, leaned himself toward the car and gave it a similar close inspection. "Is it a Daimler?"

"No, a Mercedes."

"Ooo, go oo-ver, now," he remarked in his heavy South Kerry brogue. "Is it yours?"

"For the moment."

"You mean a renter?"

She nodded.

"And what about this?" Again he held her away from him, at this angle and that. He meant the orange merino wool coat, the brown hose, the Bruno Magli shoes. Thank goodness it was growing cold now, Bresnahan thought, and she had thought to wear a coat.

"Mine, I'm afraid."

"At what cost?"

Bresnahan glanced at O'Suilleabhain, knowing his ears would be drinking in every syllable; like all good farmers, her father was a careful man and known to be close with his money, and it would be repeated how he had almost asked the purchase price of the garments she was wearing. Out of the corner of her eye she could see her mother now in the kitchen door, drying her hands on her apron before stepping out. "Paid for by my work."

"Which is?"

Tiring of his questions, Bresnahan looked up into his old eyes. "Surely you heard that Paddy Power has died."

He nodded. "But, is it murth-er, like they say?"

Bresnahan nodded.

"And they sent you, my little girl, out here to, like, invesh-tigate?"

She nodded again; there was no *like* about it.

"Hear that, Rory. Did you hear that? I can remember when you two were striplings and playing here in the barnyard, and now one of you is in the possession of the largest farm in South Kerry, and the other, who will possess the best, is out pursuing villains and thieves for the Civic Guards."

But the heels of her mother's stout black kitchen shoes were ringing on the stone. "Tom—leave off now. You'll destroy her jacket altogether with your hands." She pulled at his arms, but he wasn't through with his daughter.

"I'll say this, though. I'm partial, but I declare to God you're the prettiest sight I have seen this many a long day."

Bresnahan moved in to give him a hug.

"Oh, no, no, no," her mother admonished, and turning to O'Suilleabhain as her husband and daughter embraced. "It'll be ruin't totally, and to think what it must cost."

In the hollow of his broad chest Bresnahan breathed in the complex odor that she would always associate with her father. It was a strong, sweet smell, an amalgam of peat smoke, brown soap, Yachtsman plug-cut tobacco that he burned in his pipe, the bleach in his clothes, the barn where he had spent his early morning, and the damp earth where he passed his days. She closed her eyes for a moment and pretended that she was still his little girl and time didn't matter. They could go on forever, just the three of them, there in *Nead an Iolair* (*Eagle's Nest* in Irish) on the flank of the mountain overlooking the Kenmare River with the ocean beyond.

Close, like that, she could hear his heart beating. So strong did it sound that for a moment Bresnahan nearly convinced herself that her mother's fears were groundless, and she herself was only being senti-mental. He had whole decades before him. She could see him as a younger man, the way he had first appeared to her as she had grown conscious of his presence: the biggest, strongest man in all Sneem; a kind of tough, tireless giant who worked harder than anyone around; the man people had turned to for a right, a just, and a moral opinion on a matter in dispute, which probably had been one of the reasons she had gone into the Guards; but mostly *her father* who was always there for her, no matter what.

But when she pushed herself away, she could see that he too knew what was in the wind. For the first time ever his eyes were filled with tears. Turning his head away, he released her. "Shit," he muttered.

"Shit yourself," said her mother. "It's what I'm worried about. Stand back now you''—she meant Bresnahan—''and let's have a look at you."

Her mother, Bridie by name, was yet another tall person for a woman of her generation, but thin, for which Bresnahan gave thanks now that she herself had lost weight and, it appeared, could keep her figure. Bridie was dark with deep brown eyes, and a long, somewhat Spanish-looking face. Her hair, which was chestnut-colored and she kept tied at the back of her head like a girl, had only recently begun to gray, and she now nodded appraisingly, as she surveyed Bresnahan's coat for spots. "Divine intervention, as it turns out. Not a smudge. Let's have a look at the rest of you," and her hands darted at the loop in the belt.

Before Bresnahan could object, she had the belt undone and the coat open. "Cripes—what's this? Or what isn't it?" She stared down at what she could see of a Vittadini riding jacket that was cut only to midthigh. Fashioned from wool sateen in two tones of brown, it snugged Bresnahan's narrow waist, then flared dramatically to her shoulders.

The body of the jacket was raw sienna; the velvet collar and buttons were burnt sienna. Only fringes of the pearl silk blouse beneath were showing at cuffs and collar. Otherwise she was wearing a pair of large-circle sterling-silver earrings, burnt sienna tights by Hue, and burnt and raw sienna patterned shoes from Bruno Magli. The burnished red hair, of course, was her own.

Doffing the coat, Bresnahan took several graceful, balletlike steps such as models employed on fashion-designer runways: the front; the side; the back with a chillingly coy glance cast over a broad shoulder. "It's the latest thing in Dublin." When she glanced at them, she was presented with three different reactions. Her mother was bemused; her father was shaking his head; but O'Suilleabhain's eyes were bright with discovery.

Said her mother, "It's Dublin all right. And maybe a conference of international bankers at Parknasilla. But is it Sneem, Ruth?"

What wasn't Sneem, Bresnahan wondered, with convoys of tourists from every country in the industrialized world rumbling through town in good weather? The Ring of Kerry was a must-see on any tour of Ireland.

Said her father, "I don't know what's becoming of you at all up there in the city. Something's put you off your feed entirely, and you'll be nothing in no time unless you get some meat on them bones."

"Which is the point." Her mother glanced at O'Suilleabhain, then reached for the orange coat. "Put this back on before you catch your death and come in the house. I'll wet some tea, and you can tell us what you've been up to."

Bresnahan wrapped the coat over her shoulders and looked up to find O'Suilleabhain's eyes fixed on her thighs. "I can't stay long now. I've something on in the village at eleven."

"Mossie," her father said, and shook his head. Bresnahan waited, but all he added was, "He's not been himself since he quit the Dail. Wild, like, and unpredictable," which was about the worst thing that could be said about a doctor in a farm community and certainly the worst that she had ever heard her father say about a good friend.

"Don't you see much of him anymore?" she asked.

Her mother shook her head. "He's grown strange. It's like he's disappeared up into the mountains there where his mother's people were from. If he doctors anymore, it's to sheep and goats.

"And, Rory, you come in too now. How long has it been since you two shared a word?"

It was the real point, at least to her parents. O'Suilleabhain and she had grown up together, and it had once been an unspoken agreement between the families that the two would one day marry, which made the best of agricultural sense. Being the oldest male, Rory had inherited his father's four hundred, mostly well-drained acres, and with Ruth's inheritance they would have a stake in life that few could disparage.

Added to that was the seeming advantage in husbandry of such a match, since both had grown into strong, strapping, good-looking individuals with native intelligence much above the average. Rory had the dark, unlikely good looks that were sometimes seen in the West of Ireland: black curly and lustrous hair, green eyes, and the sort of chiseled features that seemed too good to be believed. Yet by dint of hard work, shrewd bargaining, and a natural gift for gab, O'Suillieabhain had managed to get other men to take him seriously. The women, of course, had from the start, and rumor was he had by-blows scattered throughout the county.

It had proved a problem for Bresnahan, since from the moment she became aware of the opposite sex there was nobody for her but Rory O'Suilleabhain. In comparison, all others came up short or narrow or dim or poor, and she had no spark of sense after him whatsoever. Two years older than she, Rory had only to glance her way for color to rise to her cheeks, and what was worse, he seemed to know it. With his easy way of going on, he would chat her up and be great with her when others weren't around, confident that she—and her 350 acres, her father's excellent house and barns—would be his for the asking when it suited him. But in town or at a dance or with his somewhat older friends, sure, he didn't see her at all.

Thus afflicted, Bresnahan had pined for Rory O'Suilleabhain through all of her adolescence and much of her early womanhood, wishing to make herself and her parents happy. In the meanwhile Rory was out sparking with this one and that, and his mother was sitting in the Bresnahans' kitchen representing him as the "catch of Kerry," her very words. Finally, when Bresnahan had decided that if she couldn't have Rory, she wouldn't have anybody from Sneem at all and would leave for a career in parts distant, Rory had taken her aside. But he had asked only if it "really, *truly*" was what she wanted without making any further representation of affection or desire.

A year passed and then two and three, in which her mother relayed to Dublin, where she'd begun her career in the Guards, the rumors of Rory's engagements to this one or that. Yet Rory still didn't marry, which kept a dim ember burning in her heart. Somehow in the city there was nobody as tall with the cut of his head or his shoulders or the way, when he turned his eyes and attention on her, he could make her glow.

More time passed, and finally one summer, when she had returned to help with the haying and had gone out for a late drink with a cousin, she had bumped into Rory and his mates at the bar. With the good, dry weather they too had been working dawn until dusk and—Bresnahan later tried to tell herself—the drink must have gone to his head. Loud, so they could be heard by most in the small pub, one of his friends had asked Rory when he planned to do the expected thing and "take title" to the adjoining farm.

"That's all I need of a night," he had said. "A bloody big red Guard at the door, fist in one hand, 'breathalyzer' in the other." His friends had roared, and Bresnahan, devastated by the comment, had pretended to use the facilities but instead had skulked out the back door.

Three full years ago. Before she had decided to remain in Dublin and make friends and become an active part of the city. And before she had met Hughie Ward.

Now Rory O'Suilleabhain reached out and touched the sleeve of her riding jacket, saying, "Might I have a word with you, Ruthie—before we go in the house."

"About *what*?" her mother demanded; pride had its limits.

"Ah . . . ?" His opaline eyes pleaded with her to intercede. It was a word Bresnahan had discovered in a thesaurus one lonely night years before, when she had been mooning over him.

"Ma, we'll be right in," said Bresnahan.

Her father took the mother's arm and nudged her toward the door. "Come along, Ruthie drinks coffee. I'll get out the new maker she brought us last Christmas."

"Don't be long now, standing out here in the chill. And there's the clock running on to eleven. Remember your job." And Dublin and the city, she meant.

Both O'Suilleabhain and Bresnahan waited until the door had closed. With chin raised and from the height of her recent personal and professional successes that a rude character such as Rory O'Suilleabhain could never hope to emulate, she turned and looked down her long, vaguely Spanish nose at him. How many interviews had she conducted since then? she asked herself. Dozens and dozens with every class of brazen, perfidious character. She waited.

"It's about that night, a few years back." His startling eyes flashed over at her to test her reaction, and she realized they still had their power. O'Suilleabhain was without a doubt the handsomest man she had yet to lay eyes on.

"Haven't I been hammering me head off the wall these three long years, wishing I could take back what I said. I was wrong. Worse, I was drunk, and I only hope you can find it in your heart to forgive me, Ruthie."

Still she waited, watching him squirm under her measured gaze. She tried to remember all the sleepless nights she had spent trying to conjure the image that was before her now, wondering what he was doing, whom he was with, and when she would hear at least some of the words that he was speaking to her now.

"How can I make it up to you?'

Bresnahan blinked. She had an idea. O'Suilleabhain was a . . . gadabout, to phrase it discreetly, and he would be on chatting terms with most area residents. No country *gorsoon*, if a local, would be unknown to him.

"What say?" He offered a hand. "Will you forgive me?"

Bresnahan's smile was neither conciliatory nor forgiving. Instead it was accompanied by a single arched blond eyebrow and not one but two quick squeezes of his hand. "Those green eyes—how can I resist them?"

In a flash his smile muted from gratitude, through relief, to prurient design. His eyes yet again drifted down her body.

"But there is one thing."

"You name it, it's yours. Anything."

"It's nothing, really." She stepped around him and began making her way to the house. "Just your definition of a word."

"And which is that?"

With her hand on the door, she turned to him. "Breathalyzer."

His handsome brow furrowed, and he looked away. When he got it, he began a deep, full laugh that startled the geese in a pen. "You really *have* changed," he said.

What about you? she thought. "Are you coming in?"

"I am, I am. Wait till I tell the lads what you said. They'll *love* it."

And her reputation would be rehabilitated entirely in a country where words, appearances, and gestures often mattered more than deeds and facts. Take her father, for instance. The mere presence of O'Suilleabhain at their table for would cheer him for a month.

CHAPTER 13

The Other Woman

NOREEN MCGARR THOUGHT she must be suffering acute social and ambulatory deprivation. Just to be walking through the public rooms of Parknasilla—noisy with conferees, their families, and all the talk surrounding Paddy Power and his untimely death—gave her a thrill.

At the same time she could not bear the thought of having abandoned her baby into the hands of some governess whom she did not know. Without a doubt such a person had been screened and trained by the hotel, but it was equally likely that she was a local farm girl, used to the cries of pen, barn, and field animals and not to laments of the subtlety of her Maddie's.

Thus believing that she could distinguish Maddie's cries even among a nursery filled with other gamboling tots, Noreen had placed the baby audio monitor, which she had brought with her from Dublin, in the crib that Maddie would use when sleepy. She had then hooked its remote receiver to the belt of her dress. Without the desired results.

First, all of the children sounded the same, in spite of their various nationalities. And often their shrieks rose to such a pitch that Noreen kept having to adjust the volume, if only to prevent people from turning to her as she moved from the Shaw Lounge, passed the Pygmalion Restaurant, and up the stairs to the Shaw Library. There, she examined the many photographs of George Bernard Shaw, who wrote several of his plays while staying at the hotel, and the volumes of Robert Graves, who had spent his summers here when his grandfather had rented Parknasilla as a summer residence during the last century.

Even outside it was no better. After having donned a warm winter coat, Noreen found herself having to turn the receiver this way and that until finally she ignored the thing and gave herself over to the pleasure of a long walk that led through willows to a footbridge and an island that was one dense willow grove.

Up in their suite on the bed, the dresser, and two tables, McGarr had unstacked and arranged Paddy Power's note cards. In the sitting room he had done the same with the photocopies that he had discovered in Nell Power's suite at the Waterville Lake Hotel.

Most immediately apparent was the sheer volume of the cards that pertained to Power's career. They began with a quick description of how, after taking degrees from Trinity College, Dublin, and the London School of Economics, Power had spent nearly a decade working for various banks in the City of London. He then threw over his job to return to Dublin and a post as financial adviser to the political party that Sean Dermot O'Duffy was beginning to control.

The two men hit it off immediately, and on economic matters saw eye to eye. Upon being named taosieach, O'Duffy's first act was to appoint Power to a similar position in government. McGarr then read through the cards of the subheadings that he had noticed when he first found the cards in Nell Power's suite at the Waterville Lake Hotel: ''Political Roots,'' ''Political Debts,'' ''Economic Policy,'' ''Favors Done,'' ''Election Financing,'' ''I, Bagman,'' ''Dirty Tricks.''

Under the last heading there was a section detailing how O'Duffy had by design gone after Mossie Gladden, snubbing him in party caucuses and meetings, continually selecting less senior and less savvy men for party preferment, and—worst of all—excluding Mossie's constituency, whenever he could, from any optional government appropriation. ''It was a standing order,'' Power wrote, until the ''good doctor blew up, denounced O'Duffy, and resigned.'' One of O'Duffy's supporters then stood for election and took Gladden's seat.

It was cruel really—how it was done publicly. Sean Dermot might have simply let the matter rest, but the public squelching he gave Mossie seems to have unhinged him. He's *obsessed with O'Duffy, and the other day he told me that the country would be better off without O'Duffy "one way or the other," and that anybody who "took him out" would be looked upon as a martyr in the long run. "Let history be the judge." When I asked him where he got the phrase, "took him out," he said, "From friends," and would not elaborate. (*See "Mossie" heading.)*

Under the heading "I, Bagman" there were listed thirteen—McGarr counted them—cards filled with dates and sums and nothing else. The fourteenth said.

> *What I did today has made me feel cheap. I know that politics is a dirty business, but I find it interesting to note that politicians, in order to remain above suspicion and reproach, only need to direct and not take part in the unequivocal squalidness of their practices.*
>
> *Today I was made to accept money from a Protestant religious organization which is interested in erecting a drug-and-alcohol clinic in Ballymun. I asked Sean Dermot when we had begun accepting contributions from religious groups who were trying to do good; he told me we would cease immediately, whenever that religious group became the majority religion. No matter the purpose? I asked him. "What better purpose than our own?" he answered cynically. "We always try to do good."*
>
> *In order that I not be perceived as having been a willing party to this wretched affair, I will now describe exactly from how and from whom and in what form I both received and delivered this money. Who knows, the whole thing might come to light after I've passed away, when I will have no chance to explain that in this particular case I was an unwilling messenger.*

There followed a detailed record of the entire exchange, which had occurred nearly fifteen years earlier. McGarr remembered that certain Dublin newspapers had lambasted O'Duffy for not having done more to aid the efforts of the Protestant sect when he was so solicitous of any and every Catholic health and welfare program. It had been perceived then that O'Duffy had bowed to their pressure, but here was the truth in black and white with names, dates, and pound amounts. And, of course, O'Duffy himself was prominently mentioned on one occasion accepting money directly from Power.

It was political dynamite even now, he guessed. O'Duffy might deny it, but would the much-respected Paddy Power, who had gone on to become as successful as O'Duffy in his own right, have lied to himself? There would not be many voters who would think so, especially if it seemed as if Power's death had been in any way unusual.

There was another subheading, called "Gossip," which attempted to sort out fact from fabrication surrounding the romantic affairs of the major figures in O'Duffy's early governments including O'Duffy himself, who—if Power's note cards were accurate—had had a fling with Nell, Power's own wife. "Nell can never resist a 'man-of-action,' which, I suppose, in my own time was myself. And will be again."

Even skimming each card, it took McGarr over an hour to work through that material. When he had finished, he lit a cigarette. As ever now since he had been married, he was trying to quit, but somehow he equated quiet, thoughtful work, like this, with smoking, and there was no fighting the need.

Cigarette in hand, he wandered into the sitting room to ascertain that the photocopies were the same as the cards. They were, even to pointing up the subheadings, each of which had been copied on a single sheet, revealing a methodical care.

Almost as though to clear the bad taste in his mouth, McGarr drew deeply on the cigarette and looked out at the boxwood maze below him in the Parknasilla gardens. He had always known that the politics offered for public consumption in the media was a mere shadow play of what went on, say, in the sitting room of Sean Dermot O'Duffy's cottage in West Cork, but he had not even begun to guess at depths of the intrigues, the avidity with which vendettas were pursued, enemies harried, and loyal followers—no matter how undeserving—rewarded. Fergus Farrell, commissioner of the Garda Siochana, came to mind.

True, it was the *raw* material in the strict sense of a biography or memoir that Power would have had to edit and soften. And, sure, there were innumerable references to the Dail, the *Constitution*, the high courts, law and legality, right and wrong, the structure of the bureaucracy, rule and order. But what struck McGarr most was how primitive it all seemed. It read like a narrative of a bunch of wee lads out in the play yard or, perhaps more accurately, warring factions of some primitive tribe—your gang and mine—who had agreed to fight their nastiest pitched battles surreptitiously, out of the public eye.

Why? Because they were more similar than dissimilar, and what united them in discreet, cabalistic strife was greed.

Still, would O'Duffy or anybody tied to him actually murder to achieve their ends? McGarr rather thought not. If all the skulduggery exposed in the cards was crime, it was white-collar crime. Often it had involved millions upon millions of pounds, but not once did Power mention violence.

McGarr returned to the bedroom and picked up the stack of cards that had pricked his interest and dealt with a subject Power had called "Final Tally." Some of the cards were yellowed and handworn, as though he had returned to peruse them time and again. Also, he noted how the man's handwriting had become smaller, more dense, and crabbed as he had grown older, which effectively dated them.

The grouping appeared to be Power's thoughts about what was important in life. Certain cards with quotations caught McGarr's eye as he flicked through them: by Nietzsche, "*Man is the sick animal,*" and then Power's explanation: *So many possibilities, only one life.* By Hakuin, "*Not knowing how near the Truth is,/ People seek it far away: what a pity.*" By Geulincx, "*Do not despair, one thief was saved. Do not rejoice, one thief was hung.*"

There was a longer quote from Joyce, which McGarr recognized as a passage from *Ulysses* that seemed almost prophetic, given the way Power had been found. *Ultimately, what does it all come down to?* Power asked at the top of the card. The answer? "*A corpse rising saltwhite from the undertow, bobbing landward. . . . Hauled stark over the gunwale he breathes upward the stench of his green grave, his leprous nosehole snoring to the sun.*"

Power had been a widely read and thoughtful man, who had been intrigued by the complexity of life even before his first episode with his heart. That watershed, however, was apparent even in the note cards. McGarr flicked one over that had been written on Majorca and was dated some eleven years earlier.

Like some fat, bald Theseus, I have been sitting in the sun of this foreign isle, searching blindly for an Ariadne thread to lead me out of the labyrinth of my discontent. Today miraculously, when trying to assuage Shane's urgent entreaties to return post-haste because of some Eire Bank crisis, it came to me that both thread and answer lie within.

For too long now, ever since I returned from London to join Sean Dermot and his government, I have been ignoring myself and my own personal needs. You get caught up in things and bit by bit you lose your sense of self, until suddenly it's gone and you're lost.

Card two of that entry read:

I think now I have long believed without realizing that the poets are right, and there is a still place deep in all of us, a kind of wellspring of the spirit, from which the energies of life flow to us. These are the indiscernible *means of support, without which we can have everything else and yet have nothing. Your collective energies are who you are as a person and what makes you different.*

The primary energy, which we all share no matter how blighted our experience, is love, which seeks to be realized in another person. I now realize that you can go through life only half-alive (or half-dead) without finding that other person who will make you complete.

I refer not to a love affair, which is mere captivation and when over ends. I mean a "click," a bond, a mesh—that slipping together of two persons who know in their hearts they were meant to consummate each other. I once knew that transcendent, glorious feeling, but through my own ignorance of myself, my needs, and the other let it (and her) slip away.

The cards for that entry stopped there. McGarr fanned forward, but he discovered only further maxims and pithy sayings, until he came to a group of cards that seemed to extend Power's maunderings about—what was his phrase? *primary energy*—to banking.

McGarr's cigarette was burning his fingers, and in stubbing it out, he glanced through the window to see Noreen below him, walking through the maze in the Parknasilla gardens that ran down a gentle hill to the sea. She was—he considered her appraisingly—a fine auburn-tawny, good-looking woman with the kind of quick, sure gait that suggested (but did not invite) pursuit. She had something in her hands that she kept holding to an ear.

Now, what was the chance in that, he asked himself—her being down there while he was reading just that card? Labyrinth/maze. Noreen being very definitely the "click," the bond, the mesh, in his life.

The first time McGarr had met her in her parents' art gallery in Dawson Street, he had maneuvered her on a stratagem into a back room where he had tried to kiss her and had had his face slapped smartly and was shown the door.

From that moment on his life had been changed. Totally, irrevocably. It was as though he had suffered a kind of seizure, and he would never feel so . . . transcendent again. That much he knew *and* could credit in Paddy Power's note cards.

He looked back down:

> *Borrowing, as presently constituted, is like a* bad *love relationship. Money, like love, is energy; you give it in the attempt to bind yourself to the destiny of the other person, which will make both of you better. The hope is that your combined energies will add up to more than the sum of the parts, you will make and do good things together, and you will thereby love each other more.*
>
> *But when, as often happens, some unforeseen event or set of conditions diminishes this transcendent appreciation of the bond, love dies. I have loaned you money; you owe me. You tell me you can't pay back unless I give you more. Please. I have no choice in the matter, do I? Unless I write off your debt (and you) as bad. Suspicion, ill feeling, and rancor set in. And you have had to beg.*

The second card said:

> *How much better would it be to give freely? To say, Here, I give you this because I love you, you need it, and the gift will make you better. If, later, everything turns out as it should, you might decide to give me something back, but I leave the kind and timing of the gift up to you.*
>
> *In sovereign borrowing, where there are relatively few borrowers and lenders and reputation is everything, such a system might actually work. And* would *at least for countries like Ireland, which has a history of credit accountability.*

The succeeding cards then sketched out Power's idea to swap Irish debt for equity in Irish, government-held assets. The last few under the heading ''Final Tally'' closed with further maxims, most notably

Ben Franklin's, *"Plow deep while sluggards sleep."* Which gave McGarr an idea. All this bother about love was provoking.

Wondering how long it would take Noreen to return to the suite, he glanced out the window and was pleased to see that she had made her way out of the maze. He glanced back down at the stacks of cards that had been arrayed on the bed and fought the urge to light up another smoke.

So—after Power had become aware of his heart problem some eleven years earlier, he had recuperated in Majorca where he had decided to reorder his life. It was at that time, McGarr also seemed to remember, that, after living apart for years, Power sued for divorce from his wife, Nell. Also, he began the processes that led to the formation of the Paddy Power Fund and—McGarr inferred from the cards he had just read—the steps that led to Power's proposal for restructuring the Irish debt. And perhaps the cause for his murder.

What interested McGarr most, however, was just which, if either, of the two women, who had had knowledge of his heart condition, Power had loved.

McGarr reached for the "Nell" cards that he had grouped alongside the "Gretta Osbourne" and "Shane Frost" stacks. Curiously there was no "Mossie Gladden" file, but then, McGarr supposed, in recent years Power had seen Gladden only infrequently.

Holding the stack close to his chest, McGarr let his thumb fan through the file. Few cards seemed to be narrative; most took the form of observations that Power had made about either his wife or his marriage. More slowly he scanned through them again, stopping at those that gave him some insight into the nature of Power's relationship with his wife.

> When I look back on our life together, I realize we were only happy with each other for the time that we were poor or, later, when we launched ourselves on the adventure of seeing if we could make something of ourselves.
>
> Once I did and Nell had the children, something slipped, and the bliss of confronting the intractability of the world together fled. Yet here we are years later with not even sympathy between us, hanging on to the husk of the marriage and our shared history, as sorry as it is.

McGarr paused at a further card.

A woman calls mature a man who will serve her every whim, and once he does, she no longer respects him and then will praise in his presence other, perhaps lesser men, whom she knows only partially.

McGarr then walked two fingers through the stack, choosing cards at random.

Nell is a woman you cannot do too much for. She gets simply beside herself if she cannot make every aspect of my life serve her and her children. "That's all right," she tells me, when I have to beg off from some duty she has expected me to perform. "If that's all you have to give us."

McGarr looked up; where had he heard *that* before?

Of my life and my time, she means, when in fact she already has it all. I often think that she would only be satisfied if in some public forum I dedicated my death to her.

My crime is that I married Nell and am the identifiable criminal in the tragedy of her life. No mention is ever made of the veritable fortune that I've placed before her for her use. That much was evidently expected.

I keep asking myself why Nell and I have chosen to remain together all these years in spite of the continual running battle that is our marriage. I have known—and know—other women with whom I share so much more, including goodwill. Now that New York is actually my home, it would be easy to acknowledge the reality of our situation and divorce.

I think now it is because of our history together and how in the past we shared that first bliss of our love which cannot be repeated. There are other women I prefer to be with, other women with whom I have more in common, but I will never love any of them in the same way as I have loved Nell, which makes all the difference. So what if we no longer actually love each other? What is that?

The final card said:

> I am reminded of the lyric from Tristan and Isolde: "In this world let me have my world, to be damned with it or saved."

Or murdered, thought McGarr.

Feeling rather bleak, he squared up the stack and placed it back on the bed. He desperately desired another cigarette, but, well, he was married, and—as he had just read—compromises had to be made. Or else.

He reached for the stack labeled "Gretta," which was fairly thick. But he heard a key in the door, and as he moved out into the sitting room, he chanced to look at the photocopies for the same heading, "Gretta." It was minimal and contained only three cards.

The oldest-looking said:

> I feel like the donkey in Apuleius' Golden Ass who was through the love of a woman reborn. A man needs a woman to confide in, a woman who will not break his confidence and put him down. Better, a woman who will build him up and encourage him to excel. All of us being essentially little boys who need our egos stroked by some consubstantial mammy, I fear. But not mammy, which is the point.

The next.

> Most women want a relationship of some sort that will last over time. Most men want a quickie, somebody who will be there when you need her in the way you need her. Even after whole intervals of time. When you find somebody like that, treat her right.

And the last:

> Gretta has told me she has taken a younger lover. I replied that it would be unfair of me to object. All I want is for her to be with me when I need her, and would she be amenable to that? At first she seemed almost disappointed,

but she said she would. Gretta is priceless, a gem. Without
her I don't know how I would get on at all.

Was that all Power had to say about a woman with whom he had
had a close *relationship*, whether acknowledged or not, over what
seemed to be at least a decade? Not in the originals.

"I've just discovered the strangest thing," said Noreen when she
had entered the bedroom.

Raising a hand, McGarr stayed her. The stack of original "Gretta"
cards contained at least two dozen cards. Somebody had sanitized the
Osbourne entries that had been sent to Nell Power. Why? To make
Power's opinion of her seem better than his opinion of the wife?

Had other headings been similarly expurgated? Gladden. He now
remembered that there was no heading for him in the note cards.

Back in the sitting room he discovered that there was no heading
for Gladden in the photocopies either. Which meant? McGarr rearranged the papers and set them down on the table. With the question
still in his eyes, he turned to Noreen.

"Listen to this." She held the receiver of their baby monitor
toward him and switched it on.

Instead of hearing his daughter, as he had expected, he heard a
jumble of adult voices speaking animatedly in a vowelly language he
did not know. "Chinese?"

"Japanese, I think. It's like interference," Noreen explained. "I
couldn't get the thing to work very well, and there's this channel
selector here on the side. When I pushed it from C to D, these people
came on. Have you seen the cute little Japanese baby with the group
at the Nomura Bank table? I bet—"

A phone began ringing. McGarr turned his head toward the one
in the sitting room, only to realize the sound was emanating from the
monitor. The conversation had stopped, and they now heard,
"H'woah? Ah, yes—Mistaw Flost." Because of the staticky reception
and the man's heavy accent, it was difficult to catch every word precisely, but McGarr thought he heard, "Have you studied our counter-
proposal?" And another pause. "Be happy to meet with you. Three
o'clock, then. In your room." The man hung up, and the other Japanese
burst into pandemonium, each voice trying to speak over the other.

Noreen lowered the volume and turned to McGarr. "What does
it mean?

McGarr had no idea. Perhaps the Japanese had some counteroffer
to the Power debt-for-equity swap? But why then all the . . . emotion?

Even now McGarr could hear sighs and cries and several ebullient conversations going on at once. Were the Japanese so . . . involved in everything they did? Was that the secret to their success?

Or was it . . . ?

"Eire Bank," said Noreen.

At the table McGarr began spreading out the photocopies of the "Gretta" note cards that were missing from the stack of originals. "Could you keep your ear on that thing? Maybe Frost will call back." Pity it had not been the other way around and the monitor in Frost's room. McGarr's head came up.

Was it worth the risk? Without a court order electronic eavesdropping was illegal in Ireland. Frost was a bachelor. Why would he have a baby monitor in his room?

A mistake. Ward was new to his job; he got the wrong room.

Noreen looked over McGarr's shoulder. "What have you there?"

"Paddy Power's censored opinion of Gretta Osbourne." McGarr showed her the photocopies that had been sent to Nell Power, then pointed to the additional cards that were contained under the "Gretta" heading in the note cards.

No matter how much a woman professes to be interested only in a strictly physical exchange, once carried beyond an occasional congruence, the die is cast and she feels proprietorial.

Woman always *end up owning you in some important way or other.*

Ultimately, what does a person need from others—to be loved. If she claims she does not, perhaps she cannot be loved. Or doesn't love herself. *I suppose I had some part to play in that—the fire, the scars, my insensitivity to her. But that part of my life is over, and surely I'll make it up to her.*

In spite of her smile and willingness to tackle any difficult problem, there is a negative side to Gretta's personality, best seen in what she chooses to read, hear, and sing when not working, which admittedly is seldom. It is that whole negative side to Irish culture, filled with death, love-loss, and keening. It is as though, in the last analysis, she does not want to win.

The great advantage of middle age is the capacity to look upon a beautiful thing—a piece of property or a woman—and not necessarily desire to possess it.

No act in life is pure. And no relationship. All yield both good and evil results, or at least pairs of opposites. In that way life is a muddle.

The McGarrs raised their heads.

"What horrible things to think," said Noreen. "He was a right sexist bastard, wasn't he?"

That was a change. Only a day or two ago Power had been the sort of person you could point to with pride and say, Now, *he's* Irish.

"Look at this . . . shite. 'Beautiful *thing* and ". . . not necessarily desire to possess it.' How did he know she hadn't been using him in the very same way he was using her? The *balls* of any man thinking that every woman *wants* or *needs* to be possessed! Do you think you *possess* me?"

McGarr looked away; he wouldn't touch that question with asbestos gloves.

"And all the rest of this drivel—'women always end up *owning* some important part of you.' And they weren't even *married*, for Jesus' sake. What if I were to turn this around? Do you think I *own* you?"

Body and soul, McGarr thought horribly. The former proprietorship being in sad neglect.

"Have you ever thought of a . . . you know, mistress?"

Perhaps two minutes ago, McGarr thought. But certainly not after having read Power's note cards *in company*, like this. And then there was Power's fate to consider, which was an exemplum. "I think what's most interesting is this bit—" He pointed to the reference to (evidently) Osbourne's scarred face, a fire, and Power's acceptance of blame. "As well as the exclusion of these cards from the photocopies that were sent to Nell Power. It's as though whoever sent the cards to Nell Power wished to represent Gretta Osbourne as being adored by Paddy Power, when in fact he had a"—McGarr's mind searched frantically for a Noreen-acceptable term—"balanced approach to the woman."

"I asked you a question."

Turning to look at Noreen for the first time since her outburst, McGarr struggled to keep himself from laughing. Two patches of bright pink had appeared in her cheeks. The nostrils of her long, thin nose were flared, and her green eyes sparkled with outrage. "May I make an observation?"

Her chin quivered.

"I am *not* Paddy Power—"

"That's not what I'm asking. I'm asking how you—"

"Nor am I *all* men."

She blinked.

And before she could feel affronted, having been shown the error of her way of thinking, McGarr added, "And there's no Mossie Gladden file. There's a "Nell," a "Gretta" file in two parts, and a file for Shane Frost. But nothing for Gladden, who has claimed to have been Power's best friend. And there's this—" He showed her Power's reference in the "Dirty Tricks" stack to the existence of a "Mossie" heading.

"That doesn't make sense."

McGarr waited; often another opinion on (ahem) another wavelength was helpful.

Said Noreen, "To have the file doubly expurgated. Say, Osbourne, justifiably enraged at having read this sordid afflatus, decided to murder the effing louse and place the blame on the 'other woman.' In that case she might well have edited the cards to make it seem that their mutual, conveniently erstwhile, fat, bald old man had a better opinion of her than of his wife—do you have those cards?"

Certainly bald, no longer young, and as surely paunchy, McGarr indicated the photocopies in front of him.

"And the originals?"

McGarr pointed to the bedroom.

"But why then edit Mossie Gladden's cards totally? Don't tell me one or the other of those two good women might have stooped to the likes of that psychopath?"

McGarr didn't know what to tell her, but with a feeling close to relief he watched her lower a shoulder and enter the bedroom.

Gathering up Gladden's version of Paddy Power's note cards, his eye caught on a two-line thought.

> *In banking, as in nature, trends are real, but they can vanish as quickly as they come.*

And in police work and marital relations?

CHAPTER 14

Credentials

SNEEM (*SNAIDHM*) MEANS "knot" in Irish, and the village is shaped like a figure eight. Picture-book streets of mostly attached houses and shops circle two greens.

The greens are also bisected by a river that here in the village sends water, cold from deep mountain bogs, cascading through fractured rock toward Sneem Harbor and the sea beyond. Spanning the falls is an arched stone bridge so narrow that its stone walls permit the passage of tour buses only one at a time. Even cars must slow to a crawl and ease by each other with caution. At such times tourists, who gather there to photograph the torrent below, must lean out over the parapet and pull in their legs.

There is no other bridge over the Sneem River in either direction.

Dr. Maurice J. ("Call me Mossie") Gladden had chosen the site with care, McGarr judged. Under the best conditions, the bridge was a veritable traffic knot; now it was a tight, impenetrable tangle. Cars, lorries, and buses were lined in both directions, as far as the eye could see. Uniformed Gardai had arrived to keep order.

Since McGarr was known to most of the journalists who would have been sent to an event with the news value of an alleged political murder, he did not approach the milling crowd directly. Instead he parked his car at the east end of the village and walked to the back of Sneem House, a pub that sat on the northeast bank of the river. It was also a place that Paddy Power had visited on Saturday, the day before his murder. The rear door was locked, and he had to pound.

"To the front with you now," said an older man, having opened the door only enough to see who McGarr was. Inside was alive with noise, smoke, and the acrid stench of souring lees. Spent kegs were stacked in the hallway by the door.

"Civic Guard on public-house duty." McGarr pushed his I.D. toward the man's face and shouldered passed him. "And keep this door open." He might need a convenient exit. "Fire code," he explained.

The bar quieted, as McGarr made his way through the crowd of mostly taller men with wind-mottled cheeks, rumpled work clothing, and muddy Wellies. Local farmers, gathered where they might enjoy Gladden's media event in the company of a glass and "instant analysis" from their mates. Gladden's voice would not leave their ears before a judgment was rendered.

At the window McGarr nodded to three men who made space for him. One pushed an ashtray his way. The publican then appeared at his elbow. "Sorry the old fella didn't recognize you bang off, Chief Superintendent. Will you be having something?"

McGarr felt like a victim of the "global village." "Do you have brewed coffee?"

The young man's brow furrowed. He glanced toward the kitchen, "Well, the water's hot—"

"Good. Then make it four whiskeys."

He pulled some pound notes from his wallet to show he meant to pay for the round; a local opinion of Gladden might prove enlightening.

Everybody smiled. One man offered him a smoke, which he took. Another had a light.

Exhaling, McGarr said, "Fair day."

"The luck of it, yah?" one of the men ventured in a singsong brogue, hoping for a reaction.

McGarr remembered the words of Sean Dermot O'Duffy: "Sure, Dr. Gladden is his own self entirely." He added, "A few drops wouldn't keep him away."

The others smiled, recognizing O'Duffy's statement.

"And then he's probably gotten a dispensation from some pooka for the duration of the morning."

"That would be Mossie, yah? In the company of pookas." The man who made the comment then tapped his forehead.

When he offered no more, McGarr said, "All those sheep and rocks. And dogs. Who knows what they might do to a man?"

"You mean the wild dogs he claims he sees?"

Said another, "On a still day you can hear his bloody blunderbuss three valleys away. Some class of buffalo rifle, I'm thinking."

"There's stories in the papers, but I haven't clapped eyes on a wild dog in ten years. And then only with drink on me."

"Whence her bum was duly numbered and recorded in the hall of shame," said the third.

All laughed. There was a pause while the whiskeys were delivered. McGarr raised his glass. "To medical practitioners the world over. A selfless lot."

"The best of them," one of the men added with a twinkle in his eye.

McGarr only wet his lips, so they would not think they had to buy him back.

One man cleared his throat. "As long as we're chattin', yah? I have something to ask." His was the thickest brogue, and, as though speaking in a difficult, foreign language, he kept asking if he was being understood.

McGarr nodded.

"Don't misunderstand me now. I'm not takin' away from you, yah? Mossie can be a cantankerous bastard, all here will tell you, and he probably deserved a good fist in the gob. But is he right, yah? What he says?"

About Gladden's claim that Power had been murdered, McGarr guessed he meant. Keeping his eyes on the crowd outside on the bridge, McGarr canted his head. "It's murder, I'd say."

The other men were now very quiet. It was one thing to read a report in a newspaper, quite another to question the source.

"But Paddy Power? Was he . . . by the *government*, like?" Nobody wanted to hear that. "Paddy was so natural, like anybody here. Like yourself, say. Before he took the Pledge, he'd come in here and have a session, just like any other man from the village. Which he was, of course."

"With the difference when Paddy drank, Paddy paid," another put in. "Not like some—"

"Frost," said the first man, so McGarr wouldn't think they meant him.

"—who'd come in here and splash out a few rounds, like it was his kind of welfare, then leave. Shane Frost, who hired in a gang of men from Dublin to build him a summerhouse."

Yah, thought McGarr. Something that was bad form in most country places in Ireland; something Frost would have known about and have done more out of niggardliness or as an affront than a mistake in judgment. A few serious moments lapsed while they considered the enormity of Frost's action.

"Paddy would stay and chat and and tell wonderful, grand stories about what he'd seen and done. Then, after he swore off, he didn't change a bit. Still here, still brilliant fun."

"And still with the readies." That man winked.

"Was he ever here *with* Frost?" McGarr asked.

"His protégé, he called him." The man shook his head and looked to the others, who agreed.

"With Gladden?"

One of the men began laughing. "Hasn't he told you, yah? Gladden's our local Pioneer." The Pioneers were a Catholic society who forswore alcohol of any kind. "But not like some who just don't drink and leave you alone. Mossie was always mentioning the debilitating effects of this or the harm to your liver with that. Sort of made every sip sweeter, don't you know."

The others smiled.

"What about the woman? Gretta Osbourne."

"She was Paddy's steady companion before the fire. After it, when he began staying up at Parknasilla, he came alone. Paying a call, like."

Another put in, "Back when she came, she'd sit in the lounge nursing a few drinks while Paddy carried on, then get him his hat when it was time to go. A fine-looking girl, tall and curvaceous."

" 'Designated driver,' he called her."

" 'Number-one iron,' " added another. "Paddy golfed when he was young."

"Until she went in the fire, yah?"

No. All eyes turned to him, and he raised a palm. "That was the whiskey. And wrong."

Yah. "How'd it happen?" McGarr asked.

"Him smoking in bed, was the finding. It was in his parents' house. Paddy got out. When his head cleared, he realized she was still in there, and he went back in." The man held up his hands to show where Power had been burned, and McGarr remembered the burns on the hands of Power's corpse. "By that time she was a holy mess, scorched everywhere, I know. Wasn't I along on the trip to Shannon, Paddy at the wheel, the caravan belting about the road like he'd kill us all. He hired a plane there and flew her to Dublin."

"No Mossie for *her*."

"Which Mossie n'er forgot."

"And few others. It was the beginning of the exodus from Mossie. A matter of confidence, don't you know. A new doctor had set up a surgery in the West Square, and it seemed like only a few years later there Mossie was, resigning his seat in the Dail."

"The way he did—all bitter and nettled."

"And O'Duffy, yah? He scorched Mossie worse than any fire."

All three men nodded.

"Finally upped and moved out altogether, surgery thrown in. Lives up in the mountains, but that you know." The man shook a newspaper that he was holding in his hands.

"What about Power's wife?"

The other two men turned to the oldest, who looked to be about Power's age. "A good woman, a pretty woman, I'd say. But a bit of a shrew, though Paddy was no saint and I always take the man's side. Only child, you know, Nell was. Father and mother had good custom, and they doted on her. Chemists, like Frost's father."

McGarr cocked his head, as though to say, Really?

"Sent her off to university to study it, so she could return and take over. Trinity, like Paddy. It's not where they met but where Paddy *discovered* her, don't you know. She being a little younger."

The man who had spoken least now asked, "If it wasn't the government, like Mossie claims, then who?" Murdered Paddy Power, he meant.

McGarr shrugged. Picking up his glass, he pointed to the crown of the narrow, arched stone bridge, where Gladden and another man now appeared. "Who's that with him now?"

"Kieran Coyne. He's a solicitor hereabouts. New fella—moved down from Dublin for the sake of his wife, who's a local."

McGarr knocked back his drink and began turning to signal for more, when his eye caught some movement in the crowd below the bridge. It was a new Mercedes that had eased through the gathered reporters to park across the street. Out of it now stepped Bresnahan and a young man who, though dark, McGarr thought must be her brother, until he remembered she was an only child.

"Would you look at that? Bachelor number one with bachelorette of the same order. In the matrimonial stakes," the man explained. "He's *The* O'Suilleabhain, as his mother says. Rory, by name. He's the 'strongest' farmer in every way in all of South Kerry, and a fine young buck to boot. No education to speak of, but he's got a good head all the same."

And handsome, thought McGarr, with leading-man good looks and the stature to match. Although the sun was out, it was almost cold, yet O'Suilleabhain was wearing only a plain white shirt, cut like a tunic and open at the neck. Given the breath of his well-muscled shoulders and the straightness of his back, it billowed around his torso and snapped in the stiff breeze.

Waves of jet-black hair, which he kept long like some rock star, cascaded down his back. Turning his head to reach for Bresnahan's hand and lead her through the crowd, he smiled, and his eyes, which were some light color and clear, flashed. McGarr thought of Hughie Ward.

"They say he'll stand for the Dail, yah? The very next election."

"And win too," another chimed in. "There hasn't been a man from here cut like him since Shane Frost."

"The girl—well, *woman*—I'll bet you know."

McGarr hoped well enough.

"Janie—how's she's changed, yah?"

The three men nodded, regarding Bresnahan's long brown legs, the riding jacket with its flatteringly severe cut, and how she now turned to this one and that, saying a few words, smiling.

"Not Janie at all anymore. And just what Rory'll be needing up in Dublin, I suspect."

Gladden raised a bullhorn to speak over the roar of the cataract beneath the bridge, and one of the men beside McGarr opened a window. With his voice distorted through the instrument, Gladden sounded, as well as looked, harsh and peculiar, like some large, gaunt, and damaged bird—the blackened eyes, the swollen nose angled off to one side, the spray of stark white hair that was riffling in the breeze.

"You know me, and you know what I stand for," he rasped out. "All those years you sent me to the Dail, the one thing you know you got from me was the truth. I wasn't afraid to tell it then, I'm not now."

Gladden lowered the bullhorn to show them his beaten face.

"I also stand before you a man with a heavy heart both for my

good friend and patient Paddy Power, who was murdered in Parknasilla, and for this country, which is led by the men who murdered him.
That is the truth.''

Again Gladden lowered the bullhorn and seemed pleased to see
he had the crowd's full attention. All that could be heard was the
rumble of the waterfall, the cries of gulls working the race, and the
gears and shutters of cameras.

''They murdered Paddy Power for three reasons. First, to rid
themselves of the only real political threat to the continuing tyranny of
Sean Dermot O'Duffy and his capitalist crowd. Paddy Power was
admired and loved by the people of Ireland, for whom he did and
planned to do so much.

''Second, to emasculate his conference, which would have revealed the truth about our national debt and who it has benefited. And
third, to suppress the memoir that Paddy was planning to write about
his years in government.

''Knowing the O'Duffy government as he did, fearing something
like this would happen, Paddy had given me for safekeeping his original
notes for the memoir. At the murder scene those notes were discovered
to have been stolen.

''Yesterday morning, the same government man who did this to
me''—Gladden again swung the bullhorn to the side and pointed to
his face—''the same government man who is investigating Paddy's
murder, learned that I planned to reveal the notes and give them to you
and the press here this morning.

''Yesterday afternoon without writ or warrant, this same senior
official of the Garda Siochana broke into my home and stole the cards
from me. When I attempted to stop him, he then beat and transported
me to the Waterville Lake Hotel, where—come closer while I tell you,
good people of Sneem—he attempted to frame *me*, whom you know;
me, your medical doctor who has cared for you all, no matter who,
where, or when, *me*, your *Teachta Dail* for over a dozen years; *me*,
Paddy Power's oldest and best friend''—Gladden smote his
chest—''for his *murder*, which even for those men from Dublin, even
for Sean Dermot O'Duffy, is a low, base, and foul obscenity.''

Gladden paused, as though he could not continue without gathering himself.

A man beside McGarr shook his head. ''Politician's blarney,
every last word of it.''

''The name of the man who has done, who is *doing*, this, is Chief

Superintendent Peter McGarr, and before something further happens to me, I want to tell you and the nation how Paddy's murder was accomplished and why.''

McGarr could feel the eyes of the bar on him, and he had to admire Gladden's forensic talent in setting city against country, the government against the people, and in making McGarr himself—a solitary civil servant with no political clout who could be dismissed summarily—the scapegoat. Also, Gladden's battered face and the details of Paddy Power's murder, which Gladden now began to reveal, were facts that could not be impugned.

McGarr changed his opinion of Gladden. He was not a heron. The bird he resembled most was nowhere to be seen. A phoenix, Gladden would rise from the ashes of his own abjection at O'Duffy's expense—Paddy Power's corpse and McGarr's career being merely the cinders from which he would take flight.

While Gladden continued to speak, piecing out his interpretation of Paddy Power's murder, McGarr's eyes again fell on Rory O'Suilleabhain. If O'Suilleabhain planned to run for the Dail, he would find a tough, seasoned, and nasty opponent in Gladden, who would pit youth against experience and a singular record of having put egg on the face of the Sean Dermot O'Duffy. Or, better, shit.

There was nobody an Irish electorate loved more than a sly, wily underdog who refused to be put down. O'Duffy himself had been an example early in his career.

O'Suilleabhain now bent to Bresnahan, who whispered in his ear, then smiled up at him, as though encouraging him to do something. From his height O'Suilleabhain scanned the crowd and moved away, bending to speak to this one and that.

Now, what could that be about? McGarr wondered.

Gladden had paused, and the reporters began barking questions.

''The note cards now''—Gladden's voice grated and squawked through the bullhorn—''the note cards for the memoir. Let me dispense with them and, sure, I'll answer every question you have. *I*'m not here for a cover-up.''

But still the reporters shouted away.

Equipped with the bullhorn, Gladden spoke right over them. ''As I told you earlier, the government man, McGarr, took them from me, and I'm led to believe he has them in his possession at this very moment in Parknasilla, where he is being put up at the expense of the nation.''

McGarr placed his empty glass on the bar and pointed to it.

Gladden's voice could be heard plainly there too. All were rapt, listening to him, but many an eye had fallen upon McGarr.

"But what *exactly* do they say?" somebody demanded. "Give us some details."

"Well—I remember one deal in particular." Gladden then sketched out an incident that, McGarr had thought, was nearly common knowledge to the politically astute. In return for the support of two renegade socialist T.D.'s, which gave O'Duffy a slim majority in the Dail, his government granted their Dublin constituencies millions of pounds of direct aid that was extended nowhere else.

"A payoff, as it turned out, that added to the horrendous debt that Paddy with his conference at Parknasilla was hoping to solve. What isn't known is what else those two *socialists* were paid. If my memory of the cards is correct, for the wife of one there was a cushy, no-show job in the headquarters of now Minister for Justice Harney's father's development business, and a fifty thousand pound, sub rosa 'contribution' to the campaign chest of the other."

A kind of hush seemed to fall over the crowd, as though the journalists were considering what they had heard. "Proof! Where's your proof?" somebody shouted.

"I told you. It's in Paddy's notes. We *must* get them back. They should be revealed to the nation!"

McGarr thought of Noreen alone with the note cards and photocopies in the suite. Perhaps it was time to get back. It also occurred to him that, while politically explosive, the disclosure that Gladden had just made lacked by half the probable force of some of the other revelations McGarr had read in his—what?—three-hour pass through the cards.

How long had Gladden been in possession of the note cards before McGarr took them from him? Wouldn't Gladden, a man with a political ax to grind, have pored over them and even taken notes? Why was his acquaintance with them so seemingly sketchy?

Because the cards had only recently come into his possession? If so, why hadn't Power mentioned the fact that he had given Gladden his notes? The cards that were found at the murder scene described nearly every other important activity from Power's arrival at Shannon right up until an hour or so before his death. Power's visit to Gladden in his mountain "aerie" was mentioned at some length, but not his having given him the note cards.

Power did report that he *had* told Gladden about the proposal he would reveal at the debt conference, which had enraged Gladden. Power had then wondered about Gladden's mental health. Would he then have entrusted the entire batch to such a man? Not likely.

Or carried them up over the promontory of Mullaghanattin Mountain? Even less likely still. Together the note cards were heavy, and probably weighed a half stone.

Then there was the matter of the expurgations: the note cards that were missing from the "Gretta Osbourne" heading in the photocopies sent to Nell Power; the complete absence of a "Gladden" heading in spite of the reference, "(see 'Mossie' cards)," that McGarr had found under the subheading "Dirty Tricks."

Finally there was the way in which that sack had been delivered to the Waterville Lake Hotel: by a rough-looking country gorsoon who was dressed exactly as Gladden had been on the day that McGarr had first met him. But not Gladden.

Who now seemed to be speaking about Paddy Power's proposal for solving the problem of the national debt, but curiously McGarr had heard the words before from Gladden: ". . . O'Duffy and his elitist clique who have confounded the economic potential of this country and have run the Irish people into the workhouse of foreign interests for their own personal gain."

"That's your old, tired rhetoric, Mossie," one of the journalists shouted. "We heard that from you years ago."

"*When* did Paddy Power give you his note cards?" a woman's strong voice, which McGarr recognized, now asked over the shouted queries of the journalists.

McGarr quickly returned to the window.

"I'll not take any questions from the government or a woman who is here under false pretenses. I'll take questions only from the credentialed press and other uncompromised Irish citizens."

"Then answer *me*," Rory O'Suilleabhain boomed out in a deep, clear voice. "*When* did Paddy Power give you the note cards?"

"And where are *your* credentials?"

"Right over there." O'Suilleabhain pointed to a mountain that could be seen to the southwest of the village. "Every green patch you can lay your eyes on. That's my stake in this country, and I want an answer."

Kieran Coyne, the solicitor accompanying Gladden, now turned his back to the crowd and began speaking animatedly to him.

"Is it for office you're running, Rory?" Gladden now asked.

"What about you?"

Again Bresnahan had O'Suilleabhain by the sleeve and was standing on tiptoe to whisper in his ear. "Since you won't answer that, can you tell us what exactly Paddy Power had in mind for the national debt?" O'Suilleabhain then asked.

"Gladly. 'Creditors are predators,' Paddy always said."

Nowhere in Power's notes had McGarr read that.

"His plan would have extricated the country from the grip of foreign interests and the Dublin junta who have enriched themselves and are still profiting by the debt."

"How?" O'Suilleabhain demanded.

Kieran Coyne now left Gladden and began working his way through the crowd toward O'Suilleabhain. He too was a large man, and when two photographers did not move quickly enough, he pushed them roughly aside. Like Gladden's, his face had a raw look but caused by something other than the elements.

"By writing the debt down for one," said Gladden.

"And for another?"

"If I had the specifics, I'd give them to you. As I mentioned earlier, the note cards that Paddy gave me were stolen by the government."

Bresnahan still had O'Suilleabhain by the sleeve.

Coyne had arrived in front of O'Suilleabhain, and he now said something to him.

Said Gladden through the bullhorn, "Do the *journalists* here have any additional questions?"

McGarr watched O'Suilleabhain's hand dart out and seize Coyne by the front of his jacket; on a stiff arm he swung him out of the way. "Wasn't it Power's idea to swap debt for equity in Irish assets currently owned by the Irish government? Our peat reserves, Irish television and radio, the transportation system—"

Now the journalists turned to O'Suilleabhain.

Coyne tried to pull O'Suilleabhain's hand away. His face had assumed an alarming shade, the color of old meat.

"Paddy never meant any such thing. He knew it was unfeasible. He was merely floating a trial balloon to focus the nation's attention on the debt and the narrow faction of O'Duffy supporters it has benefited."

Bresnahan said something else to O'Suilleabhain. "There's now a good chance that Sean Dermot O'Duffy might endorse the proposal in principle."

"Now that they've murdered Paddy and have made him a martyr!" Gladden roared. "Now that they've taken the matter out of his hands to do as they wish!"

"Again it comes down to a matter of proof. Your credibility is in some doubt, Mossie."

More than a few in the crowd began a laugh, which was echoed in the bar where McGarr was standing.

"You can ask the woman beside you. She and her chief have sequestered and probably destroyed the proof by now. "I'll take no more questions until that man and woman leave."

With Coyne still at the end of his arm, O'Suilleabhain only waited, smiling up at Gladden.

After a while Gladden turned and began walking toward his old Land Rover that was parked on the other side of the bridge. A few of the journalists moved after him, but the rest turned to O'Suilleabhain.

One of the men standing with McGarr at the bar window began chuckling. "Wasn't it of Mossie Rory made the fool?"

O'Suilleabhain now said something to Coyne, then let him go.

"This'll make him, yah?"

McGarr canted his head. "Make who?"

"Rory. He bested Mossie Gladden, and him with a bullhorn on the bridge."

Not without some help, McGarr thought. He watched now as Bresnahan, turning to get herself away from the media, was stopped by an old woman wearing a shawl. They spoke for a few moments, Bresnahan nodding repeatedly before leading the woman to the Mercedes and opening the rear door for her.

"And that woman speaking to Ruth Bresnahan?" McGarr asked.

"Deirdre Crehan. She's the wife of an old cottier on the Waterville Road. She's probably asked for a lift home in that grand car."

"Do you pay Ruthie that much she can afford such a thing?" another asked.

"The car?" McGarr thought for a moment, then raised his glass. "Call it a tangible, as opposed to a spiritual, benefit of the national debt."

The others laughed, but before McGarr could leave, one man took his arm. "She won't be with you for long, I'm thinking."

McGarr waited.

"What Rory wants, Rory gets."

McGarr hoped it was a local characteristic shared by both sexes.

Leaving by the back door, he found himself in better spirits than when he had entered, and not just because of what he had consumed. Say whoever had murdered Paddy Power also stole his note cards, he said to himself while walking toward the chemist shop he could see on the other side of the South Green. That person had no use for the cards himself. Why? Because he knew what they contained and that the information couldn't hurt him.

What did that presuppose? Two things: that the murderer had been sufficiently close to Power to have spent whatever length of time it might require—days, McGarr knew from his own superficial reading—acquainting himself with what they contained. And that the theft of the cards might be viewed as a motive for somebody else having murdered Power.

The murderer had then edited the cards in two ways. He had expurgated all negative references to Gretta Osbourne and completely deleted the ''Mossie'' heading. Dressed as Mossie himself, he had then delivered the cards to Nell Power, knowing she would read them and would probably try to confront Power.

Why? To make it look as if Gladden had murdered Power and had then tried to pin a motive on his ex-wife. It certainly looked that way.

McGarr glanced up. M.J.P. FROST, CHEMIST appeared in freshly painted Prussian-blue letters on a bright pink facade. As it had on the pill bottles in Paddy Power's medicine cabinet. And the plastic sack in which the photocopies of the note cards had been sent to Nell Power.

CHAPTER 15

Sin Relived

BACK AT PARKNASILLA, barman-trainee Hughie Ward volunteered for the task of transporting drinks and snacks to the suite of Mr. Shane Frost.

"But Frost is probably in conference now, and there'll be no tip," explained Sonnie. "Let one of the dining-room staff do it."

"Ah, it'll give me a bit of a break," Ward insisted. And get me away from you, he thought.

"In your back, sure, when you see all that it is. For openers there's a case of champagne."

And more with a crib and McGarr's baby monitor, which he had scarcely gotten set up and plugged in when he heard voices near the door in the hall.

"Ah, you enjoy it. Go on now, you *love* it. Don't be running on to me coy and bashful, you're a lady's man, remember? It's what you live and die for. Apart from money, of course. But then the two sometimes come together, don't they?" It was a husky older woman's voice with a playful, wheedling tone. There was a thump against the door. "You can't tell me you don't like that, now? Tell me you don't."

"But I've got the bloody Japanese coming in an hour's time. Weren't you the one who wanted that? You know how particular and observant they are, and the room's already been made up."

173

"Do we need a bed? Remember the time I had you in the press? Right up against the cupboards with Paddy holding forth in the kitchen? And now that I know your secret—"

"*Nell!*"

"Tell me you don't need me, *now*"

"But this is *important*. Didn't you tell me you wanted Eire Bank dissolved? What were your words? The last vestige of that bastard man's—"

"Bastard institution."

"—dissolved."

"But on *my* terms!"

"This is even better,"said Frost. "Think of it—a gang of 'Slants' at the helm, having bought it from you, me, and his inheritor, Gretta, the very people whom Paddy squeezed all his life." There followed a kind of pleasurable groan, as though Nell Power had acted on his suggestion. "But I don't have my key," Frost added, when he regained his voice.

Ward glanced wildly around the room. If he got caught, he could say he made a mistake and brought the crib to the wrong room, but they would lose the advantage of the monitor for the planned meeting with the Japanese.

The toilet? No, that was out, if he was right about what the woman was planning. Even the shower stall might be used. After.

Under the bed? Not there either. It was all the way across the room and too much like something out of a bedroom farce. Ward saw the doorknob turn, and he opened the closet and stepped in. He began reaching for the inner knob, when the door to the suite swung open.

"Oh, you prevaricator, Shane. The only honest thing about you is yer mahn, here. *He* doesn't lie. Or complain, I'm thinking." With one hand gripping his necktie and the other plunged deep in his trouser pocket, she swung Frost into the room. With her foot she closed the door, then looked around.

"Not the bed," said Frost, resignedly.

"No, *not* the bed. The closet? In there among your effects?"

Christ, thought Ward, not only would he be discovered skulking in the man's closet, he would be charged as a Peeping Tom. He took another step back.

"What's this, something I don't know of?" She meant the crib.

"I hope that bloody Jap isn't bringing his brat," said Frost. "He must have ordered it."

"Him? Not likely. The Japanese are *men*, Shane. They take what they want. Beside them, Irish men are mere boys to be had." She shoved him up against the low gate of the crib and pulled her hands away. "Don't move." She quickly opened the plackets of her shiny black suit and pulled open the jacket. "Now then, *down* to business."

She was a small, well-preserved woman with short black hair, wide shoulders, and the sort of well-formed, slightly bowed legs that seemed to pose a challenge, especially when wrapped in black lace stockings and raised on high heels. And what she was showing Frost now creased the skin around the corners of his eyes.

"That couldn't be a merry widow you're wearing?" Frost asked.

"Who with more right?"

Frost reached for the hem of her skirt, which was also short, but her hand suddenly lashed out and caught him smartly across the face, turning his head. "You'll wait your turn, is that understood?"

When Frost said nothing, she struck him again with the other hand from the other side. "Well, is it?"

He opened his mouth to speak, and she hit him a third time, the sound of each slap resounding around the plaster of the room. "Say, '*Please*, Nell.' "

Frost said it.

"Louder!"

"*Please*, Nell." There was definite pleasure in his plea.

What happened then Ward could not actually see, because of the angle. But fixing Frost with her bright black eyes, she moved in on him. "Can I give you a piece of advice, Shane? Don't ever lie to me again. We make a good team, you and I, but you must remember who has the upper hand. Knowledge is power—*Nell* Power—and don't you ever forget it."

Ward leaned forward to chance another peek, but all he could see was her back and Frost's legs. They were pressed up against the crib that was now rattling and creaking.

Ward felt like a character out of the *Inferno*, who was condemned to witness the preferred sin in his life over and over again without benefit of it vivifying immediacy.

Though not ceasing her exertions, he saw Nell Power pull her head back to regard Frost coolly. "Now, Shane," she commanded in a small voice that was deepened by evident pleasure. "*Now!*

Ward eased himself back into the darkened closet wall and wondered if he had switched on the monitor.

CHAPTER 16

A Prescription for Genius

THE INTERIOR OF Frost's father's chemist shop in Sneem was far different from its bright facade. After years of off-center ringing, the bell over the door had cut a deep groove in the wood. A buzzer sounded in back, but nobody came out to greet McGarr. He closed the door and looked around, trying to place the acrid stench that cut right through the pharmaceutical odor that was common to such places.

Dim, cramped, and timeworn, the shop was a warren of narrow aisles with a dusty stock of trusses, corn plasters, and tooth powders that McGarr had not seen in decades stuffed on shelves every which way nearly to the ceiling. The lino under foot was worn to the wood, which shone in an uneven path that bent around obstacles—an umbrella stand of canes; a case of luxury soaps so dusty its lighted contents could scarely be seen; an obviously new revolving display of brightly packaged condoms—and led to the rear. There McGarr could hear a radio playing.

Cat piss, he decided, following both sound and smell. No, cat piss, tobacco, and the unmistakable odor of old man that McGarr sometimes noted in his own father's digs in Dublin.

And there he was—M.J.P. Frost, McGarr assumed—asleep in a tattered Morris chair. The cat was in his lap, an ancient wooden radio on a table to one side, and the morning paper at his feet. In back of him was a tall floor lamp with a tasseled shade. A door that led to an alley in back was open. Not even the cat had opened its eyes.

McGarr flicked back the brim of his hat, lit up a cigarette, and looked around at the array of bottles, jars, boxes, tins, jugs, cartons, packets, and carboys. No space in the long, narrow room, every wall of which was shelved to the ceiling, was unoccupied. Even the chemist's work surfaces were cluttered. There were no fewer than five scales, one of which looked broken. Pharmaceutical charts had been hung from a wall, chart upon chart, and now comprised a thick mat. The first was dated 1948; M.J.P. Frost obviously threw little away.

Beside the maps were his diplomas from Trinity, Dublin, and his licenses—every one, it seemed, that had been issued in his name.

The file of "Prescriptions Filled" was similarly vast, but stated that Paddy Power had only ever purchased, "Quinidine 0.2 mg. T.I.D." and "Digitoxin 1.0 mg., Max. dose 2 tablets." Both prescriptions had been written by Maurice J. Gladden, M.D.

The log of prescriptions filled in the present year—a leather-bound journal that Frost had required all purchasers of controlled substances to sign—showed that Power had bought a three-month supply of quinidine and digitoxin some two months earlier. The only other entries of note were prescriptions for sleeping, again issued by Mossie Gladden, for Gretta Osbourne. They had begun some seven years ago and had continued to the present. The last batch of fifty tablets had been signed for by Osbourne on Friday last.

The tongue-in-groove walnut cabinets beneath the work area were filled with a motley collection of other gadgets, including several devices that were more elaborate but seemed as though they would perform the same function as the pill-making device McGarr had found in Gladden's mountain cottage. He opened a wide, velvet-lined case and discovered a variety of pill dies; behind another door were carton after carton, open and sealed, of empty ampoules.

McGarr closed the doors and straightened up. Had he seen enough?

He stepped past the old man and peered out the door into the alley, which could be reached in either direction. A wee lad, who had been kicking a ball against the wall of a garage, stopped to look up at him. McGarr waved.

"If it's Mr. Frost you're after, you'll have to shout. He's a bit deaf."

Back at the chair McGarr reached down to shake Frost, but the old man opened his eyes; they were red-rimmed with yellow scleras but looked sharp. "How can I help you, or have you done for yourself?"

"The latter. I just wanted to be sure I shook your hand before I left. You're—"

"Michael Joseph Patrick Frost, Chief Inspector. Chemist of Sneem, County Kerry."

McGarr smiled; old-timers were deceiving. "Chief *Superinten-dent*," McGarr corrected.

"For how long, I'm wondering after what I read. You should mind politicians like Sean Dermot. This entire *imbroglio* will need an answer. If not a head."

"'Tisn't a good likeness of you at all." With a slippered foot M.J.P. shuffled through the morning papers, which were scattered around him on the floor, until he came to a photograph of McGarr that had been taken from the paper's "morgue," and should have remained there, McGarr thought. It had been taken snapped several years back at a funeral. Wearing a dark chesterfield coat, a black bowler, and black gloves, he looked dour and pitiless, like an executioner.

"Have you seen your son, Shane, recently?"

"If you mean did Shane murder Paddy with something from here—" He shook his head, and it occurred to McGarr how much son resembled father. Both had the same long face, the thin, slightly aquiline nose, and pale gray eyes. "Shane would never have done anything like that. First, he lacks the cruelty necessary for the task, and, second, he's intelligent enough to know that he might have made out acceptably on his own but never in the way he has without Paddy. Paddy was special."

It wouldn't be the first time McGarr had seen jealousy as the motive for murder. And then Frost had 20 percent of the 20 percent that Power had been about to ask Irish government creditors to write down. Also, Frost might have had something to gain by Power's death; McGarr thought about Nell Power's wanting Gretta Osbourne to encourage Frost to reopen negotiations with some Japanese. And finally, Power's death by his own hand was accomplished at some distance from the murderer and therefore could only be imagined to have been cruel.

"Has he been by to see you?"

"Surely. He always stops. First thing when he gets to Sneem."

"And Gretta Osbourne?"

"She's an old friend too. The prescription for phenobarbital that

Mossie wrote for her is old, as you probably saw. Written some time after she left the burn center in Dublin and came down here to recuperate. It can be refilled whenever she needs. She also has a prescription for Dilaudid, which is a mild sedative. She has bad thoughts about the fire, she says.'' He pointed a gnarled finger at a large brown bottle.

"Helps herself?" Dilaudid might have been considered a mild sedative years back when Frost was studying pharmacology; now it was regarded as a strong drug that addicts sometimes used when heroin was in short supply.

"Under my direction when I'm off my feet, as now. I really should sell the place, but I wouldn't know what to do with my days without it.''

"Where's the quinidine?"

"Powder or made tablets?"

"Powder.''

The bottle was on the third shelf but easily reached by a tall person. "And digitoxin?"

"Three bottles to the right.''

"Have you used any recently?"

Frost the elder shook his head.

"Were I to ask you not to touch them until a lab team can get here, would you comply?"

"I promise I won't budge from this spot.''

McGarr nodded. "Pleasure.''

"All mine. I've been reading about you for years now, and, here, like in a finale, you've appeared.''

My finale or yours? McGarr wondered, the old man being much more aware than he first seemed.

Superintendent Liam O'Shaughnessy was waiting at McGarr's car. Dressed in a dark three-piece suit and wearing a homburg, he was cut out of the very pattern of the bankers at Parknasilla, even to the manilla folder that he was carrying. It contained the Tech Squad report concerning the samples of photocopy paper that had been taken from the copy machines in Gretta Osbourne's room, the Parknasilla business office, and from Taoiseach O'Duffy's house.

"No match, I'm afraid. O'Duffy's machine is even a different make and type. We're trying to run down the local dealer in Panasonic copiers, since that's what we're after. But he's up in Dublin on business and won't be back until the weekend.''

So with Frost's father's chemist shop virtually wide open, as

McGarr had just seen, and Mossie Gladden a practicing physician, the note cards remained their only real lead.

McGarr sat against the fender of his small car and faced the high-gloss facade of the chemist shop, which, having caught the direct rays of the noonday sun, looked like an emanation in pink. He pulled out a cigarette and lit it.

"Help me with this, Liam. Tell me about murder—what we know, how we should proceed."

"As it relates to this case?"

McGarr nodded.

O'Shaughnessy thought for a moment. "Murder is almost always an individual act. When it's not, the conspirators, not trusting each other, either act in concert to make sure blood is on every hand, or hire a third party to carry it out."

"Not a pill bottle carried in by one person, and then carried out by another?"

O'Shaughnessy had to think for a moment. His clear blue eyes flashed across the pink surface of the chemist shop and fell on the bridge at the other end of the green. "It's too cute, and of the four suspects—including Nell Power—only Gladden had nothing to lose but a friend, if we can believe him. Frost, Gretta Osbourne, and even the wife had gotten their positions and wealth almost exclusively from or through or because of Paddy Power. And where is their bond with each other? You don't commit murder, no matter how easy or painless, with somebody you can't trust implicitly. There has to be some tie, some glue, some—I hate to use the word—affection, since it probably has to be stronger than that."

"You mean money."

O'Shaughnessy cocked his head. "With Frost and the Power woman I'd say just that. They're too—"

Jaded, McGarr thought. "Worldly," he said.

O'Shaughnessy nodded. "From what we've learned about them so far. And I can't imagine Gretta Osbourne having much to do with Frost apart from their professional relationship as officers of Eire Bank."

Officer *ex officio* in Osbourne's case, McGarr thought. "What about Gladden—could he have stolen the cards?"

O'Shaughnessy shook his head. "If he did, he would have read them immediately and in detail. He would have been able to speak of them today. He might even have taken notes, which he obviously does not possess."

"Then whoever murdered Power—"

"Stole the cards."

"And since the cards were given away—"

"Power wasn't murdered for the cards."

"Power was murdered for—?"

A horn sounded, startling them. The Garda patrol car that had brought O'Shaughnessy was blocking traffic. "When we know that, well—" O'Shaughnessy opened the door and eased his large frame in.

Well, indeed, thought McGarr.

CHAPTER 17

On Going Long, and Cold

"IF ANYBODY CAN find out which country gorsoon was plying the Waterville Road last Sunday morning, 'tis Deirdre Crehan," Rory O'Suilleabhain had said after Gladden's press conference on the bridge in Sneem. "It's said a woman's tongue is a thing that never rusts. Hers is a surgical instrument."

She was a little shawled lump of a woman with a creased face and few remaining teeth, and she sat in the back of the luxurious rental Merc like a small, crippled bird who was happily caged. Wherever she pointed a gnarled finger, O'Suilleabhain turned. And thus they plied the laneways of cottiers and small farmers while she warbled all the while.

"Isn't it grand. Who would have thought this morning, when I set off to hear Doctor Mossie rail at the world, that I'd return in the royal plush of this motorcar with them who amount to the future king and queen of the South Kerry Mountains.

"Ah now, Rory—don't deny me my foresight. You can ask far and near, and them that know me will tell you I'm a bit of a *seanchailleach*, though I'd admit that only to you. I've got the gift, don't you know, and there you sit, more made for each other from the moment you drew breath than any two people I ever laid eyes on. Think of the wonder of it—two massive properties cheek by jowl with two only children, both tall, strong, and handsome. Have your parents seen you together again? Won't you make them proud.

"But of course they have. Didn't I see Rory's mother standing there watching him put his questions to Doctor Mossie and her shaking her head and saying she didn't want him going off to Dublin. But then, my loveen." She reached to touch Bresnahan's arm on the back of the seat. "You know all about Dublin, good and bad, and can steer Rory right when he gets there.

"Says she to me—and for your ears only, mind—'You'd think what goes long, goes cold, but from the look of him at her I'd say she's still a treasured memory in one man's heart.' "

O'Suilleabhain did not protest, and Bresnahan wondered if, when he had spoken to the old woman earlier, he had put her up to what she was saying. But he only looked away at a heron rising majestically out of a bog, and Bresnahan suspected that Deirdre Crehan would brag for the rest of her days were she able to take any credit whatsoever for arranging the match that had eluded the two families for so long.

"A mother should know. And from the cut of your stylish costume, my jewel, I'd say you've learned wonderful much in the city. My word to you is simple and plain: The ebb tide waits naught for noon." And before Bresnahan could complain that the be-all and end-all of her life was *not* the prospect of marrying Rory O'Suilleabhain, the old woman hurried on, "Now if you look you, you'll see a sight prettier than any city could possibly hold."

She pointed a bony hand to the window, where they were presented with an unobstructed sweep of mountain, field, sea, and sky. "There be a storm squall flattening the furze with slanted lashings of driven hail. While but a quarter-mile distant we behold full shafts of livid sun you can count, like bars of gold jeweled with emeralds, there where they're kissing the fields. And farther on in the turbary, them lateral bands of cut peat? Some brown, some maroon, some black. I once saw something like that in a museum in Dublin, but not real and useful, like here. No. Dead and done with a wet, oiled brush. I'll not mention the bald mountain there or the dueling tangle of storm clouds behind it or the sky farther still that's the color of a bullfinch egg. For you can see that anywhere"—she paused—"in Kerry.

"Tell me you don't miss that. Tell me that's not part of your soul," which thought suddenly filled Bresnahan's eyes and made her want to snap at the old houri, whose other hand was still on her arm.

But the old woman was too fast and lanced Bresnahan's anger

with the further thought, "And tell me your God and mine is going to make another Kerry—the most beautiful part of Ireland, they say—and put you two in it with three of your four parents alive to see their grandbabies born into beauty and wealth. *Muscha*, you've winning prospects, and I only wish I could return in another life as blessed as you."

They had arrived at another small cottage, the door of which was "standing open to the tender air," said Deirdre Crehan. Yet again she declined to go in with them, insisting her legs were too weak, though she had walked half the distance to Sneem. Instead she remained in the back of the Mercedes, every so often running her hand over the glove leather of the seats and staring fixedly at one or another of the appointments. Bresnahan could not bring herself to admit to her it was rented.

And so the afternoon wore on to twilight with Bresnahan following the breadth of Rory O'Suilleabhain's broad back and the narrowness of his waist, which she could not help but admire, to the door of one pensioner's small holding after another. "God bless all here," he would say, stepping through the door, and they could not in good form refuse at least something of what was offered without fail in even the most lowly cottage they entered. "Will I wet some tea, or will you have a drop of anything?" Usually they took the latter.

Such that around twilight Bresnahan found Deirdre Crehan, to whom drops had been taken out, fully asleep in the back of the car, and her own head filled with all the sights and sounds that she had consciously pushed from her mind for the past three years and now came flooding back. Until the woman of a small cottage said she was only after hearing her husband and his brother speaking over dinner about a strange "country man" they had seen on the Waterville Road on Sunday morning.

Neither man was still in the cottage. They could be seen, however, cutting turf in a field about a half-mile distant along a narrow, stony farm road that traced a cliff face where no car could go. Borrowing a pair of Wellies, Bresnahan set off with O'Suilleabhain in the gloaming.

The wild, changeable weather had eased, and the evening came on damp, still, and even warm. Bresnahan had to open the bright orange coat that, she imagined, could be seen—and was being watched—for miles. Above them a quarter-moon was rising with a single, bright star near its cup, somewhat like a fermata in music. Below them in the sea to the south two boats were netting mackerel, which, like the warm breeze, had been carried in by the ocean storm and were shoaling all up and down the coast, O'Suilleabhain said. "It's the last the fishermen will see of them til May. I know those men. They'll work right through the night or until their boats are filled."

As the two of them stepped through the remaining strong light on top of the cliff, they watched the red, white, and green running lights of the boats scribing careful circles in the jade water. The putting of the engines and even the occasional voice of a fisherman came to them on updrafts that puffed over the edge, as warm as heat from a register.

In the fields they were tracing, Bresnahan could hear the plaintive, puling cries of lapwing. Overhead, swallows and swifts were working the currents, streaking the sky for moths and flies that the warmth had brought. To the west the sun was just slipping beneath a dense band of clouds. Bresnahan kept her eyes on the horizon, as the brilliant tones of crimson and magenta muted through royal blue to the deeper, dun tones of purple and finally an abiding shade of mauve that would in time simply fade into starry blackness. She had seen such nights before.

"Do I take your hand?" O'Suilleabhain asked.

"Do I look as though I need help?"

"Well, I wasn't considering so much your needs as my own. I thought it might be fun."

Thought Bresnahan, It might at that. Surely it would set the tongues of those who might see them wagging, and it would stand as a test. Rory O'Suilleabhain had most likely serviced nine tenths of the accommodating women in three countries, but he had never so much as taken her hand.

His was larger than her own, which was nearly a first, and as hard and stronger yet, she imagined, than her own father's. And she entertained thoughts of what it might be like to be the chosen and the protected of such a man, though not the captive, which—she suspected—would be the case.

"Do you ever think of me?" he asked, while they were still beyond the hearing of the men cutting turf.

"Not recently, though there was a time," when she had thought of nobody else. "And you?"

"Well, to be honest—apart from the economic incentive, I haven't thought of you in years. Now I believe I'll be thinking of you for the rest o' me life."

It was a facile line, thought Bresnahan, and revealed only that O'Suilleabhain was much practiced at this sort of thing. "But *what* beyond the 'economic incentive'—as you so candidly, if crudely, put it—has changed your opinion?''

''Why, of course—how we've changed.''

Still hand in hand, they took a few more steps before Bresnahan said, ''Go on—this is all so wonderful, I'm having trouble thinking it's real. Let's begin with you. How have you changed?''

''To begin with—I've matured.''

''I can see that. When I left you, you shaved once a day. Now it must be twice.'' O'Suilleabhain had the sort of dark beard and prominent bone structure that made his cheeks look blue. The contrast with his bright green eyes was startling, and Bresnahan dared not look at him in the half-light that was now diffusing over the reach of the bay.

''I've gotten all the . . . young buck stuff out of me system, so to speak.''

And into somebod(ies) else's without doubt.

''Now it's love for me, and nothing less. I'm looking for my mate for life.''

Really, now? Christ—this wasn't a rush, it was a blitzkrieg.

''And tell me, Rory, do you know what love is?''

''I do. There are two kinds of romantic love. There's love which is lust. It can strike you heady and hot, and you know what you want and must have. Then there's the second kind of love.''

Based on ''economic incentive,'' Bresnahan thought.

''It's an unfamiliar feeling, at least to me. A kind of''—there was a long pause, while they drew all too near the men making peat—''recognition. You know, that this is the one for you. That she is the one from which your children should come. It's a more important, better, bigger love than the first, but it's a double wonder when the two kinds of love are focused on the same person.''

Bresnahan had neither the strength nor the will to resist his moving her hand behind her back and drawing her to him. Her head was spinning from all the ''drops'' she had taken in the sundry cottages they had visited, and the man she loved had never said any such thing to her. Nor even hinted.

She did manage to take a few quick steps forward, pulling O'Suilleabhain with her, and in the twilight the peat cutters looked up.

''Fine night,'' she said, breaking away from him.

''''Tis that, miss. But you should mind the company you keep,'' said the youngest of the three, who, as spreader, had the job of pitching the cut and shaped sods to the outermost edges of the turf bank for drying.

"And why is that?" The blade of the slane was about all she could see of the man, who was below them producing the lumps of peat. Like some unusual field animal, the single tooth of its right-angled blade, silvery now with the risen moon, was taking timed and regular bites through the soft, obliging bog that was here seven layers deep. The *meithel*, or turf-cutting team, also consisted of a breensler who piked the sods up to the spreader. Peat was usually harvested in late winter or early spring and disposed of in autumn, unless, of course, it was all in the way of a cash crop that your land would yield.

"Night like this, strange moon and all—the man you're with sprouts fangs as well as horns, and there's no telling whose neck he might bite."

"Not yours, Diarmuid. Which has felt neither soap nor water in a fortnight." O'Suilleabhain laughed, his perfect teeth flashing in the moonlight. He then clasped hands with the spreader and introduced Bresnahan, and reintroduced Bresnahan to the men whom she had known all her life. The slanesman even climbed out of the pit to get a look at her. "Big Tom's girl." He was the old man they had come to see. "I thought you were with the Guards."

"She is," O'Suilleabhain explained "and *this* is the new uniform."

The other young men began laughing.

"She's investigating what happened to Paddy Power." O'Suilleabhain then began speaking low and fast to the spreader, who started to laugh. "Go over now, she didn't! *Breathalyzer?* Ruthie—that's gas. You're a gem."

But Bresnahan had asked and the slanesman was telling her what he and his brother had seen on Sunday morning. "It was something to ponder and discuss, I'll say. We were working our way up to the Waterville Road and West Cove for to make a delivery." He pointed to rows of peat banks that could be seen stretching off to one side of the bog. "And me and Mick up on an ass rail of turf.

"We had no drink on us to speak of, but when we come to the Rathfield ruin, we stopped." He meant a former mansion that had been torched by the IRA. "For a call of nature, you know."

"Like Tarzan," said the young man who was known as a local wit. "Though the message wasn't vocal."

"There I was," the old man went on with a sigh, "in the ruin behind a wall bent low like, when up pulls this long red car as bright as a hen's egg. And wasn't I surprised when out steps a country man. He pulls off a greatcoat and stuffs it in the boot. Next comes his hat, and he isn't a he at all, at all. No, he's a her. The Wellies come off next, and then back into the car, and off she goes at a gallop. I don't think the whole thing took longer—"

"Than it took him to stanch his *nose*."

The old man inclined his head and smiled, as though to say, What I have to put up with.

"How did you know it was a woman?'

"By her *breathalyzer*, how else?" And the two young men fell all about, laughing.

"Long blond hair. Though, you know, trousers, like yourself is wearing."

Bresnahan was wearing tights; it was dark, but she wondered how good the old fella's eyes were. "What make, the car?"

"You'll have to ask Mick. I wouldn't know one from the other, not being in the market, so to speak."

"Mick?" Bresnahan looked at the breensler.

"He's over at the Scariff Inn in West Cove, playin' the spoons."

Said O'Suilleabhain, "I've bloody big quid burning a hole in me pocket. Tell you what, we'll pop down there and I'll lay the whole thing on the bar for all to admire. And enjoy."

Good traditional Irish music touched something deep in Bresnahan. Having been preserved with fierce racial pride, it was a mixture—curious in this day and age—of life and antiquity, and it acted upon her as a kind of aphrodisiac, especially with a drink in hand.

The deep, rapid throbbing of the *bodhran* was the wild beating of the smitten heart. The fiddle, concertina, and flute, dueling together, were the spirits soaring, while the spoons provided the crack of mental activity, of reality and the need to make . . . connections in life.

Or to dance, which she had often on the flagstone floor of her father's kitchen, while he beat time on his knees and watched with love and pride, and later in parish halls and *teach an ceoil* (houses of music) that were a feature of a handful of villages here in the West.

And standing hip to hip with Rory O'Suilleabhain, unable to keep her feet from moving as the music swelled to its rousing conclusion, Bresnahan felt more disloyal to Hugh Ward, whom she loved—or, at least only this morning had thought she loved—than when holding O'Suilleabhain's hand or at any other moment in the two years that Ward and she had been together.

Ward had once said of such music, "Crude culchie shite, every last thump of it," and most of the other jackeens she knew in Dublin thought the same. Had she been denying what was really dearest and best about who she was? Was there any need? Now.

The music had stopped. O'Suilleabhain, handing her a tray of "jars" that he had purchased for the group of players, whispered, "Now's your chance with Nick. Remember, now—I'll be watching," in a way that tickled her ear and sent a shiver down her spine. She wondered if "Now's your chance" could be prophetic. For her.

"An Audi," said the spoon player, who was a decade younger than his brother, the slanesman. "Brand, spanking new with a bumper sticker that said:

EIRE BANK

EUR BANK   OUR BANK"

Bresnahan had seen them before; every third car in Dublin seemed to have one.

"Could you recognize the person—him or her—again?"

"I didn't get a good-enough look, I'm sorry to say." He raised the creamy head of the pint and took a long drink that closed his eyes and left a buff-colored ring on his upper lip.

Bresnahan sipped from her own glass.

"I was perched on the ass rail, like I said, and my eyes were fixed on the long blond mane, me wondering if the woman was a transvestite, a cross-dresser, or off to a costume party. Like yourself, say." He paused for another sip, his eyes glinting with the gaiety of the large, packed pub. "Your father get a glimpse of you yet? I see Rory has." He winked. "Remember, it's a band"—he showed her the third finger of his left hand—"or nothing. Any other accommodation—you could have another murder to investigate, too close to home.

"Care to dance?"

Bresnahan only smiled and turned her head to the bar where O'Suilleabhain was holding forth, his handsome head thrown back in uproarious laughter. She let her eyes roam the room, noting how many others seemed to be having an uninhibited good time. They were her people all right. And his.

"Rory'll be in Dublin within the year, count on it," said the spoon player.

And what to do about that.

CHAPTER 18

Something

EARLY IN THE afternoon McGarr had found Noreen waiting for him when he got back to their suite in Parknasilla. She was standing before the sideboard on which sat three groupings of note cards and the receiver of the baby monitor that McGarr had asked Ward to place in Frost's room. Only static was coming from it now. Placed near its speaker was the tape recorder that, since Maddie's birth, Noreen had used to dictate correspondence and notes to the two employees of her picture gallery in Dublin. The device was automatic and voice-activated.

In one hand she held a tall glass filled with ice and an amber-colored fluid. The other hand was placed firmly on a hip that was sheathed in a pearl-gray chemise. A dressing gown was draped from her shoulders. Her auburn hair, which was wavy, had been freshly combed, and in all she looked provocative, apart from the determined glaze in her eyes.

With a finger she indicated the first grouping of note cards. "This is all that's said of Gladden. Here is a card that I thought germane to Power's thinking, at least in regard to this debt conference. And this last is the 'Frost' stack, which for some reason you failed to go through with the same thoroughness as you did the headings for the two women. "It's him who murdered Paddy Power, make no mistake."

McGarr removed his mac and hat and looked into the other room. No Maddie. Considering what Noreen was wearing, maybe there was hope. "It's who?"

"Frost. He's a slimy bastard."

McGarr glanced at the monitor.

"That's right. Hughie got the monitor into the room, and he's just finished boffing Nell Power, I think it was."

Who? Hughie or Frost?

"Imagine—his best friend and partner, the man without whom he'd be nowhere—isn't even in his grave, and he's out . . ."—she couldn't bring herself to repeat the word—"the widow."

"The ex-wife," McGarr corrected, glancing at the two audio devices on the sideboard. "How do you know it was—"

"*What?* Do you think I was born yesterday? It was savage, with all sorts of creaking, shrieking, and moaning, like two animals in rut. Slaps even, as though they were practicing some type of sadomasochism."

Boffing? Where had she gotten that word, McGarr wondered. Out of a mystery novel? He hadn't heard "boffing" in decades and then only on the BBC or through a wall.

"You never heard the like of what went on between them. It was—" She shook her head and drank from the glass. "Tell me something, do women often throw themselves at you?"

Only savagely. Unfortunately. Which had something to do with being short, squat, bald, and truculent. Frost, on the other hand, was tall, thin, handsome, wealthy (McGarr supposed), sometimes charming, and looked a good fifteen years younger than McGarr, though he was not.

"And, when they do, do you take advantage of them?"

"Advantage" was an interesting interpretation of having to catch a body thrown at you without breaking *something*, if only your willpower or your ego. Still, McGarr said nothing.

Noreen shook her head. "Ach—you're all the same."

Slimy bastards, McGarr thought.

Noreen turned and entered the bedroom, the silk whistling over her hips.

McGarr considered trying to find the source of the amber fluid in her glass, but instead turned his attention to the note cards.

"Excuse me."

McGarr looked up.

"Were you expecting something?" The glaze was still in her eyes.

"I don't know what you mean."

"You know, *something*."

"Why do you say that?"

"You had that look."

But didn't he always, these days.

"Well?" she demanded.

"Well, what?"

"Well, let's get to it. We might not have another opportunity like this for a while."

Put that way, could he refuse, bandages and all?

Sometime later while still in bed, he lit a cigarette and cupped a palm under his head. Noreen was dozing beside him, and he thought of how they were joined, bonded, locked (?) together for life and were performing a delicate, intricate, enormously complicated dance in step, the patterns of which would affect at least Maddie for all of her life. So far so good, largely because each had sympathy as well as love for the other. It was the given part of a good match, how two people went about their shared life together.

He also thought about Paddy Power, the note-taker, the man with a saying borrowed from this thinker and that. He had two significant others, with neither of whom he could form a permanent bond and who didn't seem to mourn him much. Yet Power had been loved by the world, or so all of the newspapers were saying. Outsiders. People who didn't know him well. Apart from Mossie Gladden, who had seemed genuinely aggrieved when viewing Power's corpse. And angered.

Which caused McGarr to remember how Power had been found, laughing wildly—savagely, grotesquely—and waving the single note card over his head, as though to say, this is the prize. There is no answer, no real knowing. Why strive? Death is the only certainty, which is the biggest and best laugh of all.

The note card, the one that he had been waving—McGarr had marked it with his pen. Easing himself out of bed so as not to wake Noreen, he padded into the sitting room and found it among the others on the sideboard.

Sunday, 3:30   Parknasilla: debt conference
Have stopped again to catch my breath before descend-
ing the narrow path through the cliff face. From time to time
the sharp report of Mossie's high-powered rifle comes to me

and then howls through the mountains. Target practice, he's told me, for the dogs that summer people leave when returning to the city. Jackals, he calls them. The wily and strong have survived and reproduce, preying on Mossie's sheep. For a time he took to trapping the dogs, but with no takers even for the pups of such animals, the local dog warden only had to put them down.

Now he uses the rifle.

Not very enlightening. Nor probably even accurate, Power merely having accepted Gladden's explanation of why he was shooting. Hadn't the farmers in the Sneem House pub told McGarr that morning that they hadn't seen a wild dog in ages, men who were out on the land much more than any doctor-politician-gentleman-shepherd or any financial wizard?

McGarr then remembered the target that he had found in Gladden's press with "Sean" duly marked on top. McGarr made a mental note to ask Superintendent Butler of the Kenmare Barracks to call in on Gladden and relieve him of the weapon, which was illegal in Ireland. He would have taken it himself, had he not been "distracted." He tugged at the bandages on his neck that had begun to itch.

Next he skimmed the cards on Shane Frost that Noreen had culled that morning. Most had to deal with Power's changing opinion of Frost as time passed. The first negative assessment was undated but was yellowing with age:

If life is most successfully perceived from a single window, then Shane's singular advantage is in viewing people and things strictly for their utility. He has no larger view than what he sees for himself, and thus is your basic, hollow 'economic' man who will work hard and devote himself only to those projects that will win him quick, substantial profits. At gaining those, he has few peers, which is why I continue to associate with him. He is utterly ruthless, and I would not want him working against me.

Some time later, Power wrote:

Shane has grown so mean and niggardly that I don't think I'm far wrong in guessing that he has never married because the very idea of sharing his wealth in any way, even

*with a wife and children, is anathema to him. I don't think
I have ever met a wealthy man so considered about every
expense. He'll pay for drinks or buy you dinner, but he keeps
a running tally on everybody, it seems, and always comes
out ahead.*

*I think of his old father dozing there in his chemist shop,
never throwing anything away, always with one eye half-
open on the door and the other on his ledger. People call
him the meanest man in Sneem and delight in telling stories
about his avarice in which—imagine!—he takes pride.*

*Already stories circulate in Dublin about Shane. Like
father, like son.*

McGarr thought of another thing he had been told that morning
in the pub—about how Frost had employed a gang of men from Dublin
to build his house in Sneem, the same who had worked on the Eire
Bank headquarters, local opinion be damned. Doubtless it was economics again, and the house was probably a "perk" of the Dublin contract,
gotten for next to nothing. Or nothing.

Other cards went on in the same vein of critical assessment, the
most recent being dated

January 22   Dublin
*I keep asking myself what happened to Shane. Formerly,
though always careful, he was a hell of a good fellow. Perhaps it is who we've become as the years have gone on, and
the system that's flattened us out. We've all had to change.
With Shane, however, the process has been rather more
severe.*

*Today I divulged to him my proposal for the national
debt, and he nearly jumped when I mentioned how necessary
an immediate write-down of no less than 20 percent would
be. "Why?" he demanded. I told him for good faith, to show
that we in the banking community were compassionate and
willing to "take a hit," as the Americans say, along with
everybody else.*

*"You mean your good faith," he replied, and then
charged me with hypocrisy in espousing compassion for the
very "yokes"—by which he meant average rate-paying citizens, I believe—whom I had formerly despised. I told him I
never despised anyone; I had simply made a mistake, as had he.*

*"On the contrary," he said. "It is you who are making
a mistake on two scores. You are being inconsistent. Worse,
you are acting against your own self-interest." I tried to tell
him I'm not, that if the country as a whole is better off, I will
be too. But he stormed out.*

So much for Frost's claim to have backed the Power proposal,
McGarr thought. He was about to reach for another group of cards
when from the baby monitor he heard what sounded like a key being
worked in the lock of a door. Frost himself then said, "Come in,
gentlemen. You'll find drinks and snacks on the bar. If you'll excuse
me for a moment, I have a phone call to make."

Another voice that McGarr recognized as that of the Japanese
banker he had heard that morning now said, "Su'ely." There was a
pause, and, when another door was heard to close, a flurry of low,
rapid conversation in Japanese ensued. McGarr checked to see if the
tape recorder was running and padded back into the bedroom for the
still half-filled glass that, he decided, Noreen had abandoned.

"Sorry," said Frost, returning to the room. "I just wanted to
make sure I have all my pins in place."

A Paddy Power expression, McGarr remembered from the note
cards.

"What—no drinks? Please, help yourselves. When I was over in
your country last spring, you weren't so reluctant."

"After hours, Shane. We w'ap this deal up, hey—we pawty."

The phrase seemed practiced and American, and McGarr wondered how many times the speaker had employed it. Japanese seemed
to own half of Dublin nowadays, and half of New York, from what
McGarr had read.

"Well—I'm going to have a drink, and I'm going to pour you
one as well, Anaki." Frost's voice sounded already a bit oiled, and,
if what Noreen had said was accurate, he was having an interesting
day on other scores. McGarr took a wee sip himself.

"Oh, you Irish," said the other man resignedly.

The curse, thought McGarr, which was looked on by most of the
cursed as a blessing. And why not? If his work had taught him anything,
it was that life *was* short and often violent. He sipped again.

"There now. Cheers."

"Chee-ahs."

Some of the other Japanese were now speaking among themselves.

"Where were we when last we spoke?"

"Forty-eight Irish pounds for *all* eight million, three-hundred-and-thirty-three shares of Eire Bank stock."

"But why *all* shares, Anaki? That will be difficult, if not impossible. Isn't it enough you'll have my twenty percent, Mrs. Power's nineteen, and the fifty-one percent that Paddy left to Gretta Osbourne? With the remaining ten percent we're certain to get a few curmudgeonly shareholders with money who will choose to sacrifice the quick profit for what they perceive as the possibility of a larger, long-term gain. Also, there's the government to consider. I'm not at all sure that they'll allow an outright purchase."

"Nonsense, Shane. One, you wouldn't be wasting our time, had you not that pin in place as you say. Two, with Mr. Powah's share soon to be in hands that are agreeable to such a sale, it's only a matter of ten percent of the shares. I can't imagine you haven't spoken to the other shareholders in detail and at length."

There was a pause in which McGarr believed he heard the distinctive ring of crystal on stone. In his own suite there was a cocktail table with a green Connemara marble top. "Fifty-two pounds per share, and I'll personally guarantee the sale. Or eat the shares."

"Eat?"

"Refund you the money for the unsold shares out of my own pocket."

"Forty-nine."

"No—fifty-two or nothing."

The Japanese banker's sigh was audible. "Then, I'm afraid, my friend, it is nothing. Chee-ahs."

Crystal again rang, and the voice of Anaki spoke in Japanese to his associates. Standing at the sideboard in his suite, McGarr quickly computed on the pad the value of Eire Bank by multiplying the number of shares by the forty-eight-pound asking price, which was a whopping 423 million Irish pounds.

Noreen had awakened and now approached him.

"I've consulted my colleagues, Shane. We can go fifty, but that's all. Our last offer."

"For Eire Bank?" Noreen asked.

McGarr nodded.

Static crackled over the monitor, and McGarr could almost feel the tension in Frost's room.

"No," said Frost. "If I am to be responsible for *all* shares, it'll have to be fifty-two to insure my exposure."

"You are a hawd man, Shane Fwost."

"No—anybody will tell you, I am an easy man who merely wants to be dealt with *fairly*, Anaki. Eire Bank will give you what you need, an unfettered toehold in post-'92 Europe. It will also get you continued government support."

"Gua'anteed?"

"I have it from the taosieach himself. Look—from the cash flow on government deposits alone, you'll have your money back in a decade. Meanwhile you have the trading and finance base. Face it, given your needs, it's a bargain price and you know it."

"How much are Eire Bank's deposits?" McGarr asked Noreen.

"Because of government accounts, billions. Since O'Duffy has been in office, tax receipts have been lodged in Eire Bank."

O'Duffy again, McGarr thought.

"Then I suppose we can't do business."

McGarr heard what he believed were hands slapping thighs. "Such is life," said Frost.

Or death, thought McGarr. Perhaps Paddy Power's for the possibility of the sale of Eire Bank. And now no sale.

Again McGarr jotted down some figures. Twenty percent of the first figure mentioned was a king's—or, rather, a chief executive officer's—ransom of some 84.6 million. Just over 80 million to Nell Power and her children. And nearly 216 million to whoever inherited Paddy Power's share. Frost had just said it was Gretta Osbourne, and, as Power's solicitor, he would know. Motive enough for murder? McGarr rather believed it was.

And Frost was willing to let the deal walk out the door? What did Frost know? How much was Eire Bank really worth? Had he another, better offer waiting in the wings?

"Let me say that I have nothing but the greatest respect for you, your associates, and compatriots."

"Good aftahnoon, Shane."

"Well, I suppose in one way it is. Paddy would have wanted Eire Bank to remain Irish, now he has his wish."

"Ah, yes. Me. Pow-ah," the man, Anaki, said. "A tragedy. He was so cha'ming."

"Good afternoon, good afternoon. Pleasure," Frost was saying to the others.

Noreen reached out and gripped McGarr's bare arm. "They don't know Irishmen."

All of whom had a bit of horse trader or cattle dealer in the blood, thought McGarr. Frost wouldn't be able to live with himself, did he not let the Japanese walk at least as far as the door.

"Anaki?" Frost said.

Noreen shook McGarr's arm.

"Fifty-one, and I swear to God they'll give you a medal when you get back to Kyoto."

A Japanese phrase that was evidently "Fifty-one" was repeated among the other men. Some discussion followed.

"And you will become chai'man and remain on the board for five years?"

"At a level of remuneration to be negotiated only upward, plus an allowance for any inflation."

"And Ms. Osbourne will agree to everything?"

There was a pause and then: "I wouldn't have brought you this far, Anaki, were I not certain."

"Well, then—" McGarr heard the door close. "Now we *will* dwink with you. May I use your phone, Shane?"

"Only if it's a local call."

There was yet another pause, in which, McGarr supposed, the man called Anaki translated what Frost had said. Suddenly the room burst into laughter, through which they heard Frost say, "I just happened to have some champagne on ice, gents. But, remember, this has to be between us, at least until Paddy is decently in the ground and has his will read and made public. If anybody asks, we're celebrating Anaki's birthday and not his great triumph in purchasing Eire Bank for what in a few years will be seen as peanuts."

"Satisfied that it's Frost?" Noreen asked.

McGarr canted his head, wishing her to continue.

"Being Power's lawyer, he knew that Power was planning to leave Gretta Osbourne his share of Eire Bank. When Power vetoed Frost's plan of selling Eire Bank, he murdered Power and stole the note cards."

"Why steal the note cards?"

"To deflect attention from himself. To make it look like it was Gladden or Nell Power or even Gretta Osbourne, considering the way he edited the contents of the cards. As I've heard you say time and again, murderers always try too hard."

Which was the problem with saying something too often. "But that only called attention to the possibility that it was murder. Without the theft of the cards, I would have reported it as a death by misadventure.''

Noreen offered a palm and smiled, as though the facts were plain for any fool to see. ''But Frost needed something to mask what we've just heard him accomplish—the sale of Eire Bank. By sending a copy of the sections that, he knew, would be incendiary to Mossie Gladden as well as an edited version to the . . . fiery Nell Power, he hoped to create a furor in which the sale of Eire Bank would seem like no big thing. If you're going to muddy the waters, make them black.''

Or mix metaphors, McGarr thought. ''What about Nell Power and her . . . tryst or whatever with Shane Frost?''

Noreen hunched her shoulders and looked away. ''Maybe the three of them were—are—in on it together.''

''Then why steal the cards to shift any blame?''

''Onto Mossie Gladden with his readily identifiable country gorsoon costume? It strikes me that he was the perfect party to blame.''

It was McGarr's turn to think. He remembered the letter that Nell Power had been writing to her daughter in America that mentioned Gretta Osbourne as ''That blessed perfectionist woman.'' Could Nell Power enter into a conspiracy with her? Not if O'Shaughnessy's theory of premeditated murder was at all accurate and could withstand the exigency of a quick £423 million.

He also thought of one of the objects that he had found in the pocket of Mossie Gladden's greatcoat. The blond wig. What use would Gladden have had for that? Did it fit in, and where?

''I suppose it all boils down to who delivered the photocopies of the note cards to the Waterville Lake Hotel. You know—who was the rough-looking country gorsoon?''

Noreen blinked. A furrow appeared in her brow, then cleared, as her green eyes brightened with insight. ''You should run a lineup, is what you should do. You know, with Gladden's hat and greatcoat, all the prime suspects, and the desk clerk from the Waterville Lake Hotel.''

''Just like in the movies.''

''Tomorrow, right before the funeral mass for Paddy Power. If Gladden won't cooperate with the coat and hat, I'm sure I could find similar objects in a shop in the village and a blond wig.''

McGarr considered the suggestion for a moment, then nodded. What would it cost? Fifty or sixty pounds. It would also obviate the need to ''disturb'' the truculent Gladden, who would be nursing his damaged image after his disastrous press conference on the bridge. "What about Maddie? Perhaps she's ready to return—"

"Oh, Jesus—I completely forgot about her!" Turning on heel, Noreen rushed into the bedroom.

McGarr turned an ear to the celebration, which was continuing loudly in Shane Frost's room. In Japanese exclusively. He checked the tape recorder to see if the reels were still spinning. It might be interesting to have it translated and transcribed, when they got back to Dublin.

CHAPTER 19

Saint Rut'ie

AT 11:07, WELL PAST the hour at which he should have been back in his dormitory digs, barman-trainee Hughie Ward ambled into the lobby area of Parknasilla and nicked a silver ashtray from the receptionist's desk. In the public toilet he washed and dried it until the surface gleamed. From the coat of his service tuxedo, he then drew a buff-colored envelope, which he had lifted earlier from one of the several writing desks that were scattered throughout the hotel. He placed the envelope on the tray, and he fitted on his white gloves.

As though delivering a message, Ward made a pass through the public rooms of Parknasilla: the sun room with its sweeping gray-stone walls and views of the dark bay and starlit sky beyond. In one corner of the large, L-shaped room a pianist was rendering classical and old Irish favorites for the bankers, some of whom were playing cards or chess; others were engaged in cigar-smoky, animated conversations, mainly in English. A fresh heap of coal was burning in the fireplace, an oily yellow flame licking at the flue. There, a group of French women had gathered, two of whom tried to order another pot of tea from Ward, who said he'd refer their request to the kitchen.

The Shaw Lounge came next, which had become a kind of reading room. Every seat, divan, chair, banquette, and sofa was taken by somebody with something legible in his hands, and the feeling was rather collegial and pleasant, Ward judged. Again he had to fend off brandy and cigar orders. There too the hearth was giving off the deep heat of a mellow coal fire, and Ward decided that someday, *if* and when all this was over, he would return as a guest. *With* Bresnahan.

But no Bresnahan was to be found there. Nor among the guests lingering over coffee in the Pygmalion Restaurant, nor in the Snooker Room, nor the Derryquin Suite, where some sort of banking meeting was still taking place, nor the swimming pool, into which he glanced on the off-chance that Bresnahan might be taking the only other sort of vigorous exercise that she practiced regularly. Bresnahan swam like a great red dolphin, taking powerful stokes even in heavy surf, the waves just washing right over her. Ward sank like a stone.

Another difference, he thought bleakly, climbing the stairs to the second floor and the Shaw Library. There, an exotic-looking Italian woman asked him if, in fact, George Bernard Shaw had actually stayed in the hotel. Ward had noticed her on the day before with an aged husband, who was now nowhere to be seen. She pointed to photographs of the dramatist, which had been hung on every wall.

"Yes. He wrote his best play here. *Saint Joan.*"

"Why *best*?" the woman asked with an intensity that neither the play nor Ward, as barman-waiter, merited. He begged off the gambit, claiming it was only his personal opinion. Smiling, he then glanced down at the silver tray with its envelope and back up into her hazel eyes that a gold choker around her neck made seem gamboge.

The woman spun around and stepped quickly back to the red chintz love seat on which she had been reclining in wait. Another country as yet unconquered, thought Ward as he withdrew strategically up the stairs toward Bresnahan's room. He wished he had fifty pee for every opportunity he had ignored in the past two years; he'd have enough money for a holiday in Trieste, which was where the woman's husband owned his bank.

Ward was about to step into the hall on which, he had earlier learned, Bresnahan's room was located, when he saw her, or at least he thought he did: her wide shoulders, thin waist, that certain athletic swing to her stride that he so much admired, even the unmistakably particular aroma of her costly perfume, which had been recently applied and now pervaded the hall.

Ward opened his mouth to call out, but restrained himself. What if her "sugar daddy," as it were—the one who had "sprung" for all the designer "threads" and the Merc—was in residence at the hotel and that was the reason she had been avoiding him. His heart pounding in his temples and with all his senses jacked up to ring-readiness, Ward followed in her spice-musky train, employing the even deeper shadows along the sides of the walls to conceal his pursuit.

In the stairwell he waited until she had passed beyond the rail where she might look down and see who was behind her. But she neither stopped nor turned her head left or right. Instead she made straight for Frost's door. There she raised her hand to knock, but the door opened, and Frost—reaching out—pulled her to him and kissed her.

Ward was on the final stair, and his entire body went taut. The pattern of the carpet spun before his eyes, and he felt lightheaded and weak in the way that was disastrous in the ring. Control. He did not know if he could keep hold of himself, job *and* profession be damned. How could he work with her, how could he go back to Dublin, after this . . . mockery of their relationship. He'd make hash of Frost, so he would. And resign.

Ward's right calf tensed, and he was about to propel himself forward when she pushed herself away from Frost, saying, "Get away from me, Shane. You've been drinking. If I've told you once, I've told you a dozen times, I will not confer with you while you're drunk."

"Who's drunk? I'm just celebrating. We've done it—fifty-one bloody pounds per share, outright purchase! Even Paddy could not have refused that." In the brilliant light spilling from the doorway, Frost raised both arms, his mane of silver hair lapping back over his bare shoulders. He was wearing only shorts, and his tall, square body looked lean, well exercised, and deeply tanned. One hand held a bottle of champagne. "Well . . . ?" he demanded.

"I've changed my mind. I've decided not to sell."

Ward's eyes cleared. It was *not* Bresnahan after all, but rather the other tall woman—Gretta Osbourne, Paddy Power's former . . . assistant.

"*Why*, for Jesus, sake?" Looking up the hall in one direction and then—Ward flattened himself the against the wall of the staircase—the other, Frost closed the door.

Ward's body was tingling, and sweat—something that usually took as many as two rounds to gather—now beaded his forehead and upper lip. His arms were shaking, and, when he looked down, he saw that his hands were still knotted in tight white fists. He told himself to relax, and he did.

Until he turned to descend the staircase and, looking out the casement window, saw the Merc that Bresnahan had been driving. It wheeled around and came to a stop with its lights focused on the back bumper of a red Audi.

Bresnahan, who was sitting in the passenger seat, now got out and approached the Audi, walking through the beam of the Merc's headlamps. She glanced down at the bumper sticker that Ward knew from its shape said.

EIRE BANK

EUR BANK   OUR BANK

Then she copied something into her notebook. Probably the plate number.

The driver's door of the Merc popped open, and out stepped a man who looked enough like Bresnahan in height and build to be related. But for his black, wavy mane, they were a pair.

Bresnahan raced around to the other side of the Audi to copy the information on the tax stamp and to check the doors there. She then said something to the man, pointing to the empty slot beside the Audi. He parked the Merc, got out, and, taking Bresnahan's arm, led her toward the hotel.

Some cousin? Some friend? Ward was so relieved that Bresnahan was not the woman who had entered Frost's room that he was nearly dispassionate in considering who the tall young man might be. The owner of the car? No, he was around Ward's own age and too young to be able to afford such an extravagant machine.

"What are *you* doing *here*?" A deep voice asked from the stairs below. It was Sonnie, carrying a tray with a wine bucket and the towel-wrapped neck of a champagne bottle protruding from ice.

Ward showed him the silver tray and envelope. "Mr. Feeney asked me to deliver a message."

"Mr. Feeney went home hours ago," said Sonnie skeptically. "But as long as you're still here, go down to the kitchen and fetch the cart that's been ordered for Mr. Frost's room.

"But I'm—"

"Nonsense, man. You're in service now, and you should resign yourself to the idea that your time is no longer your own. And a piece of advice—when you're to go home? Go Home. Don't linger around."

Sonnie swept by him, and knocked on Frost's door.

Frost appeared, still nearly naked. He handed Sonnie a tip, took the tray, and closed the door.

Sonnie snapped a five-pound note before Ward's face. "This from him is like a gold scapular from the pope. He's drunk, I'd say, and there's probably one of these in it for you, if you hurry."

Enough said; Ward turned on heel.

O'Suilleabhain directed Bresnahan beyond the trapezoid of yellow light that was spilling from the main entrance of the hotel and the eyes of the doorman, whom they both knew.

In the shadows he pulled her to him. "Give us a kiss."

"Are you singular tonight, or is there more than one of you, as usual?"

O'Suilleabhain smiled understandingly. "Fair play, but, you know, people can change."

"And for the worse, as well." Bresnahan had both hands on his chest, and she pushed herself back to look up at him. "Let me ask *you* something. How old are you?"

Working back and forth as though attempting to cast a spell, his green eyes fixed in hers. "You know as well as I. Two years older than yourself."

"Thirty."

O'Suilleabhain nodded.

"Don't you think it's time to stop playing games?"

O'Suilleabhain pondered that for a moment, then said, "But isn't life one big game? Isn't that what makes it fun?"

"Like hide-and-go-fetch?"

"Well, tonight I had in mind something more like tag."

Bresnahan fixed his gaze and wondered how long, if he were to pursue her, she could avoid the lure that Rory O'Suilleabhain represented. In every way he was—or at least had been—so right for her, and after all the years she had pined for him, she could not keep herself from wondering what it would be like to realize those not-entirely-forgotten dreams. Perhaps Wilde was right and she could cure herself of the temptation only by yielding to it.

But it occurred to her as well that any such concession, no matter how slight, would be the death of her love for Hughie Ward. Or at least would begin the process. Things between them would become immediately different and . . . diminished. And yet she wished to live and experience and possess life in all its forms, especially that which had been most appealing to her for so long.

Perhaps she couldn't have it both ways. She knew this: You had to pick and choose, and then live with your choices. But at what cost?

She reached up and seized O'Suilleabhain by his long, chiseled nose, which she squeezed. "Suffer, sinner." And she broke away from him, stepping back into the light where she could be seen by the doorman.

O'Suilleabhain followed her. "Didn't Martin Luther say something like that?"

"No, he said, 'Sin bravely.'"

"And look what it got him. Another religion."

And centuries of religious strife that had not yet ceased, at least in Ireland. Life was too complex to be reduced to riposte or a dalliance for all the *right* reasons.

"Well—how do I get home?"

She was tempted to tell him on his two feet, but she had no reason to be angry with him. He was who he was, and there was no changing that. "You have the key to my car. I'll need it again tomorrow, before the Power funeral."

"Are your folks going?"

"Of course. Wasn't his eldest sister maid of honor at my mother's wedding?"

"I'll give them all a lift, then." Together with his mother, he meant.

So, he *was* serious; their parents' presence would make tongues wag and seriously curtail any protracted "sparking" he might be engaged in at least locally.

"Michael," she said in greeting to the doorman, sweeping by him.

"I see Rory's found you, Ruthie."

"Did you think he wouldn't?" she asked.

"They say he's got radar." He canted his head to add confidentially, "A word to the wise."

Bresnahan raised an eyebrow, thanking him, and walked into the lobby, which was empty. But she had no sooner climbed the deeply carpeted stairs to the second floor, when she saw Hughie Ward, pulling a laden cart down the hall. "Can I give you a hand with that, waiter?" Like a matador(a), she opened the fire door and tilted her smiling face to him as he wheeled the cart through.

Ward caught a glimpse of her gray eyes, which the red illuminated Exit sign flecked with bits of ruby light. Jesus, how had he gotten himself into such a mess? He punched the Up button on the elevator that would take him to the second story and Frost's suite. He glanced up at the lights of the floor monitor; he couldn't look at her while deciding, but he had to face this thing straight on and then act according to his determination.

This was—he took a deep breath and then abandoned himself to his fate—love, for Christ sake, and love was trust, sharing, and mutual respect. Love was help, encouragement, and support. Love didn't go around suspicious, distrustful, and bitter. Having only his hard self to guide him and the sorry history of his past, failed affairs—all of them 100 percent ruined by design—Ward didn't rightly know how to proceed, but he suspected it was a matter that couldn't and shouldn't be planned.

Instead he'd wing it. He'd speak and act, not think, and see what came out. The point was to be light, not heavy. Any time a woman had become serious with him, he had split, especially when he had had a choice. He thought of the tall, dark, handsome man who had brought her home.

The elevator slid open. Ward put a foot in the door and turned to her. He smiled and let his eyes roam her powerful body, every inch of which he knew perhaps better than his own; Ward was nothing if not an attentive lover. "So—how went your day? Make Gladden's press conference on the bridge?"

She nodded and told him how Gladden had painted Power as martyr and himself as scapegoat in a government cover-up led by McGarr. "He also didn't seem to know much about Paddy Power's note cards. It was as if he never really read them thoroughly. When the Power proposal for the debt was brought up, he stormed off. You know, swapping debt for equity."

"Brought up by you."

She smiled, wondering if perchance Ward had been running some message in the village for Sonnie and had seen her and O'Suilleabhain, and she felt almost guilty. "In a roundabout way."

"I'd be careful of him, were I you. Gladden's no fool, and more dangerous than he appears. He's bent, I'd say." On his midday "break" of two hours Ward had skimmed Paddy Power's note cards in McGarr's room.

"Mossie Gladden? Come now, he attended at my birth."

"Proof positive," Ward continued in the same jocular vein.

"Anyhow—I've solved the case, and it wasn't Mossie."

Ward's eyebrows arched.

She told him about the balance of her day—interviewing old cottiers and small farmers along the Waterville Road—and the description of the country gorsoon who climbed out of the car by the Rathfield ruin to doff greatcoat and hat. "A rough complexion and long gray-blond hair. Driving a new Audi with an Eire Bank bumper sticker. Sound familiar?"

"You mean Gretta Osbourne without any makeup on her face?"

"Precisely. She had every opportunity to steal the note cards and unlimited access to Power's medical cabinet."

"And she had a hell of a motive," said Ward.

Bresnahan waited.

"I overheard Shane Frost . . . speaking to Nell Power about Osbourne inheriting Power's share of Eire Bank."

"*Voilà!*" She glanced down at the food, which smelled delicious. She lifted the cover off one of the oval plates. It was an entrecote of beef topped with a bordelaise sauce. Suddenly she was famished, and she thought briefly of ordering something from room service on the chance Ward could be sent on the delivery. But no. That would be wrong; she had her parents to think of.

"But why would she have delivered the cards to Nell Power dressed up like Gladden?"

"To cast suspicion on him, of course. How many men go around like he does, these days? And to rub the wife's nose in Power's poor opinion of his marriage and her. A woman's thing altogether."

Ward was glad she said that, not he.

"The giveaway was her expurgating any negative cards that Power might have written about herself, while including the full stack about Nell."

"Where'd you learn all this?"

"After I found out about the Audi and the long blond hair, I phoned the Chief and got Noreen."

Who, of course, provided Bresnahan with an inside scoop, woman to woman. "Why the cards to Gladden, then?"

"Don't you see that she stole the cards before Power was actually murdered, most probably on Friday night or early Saturday morning when he went into the village for a session with his old friends at the Sneem Inn. She didn't have much time, but the point was to make it appear as if Gladden had murdered Power to get ahold of the note cards that she knew he wouldn't be able to keep himself from making public. It was just the chaff that he had been waiting for these last three years, what he could and would use to gain media attention and smear O'Duffy.

"But the photocopies took time. Editing the "Gladden" heading—there had to be one; every other important person in Power's life is mentioned, and there Gladden was keeping Power alive—well, that was easy. All she had to do was grab the stack and chuck it into one of the fires that're burning in all the public rooms all the time. That way, if or when the cards *or* the photocopies were examined, no Gladden heading would be found, and further suspicion would be cast on the daft doctor. As I said, her removing the derogatory cards from her own stack was her mistake and probably an afterthought."

"So the point was to pin it on Gladden."

"Who better? Certainly not Frost, with whom Osbourne was—*is*, I'd hazard—having an affair."

Why *is*? Ward wondered. Could a woman tell by looking at another woman?

"And not Nell Power, who is also a significant shareholder in Eire Bank, which Frost not more than a few hours ago sold to the Nomura Bank of Kyoto for—are you ready for this?—over four hundred and twenty million pounds."

Ward's head went back. It was obviously more sororal insider information that she had gleaned from Noreen. How could a lowly waiter compete?

"Paddy Power, you see, didn't want to sell. Motive enough, I'd say."

Ward nodded and struggled to hold his smile. But he could not keep himself from thinking about what he had just heard—Gretta Osbourne telling Shane Frost that she did not want to sell her majority share of Eire Bank to the Japanese.

Also, there was a reference in Paddy Power's note cards—one of those that had been found beside his body—to Power's having looked for and not found Gretta Osbourne's red Audi in the Parknasilla car park. It was on Sunday morning, exactly at the time that the sack filled with the photocopies of the cards were being delivered to the Waterville Lake Hotel. But Gretta Osbourne was still at Parknasilla. Power had asked her for the keys and had then gone directly to the car.

But Ward said nothing. His last wish was to deflate her buoyant mood.

And that's all you want-ed?" She pulsed her eyes at him. "To know about my day? I'd ask you about yours, but I know you're too considerate to bore me with all the thrilling details of pouring whiskey and beer. And the point is now moot, is it not?"

"Case closed, you mean?"

She nodded.

Even across the serving cart with its rapidly cooling edibles, Ward could catch the inviting scent of the distinctive and obviously priceless perfume that Gretta Osbourne also wore, which reminded him of the Merc and Bresnahan's new designer costumes. His glowery mood threatened to return, but he fought it off. "Oh, I dunno—I just wanted to share a few words, I guess." With his foot still in the door he pulled the cart onto the elevator.

"You mean, your sole reason in waylaying me, like this, was . . . communication?"

Ward hunched his shoulders and scanned the control panel for the Up button. *Waylaying* who?

"Nothing else?"

His mouth formed an inverted U; he shook his head.

Well now, thought Bresnahan, this was different. Perhaps something *had* changed or changed him. But what? The job of work here in the hotel? Had it given him a bit of perspective, such that he realized how lucky he was back in Dublin and *in love* with herself, though he couldn't bring himself to form the words? Were they getting close and, once said, how would that change things? Ward was so . . . elusive—she believed the word was. Dodgy, skittish, particular—that she wondered if it needed to be said. Or should.

Bresnahan had been leaning against a jamb of the elevator, and she now straightened herself up from the cart and looked down on her small, square, *fine* man with his dark good looks. What she wouldn't give to see him all done up, like one of the bankers, and part of a conference, such as this, where his quick mind could show. Maybe that was the problem he was having. Maybe he—or at least one of them—should now resign, and begin something else, like banking. It was the proper thing to do, now that they were semipublic knowledge.

"Look—I thought of trying to pull you away last night. For a drink. But I figured you would be—" She tried to find a word that would bruise his masculine pride least.

"Shattered," he prompted.

What was this? Ego honesty? Once, after having sustained a concussion in the ring, Ward had admitted to being "a bit dizzy."

"—from the work, and then a drink was probably the last thing you needed. Right?"

"Ask me the first thing."

"And that too. Country people, as I told you, are keen observers. If I dragged you into a pub, they'd know. If we pretended to meet at the bar and then left together, they'd think even worse of me. If we even merely met on the road and somebody saw—" She shook her head. "And, trust me, people around here *see*. Think of Gretta Osbourne in the Rathfield ruin. Can't we pretend we're on holiday from each other? Surely you can get through a week."

Ward canted his head and smiled at her, his eyes moving down her body and then up again. "It would be one thing, were we actually *on* holiday, but with you around and looking so . . ."

Bresnahan waited. "Go on. So—?"

"Do I have to say it?"

"Yes, you do."

"Delectable. Sexy. Smart. Provocative."

"That's all?" She turned from the cart and began a model's strut toward the stairs.

Seen from Ward's perspective, she was all long, shapely deep brown legs. The flared jacket. The nip of her waist. Those shoulders. The wild, unlikely hair. "What?" he asked. "No kiss?"

It was the same question that Rory O'Suilleabhain had asked, and Bresnahan wondered if they could be merely different, handsome forms of the same exploitive, macho-sexist personality. "Blow me a kiss from across the serving cart, Give me your service tux to cry on," she sang, paraphrasing one of the pop records that her mother—a devoted country-and-western music fan, like so many farmers' wives in the West of Ireland—had played over and over in their farmhouse kitchen before television had arrived in Sneem.

"You sound like Bernie," Ward observed in a different, disconsolate-but-resigned tone.

At the stairs she waited.

"You know—life as a sudsy, sardonic, upbeat ditty."

Bresnahan tilted her head, considering. Drop the sudsy, and there was little wrong in that. From all she could know, it was the way people were, at least in Ireland. And Ward usually as well. There was nobody more . . . buoyant, when he was in good form.

"Can I ask you something?" he went on, adjusting the fit of the serving cart in the elevator. He was behind it but still had managed to keep his foot in the door. "Is the vent of that jacket tacked or just, you know, open-to-hand?"

Bresnahan's brow furrowed. She twisted around to see what he meant by open-to-hand, and out of the corner of her eye she saw him perform a remarkable feat. In one movement Ward vaulted over the height of the serving cart and pulled it forward, such that he landed squarely on the carpet out of the elevator, and the cart jammed between the closing door.

She knew what that meant and took two long, quick strides up the stairs, trying to flee, before she felt his hand snag her leg and she fell on the carpet of the landing. Ward was quick and deft, and she knew what he intended. She let out a squeal of delight, but of pique too. It was the game they sometimes played on the long staircase up to his loft on the quays in Dublin where you could be free and nothing mattered.

In a trice her little monkey of a man was upon her, and she couldn't resist. She rolled him over and pinned his arms to the carpet. But, just as she was bending to give him the deepest, best kiss that he had ever received, she heard.

"Children?"

She looked up, and there stood McGarr, a bundle of what looked like photocopies under each arm. He had spent the last several hours making his own copy of Paddy Power's note cards.

"Ah, Chief," said Bresnahan, climbing off Ward. "Just the man I've been looking for."

She saw McGarr's eyes float toward Ward's; he then continued his transit up the staircase.

Bresnahan picked herself up, straightened her *riding*—ahem!—jacket, and followed, saying, "Chief—one moment. It's not been *all* fun and games. I've something further to tell you."

Ward quickly descended the stairs toward the elevator and the now-cold food meant for Shane Frost, Eire Bank purveyor. The elevator door was opening and closing on the cart, making a racket that sounded like something from the "Anvil Chorus."

THURSDAY

"Love is death, come upon with passion."

Djuna Barnes

CHAPTER 20

Wig

"DIDN'T I KNOW it was her all along," whispered Bernie McKeon, when shortly after nine the next morning McGarr, Bresnahan, O'Shaughnessy, and he had gathered in front of Gretta Osbourne's suite.

McGarr knocked and turned an ear to the door; he had tried to reach her by telephone at 7:30, 8:00, 8:30, and 9:00 A.M. He had arranged for the desk clerk at the Waterville Lake Hotel to meet them at the church in Sneem. Like most area residents, the clerk had said she would be attending Paddy Power's funeral. Over his arm McGarr carried a greatcoat like Gladden's; in that hand he held a farmer's hat. He knocked again.

"Potato-puss hex complex," McKeon went on. "Guilt written in lumps all over her face."

O'Shaughnessy's head turned to him.

"Consider the parallels. Power was old enough to be her father. They had carnal relations, or so I imagine, which in this country always results in guilt and a man paying, one way or another. Didn't Power and her then attempt to purge themselves with fire? No luck. She survived and, worse, was disfigured. Power tried money next, whole gobs of it, to be paid at some time in her future, not his, which was his mistake. When he rejected her in the end, she did him dirty." Unable to contain himself, McKeon began chuckling.

"Didn't you see the play at the Abbey a coopl' a years back? Freudened the hell out of me with twelve 'Jung-ans,' not one of whom I named Eddie."

Puffing his cheeks, O'Shaughnessy passed wind between his lips volubly.

"'Twas the beginning of language, I'm told," McKeon observed.

McGarr knocked once more and, still hearing nothing, turned to the hotel carpenter, who was standing behind them, holding a ladder and a toolbox.

Osbourne's red Audi with the Eire Bank bumper sticker was still in the car park. None of the Parknasilla staff had seen her leave the hotel. Like Paddy Power's room three days earlier, the door was locked from the inside, both door latch and dead bolt.

But not the night chain.

Gretta Osbourne was seated at the head of the conference table that filled the sitting room of her suite. She was wearing a black, patterned dressing gown. One arm was thrust out before her; on it rested her head. The bun at the back of her head had become undone, and her long gray-blond hair had spilled over the edge of the table.

The eye, which was visible, was open and staring down at the grain of the table as though trying to divine some mystery that was locked in the wood. Near the fingers of her right hand was a large black fountain pen, on the gold nib of which black ink had dried. The note card near it said:

I think it is only appropriate to use this form to say I never knew how much I'd miss Paddy. I feel so guilty that

There was no more.

"See what I told you? You never listen to me," McKeon whispered to O'Shaughnessy. "Guilt rules all. It's the reigning emotion, at least in this country."

With weary eyes McGarr regarded McKeon, who tried to look guiltless.

A reach away from the woman was a champagne glass and a magnum of Veuve Cliquot Ponsardin: both empty. Near the last was a small vial of pills, the label of which was turned toward the corpse and said:

M.J.P. Frost, Chemist
Sneem, Co. Kerry

From: *Dr. Maurice T. Gladden*
For: *Miss G. Osbourne*
Rx: *Phenobarbital to induce sleep:*
100 mg. Max. dose 3 tablets.
DO NOT USE IN COMBINATION WITH ALCOHOL

"Tech Squad," said McGarr, and McKeon immediately left.
"And the door." Bresnahan stepped to the open door, in which bankers, who had been passing in the hall, now stood. She asked them to
move on.

McGarr raised himself up and looked around at the rest of the
room, which, with copy and fax machines, a computer terminal, and
three rows of filing cabinets, looked more like a tastefully decorated
office than a hotel suite. On a sideboard sat a notebook, a kind of
diary, that was written in longhand.

McGarr glanced at the note card and then walked over to the
diary: same ink, same hand, it appeared, though an expert opinion
would be required.

Ward appeared by his side bearing a tray with three cups that
contained a small amount of coffee and a rather large splash of malt
whiskey. McGarr poured McKeon's measure into his own cup and
handed the third to O'Shaughnessy, who drank his off quickly and
replaced the cup on the tray.

McGarr turned to Ward. "Rut'ie told me you were on your way
to Frost's suite with that cart last night."

Ward, giving his back to the crowd at the door, then told McGarr
what he had seen and heard: Frost in his skivvies waving a champagne
bottle; Osbourne saying that she had changed her mind and no longer
wished to sell *her* shares to the Japanese; Sonnie delivering an un-
opened refill.

Later, when Ward arrived with the food, Osbourne was sitting on
a couch, a full champagne glass on the table beside her. Frost was still
nearly naked and very drunk. "He gave me a tanner and the advice to
go into business for myself, which was 'the only way.' " Ward meant
he was given a ten-pound note. "I had the feeling there was somebody
else there, maybe in the bedroom. But the place was a mess from
Frost's afternoon party," and perhaps it was only his imagination after
what he had witnessed Frost engaged in earlier in the day.

McGarr glanced down at the bottle, then advanced on the small
portable bar that had been pushed against a wall. No champagne there,
and none of the glasses looked to have been used. More to the point,

there were no champagne glasses, which suggested that Osbourne had taken the glass on the table from Frost's room.

And the magnum as well, which was fifty ounces. With an alcohol percentage of—11 percent, that made 5.5 ounces. Not a whole lot, even if she had drunk it all, which was unlikely. But combined with the phenobarbital? Again, he would have to wait for a professional opinion.

One thing was certain. She had arrived at the room well enough to have thrown the dead bolt and perhaps written the beginning of the message on the note card in front of her. McGarr moved to the windows in the sitting room and then those in the bedroom and toilet—all locked from the inside. The bed had been unslept in, the costume that she had been wearing on the day before had been left out on a clothes horse for the morning maid to take to the laundry.

When McGarr returned to the sitting room, he found Frost standing by the table, looking down at Gretta Osbourne's corpse. He was dressed all in black, and the skin of his long, handsome face was both flaccid and flushed. When his eyes rose to McGarr, they were netted with broken capillaries from his celebrations of the day and the night before. Clearly he was in pain; there was no faking the tremor in his right cheek. McGarr handed him his coffee cup, which he had not touched.

Frost looked down into the dark fluid, raised it to his nose, then smiled. "You're a right man, McGarr." He sipped, then drank. Straightening up, he tilted his head from side to side in a practiced manner, as though assaying the limber of his neck or easing the passage of the alcohol into his system. He then looked back down on the woman who had been his colleague, and lover, McGarr supposed.

He cleared his throat and squared his shoulders before saying, "Gretta was one of those persons who kept everything inside. She was sensitive, but she made a point of never showing her emotions. You know, so as not to be branded a *typical* woman."

He finished the coffee, then placed the cup on the tray that Ward was still holding. He touched a hand to his chest and waited until he could speak again. His bruised eyeballs were at once glassy, opaque, and swollen.

"I'd no idea Paddy's death had affected her so. She'd had counseling, you know."

McGarr waited, regarding him.

Out in the hall Bresnahan said, "Move on now. This is none of your concern."

"For depressions. Years of it, after the fire." He pointed to the scars on her face, which seemed more conspicuous now in death. "I can dig up her psychiatrists' names, if you like. Perhaps they can explain . . . why, when she had so much to live for."

Like 216 million pounds. McGarr stepped to the bar where he had seen a bottle of malt. Back in front of Ward and the tray, he poured two large dollops of malt into the coffee cups and reached one toward Frost, who looked down at it with fear and longing.

"Ah, no, Superintendent—I couldn't. The first bit was enough. I've got Paddy's funeral—"

Couldn't miss that, McGarr thought. Sean Dermot O'Duffy and his entourage of movers and shakers would be there, and Frost—certainly a celebrity after the sale of Eire Bank that would also have enriched the "government insiders," Gretta Osbourne had called them, who owned 10 percent of the shares. McGarr made mental note to obtain the list of Eire Bank stockholders, by court order if necessary.

"Well—one more can't hurt." With both hands Frost reached for the cup. "Set me up, don't you know."

McGarr was hoping. "Been celebrating?"

"A bit."

McGarr waited, but Frost said no more. Again he had turned toward the figure at the table.

"Did you see her last night?"

Frost's eyes shied to Ward, before he nodded.

"Where?"

"My room. It's where she got the champagne."

"For your celebration," McGarr probed.

Frost only nodded. "I'd had a bit of a lead on her. She said she'd do me a favor and take the bottle with her."

"What time was that?"

Frost's eyes floated up into his skull. He shook his head to say he could not remember.

"What sort of automobile did Ms. Osbourne drive?"

Frost had to think. "It's a red Audi, I believe. New. I don't think it has a thousand miles on it. She hated to drive and only brought it out with her this time because connections between here and Dublin are otherwise dreadful."

"What would she have been doing on the Waterville Road on Sunday morning?"

"But she wasn't. Sunday morning we went sailing bright and early. It was a glorious day, and, as perhaps you know, I have a house here in Sneem on the harbor. Sailing was one of the few ways Gretta could relax.'' His eyes turned to the woman again. ''You know, no phone, no computer, only the elements and the boat to contend with. She really worked too hard.''

''But she and her car were seen at the Rathfield ruin.''

Frost cocked his head. ''The car, perhaps. But not Gretta.''

''Go on,'' McGarr had to prompt.

''I don't know what you're getting at here, but Gretta had asked Mossie Gladden to stop by on Friday and take a look at Paddy when he arrived. She was worried about him, she said, his having seemed so peaked when she had last seen him in London. Gretta was the advance person—you know, to make sure everything was ready for the conference.'' Frost flicked a wrist at the machines in the room.

''Anyhow, after examining Paddy, Mossie gave him a sedative and then prescribed an antibiotic that he said was only available in Kenmare. Nevertheless, I rang up my father, but sure enough, he didn't have it. The old fella's getting on now, and he doesn't fancy splashing out for every new drug that comes on the market.

''By then it was midafternoon, but Mossie said he could get the stuff, could he get there in time. Problem was, he didn't trust that old banger of his to transport them there and back. Gretta said, 'Take my car. I won't be needing it for the rest of the week.' I don't know when Mossie got back. I had other affairs to attend.''

All 423 million of them, McGarr thought. He also remembered that Kenmare and Waterville, while in different directions, were just about equidistant from Parknasilla. ''Did he return with the antibiotic?''

Frost shook his head. ''I don't know, but I didn't see any such thing in Paddy's medicine cabinet when we—'' When he and McGarr looked after Power's death, he meant.

But Gladden had *not* been the country gorsoon who had dropped off the photocopies of the notecards at the Waterville Lake Hotel; the desk clerk knew Gladden and would have recognized him, had it been he. Could she have been lying? McGarr didn't think so.

As though a sudden thought struck him, Frost's head went back. ''Why all the questions?''

McGarr hunched his shoulders. ''Here we have a bottle of champagne, here a vial that says it contained phenobarbital, and here a dead woman. At the very least an autopsy is required.''

Whether from genuine grief or merely alcohol, Frost's eyes suddenly filled with tears; one splatted on the surface of the table. Frost stepped back, reached inside his black topcoat, and removed a handker-chief. "I'd just come down to pick her up, and—"

They waited while Frost blew his nose. "Look—I'll be right back to handle whatever has to be done. Gretta had no family that I know of, and I was both her friend and solicitor. I'll see to the . . . arrangements. But right now I've got Paddy's funeral." He glanced at his watch then made for the door.

"Who inherits her fifty-one percent of Eire Bank that with power of attorney you'll now sell to the Japanese?"

Frost neither turned nor stopped. "That, I'm afraid, is privileged information. Or are you claiming this is murder too?" He pushed past Bresnahan, saying, "What—not going to Paddy's funeral?"

"See you there, Mr. Frost."

"Shane. I told you yesterday, it's Shane."

"The day before, I believe it was."

"That's right. How could I have forgotten?"

The funeral. It gave McGarr an idea. Gladden would not miss the opportunity for a confrontation with Sean Dermot O'Duffy, given all the media that would be present. Somehow McGarr was missing something, and he didn't think he'd find it here in spite of the several anomalies that he could see before him.

If Gretta Osbourne had collapsed while writing the note card, why was the pen not still in her hand? Instead it was placed neatly, nearly lined up in the same plane as the note card. At the very least McGarr would have expected a scrawl or line or ink mark on the note card or the table. Or some ink on her right hand, which lay limp near the pen. There was none.

The bun at the back of her head. How had it become undone? Besides the pen, it was the only detail in the entire room that was out of place. McGarr moved toward the chair, over which he had placed the greatcoat that looked like Gladden's. He removed the blond wig that Noreen had also purchased. Back at the table he compared it to the strands of Gretta Osbourne's hair that were hanging over the edge. It was not a perfect match, but close enough, especially if the plan had been for it to be seen at a distance late in the afternoon.

Plan. Surely something like that was at work here, right from the careful execution of Power to what now amounted to the felicitous removal of the one other person apart from Paddy Power who had been standing in the way of a windfall for Frost, Nell Power, and a handful of other government insiders and cronies.

McGarr felt somebody beside him, and looked up to find Bresnahan, who was also garbed in something black but tight and eye-catching. She was wearing a small pillbox hat and a face net. "I'm off now." Her eyes flashed at the door in which stood the same young man McGarr had seen her with at the bridge in Sneem yesterday.

Ward forced his eyes down onto the tray in his hands.

O'Suilleabhain glanced around the room with interest, until he saw the corpse sprawled on the table.

Said Bresnahan, "When I interviewed Ms. Osbourne, she wrote in this diary." A spiral wrap of something like crushed silk, the dress was tight and made the sway of her shoulders yet more apparent as she moved toward the sideboard, where sat the notebook that McGarr had used to compare Osbourne's handwriting with the note card on the table. Taller than McGarr, her gray eyes flickered down on him.

"She wrote this with her left hand." She pointed to the entry that bore her own name. "When she drank from a glass, she used her left hand. The phone—when she reached for that, it was with her left hand." Bresnahan turned her head to the table where the fountain pen rested by Osbourne's right hand.

"Hughie?" McGarr said, and Ward joined them at the sideboard. "Get right on Frost. Indentify yourself, then ask him to empty the contents of his pockets."

Ward smiled; there went his cover, right out the window. And his bar job. Sonnie be praised!

"Any keys, bring him and them back here, then go to his room. Check to see if the baby monitor is still there and functioning." He had kept a tape recorder on all night. It was voice-activated and might have picked something up, if Frost hadn't pulled the plug. "The dining cart you delivered last night? Stay with it until the Tech Squad can get here.

"Meanwhile, toss the room. Again you're looking for keys that fit this lock and the lock of Power's room. You're also looking for phenobarbital in pill, tablet, or liquid form, and digitoxin or digitalis. Set aside any unmarked substance, and don't spare anything—the linings of his cases, clothes"—he swung his hand at the machines—"cabinets.

"Then you're to get yourself out of that monkey suit. Knowing the hotel as you now must, find out if Gladden or Nell Power were on the premises last night."

Ward's eyes slid off Bresnahan's as he turned toward the door. There, he held out his hand. "You're—?"

"Rory O'Suilleabhain." O'Suilleabhain looked down at Ward's hand, as though trying to decide if he should shake hands with a waiter.

"And how are all the little O'Suilleabhains?"

O'Suilleabhain's smiled crumpled. "I don't understand."

"Just as I thought. Good for you. Stick to your gun, and don't let any little gurrier tell you otherwise."

Ward left O'Suilleabhain with his hand in the air.

Bresnahan tried not to smile, but McGarr had not seemed to have heard the exchange and was still staring at the woman at the table. Power had written:

Like some fat, bald Theseus I have been sitting in the sun of this foreign isle, searching blindly for an Ariadne thread to lead me out of the dark labyrinth. . . .

Which, but for the setting, was McGarr's position exactly. He was missing the thread that would bind together the tangled pieces of the investigation and lead him from the maze of the murderer's plot. If Gretta Osbourne had been sailing with Frost, she could not have been the person who had delivered the photocopies of the note cards to Nell Power. With the tip of his own pen, McGarr turned the pages of Osbourne's diary back to Sunday, and there it was. *"Sailing with Shane"* occupied all of the Sunday morning entries.

Again he examined the acrylic strands of the blond wig. If Frost could be believed, a wig such as that had been used along with the red Audi to cast suspicion on Gretta Osbourne by whoever had delivered the photocopies to the Waterville Lake Hotel. But why dress up like Gladden unless to cast suspicion on him?

It had not been Gladden, however; that much was already established. And Frost had as much as eliminated Osbourne and himself, again if he could be believed. Why would he lie? It could easily be checked; somebody was certain to have seen them sailing.

Who else was tall—"A rough-looking fellow with hardly a word on him," the desk clerk had said. He had handed her a note asking her to deliver the sack to Nell Power. Why a note? Afraid to speak because of some accent?

Who else would have had access to both Osbourne's Audi, which Gladden had borrowed, and Gladden's greatcoat with a wig inside the pocket?

McGarr turned to Bresnahan. "If you see Noreen in Sneem, ask

her to return here and transcribe the tape on the recorder she placed by
the baby monitor.

"And save a place for me."

"In the church?"

McGarr nodded; maybe if he saw everybody together . . .

On the way to his room he was handed a note by a uniformed
Guard. It was from Superintendent Butler of the Kenmare Barracks,
saying that he had sent a squad to search Mossie Gladden's mountain
farm for the high-powered rifle that McGarr had seen on Tuesday, but
they could not find it.

CHAPTER 21

On Bridges, Rivers, and No Turning Back

WITH AN OVERWHELMING sense of *déjà vu*, Ruth Bresnahan lowered herself into the front passenger seat of her rental Merc and watched Rory O'Suilleabhain close the door. The ease of how they were together and the . . . usualness of being a part of each other's life was so winningly comfortable that it almost felt as if she had never actually been without him.

It was as though—after some dark passage in which, while with the Guards, she had taken the long way round through various cow towns and finally Dublin, she had arrived suddenly back on the main road of her life, crossed a bridge, and there was no turning back. Things were now hurtling forward with all the headlong inevitability of predestination. *This was how it was meant to be*, she kept thinking. Her life.

But for her St. Laurent dress, the car itself, and the weight of the Gluck automatic pistol in her purse, she could have believed it was a decade earlier, and she had never left Sneem and the South Kerry Mountains.

The three parents were sitting in back, and little was said at first, apart from Agnes O'Suilleabhain remarking on how "womanly" Bresnahan looked. "And beautiful," her own mother added, on the principle that you should never allow a prospective buyer to derogate your calf.

"Not like a girl at all."

"Well, she's not one, is she?" Through no fault of her own, her mother meant.

Said O'Suilleabhain himself, "The little fella—he a cop too?"

Which little fella? Counting McKeon, there had been three of them. But she nodded, knowing he meant Ward. They were approaching the outskirts of Sneem, and the mounded sides of the narrow road were lined with parked cars.

"Junior man, I'd say. Looks hardly out of his teens."

Bresnahan did not know why, but it irked her to hear O'Suilleabhain slag Ward so. "Actually, he's not. He's a full rank above me and currently in line for even higher position." She let that sink in. "It's the tux. Short notice. He had to take what they had."

"The smallest size. Something tells me he fancies you." There was a glint of derision in O'Suilleabhain's thin, sidelong smile.

Bresnahan felt her nostrils flare. "Something comical in that?"

"No—nothing. Don't get mad. It's just there's such a difference, you know, between you."

Bresnahan knew well the differences, which, granted, were many, but she wanted O'Suilleabhain to tell her what he thought they were.

"—height and such."

"Do you follow boxing, Rory?"

"You know I do."

Vaguely Bresnahan seemed to remember he did, but the egotism of his assuming that she had treasured the least bit of information about him was galling. "Have you ever heard of 'Whipper' Ward?" which was her pint-sized pugilist's ring moniker, and which she personally thought was ludicrous.

"Of course. He was one of the finest fighters Ireland ever produced."

"*Is*," Bresnahan corrected.

"Up until four, five years ago, I'd say."

"Who?" her father asked from the backseat.

" 'Whipper' Ward, Tom," O'Suilleabhain explained. "D'ye remember him? Cute little dodger from Dublin in the seventy-kilo weight class. A *boxer* in the strict sense. Won the Euro games twice, I believe."

"Three times," Bresnahan corrected, but as she was a woman, her comments on a male subject were not being heard.

Said her father, "That Dutchman, now—remember how Ward came out in the third? He took your man's measure for nearly the entire round. Everybody thought he'd lost it for sure. Then with a flurry at the bell he put the Kraut right through the ropes and out of the ring.''

O'Suilleabhain smiled and shook his head. "He was a great one, all right.''

Is. *Is,* Bresnahan thought without wasting her breath.

"So?'' O'Suilleabhain finally demanded. His mouth then dropped open. "You don't mean to say *that* was 'Whipper' Ward?''

Bresnahan had not meant to say anything whatsoever about 'Whipper' Ward, and she pointed toward the windscreen of the car. Standing in the middle of the road was a tall Guard in dark blue overcoat, marked out by a white garrison belt. He had raised one white glove, and O'Suilleabhain slowed, approaching him. "You're not kidding, are you?''

Bresnahan's smile was brittle, as she opened her purse and extracted her photo I.D.

"Hear that, Tom? 'Whipper' Ward is back at Parknasilla.'' And to Bresnahan: "I wish you'd told me. I'd've gotten his autograph.''

Maybe tattooed across your nose, she thought.

"He in training?''

Something like that, but not for a fight.

The car pulled up beside the Guard, who said, "Sorry, folks. I'm afraid the village has as many cars as it can hold today. There's a funeral in progress with dignitaries and all. If you're here for it yourselves, you'll have to park—''

He handed Bresnahan's I.D. to the Guard, who studied it, said, "Changed your hair, I see,'' to O'Suilleabhain, and waved them through.

"Marvelous what a little pull will do,'' her mother said proudly.

"Sure—Rory only had to tell him who he was, and we would have sailed through fine,'' his mother countered lamely.

Ah, shit, Bresnahan thought, imagine two years of that, or ten, or twenty?

O'Suilleabhain handed the I.D. back, but Bresnahan did not put it away. In front of them were more blue uniforms than Sneem had seen in a decade.

Already several uniforms had broken from the blue line; one raised a hand. Other Guards were carefully checking the cars that were parked along the square. Out of the corner of her eye Bresnahan saw a silhouette blocked out against the winter sun on the other side of the square. It was a soldier—obviously part of the taosieach's security force—actually walking the peaks of the buildings on the other side of the square, checking rooftop coverts and aeries.

"Park there." She pointed to an empty slot in front of M.J.P. Frost's chemist shop.

Even before O'Suilleabhain turned in, one of the Guards began shaking a hand at them.

"You can get out, people. I speak their language."

"Apache?"

"No—it's a tongue that originates in Phoenix Park," which was headquarters of the Garda Siochana. "Pol-eash. The words are weighted by chain of command." It was a Murder Squad in-joke that Bresnahan had not entirely appreciated until that moment. One thing she could never deny, no matter what else might happen in her life, was the fact that she had matured and become very much a confident, competent woman in "the Guards."

"So—it's you."

Bresnahan glanced up at the sergeant who was studying her I.D. Did she know him? Scrupulously shaven, pink flesh lobbed over his black chin strap. Four other pair of judgmental eyes devolved on the line of her body.

"The Ban Gharda who put the questions to Mossie Gladden," he explained. "Haven't you seen the papers this morning? He's demanding you be fired, along with your chief there. McGarr. Some say he's muffed this one."

Gladden or McGarr? Bresnahan wondered until another of the Guards began sniggering.

He returned the square of laminated plastic to Bresnahan, who slipped it in her purse. "Nice duty, the Murder Squad."

"Umh-uh-uh," said another, watching her walk toward *the parents*, Rory O'Suilleabhain, and Noreen McGarr, who was holding Madeleine by the hand.

By the time McGarr arrived a half hour later, Sneem looked as though it had been invaded by two rival armies—one blue, the other olive drab—who were preparing to contest the green. In Ireland terrorists were always a threat, and the security force, which accompanied the taoiseach, had evidently completed their sweep of the village and were awaiting the end of the funeral mass to resume their places.

A third group of journalists and media personnel with their large, lumbering, and brightly painted remote vans had gathered in the laneway that led to the church.

McGarr had read that O'Duffy would eulogize Paddy Power not from the pulpit of the church but rather from the arch of the narrow bridge over the Sneem River from which Mossie Gladden had launched his accusations of the day before. He had promised he would answer Gladden and "all other questions relating to Paddy Power's sudden, tragic death" at that time. McGarr wondered how, since nobody had consulted with him apart from Commissioner Farrell, who had only voiced his displeasure with McGarr's conduct of the investigation and demanded he turn over "all evidence gathered in the case so far," by which he meant the note cards. Before ringing off that morning.

McGarr lowered the visor with the chief superintendent's shield on the back and slowly eased his Cooper through the respective authorities, who waved him on. The press was an agency that respected no authority, however; they surrounded the Cooper, and McGarr had to throw his weight against the door to climb out. There, questions were barked at him, flashguns popped, and microphones were shoved in his face.

Swirling his shoulders to clear a space in front of him, he sent one microphone sailing off into the crowd. He then snapped his head in the direction of the uniformed Guards, who were watching what amounted to his being mugged by the Fourth Estate. "You!" he shouted, pointing at the Guard with the bright sergeant's chevrons on his arm. He then pointed to the press, jerked a thumb over his shoulder, and waited while the gaggle of Guards broke toward them, voices raised.

"Get out now! Get out! The chief is on official business."

"Go to many state-sanctioned funerals, Chief?" one journalist asked.

"Sure he does. Great place for a cover-up. Appearance and reality are one."

"Mossie Gladden says you stole the libretto for this opera, but Phoenix Park claims they know of no such evidence. Any chance of *our* getting a copy?"

"You'll need friends. We could make it worth your while."

McGarr tried to put a face with that voice, but he kept moving, now that he could, toward the church of gray stone that looked like a part of the crag on which it had been built.

So—Phoenix Park had begun to comment on the case, again without consulting him. It was a public warning from Farrell and O'Duffy that they would announce their own findings with or without him. Unless, of course, McGarr could come up with a murderer. And, more, *proof* of a murderer.

The people who had gathered in front of the open door of the church now turned to him; worse, they stepped back to let him pass, which was extraordinary for an Irish crowd. Feeling like a man condemned, he moved through the vestibule and down the aisle, picking up speed when he noticed a priest moving toward the pulpit. The sermon in eulogy was about to begin, and nowhere could he see the bright patch of Bresnahan's orange hair until he had nearly reached the chancel rail.

By then, every eye was on him, including those of the priest on the pulpit. Even O'Duffy, Minister for Justice Harney, and Commissioner Farrell turned, regarding him without expression. But there was Bresnahan with her hand raised to signal him. McGarr entered the pew.

"All here but Gladden," Bresnahan whispered, as the priest in the pulpit gathered himself and adjusted the microphone.

A line appeared in McGarr's brow. Why? Gladden was missing the opportunity of a lifetime. Or had he allowed the presence of Sean Dermot O'Duffy to keep him from the funeral of his self-described best friend? No, McGarr decided—Gladden would make his appearance later, with the press in attendance, outside the church or at the bridge.

"Frost and Nell Power." Bresnahan inclined her head to one side where in the first pew they sat together. "With Power's children." She meant the five younger people beside the woman. "Even Gladden's solicitor, Kieran Coyne." Bresnahan's head moved in the other direction and turned her body to look behind her. "The tall fella with the rough-looking face."

McGarr searched through the church of faces until he found the gaunt face, hollow cheeks, but bright red complexion of the man he had seen with Gladden yesterday. One of Coyne's eyes was blackened and that cheekbone swollen. And McGarr had seen the look on Coyne's face more than a few times before; without a doubt it was guilt, which made McGarr curious. Turning back to Bresnahan, he said, "I heard yesterday he was a blow-in from Dublin."

"In the name of the Father, the Son, and the Holy Spirit," the priest said into a microphone.

"His new wife is from Sneem, Rory tells me." She leaned her head toward O'Suilleabhain, who was sitting on the other side of her. "He's trying to make a go of a law practice down here for her sake."

"We are gathered here today to mourn the passing of one of Sneem's most illustrious sons and to celebrate his passage to a higher plane, which is his—and will be our own—ultimate reward."

McGarr thought of how, three days earlier when Frost had confronted Gladden, Gladden had threatened to put him on the flat of his back. "I wonder how he got the shiner?" When McGarr turned to look back again, Coyne was gone.

McGarr spun out of the pew and was down the aisle at a jog in time to see the vent of Coyne's overcoat disappearing into the crowd at the back of the church. McGarr raced forward, wanting to stop the man in the vestibule, before he could get outside among the press. But the crowd, having turned to Coyne, had closed, and McGarr had to shove people out of his way. "Police. Police business!" he shouted. "Make way!"

McGarr grabbed the collar of Coyne's overcoat, just as he reached the periphery of the assembled reporters. He spun the tall, lank man around and threw him toward the church. With a sickening, hollow sound Coyne's head struck the gray stone gable of the church, which was brightened by the flash of cameras; Coyne's soft hat fell off and was carried away by the breeze.

"See this?" From the pocket of his mac, McGarr pulled the blond acrylic wig and held it in front of Coyne's face. "I want you to tell me about this. I have witnesses that place you with a photocopy of Paddy Power's note cards, in Gretta Osbourne's red Audi, at the Waterville Lake Hotel, and later at the Rathfield ruin. She's dead, and at the very least there's the charge of complicity in a double murder."

Coyne's bony hand had wrapped his forehead. The blackened eye had opened and was staring down into the blond wig, which a further burst of electronic light blanched. "Can't we—"

"No!" McGarr had been filmed collaring the man; now he would let the press witness why. "This is your only chance to tell me the truth. Otherwise it's a charge and Dublin. Think of your law practice. And your family." He waited until Coyne blinked before releasing his hold on the overcoat. He stepped back.

Coyne straightened up and turned around to face McGarr and, over McGarr's shoulder, several score of the country's press. In the doorway others had turned their attention from the funeral to him. From the church McGarr could hear the voice of the priest on the pulpit asking if the vestibule doors could be closed.

Said Coyne, "I didn't think much of it at the time. Mossie said it was a kind of joke, and he'd pay me for my time and all." Coyne's eyes rose to McGarr, pleading for him to understand. "It was only later that I realized it might be connected to—"

"Paddy Power's murder," McGarr prompted.

Coyne nodded.

"Why didn't you come forward?"

On his scrawny neck Coyne's head swirled. "It wasn't like Mossie or I were part of the murder itself. It was just . . . an opportunity. For Mossie."

McGarr waited.

"Look—it was early Saturday evening. I was in my office." His eyes flickered down into the laneway to the building on the corner. "I was about to go home to my dinner when Mossie knocked. He wanted to use my copy machine, which he sometimes did. When I first settled here in Sneem, Mossie got me clients, he provided my family free medical attention, he helped us out every way he could. Without him I would have gone under." And might still, the expression on Coyne's haggard face said. "Anyway, I let him in, switched on the machine, and we waited, talking, while the thing warmed up.

"Maybe a minute later, we heard a knock on the door—just one, like a thump—and when I opened it, there the cards were in a plastic sack from the chemist across the street."

"Go on." McGarr said.

"But there was nobody in the hall. I thought it strange and had no idea what the sack contained, but Mossie took one look and knew from the handwriting what they were. He went right to my desk and began spreading them out. The phone rang, and it was my wife, telling . . . *asking* me to come home to my supper. Mossie wondered if he could stay in the office, and would I mind if he used the copy machine. I filled it with paper, set the counter, and left. Much later—nine, say—I went out for a pint, and when I drove by, I saw the light still on in the office and Mossie's old Land Rover parked out front.

"Next day, Sunday, I got down here to the office early so I could do some work before Mass. I saw that Mossie had used all of the paper in the copy machine and half of the box that remained. He'd left some money—a hundred pounds—which was needed, let me tell you." Coyne's eyes glanced off McGarr's and swept the journalists; he sighed. "And since I can't afford any office help, I launched into my paper work for the week—the typing and filing.

"Maybe around nine, Mossie arrived. He said he had something 'unusual but harmless' to ask of me. He put two hundred-pound notes on my desk and told me what he wanted. 'A kind of joke,' he called it. He said I was to put on his greatcoat and hat and deliver the sack of note cards to the Waterville Lake Hotel, using the car he had outside. He laid the keys on the desk, and I could see they weren't for his old Land Rover that I'd used a couple of times to haul feed.

"When I got to the hotel, I was to say as little as possible. He even provided me with a printed note. 'Just hand the note to the desk clerk and leave.' He showed me that too. It said the sack was to be delivered to Nell Power, which seemed aboveboard and easy enough. The tricky part, though, was in coming back."

Coyne shook his head. "I don't know why I agreed to it. At that point, you know, Paddy Power was still alive. It wasn't until a day later that he was discovered. And—" Coyne passed a hand across his upper lip, which was sweating. "Mossie wanted me to keep an eye out for some locals, who were either out working in their fields or traveling along the road on a bicycle or cart. At that point I was to put on that thing." Coyne pointed to the wig. "You know, up under the hat. I was to stop the car in plain view, get out, and change out of the coat and hat. Then, without taking the wig off, he wanted me to get back in and drive away, making sure they got a good look at the car.

"I thought that would be the hard part, but, it being Saturday and people on the road—" He shook his head. "I had the choice of dozens. I chose two men I'd never seen before."

"Didn't you ask Gladden why?"

Coyne nodded. "He said he didn't know who had dropped the sack off at my office, but he knew it had been intended for him and why. It was political dynamite and implicated O'Duffy in a whole bunch of matters that had never before surfaced. He was going to make the most of it, and what I would be doing for him was both insurance and would 'promote controversy,' was what he said."

"Insurance?"

"That what was contained in the note cards would see the light of day. At one time, it seems, Power had been kind of a rake, and the wife hated him 'for all the best reasons,' Mossie said. Were Power to deny that Mossie's copy of the cards was his, she would be certain to come forward. 'She's a woman of passion who has been scorned,' he said. 'All the more so when she gets a look at these cards.' "

"But why set Gretta Osbourne up?"

"The Audi and the disguise were the only way we could think of getting Nell the copy quickly without incriminating ourselves in the theft. The gorsoon outfit was Mossie's idea. He said, if Power reported the cards stolen and the police were called in, they'd discover that a country man in a costume like his own had dropped them off. Without a doubt they'd drag him in for an identification, but the desk clerk, who knew him, would swear he wasn't the one. 'But we'll get the headline,' said Mossie, 'and that's all I'll need. One session with the note cards and the Dublin press.' ''

With proof of his allegations, McGarr thought. "But why did Gladden have such a sketchy knowledge of what the cards contained?"

"I don't think he ever had time to read them. He spent most of Saturday night copying them. Then on Sunday he had Paddy Power drop in on him up in his mountain farm, and later he attended Power's reception at Parknasilla. As I understand from local gossip, he was then called away on a medical emergency."

"Of what sort?"

Coyne's eyes shied. "He didn't tell me exactly, but I don't think he got to sleep on Sunday night either. Even though he still looks strong, he's a man of certain age. He probably never had time to go through them thoroughly."

McGarr thought of how glassy Gladden's eyes had looked on Tuesday morning. "Did he tell you why he decided to turn against Paddy Power?" His lifelong friend.

"I think it had to do with two things. I was still in the office when Mossie came upon the section of the cards that dealt with himself. 'No,' he kept complaining. 'That's not me at all.' And, 'You have me on the wrong foot altogether, Paddy.' He was like a man in a rage. He was getting up every few minutes and marching from one room to the other. Finally he just picked that stack up and chucked them in the fire.

"The second thing came just as I was going out the door. 'Jesus—' '' Coyne glanced up at the church and did not repeat the rest of the imprecation, '' 'Power's worse than O'Duffy and his tribe. D'ye know what he wants to do with the debt? Give the country away for it, and that bastard O'Duffy will reject every word of his proposal and then quietly do just that. It's perfect for him and his crowd. They hold as much debt—more,' he shouted, 'than the foreigners. They're the worst kind of people to have in a society. Jackals. They'll eat as much as their bellies can hold, then spit up and take another meal.'

"Did you see how he was on the bridge yesterday when the proposal was mentioned? He was so . . . livid he could no longer speak. He's like a man possessed, and I have no idea what you can expect from him next.''

"Is that how you got the eye?"

Coyne nodded. "Yesterday, after the bridge. I drove around, trying to find him. When I didn't, I went all the way up to his farm. I wanted to tell him that I'd had enough of the ruse and was going to look you up—" Coyne's eyes scanned McGarr's impassive face. "Honestly, it's what I said. What I intended. But I no sooner got it out of my mouth, when I found myself on my back with the cross hairs of his target rifle right here." Coyne pointed to bridge of his nose between his eyes. "He said he'd shoot me and everybody in my family, were I to divulge a word. And look at me" When McGarr, who was now lost in his own thoughts did not, Coyne shook his sleeve. "I believe him."

McGarr thought for a moment. Jackals. Where had he seen or heard that word in the recent past? He looked away, down into the square where the blue and olive-drab security forces had gathered.

"Where is he now?"

Coyne shook his head. "I have no idea. I thought for sure he'd be here today." He too now looked into the square.

McGarr nodded. From the church behind them he was hearing an organ playing the *Missa Solemnis*, which, he assumed, announced the end of the funeral mass. Still, none of the crowd immediately in back of him had moved. The last thing he needed was to create another scene, especially with the personages in attendance. Taking Coyne's arm, he led him out through the journalists, a few of whom were torn between whom to follow. Questions were shouted, which McGarr ignored.

"Am I under arrest?" Coyne asked. "Because, if I'm not, I'd like to get home and—"

"Quiet," McGarr said. He was trying to think where he had come upon the word "jackals." While arguing with Frost over Power's corpse on Monday, Gladden had said, "You and your bloated sow of an Eire Bank. You and O'Duffy and your pack of slavish jackals are thieves, every last one of you. You stole the wealth of this country and its future right out from under the nose of the poor, hardworking common man, and you'll do anything, even commit murder, to keep it in your grip."

But somebody else had also mentioned the word. *Jackals.* McGarr looked back and saw Nell Power, Shane Frost, and Power's children in the doorway with Sean Dermot O'Duffy, Harney, Quinn, and Farrell immediately behind them.

"I mean, if he's seen us together—"

The note cards. Paddy Power had written:

> *Target practice, he's told me, for the dogs that summer people leave when returning to the city. Jackals, he calls them. The wily and strong have survived to reproduce, preying on Mossie's sheep.*

McGarr then thought of the targets he had discovered with the target rifle inside the back door of Gladden's mountain retreat. Below the picture of the first, which pictured a sheep, somebody—evidently Gladden himself—had written "Sean" in ornate Gaelic script. McGarr now wondered if the other targets were titled "Dermot" and "O'Duffy."

McGarr turned to Coyne. "You know Gladden. Do you think he killed Power?"

Coyne was now plainly distressed and wanted to get away from McGarr. "You don't know how many times I've asked myself that. You know, has Mossie involved me in murder? But"—he looked away, wildly now, his eyes scanning the small section of green that they now could see—"I don't think so. Mossie is a moody man, and you can tell from his moods what he's about. On Sunday when he put the proposition to me about the note cards and car and so forth, he was upbeat. It was an opportunity, is all, I think. Like I said. For him to make political hay of the thing.

"But his frame of mind crumbled entirely when you discovered his photocopies of the note cards and then rounded up the originals. And finally there was his debacle on the bridge, which I advised him against wholeheartedly. I pleaded, I *begged*, him not to stand up in public with no proof, which was just what he had done a few years back with results so disastrous that he was still under a cloud.

"But, like I said, he was possessed by Power's 'murder,' he kept calling it, and his having lost the note cards. And you—Jesus—he *did* say he'd murder you himself."

"But was that rhetoric or do you think he *could* kill? Wantonly."

Now funeral-goers were streaming passed them toward the bridge where O'Duffy would speak.

"In the two years I've known him, I've seen him decline so much that I'm really not sure. First he quit his seat, then gave up his medical office, and finally moved out of town to that jakes of a place in the mountains. And the way he goes round. Him a medical man.'' Again he shook his head.

"What about him and the IRA?"

"I know nothing about that," Coyne said, too fast.

"How long has he been taking care of their wounded? Is that what he was doing Sunday night?"

Coyne nodded. "I don't know exactly. Years, I'd say. Two. Three."

If the faction Gladden was aiding had been involved in the recent spate of terrorism in the North, then certainly Gladden—the medical man who had taken an oath to further human life—had to know he was serving death as well.

"Can I go home now?"

McGarr scanned the crowd and picked out Shane Frost standing with Nell Power and her family. Also standing by the bridge were Bresnahan, Rory O'Suilleabhain, and some older people who could only be their parents.

McGarr scanned the church, the village green, the security forces, the narrow bridge where O'Duffy, Harney, and Quinn could now be seen. There microphones on stanchions bristled like a patch of metallic cattails framed by the black boxes of public-address speakers. The sky beyond was leaden, and a cold wind had sprung up. It would rain soon or snow.

But no Gladden that McGarr could see from where they were standing.

The security forces would have swept the village, looking for arms and snipers, people who should not be there. But, what about somebody who, say, had surfaced after their sweep and while everybody else had been in church? He would have been stopped and his identification checked. But a doctor and former T.D., who was known to hail from Sneem and was sure to put up a bit of a stink were he to be kept from the proceeding, would be let through. He might be followed and watched, but he would be allowed to pass.

Also O'Duffy, who was most certainly a master of debate, might have instructed them not to hinder Gladden in any way. A final, terminal squelch would put Gladden out of the political picture for keeps.

"Does Gladden still have a house here in the village?"

Coyne shook his head.

"What about your office? He have a key?"

Again a head shake. "But he knows where the key is."

"Yesterday—was he there?"

"Last night. He rang me up to ask if he could use the typewriter and phone. He said he had something important to write, several people to call."

"Always leaving a bit of money," McGarr prompted.

"It pays the rent, most months."

"Come on." McGarr pointed to the building on the corner where Coyne had said his office was.

"But I can't. I really must get home."

"What about the matter of theft?"

"I didn't steal anything."

"You just admitted to me that Gladden recognized the note cards as Power's. Instead of returning them, you knowingly delivered copies of them to somebody else. Certainly, Counselor, you must have known *that* was wrong."

As they reached the top of the stairs leading to Coyne's office, McGarr heard O'Duffy's amplified voice from the bridge saying, "Paddy was the true architect of the economic renaissance of present-day Ireland, and we can never thank him enough. Other countries, such as Namibia, Honduras, and Portugal, owe him a similar debt of gratitude for the services he rendered them while with various international banks and . . ."

Coals were still glowing in the hearth of Coyne's office, and the room was warm, in spite of the cold wind that was fluttering hems and causing people to turn their shoulders to the blast, when McGarr peered out the windows toward the bridge. There, O'Duffy was positioned before the microphones, his voice—amplified through the speakers—coming to them plainly as McGarr made a quick survey of the room. Wide flakes of swirling snow shot by the glass.

"Did you start a fire this morning?"

Coyne shook his head, his eyes surveying the room warily.

Which meant Gladden had spent the night there.

O'Duffy was saying, ". . . and so that Paddy Power's death from whatever cause, which, I trust, will soon be determined, will not have been in vain, we in government have decided to explore the possibility of implementing at least part of the proposal that Paddy put forward at the conference of bankers held here in Parknasilla this week. Internationalizing unproductive Irish assets while retiring Irish debt is an idea that only somebody with the genius of Paddy Power could have created, and an idea whose time has come. Maintaining Irish control, of course.''

It was Frost's prediction right down to the way it was being offered to the Irish people—as Power's idea but changed even to its wording.

O'Duffy went on, ''Along the line of Ireland becoming more international in outlook and trade, I'd also like to announce that Mr. Shane Frost, chairman of Eire Bank, has applied for and been granted permission to sell that concern, which is privately held, to the Nomura Bank of Kyoto, Japan, for an unspecified sum.''

That was fast. *When* exactly had Frost applied to the government? Yesterday by phone?

''Eire Bank, as you know, was founded by Paddy Power, and his family and heirs have agreed to accept the Nomura offer for the assets that they hold in the bank.

''I would like to close my remarks by stating that, in spite of what you may have read or heard regarding the manner of Paddy's death, there still has been no determination in that regard. As far as we know to date, Paddy died of the natural cause of heart failure perhaps brought on by his having mistaken the medicines he was taking. Paddy had a long history of heart trouble. The investigation is continuing under the direction of Chief Superintendent McGarr, one of our senior-most police officials, who enjoys the complete confidence of both the Garda Siochana and this government. His final report will be made public in its entirety.''

McGarr would try to hold O'Duffy to that.

''Now I will attempt to answer any questions.''

On the desk was a single typewritten sheet of paper, signed by Gladden.

What I do, I do out of love for my country and for the good of all Irish people who wish to keep Ireland in Irish hands. And so that generations from now there will still be an Irish people, proud in their culture, traditions, and patrimony, who will be free to determine their own destiny.

What's needed is a government run by persons who are patriots first, last, and always, and not merely capitalists interested only in enriching themselves and their friends no matter the cost to the country.

The evidence that I needed to prove that Paddy Power was murdered to remove him from the political scene was contained in the notes that he had written for his memoir. They were stolen from me, sequestered, and without a doubt destroyed by Chief Superintendent Peter McGarr of the Garda Siochana, acting upon the direct orders of Taosieach Sean Dermot O'Duffy.

It was signed by Gladden.

"Have you seen this? Have you read it?" McGarr asked Coyne, who was standing on the other side of the desk.

Coyne blinked, which meant he had, but said, "I need glasses for reading, more so upside down."

"Good man." McGarr buried the sheet in the pocket of his mac.

Out on the bridge O'Duffy was answering a question. "As I stated yesterday afternoon and was printed in this morning's newspapers, the government has no knowledge of these note cards that Dr. Gladden alleges were stolen from Paddy Power around the time of his death. Personally I know that Paddy *was* compiling notes to write a memoir, but nothing of the sort has been entered as evidence in the inquiry into his death. Nor lodged with the property division of the Garda Siochana. If Chief Superintendent McGarr has Paddy's notes, he has neither surrendered them according to procedure nor made mention of them in his daily reports of his investigation into Paddy's death. Again, according to procedure."

There it was—the basis for dismissal and the tag of scapegoat.

It was then, however, that McGarr heard the loud, angry snarl of an unmuffled diesel engine, shouts, and then gunfire from down in the street near the green. He spun around to the window where he saw Gladden's tall, battered Land Rover bearing down on the line of policemen and soldiers that stretched across the street. Some had turned to fire, and several were caught off-balance, directly in its speeding path. Sheets of rusty metal covered the radiator and most of the windscreen, and, in spite of the rapid fire, the vehicle hurtled forward.

Beyond the soldiers stood the crowd of onlookers from the funeral, the press with its television and other cameras, and on the bridge the bristling patch of microphones, and the taosieach, his two ministers, and some of their local supporters.

A few in the crowd, understanding what was about to happen, turned to flee, but found no place to run. There were simply too many people cramped into the funnel made by the buildings and the chest-high rock wall of the narrow bridge, and those there—"*Gladden!*" McGarr shouted; who else could it be?—were doomed.

McGarr wrenched free the Walther he had slipped under his belt and with its pommel dashed out the pane of the window. But already the Land Rover had burst through the line of soldiers. With the crowd only a dozen yards away, McGarr dared not fire and could only watch the catastrophe unfold.

"No!" McGarr shouted.

In the crowd an old, shawl-draped woman had fallen, and a child turned back to help her to her feet.

It was then a figure darted from the shadows and hurled himself at the door of the speeding truck, smashing something through the window and with the other hand clutching at the roof rack. It was a remarkable athletic feat, and his body was thrashed against the side of the truck. But he hung on, recovered his balance, and lunged at the steering wheel.

CHAPTER 22

Bridge Burned

HUGHIE WARD HAD walked into Sneem. Now that his cover was blown, he wasn't about to spend one additional minute serving drinks and running errands. Sonnie had looked down at Ward's Garda I.D. and said, "Wouldn't it have been easier, had you just told me, ah, er—"

"Detective Sergeant," Ward suggested. "Maybe, but after I became acquainted with your *modus operandi*, I couldn't be sure you weren't our man."

"Fair play," Sonnie had said to his back. "Fair play to you." And when Ward was nearly out the door, "What about your wages?"

Stuff 'em, Ward had nearly said, but had only waved, happy to be out in the new day, sailing on the wings of morn' the two or so miles into Sneem. His joy was visceral and scarcely permitted thought, until he caught sight of the cars, parked up on the banks of the drainage ditches and the blue overcoat of the first of what would prove a gauntlet of Guards and army thugs.

"Where'd you get this?" one Guard asked, meaning Ward's Garda I.D.

"Where you got that." Ward pointed to his uniform.

It was his credibility problem again, and even without the oversized service tux. Ever since his recent promotion to detective sergeant—*on merit*, he did not think he should be forced to

242

divulge—people simply did not believe he was who he was. It had something to do with the photograph, which was a bleached-out head-and-neck shot that looked like a snap from a sixth-form yearbook. Also, the rank of detective sergeant was seldom achieved before forty. Ward was wearing a light green warm-up jacket, jeans, and a pair of Everlast ring shoes.

"I don't know—" The Guard tapped the I.D. on the back of his other hand and turned to look toward the village, as if for help.

"Precisely why you're standing here in the middle of a country road," Ward observed, snatching back the I.D. "Any farther west and you'll be in the drink." He pointed toward the harbor that could just be seen in the distance.

The other checkpoints were similarly bothersome, but had he not been hassled by an army lieutenant, who kept asking dumb questions about his "duty station" and "superior officers," Ward would not have turned to look back. His eye caught on a battered Land Rover. It had just cranked over, and its vertical exhaust pipe was gushing a dense cloud of diesel smoke.

Mossie Gladden got out of the truck and began lowering a steel plate over the radiator. At first Ward thought little of it, since winter was now upon them and a grill cover was one way of skimming a bit of heat off an engine. Until, looking back again, he saw Gladden lowering some other rusty plates over the two panels of the windscreen, such that only a slit was left to peer out. Gladden quickly climbed back in.

By then two soldiers, who were closer to the Land Rover, had begun to move toward Gladden. Suddenly a boil of black smoke broke from the stack, the engine roared, and the truck shot out into the road, right at them. They threw themselves to either side, and other soldiers shouldered weapons, unsure whether to fire until the truck broke the final line of blue and drab uniforms.

Gunfire erupted, a staccato gout of deafening noise that was over as quickly as it had begun. Once the truck hurtled by them toward the crowd, the soldiers had to jerk their weapons skyward.

Ward had his Beretta out, which was virtually useless against the truck. He glanced at the crowd, then back at the careening Land Rover that was bearing down on them. He didn't know what he could do, but suddenly he was sprinting off on an angle that might get him to the truck before it reached the crowd.

And did. At the last moment, just as the truck was about to sweep by Ward, Gladden jerked the wheel to catch a soldier with the bumper. It was then Ward launched himself at the side of the truck, grabbed hold of the roof rack, and smashed the twenty-three ounces of his Beretta through the side window.

Bits of glass sprayed over Gladden, who was crouched behind the wheel. There was another man in the truck who had fallen to the floor. They were still speeding wildly forward, and Ward lunged for the wheel, trying to turn the Land Rover away from the crowd and into a building.

But Gladden swung the wheel violently, attempting to shake Ward off. Yet Ward held on and manage to jerk the wheel, aiming the truck at an open space in the crowd and the thick stone restraining wall of the bridge beyond.

Striking it at an angle, the Land Rover was carried by its momentum along the line of the wall, jouncing up onto the bridge and bursting through the thicket of cameras and microphones that had been grouped there for Taosieach O'Duffy's speech in eulogy of Paddy Power.

Before he lost his grip and tumbled from the running board, Ward saw two men, frozen before the oncoming truck. One of them was O'Duffy.

It was strangely quiet for the several seconds it took McGarr to sprint to the bridge. The living and uninjured had been stunned into silence. Those who could act seemed hesitant, as though not knowing who of the fallen to help first. He heard a moan here, a whimper there, but mainly the harsh winter wind soughing over the bridge.

Then suddenly as one, nerves broke. McGarr heard a cry of grief from behind him, which was picked up and echoed by others from every side. McGarr caught sight of Ward, who had fallen in the road in the middle of the bridge; McGarr began running toward him when the concussion of the colossal blast tremored the macadam beneath his feet.

McGarr snapped his head to the west. There, perhaps two hundred yards away, a greasy orange fireball from an exploded Garda patrol car was burning black into the western sky.

McGarr only glanced at Ward, whose eyes were beginning to open, and at the two men whom the truck had knocked over the wall into the rocky Sneem River below. Some photographers were scrambling down steep banks to help them. Others were already aiming cameras at what they could see:

Sean Dermot O'Duffy was spread out on his back on a flat rock, his legs and feet being whipped about in the boil of the swift river. His eyes were open and unblinking in the spray of rushing water. Crumpled near him but submerged in a shallow pool made pink by his own blood was Minister for Finance Quinn, his long gray hair swirling in the livid water.

McGarr saw Noreen next. She was holding Maddie's face away from the heat of the burning car.

"What are you doing here?" he demanded. "I thought you were back at Parknasilla."

"We bought"—Noreen's eyes flickered down on the fisherman's knitted tam and jumper that Maddie was wearing—"but by then microphones and so forth had been set up, and they wouldn't let cars back over the bridge."

"What happened here?" He pointed to the burning patrol car.

"Gladden. He stopped, pointed a rifle out the window of his Land Rover, and fired at the petrol tank. Two shots is all it took."

"Anybody in it?"

"Not that I could see."

"Where's our car?"

Noreen pointed across the square.

"Get ahold of a senior Guard, somebody like Superintendent Butler. Tell him I said to seal off the Ring of Kerry. Gladden's driving either that Land Rover or a gray Ford Granada with Northern plates," McGarr remembered from the car he had seen in one of Gladden's outbuildings. "Helicopters, airplanes, anything they can throw in. The taoiseach has been killed." He could not bring himself to use the accurate word that now would not be avoided.

Noreen reached for his arm, but McGarr turned and broke for her car. Gladden had now achieved his secret desire, McGarr thought as he eased Noreen's large sedan past the fiery wreck and then accelerated down the Waterville road in pursuit of the Land Rover. He was now pariah complete, to be put down with the same dispatch as he had hunted the wild dogs that had preyed on his sheep.

Now Gladden had a lead of—what?—seven, eight, maybe ten minutes, McGarr estimated, as his powerful car clipped along the narrow, winding road. The truck Gladden was driving had to be damaged in some vital way, and what were Gladden's options?

None by the main, traveled roads that could lead him most quickly out of the peninsula that was the Ring of Kerry. It was twenty-five or so steep, sinuous miles to Waterville alone, where Gladden would then have to choose between shore or mountain routes, which were some thirty-five or forty additional miles long, if McGarr's knowledge of geography served him well.

But something else occurred to him: Throughout history the mountains of Kerry had served as a refuge for outlaws of every stripe. Certainly Gladden would be acquainted with at least a few of those mountain sanctuaries, and Gladden could probably either live off the little that was offered there or had already prepared for the eventuality.

Also, Gladden had a connection with elements of the Northern wing of the IRA, among some of whom the solitary, daring act of having assassinated Sean Dermot O'Duffy would be accounted a stunning tactical achievement. O'Duffy's internationalist, free-market economic policies had been diametrically opposed to the insular and socialist IRA, and O'Duffy had endorsed agreements concerning Northern Ireland that previous taosieachs had entered into with the British.

But there was yet another alternative. As McGarr swung around a broad curve in the middle of the mountain, below him he saw black sooty smoke rising in a flame-driven plume. A tour bus was stopped, and the driver and several of the passengers were staring down the sheer face of the mountain at a burning wreck below.

McGarr parked the sedan and got out. It was the gap in the rock restraining wall where on Tuesday Noreen had surveyed the view below. The wind sweeping along the road was fierce enough to stagger him, and he had to snug his hat over his brow and turn his back to belt his mac.

Plainly it was Gladden's Land Rover that was burning in a twisted pyre. The cab had kept some of its boxy shape, in spite of having plummeted several hundred meters to the rocks below, and McGarr could see a steel plate covering one side of the windscreen.

McGarr flashed his identification at the others and tried to shout over the roar of the wind, "What happened?"

"Poor bastard came right out in front of me, you can ask this man here," said the bus driver, who was British. "He was sitting in the front seat. And him." He pointed to another man, who nodded. "I was going dead slow, as it was. Because of the road," which along the stretch that followed the cliff face was just wide enough for the passage of the bus itself. Otherwise, there were step-asides—such as where McGarr had parked the sedan—for cars to pull in until a bus or lorry had passed.

"But it was a wreck even before it went over, if you want to know the truth. God—I never seen the like. Smoking and spewing steam, all . . . *shot* up?"

"Bloke was slumped over the wheel," said one of the other men. "Must have had a heart attack or—"

"There was somebody else standing here by the side of the road who must have seen it go over. A local, by the look of him. But—" The driver turned to look behind him, as for that witness.

McGarr moved first to one edge of the gap in the wall and then to the other to see if the Land Rover had struck the rock. No. As Noreen and he had imagined on Tuesday, the truck had sailed cleanly off into the ether toward the tan beaches and cliffs on which the surf was breaking in silvery lines.

McGarr wandered back along the road to look for skid marks, signs that Gladden or . . . whoever had tried to save himself. He could not believe that the man would have taken his own life without finishing the business of providing a motive—or, at least, the semblance of one—for the atrocity he had committed back in Sneem. Gladden was just too . . . rationally deranged for that and had nothing to lose, not even his life, now.

But there was nothing to indicate that the Land Rover had braked or swerved or skidded. There was, however, a fresh pool of motor oil or coolant, some rainbow-tinged viscous substance oozing down the road. Which had dropped in a clump on the road while the Land Rover was speeding past to its doom?

Back with the driver and his witnesses, McGarr asked, "How fast was the truck going?"

The driver shook his head and tried to remember. A car behind the bus began honking.

Said one of the other men, "A moderate speed. Not enough to have lost control."

"Or skidded," McGarr prompted.

"That's how we got a look at the driver. Had it been speeding, I don't think we'd have seen him at all."

"What about this local, where was he standing? Here?" McGarr pointed to the area near the gap. "Or there?" He swung his finger to a spot of oil.

"There," all three said, the driver adding, "I said to him, says I, 'You see that?' The man tightened his hat over his brow and crossed the road."

"Toward the step-aside?" Where McGarr had parked the sedan, he meant.

All three men nodded.

"Was he also wearing a black farmer's great coat?" McGarr prompted. "Wellies on his feet. The hat is dark brown, good quality, wide brim."

One man nodded. "Except for the Wellies. What he had on his feet was more like hobnail boots. They bit and scuffed on the road, I remember. When he moved to the other side."

For climbing, McGarr thought. He raised his head and scanned the side of the bald gray-green mountain. There near the pinnacle was a figure in a black coat and dark hat who had himself stopped to look back at them. He had something in his hands that he now raised to his face.

It jumped, and the step-aside was filled with the yellow light of the sedan exploding. The concussion blew them back into the grill of the bus as Noreen's sedan burst into a sheet of flame, the howling report of the high-powered rifle echoing through the mountains to the east. When McGarr looked up again, Gladden was gone.

Why shoot the car and not McGarr himself? He had been standing exposed for whole minutes now. The note cards. Contained in them was the only—justification was too definite a word—that Gladden's atrocity would ever garner. And if McGarr and *not* the Garda Siochana had them, Gladden might have a chance of getting them back. McGarr allowed himself a thin smile.

Arriving back in Sneem a half hour later, he found Noreen nearly where he had left her—on the north side of the bridge. Maddie was now asleep in her arms.

"How many died?" he asked, relieving her of the burden of the child.

Noreen shook her head. "On this side of the bridge everybody's been concerned with Sean O'Duffy and Patrick Quinn, who were killed outright. I've heard two or three others, but it could go higher. Some people are badly injured."

McGarr led them past the cordon of police, and they climbed the arc of the narrow bridge. The wind was still fierce and bitter, and McGarr imagined that the pretty little village would never be the same. "What about Hughie?"

Noreen tried to smile. "No concussion, but a broken leg for sure. And scrapes."

"He's a brave wee man."

Noreen nodded. "He must have saved"—again she shook her head—"at least all those people on the other side of the bridge. What about Gladden?"

"Got away, at least for the moment. They'll think he died in a fiery wreck, but they'll discover it's somebody else, most likely some gunman from the North who was already dead."

"They?"

"Whoever investigates this entire thing. I have a feeling my career in the Guards is just about over." McGarr moved his chin toward the other end of the bridge where Garda commissioner Fergus Farrell was waiting, his red face set in grim resolve.

"But *why*? What did *you* do?"

"It's more a matter of what I didn't and won't do."

"You mean, you didn't arrest Gladden when you had the chance? But they wouldn't have wanted that either then."

Which was precisely the point. Farrell and the politicians he represented could never be wrong, as long as a scapegoat could be found. "Also, there's the note cards."

"That they'll want to suppress even more now, because of Power's unflattering portrayal of Sean Dermot O'Duffy."

McGarr turned his back to Farrell, who was now approaching, so he might speak to Noreen without being overheard. "Listen to me closely and do exactly what I say. I'll explain it all later, but if I've got any chance at collaring Gladden, I'll need your unquestioning cooperation."

Noreen blinked.

"Find a car that will take you back to Parknasilla. Pack up our belongings along with the photocopies of Power's notes that I made last night. It's on the top shelf of the closet. Then have the hotel get you a rental car. Say it's an emergency, and you need it immediately. Then go someplace I've never been and people don't know who you are. Use your maiden name, park the car where it can't be seen, then phone your mother and tell her where you are. And just wait. I'll be in touch."

"But—"

McGarr handed Maddie to her and turned to Commissioner Farrell, who said, "May I have a word with you. Private, if you don't mind."

"But I do." McGarr began walking toward a group of reporters who were interviewing an emergency-medical officer. He needed an impartial witness with a large national following. There he reached for the arm of a reporter whom he had once treated unfairly. "Got time for a scoop?"

Through thick lenses her eyes tried to read McGarr's face, but she stepped away from the others with him. She was a thin young woman with a large, round face and pug nose.

"You remember the commissioner, don't you? Go ahead, Commissioner—shoot."

Farrell glanced at the reporter, but her presence suited his needs as well. "Nell Power tells me Gladden assaulted you on Tuesday. You had a chance to take him into custody, and you didn't. Why?"

"Because you didn't want me to."

"What? Did I ever say that?"

"No, you didn't. But Taosieach O'Duffy did, when I spoke to him on Tuesday night in his West Cork bungalow about Paddy Power's murder."

"Murder?" the young woman asked, writing furiously in her notepad. "Was Paddy Power murdered? Officially?"

"Semi-officially, you might say," said McGarr.

Farrell's nostrils had flared, and his eyes drifted down onto the reporter's pad. "I wouldn't make accusations that you can't prove, were I you."

"But you're not me, and I can." McGarr tapped his chest pocket. "Wire."

"You recorded your meeting with the taosieach?" Farrell demanded indignantly. "Without telling us?"

"No, but there's proof." McGarr winked at the reporter, before asking, "Can I say something to Commissioner Farrell strictly off-the-record?"

"Of course," she replied, though her pen did not leave the pad.

"Try me, Commissioner, and I'll take you down. You, Harney, and whatever's left of your government." Their eyes met for a moment, and McGarr hoped an understanding passed between them.

"The note cards. I want them."

"Mossie Gladden does too."

"What does Mossie Gladden have to do with the note cards?" Farrell, enraged now, demanded. "Those note cards are evidence in a murder case that is directly linked to the assassination of the taosieach. As such, they are the property of the state."

"And they made *him* commissioner," McGarr said to the reporter. "Shall I explain it to both of you?"

She nodded.

McGarr swung his face to Farrell. "If I give them to you now and you say you have them, I won't get Gladden. But if, under the present circumstances"—he pointed to the reporter's notepad—"I refuse to give them to you, I well might. In other words, the note cards are neither evidence nor the property of the state, but rather bait. Is that plain enough for you?" McGarr waited, but when Farrell said nothing, he muttered, "I wonder if we speak the same language." Then. "You know, it might be better if you sacked me."

"McGarr—you're sacked. As of this moment I'm relieving you of your duties."

McGarr turned to the reporter. "There you go—I promised you a scoop."

"There'll be a disciplinary hearing," Farrell shouted at his back. "Charges will be brought."

"You'd better check that out with your masters. Who are they now—the Harneys? Remember, I hold the cards. A whole big box of them."

"Look—I can help you," said the reporter, reaching for the sleeve of his mac. "I have a million questions, and—"

But he was already by her, weaving through the milling officials near the South Green, where he stepped over the chain and walked toward M.J.P. Frost's chemist shop.

A woman and child had just come out the door, yet McGarr found the old man as he had left him the day before: asleep in the tattered, stuffed chair; the cat in his lap; a newspaper at his feet; the ancient wooden radio on the table telling from Dublin of the events that had occurred a hundred yards from his door.

McGarr turned to the jars, boxes, and bottles of pills. He scanned through three rows before the old man said, "Phenobarbital is the third bottle on the last shelf. Pills. Powder, one down. What you do is, take the date off the bottle, then refer that to my prescription book. Add up all the tablets I've sold to the present, subtract that from the original figure, then count the tablets, which should match. It's the same procedure for the powder, but more time-consuming. One has to measure by weight. The scales are over there." He pointed toward another counter in the cluttered back room of the chemist shop.

"What about in solution?"

His smile was more a baring of tea-and tobacco-stained teeth, and the ammoniac smell coming off him was daunting. "Sodium barbital is soluble in water. Or champagne. You'll find Gretta's name down for it rather often. Refills. High doses. From Mossie.'' He waited while McGarr thumbed through the book. ''Care to hear my theory?''

McGarr was all ears; so far Frost had not mentioned Sean Dermot O'Duffy or the others, probably many from Sneem, who had been killed or injured at the bridge. Gretta Osbourne's death was obviously on his mind.

''It was neither suicide nor murder but merely a . . . how do you term it? A misadventure with her medicines.''

Another misadventure with medicines, thought McGarr.

''It was close to bedtime. Gretta had been taking the substance for years now, and had built up a kind of tolerance to the effect of the drug, which masked the actual quantity in her body. Her blood and organs and such.

''A couple of glasses of champagne and—'' He hunched a bony shoulder.

McGarr wondered when Shane Frost had stopped in to visit his father? It could not have been before Paddy Power's funeral, since Frost had been late already when he arrived at Gretta Osbourne's door. And certainly not after, since Frost had accompanied Nell Power to the bridge, and McGarr had seen them standing there before Gladden struck. Therefore, it must have been sometime after the horrific event at the bridge that Frost visited his father with the details of Gretta Osbourne's quiet demise in her suite at Parknasilla. ''What about the suicide note?''

''That was no more a suicide note than any of the note cards in Paddy Power's file. I doubt if it was even written at the time she was dying. I think she got it out to, you know, add something to it. Or complete the thought. Shane tells me her pen was found on the right side of the card. And there Gretta was a lefty all the way.''

Which was what had been bothering Frost, such that he sought out his father to discuss the particulars? And why still no mention of Sean Dermot O'Duffy? ''He tell you the good news?''

''About Eire Bank? Yah—a coup, isn't it? Never in my wildest dream did I think Shane capable of a deal of such magnitude. I only wish I could drink champagne, but I can't. Mossie says—But then, of course, it wouldn't be decorous, would it? Now.''

McGarr waited, watching him closely. M.J.P. Frost was both a sly and a silly old man. For a moment there he had been taunting

McGarr, rubbing salt into the wound, which was Power, Osbourne, Gladden and the bridge, his son's £80-million-plus deal that had been worked right there in Parknasilla under McGarr's nose.

"Mossie has been off his chump now for years. The only reason he was even tolerated is he was a medical doctor and gave away his services free. But in taking on the likes of Sean Dermot O'Duffy, he went to hell altogether, didn't he now? Making those foolish accusations in public *twice*, no less, and finally this thing, which is straight out of the IRA. You know, the new gang from the North that Mossie was always helping. I wonder if ever they helped him?"

McGarr himself wondered what he was hearing—a simple explanation of the massacre at the bridge? One that excluded the complications of Power's and Osbourne's murders and the theft of the note cards and what they contained? One that would be acceptable to the surviving government and believed by the Irish people who would want to hear some "soft" truth and were inured to the depravities of the IRA? Again McGarr thought about the body that would be found in the Land Rover, doubtless that of some gunman from the North.

"What I came for were some sacks. You know, your plastic sacks with the name of the shop on the side."

"They're under the counter, there as you go out."

"I'm going to take several, and these note cards here." He meant the packets of blank note cards that were being offered for sale.

"Do you know that Paddy asked me to get them for him some years ago. Now that I come to think of it, they're probably the very material from which he scratched out his potentially scandalous notes. Take them, go on. Again, no charge. I'm always happy to help the police."

Now that your son is rich, McGarr thought. By the felicity of two murders.

Outside near the church McGarr found McKeon and O'Shaughnessy waiting at his Mini-Cooper. "Commissioner Farrell told us you were here, then ordered us off the case and back to Dublin. Told Liam and me to write up everything we could remember about the past week." McKeon flexed his elbow. "Short list for me."

McGarr smiled. "At least we now know the enemy."

"Having seen the not-so-whites of his shifty, politic eyes."

"What about Gladden?" O'Shaughnessy asked.

McGarr filled them in, saying that he had Paddy Power's note cards—"The originals and Gladden's photocopies"—in the boot of the Cooper, and he would return to his house in Rathmines. "As per the commissioner's orders."

McKeon smiled. "*With* the cards."

"Gladden will want them, but understand this—he's mine. Alone."

"Where's Rut'ie?"

McKeon looked toward the bridge. "I dunno—went with some of the injured, I suspect. I saw her and the big fella—"

"O'Suilleabhain," O'Shaughnessy supplied.

"—bending over some of the fallen."

Who would be known to her, McGarr concluded.

FRIDAY

"Leave me, O Love, which reacheth but to dust"
Sir Philip Sidney

CHAPTER 23

Death

WHEN MCGARR GOT back to Dublin just after midnight, he again had to refuse offers of help from McKeon and O'Shaughnessy, telling them that Gladden would probably not be able to leave the Kerry Peninsula for several days, and he had his own preparations to make. Also, they could better serve him by manning their desks at Dublin Castle.

"But how do you know he'll come alone?" O'Shaughnessy asked. "If he has an IRA connection, he might get help, and he—or they—could be here any minute."

McGarr did not think so. Gladden might have sought IRA assistance, but no earlier than Wednesday, when after his "press conference" he had decided on extreme measures. Up until then Gladden had hoped by some means, if only press and media pressure, to get the note cards back. And Gladden would not allow them to fall into somebody else's hands, not after what they had already cost him. And others.

And then Gladden might not get through what the radio was even now calling "the biggest manhunt in the nation's history"?

Even so, McGarr took his own precautions. After having dropped off McKeon and O'Shaughnessy at the Castle, where they collected O'Shaughnessy's car, McGarr drove around Belgrave Square twice, looking for details that were out-of-place. It was late and cold, and yet there was at least one light in every house, as—he supposed—people followed the hunt for Gladden, which was being monitored by every Irish radio station on the dial.

Pausing beside an ambulance that said, "ST. COLUMBA'S EMERGENCY SERVICE, BLACKROCK, CO. DUBLIN," McGarr heard the boyish, insouciant, and—was it even?—happy voice of Minister for Justice Harney promising, "We'll have the man in short order." If not, Harney would hatch him from an egg, McGarr thought, trying to remember if he had seen the ambulance before. Some medical students had rented one of the large houses in the square, and, as usual, lights were burning in nearly every window, even now at—McGarr checked his watch—1:45 A.M. Perhaps one of the students was moonlighting as an ambulance attendant. He crept slowly by.

Otherwise, every other car was familiar to McGarr, and only the occasional taxi was passing through the windswept winter streets. Nevertheless, he took his own precautions, parking in a cul-de-sac three blocks away and leaving the note cards and photocopies in the boot. He removed only the five plastic sacks from "M.J.P. Frost, Chemist, Sneem, Co. Kerry," which McKeon had stuffed with blank note cards on the long trip up from the country. He also approached the house through back alleys and laneways, and took the final precaution of entering the back garden not of his own house but of the house next door.

A light was on in the kitchen, and, when he knocked, Sol Viner answered the door. A large, lumbering man with full dark beard, wire-rim reading glasses, and black yarmulke even at the late hour, he stepped aside and bid McGarr enter his large, modern kitchen. On the table McGarr could see, Viner had a stack of newspapers and magazines not all in English; low, funerary music was coming from a radio on the sideboard.

"Ah, *former* chief superintendent McGarr. Just the man whose career I've been mourning. I've always admired the literal approach to life, but, I wonder, could you be taking it a bit far?" He pointed down at the sacks that McGarr was carrying.

Rabbi of a small congregation, Viner was, like McGarr himself, a native Dubliner; he now closed the door behind McGarr and stepped back to take a look at his friend. "What will it be—a nice cuppa or a little something to take the edge off the wind?"

McGarr shook his head. "I just stopped by to say we might be having a visitor here in the neighborhood sometime soon. It being the weekend, I was wondering if you, the missus, and the kids might be off to Arklow," where Viner's wife's brother lived and they often visited.

"You mean Mossie Gladden, the mad doctor?" Viner's eyes again fell to the sacks, then quickly returned to McGarr's. "Yer coddin' me." Viner prized the least detail that he was able to extract from McGarr about his investigations, and here he was in the middle of what loomed as the major criminal event of the decade. "Sit down. Sit down, man." He swept a hand at the table. "Really—have a seat. I'll put on a pot."

McGarr shook his head. "I just thought I'd let you know."

There was a pause in which McGarr could almost hear Viner's quick mind scanning through what he had recently heard and read. "You mean about the evidence that you've sequestered and refused to turn over to the government? It just came over the one-thirty date. A kind of teaser let drop by some woman reporter. You know, details to follow in the morning's *Times*." There followed another slight pause, then, "But do you mean Gladden *here*?"

McGarr blinked.

"And him after Paddy Power's note cards? It's in the papers." Viner flicked his hands at the newspapers on the table. "What about Gladden's IRA connection—is it for real?"

McGarr turned and reached for the handle of the door. "You should visit Phoenix Park on Monday and fill out an application. I understand there's a position open."

"Peter—tell me this before you leave. Have you read Power's note cards?"

McGarr stepped out into the darkness, where he saw that it had begun to snow.

"What's in them? Is it the—*right* stuff?"

It was that all right, Dublin style: filled with all the revealing, *quiet* detail that could bring charges, ruin careers and perhaps even lives.

"And not a morsel will you let drop to me, your friend, neighbor, and confidant—a man of the cloth, for Jimminy sake—at two in the bloody morning with no bloody body about. You'll get no points with 'Yer Mahn' for this night's work."

But McGarr kept walking.

Maisie Edgerton-Jones, McGarr's other contiguous neighbor,

came next. A woman well past seventy, she slept poorly, and her light was often on at this late hour. Knowing that her back garden would be a soup of partially frozen water and ice, McGarr walked round to the front of the house to pass under the bows of yews that bordered the side of the house. They had not been cut in a decade and had attained the height of small trees. In such a way McGarr arrived at the old woman's back door.

Through the lace curtains covering the back door, he could see that her kitchen table was already set, until he knocked and the pleasant scene of hot toast, tea, and a few sausages set on a warming tray was replaced by the wolfish head of a large Alsatian dog. Recognizing McGarr, the dog backed away from the door and sat, his bushy tail sweeping the tiles by the stove.

"If it isn't the Chief Superintendent. We've just been hearing about you. Over the wireless." She pointed to an ancient radio set with a dim yellow dial and a carved oak cabinet. "You're just in time. I've got everything laid out, and you can have the lad's portion of sausages."

McGarr glanced down at the dog, which had seemed to understand what she had said.

"He likes them just as well raw."

Or any way he can get them, McGarr judged. Did the dog smile, watching her shuffle toward the fridge? McGarr thought it did.

Miss M. E.-J., as she was known to the neighborhood, was a tall woman with a long, haughty face and snow-white hair that had been gathered into a braid that flowed down her back. Tonight she was wearing a crimson velvet housecoat, buttoned to the throat, and what looked like Christmas stockings stuffed with felt that made her old legs appear birdlike and frail.

Apart from the dog, the kitchen was presided over by an ancient coal stove with crazed green porcelain griffin's feet that always caught McGarr's eye. It kept the room torrid in every season, and McGarr, taking a seat at the table, settled into the comforting warmth.

The dog was a Bomb Squad veteran that McGarr had given to the old woman for companionship and mutual assistance. After having been injured in a blast, it limped noticeably and could barely hear; but, unlike the old woman's sight, the dog's was excellent and they complemented each other well.

Apart from scenting, the dog had been trained in perimeter security and personal protection; it had also been praised by its trainer as "a dog in a thousand. A kind of dog genius. A big, gentle brute of a fella that should *not* be put down.'' Which would have been its fate had a collection not been taken up and a home found.

In a kind of soldierly salute the dog—called "Wellington,'' by Miss M. E.-J.; the "P.M.'' (of Belgrave Square) by Square residents—nuzzled McGarr's wrist, then sat far enough from the table not to appear to beg.

Which was genius enough for any nine-stone Alsatian, McGarr imagined, reaching for the tea that the old woman now poured.

"So, tell me,—how's the wee bairn and our darling Noreen?'' In spite of the continuing radio updates, she would ask no direct question about what had happened in Sneem, which was the reason McGarr had settled at her table so readily. It was the way *her* people, who were decidedly West British, comported themselves, and not for the first time McGarr thought there might be some basis for Maisie Edgerton-Jones's assumption of superiority.

Thus they ate virtually in silence, discussing only the weather and the snow, which, they could see through a kitchen window, was now falling heavily, and the differences between city and country, which neither McGarr nor the old woman cared much about. "I hear Noreen lost her lovely big car.''

McGarr nodded; the early reports were more detailed than he had expected. "We'll get her another.'' How, he did not know, but they would.

It was her only reference to McGarr's situation, and he followed her suggestion to take his toddy and smoke to the Morris chair. There, before nodding off, he heard the solemn music interrupted; the voice of a newscaster then announced that a car, answering the description of the Ford Granada that McGarr had glimpsed in an outbuilding of Gladden's mountain farm, had been found in Carlow. "It's believed that the car has been there since sundown.''

"Goodness,'' said Miss M. E.-J. as she washed the dishes, "that's more than halfway across the country.'' Her tone was vexed and supportive of McGarr, as though to suggest that the police without him were surely incompetent.

Granted Gladden had had a jump on them, but he was either lucky or—

"I imagine he's had help.''

McGarr nodded, thinking that he'd sleep an hour. Two, at most. But when he awoke, it was first light. A blanket had been snugged over him, and the P.M. was lying on a pallet by his feet, its eyes half-open.

McGarr decided to let him out and keep him there for perimeter security. "Ready to be reactivated?" he asked, fetching the plastic sacks and opening the door. "Cold, dark duty, but we haven't long to wait, I suspect."

The snow had changed to sleet, and McGarr's brogues bit through the glittering crust. On top of the stile in the wall that separated their properties, McGarr stopped to survey his back garden. When the new day dawned in an hour or so, rain would turn the three or four inches on the ground into an ankle-biting bog of frigid slush that would linger for weeks and was the worst feature of a Dublin winter. Seldom was it cold long enough for snow to remain snow, or warm enough for the city to be spared an icy cover.

There were no footprints leading from the laneway to the back door, nor—on the other side—up the tall staircase to the first floor of his Georgian house. Feeling refreshed by his sleep and invigorated by the nip of the cold, icy wind, McGarr carefully lowered himself down onto his narrow side lawn and walked round to the garden basement door. Saying, "Watch," to the P.M., he let himself into the warmth of the room that he used as a kind of hothouse to germinate seeds and grow shoots for spring planting. He flicked on a light.

Everything seemed in place, and he climbed the stairs to the kitchen, where he put on a pot for coffee, then moved into his study to switch on a radio. But the telephone began ringing at—he checked his watch—7:10 in the morning. Who could it be? He had instructed Noreen not to call him, and, like many senior policemens', his home phone was unlisted. Only staff and close personal friends knew the number. Gladden maybe, ringing to see if he had reached home? How would Gladden have gotten his phone number? How would anybody else?

Deciding it had to be staff at such an early hour, he picked it up and listened. It was a reporter from Minister for Justice Harney's father's newspaper, wondering if McGarr would answer a few questions. He hung up and switched on Noreen's answering machine.

Next came the box that was attached to the back of the front door and was crammed with mail, old newspapers and, felicitously, the morning *Times*. It was the only morning paper that was delivered to the house, mainly for Noreen, and was still spangled with sleet, obviously having just been dropped off. The other three morning newspapers McGarr read at work.

The phone rang again, and on the fourth double-jingle McGarr heard Noreen's recorded voice mixing with the voice from the radio, saying that she couldn't come to the phone at the moment and—McGarr waited until he heard the same reporter say, "Aw, c'mon McGarr. Give us a break. You playin' favorites with the *Times*, or what?"

Or what, exactly.

"Dr. Maurice J. Gladden, a former T.D. and a longtime political foe of Taosieach O'Duffy is suspected . . ." the deep, disembodied voice of a Radio Telefis Eireann newsman droned on, recapitulating the events of the day before. McGarr kept half an ear on that, waiting for any details that he had not heard before.

Back in the kitchen he poured the now-boiling water into a plunger-type coffee maker, and turned to consider his strategy for the blank note cards while the coffee steeped. He would hang one sack on the back of the door to the basement where there was little light and the landing creaked. He would cram another into the mailbox on the front door, leaving the hatch open, as if the sack had been squeezed through from the outside and its bulk had forced the clasp. Another he would place on the long table in front of the windows in the study where if Gladden got that far, he would have his back to the door while he examined it. The other two he would put someplace upstairs; once Gladden got that far, he would leave the house either disarmed or feet first.

McGarr poured himself a cup of coffee, then carried the paper into the study to learn how much time he had. He opened his jacket and rearranged the weight of the Walther that he had slipped under the waistband of his trousers hours before and was now chafing his paunch.

". . . all ports and airports have been closed indefinitely by the minister for Transportation, stranding thousands of travelers. . . ."

McGarr turned down the volume and spread the newspaper on the table in front of the windows there. It was growing light now, and he could just see the figure of the P.M. making a transit of the side lawn, its head raised as though looking up at the house.

McGarr's eyes lit on the front page of the *Times* that was filled with a blaze of banner headlines:

O'DUFFY ASSASSINATED
QUINN DEAD
FOUR OTHERS KILLED WHEN MAD DOCTOR RUNS AMOK
SEVEN CRITICAL

He scanned those articles that capsuled the events of yesterday in Sneem. To prove its claim of assassination, the newspaper detailed the evident planning involved in cutting and fitting the steel plates that Gladden had fixed to the Land Rover, in the fact that he had not once tried to change direction in spite of Ward's efforts, and in the corpse of the other man found in the truck, who had died of traumatic injuries a day earlier. "The premeditated murder of a political leader is called an assassination. Taosieach Sean Dermot O'Duffy was assassinated by Dr. Maurice Gladden. Would that Dr. Gladden could tell us why."

The headline lower on the page said:

GARDA CHIEF FIRED
WORLDWIDE MANHUNT LAUNCHED

It was Farrell's version of McGarr's suspension. Ward's heroics were again mentioned, but nothing of McGarr's own chase. "Chief Superintendent Peter McGarr was suspended without pay for two violations of Garda Siochana procedures, which Commissioner Farrell refused to discuss publicly beyond stating that the matter will be dealt with in an administrative hearing. 'Criminal charges may be brought,' said Farrell."

In parentheses the reader was directed to page 3, on which one Moira O'Boyle—bless her hazel eyes and quick hand—rendered without flaw or favor the reportable parts of dialogue in which McGarr had engaged Farrell. And unlike Farrell, she understood the concept of bait. The article closed with:

> McGarr stated he was in possession of note cards that Paddy Power, a former O'Duffy insider whose death he was investigating, had amassed for a planned memoir. When asked to surrender the cards as evidence, he refused, saying that he had not yet completed his investigation of Paddy Power's murder. It is to be supposed that McGarr's failure to arrest Dr. Gladden for presumed cause two days earlier was the second reason for his suspension.

Page 3 also contained editorials, the last of which asked if the government was already engaged in a cover-up of the events leading up to the slaughter in Sneem and why McGarr,

> . . . one of the Garda's most senior and certainly most respected officers, has been summarily dismissed during such

extraordinary circumstances without an official Garda statement of cause. If the byplay witnessed between the Commissioner and his Chief Superintendent is accurate, much needs to be explained, both by the Garda Siochana and now-suspended Chief Superintendent McGarr.

The *Times* was not the newspaper owned by Minister for Justice Harney's father, and McGarr had his supporters too.

McGarr's eyes worked down the rest of the page, which was filled with eyewitness descriptions of the disaster, follow-up stories on victims and survivors, and a list of the injured. He kept turning the pages, looking for any report of O'Duffy's having announced the Eire Bank sale, wondering if a multimillion-pound sale to the Japanese of an institution that had been so favored by successive O'Duffy governments and so controversial throughout its existence could have gotten lost.

No, there it was at the top of the Financial Section. "ONCE RUMOURED SALE ASSASSINATION-DAY ACTUALITY, the headline said. The article went on, "In an intriguing about-face which occurred moments before the calamity in Sneem, County Kerry, Taosieach O'Duffy announced the sale of Eire Bank to Nomura Bank of Kyoto for an undisclosed price." There followed a brief history of Nomura Bank's interest in Eire Bank, which dated back five years.

Beneath it was another small story about O'Duffy's having ". . . endorsed Paddy Power's call for a debt-for-equity swap of the national debt under the rubric of '*internationalizing* the burden of past, public borrowing.' "

McGarr began turning the pages back toward the beginning of the paper. Preoccupied with finding the Eire Bank story, he had seen but had passed over something else of interest. But what and where?

It was growing lighter outside, and again he saw the P.M. pass by the window, limping on its one gamy leg. Its head was lifted toward the windows, its wet, gleaming nose pulsing as it scented the air.

The phone rang again, but once only, before Noreen's voice intervened and the same reporter—who judiciously had yet to give himself a name—came on to harangue McGarr about his duty to the reading public and the nation. Before hanging up, he added, "I'm going to keep ringing this fecker until you pick up. You're gonna need us, you bastard. Every miserable line you can get."

There was a time a mere day ago, McGarr thought, when no reporter would dare speak to him like that. Under the pain of being ignored for whole years, which made him think of Gladden, who had not been able to endure such a fate. What about himself? After years in the public eye, could he suffer being just another ordinary citizen? Or, worse, an outcast citizen who would be forced to live under an extraordinary dark cloud of suspicion and supposed guilt? He thought of Maddie and how cruel children could be to pariahs, or, rather, to the child of a pariah.

His eye then caught and riveted on one name in the list of those who had been injured at the bridge. "T. Bresnahan, Sneem. Critical." Among the dead was a Mrs. Agnes O'Suilleabhain.

The radio was saying, "The manhunt has shifted to the Dublin Metropolitan Area where, it is suspected, Dr. Gladden has arrived with the help of Northern elements of the IRA. A Garda spokesman in Phoenix Park has reported the theft of an . . ." McGarr switched off the radio and reached for the phone before it could ring again. In the directory he found the hospital in Tralee where T. Bresnahan would have been taken. He dialed the number.

Not knowing if the call would still be put through under his own name, McGarr began to say, "This is Superintendent Liam O'— No," he corrected, "This is Chief Superintendent Peter McGarr of the Murder Squad of the Garda Siochana. Please put me through to Detective Inspector Ruth Bresnahan. Her father, Tom, is a patient of yours, and she's probably with him now."

There was the slightest pause, then: "Yes, Chief Superintendent, I'll ring the floor directly." There was a long wait in which McGarr listened to the static crackling over the line and wished he had thought to get himself another cup of coffee.

There went the P.M. again, now lifting his entire body onto his haunches as he limped by, as in a strange, spastic dance. Why? McGarr wondered. Some effect of his injuries, no doubt. He had never seen the beast so curiously . . . animated, and he speculated that perhaps animals knew more than humans gave them credit for, and he was merely responding to challenge of the command McGarr had issued. Watch!

"Chief?" Bresnahan asked.

"Is it your father?"

"Yah."

McGarr waited, but when she offered no more, he asked, "How is he?"

Bresnahan didn't know what to say. She had been on her feet for nearly twenty-four hours, having to deal with her father, which had been easy enough physically, and her mother, who had gone to bits entirely, and O'Suilleabhain, who had maintained a grim smile through it all but was in a kind of emotional shock, she could tell—because of his mother.

All he had said was, "You know, my father died so early in my life that she was the only parent I actually had. Apart from your father, of course. But—" He would not survive either, and neither the doctors nor Bresnahan knew exactly why, which troubled her most.

When the speeding Land Rover, driven by Gladden, had breached the line of soldiers and bore down on them, Bresnahan had pushed her mother away from it and had then reached for her father, who had been standing on her other side. But he had ahold of Agnes O'Suilleabhain, who had stumbled.

It was then that Bresnahan glanced up and saw Ward hurl himself at the truck where, had he not turned the wheel, they all—Rory and herself included—would have been killed outright, caught flat-footed in the direct path of the maverick machine.

Instead the headlamp and bumper struck Agnes in the head and shoulders, and her body was shot, like a bail from a binder, into Bresnahan's father, who also went down. He got up—too quickly, Bresnahan now suspected—clasped his neighbor to his bosom, and took a half-dozen faltering steps away from the horrible scene toward the church where they had parked. But there were too many bodies and too much blood; his legs were weak, and he finally stumbled and fell.

By that time Bresnahan and O'Suilleabhain were standing over them, and they rolled her father off the even-then dead woman. His eyes, which were half-open, were dim and glassy, and there was a fleck of spittle on his chin. But otherwise the blood was hers, and O'Suilleabhain was saying, "You take Ma. I'll take Tom, and we'll get them help before—"

Pandemonium broke out: There were people running toward the bridge, and from off on the north side of the village an enormous explosion erupted. The next thing she knew she was in the car, and they were far from Sneem, O'Suilleabhain at the wheel and beating the quick, surefooted car over the unpaved narrow mountain roads to Tralee.

"Pa! *Pa!*" she kept saying to her father, but it was as if he couldn't see or hear. Or as though what he had seen and heard had been too much for him, and he had simply quit, which was the gist of what he said to her later.

"The shock and his heart—" the doctors had told her. "I'm afraid there's little we can do but revive him for a time, so—" *you can at least say good-bye* went unsaid.

Her mother couldn't. "I knew it was coming, but I just can't bring myself to face him, knowing I'll not see him again. And it should be peaceful with no weeping, which he always hated." And, like a child, she had come apart altogether, making it clear to Bresnahan that the tables had turned and her daughter was even now in charge.

And then, after they gave him the last injection of digitalis—a coincidence not lost on Bresnahan in spite of her anxiety and grief—he said he wanted to speak to "Ruthie alone. With the door closed."

Bresnahan had then entered the room as though stepping onto a stage to play a scene that she would reenact—she knew even then—over and over again for the rest of her life.

The nuns and nurses had propped him up on the pillows and even combed his thick, steely hair. But for the cardiac monitors taped to his hairy, bearish chest, his torso was naked, and he looked, as she had always thought of him, immense: at once square and wide and strong, and certainly not about to die. She was tempted to rush out and try to find some other doctor, who would see how sound he was and could save him.

But he had seen her, and that same substantial chest was heaving, his eyes were now wide open but glassy, and when he spoke her name, his breathing was labored.

He opened his hand, and she took it.

"Well, Ruth Honora Ann—here we are."

At the end of the road, she supplied without having to say it. Not being able to help herself, she felt tears streaming hot down her cheeks.

"It's all right, really. I've been lying here thinking that the least that can be said about me is I was fierce proud and never lowered myself." He kept having to pause to gather breath, like a runner at the end of a long race. "I did my duty, like my father and his before him. You know"—his eyes cleared for a moment—"living here between the mountains and the sea where we've lived since time out of mind." Another pause. "Not like some, who don't know or care where they live or why." His eyes closed and his chest tensed, while the heart monitor drew some lines shaped like gentle waves; Bresnahan squeezed the rough calluses of his hand, but he did not respond for what seemed like the longest time.

When his eyes opened again, they were more distant. "It's an important thing you do. I saw so today at the bridge. Mossie—" He tried to shake his head; there was yet another long pause in which Bresnahan tried to listen to the sounds of the hospital so that she would know that it all was real: a metal trolley passing, like a set of cymbals, in the hall; a nun's beatific voice speaking a prayer over an intercom that could not be stifled completely; the clank and knock of the central heat, warding off the winter cold.

"But I'm leaving you now. Comfortable enough, you'll see, at least for your ma." His eyes tried to scan the room but quickly narrowed again. "Where she is. You do what you want, but I have one thing to ask you." His head turned fully to her, and his eyes fastened on hers. "Promise me you'll keep at least a piece of the place, even if it's just a cottage on the mountain that we've loved. And the name." He then eased himself back into the pillow. "*Nead an Iolair*," Bresnahan had said to herself. Eagle's Nest.

It was the last Bresnahan heard from him. Or would, she suspected. Now he was just lying there, waiting for the spark to go out, which she now told McGarr, who did not reply.

Only when she asked, "Chief?" did she realize that McGarr had long since left the line.

And was already hanging from his own handcuffs. His wrists had been clasped behind his back, and his body had then been raised on a length of line from a rafter in his basement.

It was an interrogation technique—torture, to be precise—that British forces had practiced on terrorists in the North, and they now used themselves. The purpose? To gain information, such as the question Gladden asked before McGarr had passed out from the pain. "The note cards. You can tell me now or after your shoulders are dislocated. But tell me, you will."

CHAPTER 24

Cuffs

DETECTIVE SERGEANT BERNIE McKeon's wife and four of his twelve children met him at the door of his house in Rings End, a working-class section of Dublin. They had been gathered around the kitchen table, listening to the radio reports of the manhunt for Dr. Gladden.

Upon giving him a kiss, his wife had said, "But the sh-tink of you! Janie, what is it?" She lowered her nose to his overcoat, then grabbed hold of his full shock of blond hair and pulled his head down where she gave it a sniff, tossing it roughly from side to side as she would the hair of one of the children. "Booze, and plenty of it. But that's a given. And . . . *perfume* is what it is."

"Now, I can swear to you one thing—I didn't drink a drop of perfume in me entire time down there. But I did give me mop its yearly rinse." From a coat pocket he extracted a handful of small vials of fancy shampoo that had been left in his room at Parknasilla; from another pocket he produced the complimentary soaps put up in pretty octagon packets. Four pairs of small hands shot out, and a squabble ensued until each child had one soap and one shampoo apiece.

McKeon regaled them in his usual fashion about what he had witnessed in Sneem, but his wife's comment about the drink had hit its mark. Perhaps if he hadn't spent most of his waking hours in a pleasant pickle, he might have done more to avert the tragedy, the like of which the McKeons themselves had experienced. Seven years earlier his eldest son and firstborn grandchild had been shot to death—executed, bullets to the backs of their heads—by terrorists whom they had surprised burying land mines on a road that ran past their family farm in Monaghan.

McKeon had not, nor did he suspect he ever would, completely recover from the tragedy. It had something to do with the fact that he was still alive, and his strong, handsome son and his innocent, beautiful child were not. How much more severe his discomfort now to think that many of the people who had died or had been injured in Sneem might now be whole *had he been sober*. McKeon had guessed when he saw Gladden outside of Parknasilla that he was some sly class of culchie madman.

With that exact thought in mind he heard the radio announcement about the gray Ford Granada with the Northern plates that had been found in Carlow. Without a doubt it was the same car that McGarr had discovered in an outbuilding on Gladden's farm. McKeon reached for his hat and the telephone in that order.

"What—going out again?" the wife asked.

Glancing from her to the children, McKeon could read the disappointment in their upturned faces. They got to see him seldom, and they had been fascinated by his description of the scene at the bridge and innocently proud that their father had been party to such a momentous event.

"I'm going to arrest Dr. Gladden," he told them.

"You know where he is?" the littlest lad said with wide, frightened eyes.

"I have a good idea that I do."

"Ah, g'wan wid' yah," said the wife. "Don't be leading them on. Aren't we after hearing you've been taken off the case? You're just off now for a bit of booze. We've no room service here."

Which was the cruelest cut, there in front of the kids. But warranted, he judged.

McGarr's phone was connected to his answering machine. O'Shaughnessy picked up on the first ring.

"Can't sleep," said McKeon. "You hear the latest?"

"About the Granada? I was just out the door myself. Do I pick you up?"

"No—a cab'll be quicker." McKeon did not own—because he

could not afford—a car, and O'Shaughnessy lived on the other side of
Dublin. "I'll approach the house from the back. If they're already
there, I'll try to flush them out the front."

"Right."

But McKeon could not seem to find a cab, and when he did by
phone, the driver had to stop at every police barricade—"with even
the boot being searched," he said. "Traffic backed up for blocks. That
man will never get into this city."

Already had, McKeon decided, when he saw the ambulance
parked on the quietest corner of Belgrave Square. O'Shaughnessy had
not arrived yet, and McKeon had the cabbie let him out beyond sight
of the house in an adjoining street. He wagged an extra five-pound
note at the man. "Do me a favor?"

The man nodded.

"Drive down to the Murder Squad office in Dublin Castle and
give this to the man at the desk." On the back of one of his cards he
wrote the license number of the ambulance and added, "Belgrave
Square."

Trying to keep himself in the shadow of the back-garden walls
along the laneway that led to McGarr's gate, McKeon had to step
through ankle-deep, crusted snow and hop over slush puddles and thin,
treacherous ice. It was only first light, and with sleet now falling in a
biting slant, even the visibility was against him.

At the gate he put an eye to the crack but had to wait an eternity,
it seemed, for the sky to brighten. He then saw no footprints from the
gate to the house, but a definite track from the door to the stile in the
yard wall that led to the house of the old woman who lived next
door. And the Alsatian—the former Bomb Squad dog that was now
hers—was pacing around and around McGarr's house, its nose pointed
strangely toward the windows and the basement door, where it stopped
each time and sniffed further.

There was a light in the basement and others in the kitchen and
around the side of the house, but McKeon could detect no movement
within.

What to do?

If McKeon was any judge of dogs—and fifty-three years of almost
exclusively negative betting experience told him he was not—the dog
had lost his talent for sniffing and just wanted to get into the house for
some heat or a tidbit or both. On the other hand, McGarr might have
placed the dog on "watch," and now the beast suspected something

within. But how to approach the house or him without getting ripped apart or, worse, shot?

The old woman. Over the top of the wall McKeon could see the glow of lights from her kitchen. He'd get through her back gate, cross her backyard, and be in her door before the bleeding dog—who was deaf, he seemed to remember—knew he was there.

But the gate was locked, and, when he put a shoulder to the wood, he found it made of some tough stuff, like teak, the lock stout and sure. In his bare hands a skeleton key, even though warm from his pocket, soon burned his fingers like a shaft of frozen mercury. And once in, he turned to find her back garden a bog of thin ice that first sagged and then collapsed under his weight, making each step a bit of loud, low, unlovely comedy. When finally he arrived at her back door and pulled an ancient brass chain that rang a bell in the kitchen, his shoes were brimming with frigid water.

"Who is it?" the old woman called out.

Even with the gate and the ice, McKeon's luck was holding in regard to the dog. Without uttering a word, he dug out his Garda I.D. and pressed it to the glass, only to realize from the way she squinted and tilted her head, that the woman was nearly blind.

He then heard what sounded like the basement door open in McGarr's house and a voice that he didn't recognize call out, "Here, doggie. Here doggie, doggie. Cum an' git y'ere lee-ad." A Belfast accent if McKeon had ever heard one.

"Lemme in, for Jesus' sake," McKeon averred under his breath, pointing to his own chest and then toward McGarr's house.

She only regarded him severely down the length of her long, bony nose.

Having tried all else, McKeon opened his coat and showed her the pistol that was tucked under his belt; when he looked up, miraculously she had opened the door.

"You're one of Peter McGarr's men, aren't you? I recognized you by your hat." She pointed to his bowler.

McKeon again heard the voice calling for the dog and what, immediately after, sounded like a muffled gunshot and a yelp. Suddenly the dog was on top of the tall wall; it paused there, as if wanting to jump, but instead flopped roughly down into the snow onto its back and neck. There, it tried to get up but staggered and went down again, its eyes blinking once, as though to say, No—I can't.

McKeon heard the door close on the other side of the wall.

"Wellie!" the old woman shouted and pushed past McKeon, half slipping down the snowy stairs and out through the crusty snow and ice onto the side lawn. "Ah, Wellie—what have they done to you?"

McKeon had an idea. And another about what was going on in the house. It had something to do with shooting what, they thought, was McGarr's dog: a threat that had been acted on. Now, if they saw the old woman, something else would happen, and soon.

Out in the snow McKeon had to pry the gnarled hands of the grief-stricken woman off the panting animal. He then squatted down and forced his hands between the frozen snow and the dog's blood-smeared body, hoping it wouldn't turn and sink its creamy fangs, which were visible as it struggled to breathe and live, into his arm.

McKeon, though short, was a wide, strong man, but he was sure, as he lifted the brute, that he felt the sharp pain and even heard the pop of his stomach wall giving way. A fecking hernia, he thought. The last thing he needed, though maybe he'd be lucky to get out of it with just that. It was nearly daylight now, and if either the old woman or he had been seen, whoever was in the house would be back, and McKeon would need to be prepared.

Carefully he negotiated the slippery stairs and swung the bloody cargo past the old woman, who was holding the door, and into the house.

All that McGarr watched from a dark nursery window that looked out over the side of the house. Gladden and some younger man, both dressed in the white uniforms of ambulance attendants, were standing behind him. They had let him down from where they had hung him by the handcuffs in the basement, and had pulled, kicked, and dragged him up to Maddie's bedroom so he could watch the dog be shot. His hands were still shackled behind his back, and Gladden was holding a gun to his head. "Who's that?" he asked, pointing to McKeon.

"Her son," lied McGarr.

"Will he be over here soo-ehn?" asked the other man, who was obviously from the North.

"Not likely," said McGarr. "He's a bit of a poof, and guns—"

Said Gladden, as though pleading a point, "If they didn't hear the shot, they'll think it's a road accident. Or the fall from the wall." He wanted the note cards and the time to get them.

"A fookin' strong fookin' poof," said a third man from the door. "That dog must weigh ten stone. See the way I drilled him, Sahmmy? One shot freehand and him going over the wall like a snipe. Me with the silencer and all.

"What's next, the rope trick again?" he asked, like a child bemused at play.

The man Sammy spun around and delivered a blow that drove the other man out into the hall. There, beyond McGarr's sight, he heard two further punches and the advice, "Bring back the old woman and hope, *pray*, they haven't phoned the police. Double quick, now. Run, *run!*"

Gladden jerked up on the cuffs, and a bolt of pain shot across McGarr's shoulders. He was directed out into the hallway and then shoved down the stairs to the first floor and then back down the cellar stairs to the basement.

They had been in the house all the time, having arrived in the speeding ambulance sometime during late afternoon or early evening, before the snow had begun to fall. They had waited for McGarr to arrive, even waited through the beginning of his phone call to Bresnahan, hoping he might tell her the location of the note cards.

While the other man now tied a length of line to the handcuffs and walked the free end up the cellar stairs, Gladden asked, "I ask you again why you think you should protect O'Duffy's reputation and scum like that Harney and his father. O'Duffy was planning to sell you out. Now Harney will."

There was much that McGarr would like to ask Gladden, but he was in no position. He knew that his left shoulder was already dislocated, and even the slight pressure of the line on the cuffs was galling.

"Do we wait for Mick or—?" the other man jerked on the line, and McGarr's eyeballs floated up into his head. Every time his yoked arms were raised beyond a certain point, it felt as if they were being prised from his shoulders.

And ripped, when Gladden pointed down, and the other man, using his own body as a counterweight, jumped from the landing while holding on to the other end of the rope. McGarr was jerked off his feet and left dangling.

The pain was blinding, horrendous, a flash of livid light that seared through his back, shoulders, neck, and head. He couldn't breathe for it. Nor see with his head lowered to his belly and his body swaying wildly on the pendulum of the rope. He kicked out and scattered the plants on the table. He tried to lift his head and breathe, but the pain only became more severe, and he felt himself passing out.

Before he could, they dropped him into the dirt of the scattered plants.

"So, we ask you yet again—" Gladden said in an even and dispassionate tone, "—where are the note cards?"

McGarr shook his head. The pain was still with him, but without the tension on the rope he could at least breathe. And think. "I told you I don't have them."

"Even if I believed that—and I don't—sure, you would have kept a copy for your own protection. From Harney." There was a pause and then: "You a man with a family and a career. I saw the pictures upstairs. What do you want your child to know about you?" *When you're gone*, he meant.

McGarr shook his head again, and the other man began climbing the stairs. McGarr tried to gain his feet, if only to lessen the distance that he would be hoisted.

"Without those cards they—not you or me—will judge what went on in Sneem and your role in it. I have my side too, you know, which must be told."

How it felt to run down all those people, McGarr thought. Or, rather, why he decided they were expendable to get to O'Duffy. McGarr had read Paddy Power's note cards, and whereas there was plenty of skulduggery, malfeasance, and graft, there was nothing in them even remotely approaching murder. Or, rather, mass murder.

"And you yours."

What was McGarr hearing, compassion?

Gladden looked up at the other man, who had reached the landing. "Where's Mick? Shouldn't he be back by now?"

"Thing like this, he likes to linger. Don't worry, he's thorough for all his child's play."

Gladden nodded, and just then Sammy, yelling "Whoopee!," jumped from the landing.

In the deep shadows of the tall yews that separated McGarr's property from the old woman's, Bernie McKeon was waiting. With black bowler, black overcoat, and dark gray trousers, he was garbed nearly like an undertaker, he thought.

Apart from the shiny Colt Python. It was warm and dry where it belonged, under the belt of his trousers. When provided the opportunity, McKeon's approach to justice was swift, summary, and sure. Every other life form reserved the right to protect itself from predators, and the only sure protection was death. In such a way McKeon looked upon himself as one of society's fangs.

From over the wall he again heard the squeak of McGarr's basement door opening and the slap of it meeting the jamb. No caution there. With impunity a predator was now prowling the sleeping neighborhood, its prey an old woman and her wounded dog.

He listened to footsteps approaching through the crusty snow. Still without moving, he waited. Whoever it was would climb the stile in the wall, then pause at the top to look down before descending the icy stairs on McKeon's side. McKeon wished him to see only friendly darkness and shadow. He pulled in a large chestful of air and held it so the vapor from his breath would not give him away. Still he did not reach for the Python.

"Ah, fook." The man had slipped on the icy stones of the stile. McKeon heard him grunt as he began climbing again. And his breathing on the top of the wall, as he looked down. Then one step down. And another.

A scuffed black shoe and white sock appeared at the level of McKeon's eyes.

Before it could leave the shelf of stone, McKeon's left hand shot out and grabbed the ankle. Raising the Python and glancing up, McKeon saw a young man with a great mass of curly brown hair on which sat a white campaign cap of an ambulance attendant. Holding what looked like an automatic fixed with an equally long silencer, he teetered there and tried to point the weapon down. Pulling up, McKeon wrenched the foot away from the stone, and the man fell.

With the barrel of the Python, McKeon followed the back of the curly head down into the snow, where he squeezed off a shot that roared in the narrow space between the rock wall and brick house of the old woman. The curly mop jounced in the snow.

McKeon rolled over what was now a corpse with a gaping third eye in its forehead. He began stripping off the white jacket.

"What was that?" Gladden asked, as he rifled through the desk in the study, looking for anything—a garage rental slip, an automobile registration—that would tell him where the note cards were.

"Mick, I guess."

"I thought he had a silencer."

Sammy hunched his shoulders and turned to the television set, which he had only just switched on. "Likes the noise. He's the best I could get on short notice."

Gladden straightened up. A news announcer was saying, ". . . suspended for failing to follow Garda procedures in two separate matters related to Dr. Gladden."

Which meant McGarr had the note cards, Gladden thought. He was letting McGarr hang for a while. It would make the pain all the more severe when they brought him down and questioned him with the old woman there. Whose house he had come from.

A relative? There she was in a photograph on the desk, standing with the dog and a red-haired woman whose portrait was in other places in the house and was obviously McGarr's wife.

It was then that another, smaller-framed photograph sitting on top of the television caught Gladden's eye, and he advanced on it: McGarr standing by the side of an older forest-green Mini-Cooper. An antique. Gladden had seen a car like that at Parknasilla. Could he have left the actual copies in the car, parked somewhere suitably far away from the house? It was a possibility.

"Better check on McGarr," he told Sammy. "And Mick and the old woman." Now that he knew the question to ask.

McKeon heard the order, and he raised his arms over his head. He was standing in the shadows at the top of the stairs in McGarr's basement.

Below him in the shadows McGarr was still unconscious, swinging from his handcuffs, which had been clasped behind his back and attached to a rope. The rope had then been pulled over a rafter, jerking his arms up and his feet out from under him. Evidently he had passed out from the pain, and McKeon hadn't dared let him down for fear he might groan or cry out. But the handcuffs had given McKeon an idea how he would pay one of them back. In kind.

In each hand McKeon now held an open ring of his own handcuffs that he had adjusted down to their shortest length. He had switched off the basement lights, and when a figure pushed opened the door and began feeling for the switch with his head and neck bent accommodatingly forward, McKeon looped the cuffs under the chin. Pinning a knee to the small of the man's back, he then tugged up with all his force and caught, clasped, and locked the cuffs. "So much for police practice," he whispered in the man's ear.

Choking, his hands clawing at his throat, the man spun around and staggered, as though he would plummet backward down the cellar stairs, which McKeon could not allow. Instead McKeon kicked opened the door and shoved him out into the hall.

Tearing at the handcuffs while issuing a thin, high, liquid sound, like steam escaping from a pressure pipe, the man blundered toward the study, slipping on a throw rug and falling on a hall table that splintered under his weight. Python in hand, McKeon followed at a cautious pace.

It was then McKeon saw Gladden standing by the front door, a rifle raised to his face.

McKeon threw himself against a wall, the rifle roared, and a plate-glass window at the end of the kitchen shattered into silver fragments.

Gladden opened the front door and stepped out of the house, closing it after him. He had McGarr's key chain, and he would cruise the neighborhood in the ambulance, looking for the Mini-Cooper. In it he was now certain he would find the note cards. McGarr would not have trusted anybody else with them, and Gladden knew he had not brought them home.

The man in the house was obviously some other Guard, but he would not soon step out onto the exposed landing of the Georgian town house, knowing about the target rifle that Gladden now slipped under his greatcoat.

Gladden turned around to hurry down the stairs when he saw, standing below him in the middle of the footpath, a tall, well-dressed older man wearing a pearl-gray homburg hat and topcoat to match. The fingers of one hand were inserted almost casually in the slit of a side pocket, and his feet were planted wide. There was something in his other hand, which now came up.

Without announcing who he was or that Gladden was under arrest or, in fact, saying anything whatsoever, O'Shaughnessy raised his revolver and emptied all six of its .357 magnum rounds into Gladden, tacking him to the heavy white paneled Georgian door. Against it Gladden slumped, his strange bald blue eyes raised to the biting winter sleet.

The target rifle clattered down the stone stairs and came to rest at O'Shaughnessy's feet. The door was now pink with Gladden's blood.

FALLOUT

"It was like honey for my poor tormented heart to rise up on the shoulder of the mountain footing the turf or gathering the sods on each other. Very often I'd throw myself back in the green heather resting . . . for the beauty of the hills and the rumble of the waves that would be grieving down from me, in dark caves where the seals of the sea lived—those and the blue sky without a cloud travelling it, over me—it was those made me do it, because those were the pictures most pleasant to my heart. . . ."

Peig Sayers

CHAPTER 25

Deal

MCGARR AWOKE THE next morning in a hospital bed. He had been X-rayed, strapped, and given a powerful sedative that was still with him. He felt groggy and sore.

He tried to sit up, and Noreen, who was standing with Maddie beside the bed, moved to help him, saying, "I don't know why I'm doing this. Jesus—when I heard, I could have murdered you with me bare hands. I drove all the way here from Mayo in a rage."

McGarr looked down at his little girl who, clutching a small black stuffed dog with a beige bone clenched in its mouth, now stepped toward the bed. "Hi," she said, and smiled, happy to have uttered the greeting.

"Hi," he said back. "How's Tricks?" which was the name of the dog. And to Noreen: "Could you run that by me again?"

"You *knew* Gladden would come for the note cards, which was why you sent us away with the photocopies." She pointed to a plastic tote sack on a chair that contained a thick, banded sheath of photocopy paper. "Why in the name of hell didn't you surround the place with bloody Guards?"

McGarr wanted to reach out and lift Maddie onto the bed with him, but his upper arms were strapped to his chest. He had a complete shoulder separation in the left arm, and a partial with much muscle tearing in the right. His neck and back muscles were also strained, and he had been told he would be lucky to mend without some permanent problem.

"You risked yourself, Maisie, the P.M., and who knows how many others. Our house. The neighborhood. *Why?*"

He wanted to say: because he couldn't have risked the possibility of scaring Gladden off. Because he had been suspended and was no longer a Garda officer. But mostly he, like her, had read the note cards and knew what they contained, and he did not still know if that information should be made public. Other cops, acting on Farrell's orders, would have wanted to know where they were; they would have searched and found them.

"You know what they're saying?"

"Who?"

"Some of the press. That it's like what happened to John Kennedy in Dallas. All the conspirators are dead, and key evidence is missing." She reached for a newspaper and showed him the headlines:

O'DUFFY
ASSASSIN, ACCOMPLICES
KILLED IN
RATHMINES SHOOT-OUT
New Questions for McGarr

McGarr glanced at the bedside table. "Do you think I could get a cup of coffee around here?"

"With or without?"

McGarr's eyes met hers. Was there a possibility?

"In addition to the reporters who've staked out the lobby, waiting to speak to you, there's also a man outside with a present that looks like a bottle. He'd like a word."

McGarr raised an eyebrow; any of his former staff would have been allowed into the room.

"Harney the elder."

Daddy of O'Duffy's heir apparent. "What is his newspaper saying?"

"That the *government* has brought the unfortunate episode to a decisive close. His son, of course, is responsible for the quick action, having directed the search for Gladden from start to finish when," she read from the paper, " '. . . on-duty Garda senior officers Superintendent Liam O'Shaughnessy and Detective Sergeant Bernard Q. McKeon shot and killed Gladden after he fired upon them.' ''

"And Farrell?"

"I didn't see him mentioned anywhere in Harney's paper."

McGarr thought for a moment. Were they still certain about branding him with Sneem, Farrell would have been prominently mentioned; obviously Harney had something to offer him. "I've never been much for roses. Or chocolates. At least he got the present right."

He glanced down at Maddie, who was rubbing an eye. "How long have you been here?"

"Most of the night."

"Want to go home?"

"Yes, if there's any of it left. Last time I checked, some of Commissioner Farrell's men had declared it a crime scene and told me they'd phone here when I would be 'allowed' to return."

They were searching the house for the note cards that McGarr had had McKeon take to the safest place he knew, where no 'government man'—Gladden's phrase—would think of looking: behind the bar at Hogan's, the pub in Greater St. George's Street that functioned as the Murder Squad's second office. "Wouldn't your parents' place be better for the moment? There's bound to be—" *blood*, he did not say, "—and I think I remember that the window in the kitchen is shattered."

"All the more reason I want to return. It's winter, if you can remember, and all our pipes will freeze."

"Didn't they board up the window?"

"Not when I was there. The place had the feel of a morgue."

Which gave McGarr a taste of what being an outsider would be like; in any other situation, the commander there would have taken steps to safeguard the home and possessions of a fellow Garda officer. He also thought of his desk in Dublin Castle, which he had been ordered to clean out, and his personal files.

McGarr glanced at the phone on the bedside table. "I'll see what I can do."

Before leaving the room, Noreen clasped McGarr's bald head to her bosom. "Ah, Peter—what would we do without you?"

Or himself without himself, he thought.

"Maybe we should think of doing something different."

We, was it? "I'm open to suggestions from the chin up and the waist down."

"You know what I mean. Haven't you had enough of this work?"

He had, definitely, but it remained outside in the hall, waiting for him. "Look—do me a favor before you go. There's something you can get me." He raised his head and whispered in her ear so Maddie and anybody else who might be listening would not hear.

She regarded him. "Do you think you'll need it? With him?"

McGarr did not know, but his mobility was limited. She too had read Power's note cards, which had described Harney as "the worst kind of thief, the one who will steal friendships with a wrong word slipped here and there." And a thief was a thief was a thief, no matter what it was he stole.

A few moments later Harry Harney entered the room and looked around, smiling to see that they were alone. He was an immense, flame-faced man with a bald head and his usual large cigar, which was his signature prop in a country where sin taxes made tobacco of quality a conspicuous extravagance. Closing the door, he pulled out a fresh one. "Smoke?" In the other hand he held a wrapped bottle. "Drink?"

"Yes, Doctor," said McGarr. "Whatever you say."

Harney's laugh was as large as himself, hearty, rollicking, and orotund of the sort that would make most other people smile. "I knew you were a man I could talk to." He rolled forward, new heels clacking on the tiles of the hospital-room floor. His upper body, swollen like a robin, was bound in the precise pleats of a gray, pinstriped, double-breasted suit; in his lapel was a single black carnation. "Is there a second glass? I can't have you drinking alone."

McGarr tilted his head toward the sink, and while Harney went to fetch the glass there, McGarr reflected on what he knew of the man.

In his note cards, Paddy Power had said that Harney was a consummate salesman, a man whose singular talent was the ability to convince others to go along with his schemes, which ranged from the sprawling housing estates that now ringed Ireland's larger cities to shopping centers, high-rise buildings in Dublin, and, of course, his newspaper. This last he controlled as if it were an organ devoted to the whims of his personality, and yet for all its quirky newness, the *Irish Spectator* was a roaring success.

"I know the Irish people countrywide and not just here in Dublin," he had told a television interviewer. "What we want to read and know and wonder about." And now with Sean Dermot O'Duffy and Paddy Power out of the picture, McGarr suspected, who they should have rule them—his son.

"Wasn't that Noreen Frenche I saw leaving the room? Your wife, I understand," he said, unwrapping the bottle that proved to be—McGarr's eyes widened—Hogan's Own, the whisky that years ago the pub had bottled and was now a collector's item. Having been first aged in sherry casks, the malt had its own distinctive reddish color, a somewhat sweet flavor, and a bouquet like none other. McGarr had not drunk any in, oh, years, and he wondered if it was just a coincidence—the gift bottle and where he had stored the note cards—based on the fact that it was general knowledge he frequented the pub. In any case, he appreciated how well Harney had prepared himself for the visit.

"Wonderful family, the Frenches. Fitzhugh is a good friend of mine." His bulging arms worked the cork, and he poured two large drinks. "Have you heard about Eire Bank? But of course you have, having been in Sneem. I suppose it's in suspect taste to mention deals, given what's transpired, but life must go on, and even with all the . . . distractions, Shane Frost surely worked a miracle out there at Parknasilla."

"Do you own a piece of Eire Bank?" McGarr asked.

"Did. I *did* own a piece of Eire Bank. Three percent. Wish it was three hundred percent, but it's a done deal, don't you know. That's catchy, isn't it? Somebody ought to write a tune with that line. You know, 'It's love/ I snatched her flower/ It's a done deal, don't your know.' "

Harney looked down on the bandages that sheathed McGarr's upper body. "Do I hold the glass to your lips?"

"Straw," said McGarr, picking up one on the hospital-bed table and lowering his mouth to its end.

"Now, that's a first. Hogan's Own through a straw."

"Better than a needle," said McGarr, which caused Harney to laugh overloud and overlong.

Pulling up a chair, he had to remove the plastic tote sack with the bound sheaf of photocopies before sitting. The printing on the sack said, PARKNASILLA in tangerine letters on a buff background. A GREAT SOUTHERN HOTEL.

"So—you got Gladden and the others." Harney's girth was such that his breathing was voluble, and his eyes narrowed down on McGarr in a kind of sly smile. "To your continuing good health and progress in the world." He raised his glass.

McGarr closed his eyes and pulled on the straw; he wondered how many of his clothes he could manage to put on by himself. He would close the door and leave a note that he had taken a stroll and would be back soon, which would give him something of a lead. It would take him—what?—a half hour to walk to the Castle, and he might be lucky enough to catch a cab outside the hospital, if there weren't any reporters about.

"May I be frank?"

Better than Francine, McGarr thought, the warm seep of the malt making him feel momentarily buoyant in spite of the continuing pain.

The new cigar was out, Harney holding the flame from a large gold lighter to its end. "Paddy Power's note cards—do you have them?"

McGarr blinked, but he did not glance at the sack that had been placed against the wall.

"Did you *read* them?"

Again.

"Can you tell me what they say?" Harney swirled the cigar. "Generally, I mean."

"Generally, they're"—McGarr rejected the words explosive, inflamatory—"revelatory."

"Of what? Give me an instance."

"The debt. How it was derived, who particularly it has enriched, and who is *not* paying it back." He watched Harney's smile sag. "Other matters—government participation in your housing scheme in Clondalkin and elsewhere. How the permissions were gained, roads built, palms greased—that sort of thing. Eire Bank, as you would suspect, merits a full heading. Stack of cards so big." McGarr held out two index fingers to demonstrate the size. "The only heading larger is that for Sean Dermot O'Duffy," *who would be canonized in your newspaper*, he did not add. McGarr tugged on the malt.

Harney extracted the cigar from his gob and examined its gluey end. "Which is why you didn't turn them over to Farrell."

Or anybody else.

"Which is why you even risked your career to keep people from reading them?"

McGarr only tilted his head.

"Who else has read them?"

"Gladden, Gretta Osbourne perhaps, and certainly Nell Power. She had them long enough to read them in their entirety."

"I've spoken to Nell," *who would do nothing to jeopardize the Eire Bank deal*, he did not have to add. "Shane Frost?"

McGarr thought for a moment. If Kieran Coyne could be believed, somebody had dropped the note cards off in the hallway outside of Coyne's office. If it had been Frost, would he have had the time or inclination to read them? Why, when he probably knew most of the revealing information that the cards contained? "Maybe."

"Anybody else at all?"

McGarr shook his head.

"Not your wife?"

McGarr only stared at the man. He did not want to make Noreen a target. Harney was not a gunman, but with the stakes high, so too was the propensity for risk. Again he thought of Eire Bank and Shane Frost. What was the price of two more lives? Or three, counting Nell Power.

With the cigar in the center of his mouth, Harney leaned back and folded his arms across his considerable chest. "So, what now?"

McGarr did not honestly know. He would consult with McKeon and O'Shaughnessy, who, apart from Ward, were the only two men he trusted. Only then would he decide.

"Farrell won't last forever," Harney went on. "In fact, there're some who think he got it all wrong—how you handled the Power investigation, Gladden, and surely the note cards. Already the *Times* is indicating—"

McGarr nodded. Thank God for the *Times*.

"You saw it? And I've heard other rumblings. You know, from Joe and Jane Soap. Nobody can protect a public figure from a Gladden or an Oswald, who will find a way to do what they will, regardless. Which wasn't your job anyway. You were investigating what Gladden was calling a murder, though there's plenty to say he was the murderer himself. And then it wasn't as if Farrell had had no warning, was it? With Gladden ranting the day before and the village crawling with the police and the army. And his rifle, of course. He might have used that to assassinate the taosieach and not your wife's Rover."

Harney straightened up in the chair and pulled the cigar from his mouth. "It occurred to me immediately, you see—why was the vehicle not searched? And in it both the rifle and the dead man he had been secretly treating and he hoped the Gardai would mistake for himself, after he drove the Land Rover over a cliff."

McGarr knew why. As a local and a medical doctor, Gladden was probably known to the Guards who had been assigned that end of the village. He might have told them that the man was sleeping or had been sedated, and he was only waiting for the bridge to be cleared so he could drive him back to his house in Waterville or some other place to the west.

Harney stood and began pacing. "No—your command was—is—the Murder Squad. Also, you had earlier conferred with the taosieach who had advised you *not* to hassle the poor demented Dr. Gladden. My own son was a witness to that. In retrospect, it was a mistake on O'Duffy's part—one of the few in his illustrious career, which is unparalleled in modern Irish history—but certainly it wasn't *your* mistake. You didn't take Gladden in for assaulting you because his arrest would have provided him the—"

"Forum," McGarr supplied.

"—that he so desperately desired. The note cards? Well"—he turned to McGarr—"the reason you didn't turn them over is there *were* none. They got destroyed in your wife's car, the one Gladden fired at. From then on it was nothing but a brilliant, brave, and selfless ruse designed to lure Gladden back to Dublin, which worked. You had to lead Farrell and the government and the press and the people on, even to filling those three plastic sacks with the blank note cards from Shane's father's chemist shop and carrying them with you to Rathmines."

Again Harney examined the cigar. "Did I give you one of these, Peter? They're grand and help a fella muse and speculate." Out of his jacket he pulled a fistful of cigars that he placed on the bedside table. From the bottle he topped up both glasses and drank off his own in a swallow.

"What we *would* have to know, however, is that the cards—*all* copies—are destroyed. Utterly."

But then, thought McGarr, he'd only have Harney's word that the "government," as it were, would fulfill its side of the—was it?—bargain.

"There'd be hell to pay, if they ever came back to haunt us." Harney reached for his hat and topcoat. "Well, now—I'll let you think on the matter. I must be off. You can reach me anytime through the *Spectator*. Just tell them who you are, and somebody will get back to you with a place we can meet."

Harney began stepping toward the door but turned back. "Did I ask you how old you are? Fifty-one, I'd hazard. Four years from retirement, if you choose. Think of it, four years as commissioner and then on to something else, like the Dail. Given the publicity and how you bagged Gladden, you'll be a lifelong hero and simply unbeatable from wherever you choose to stand for election.

"Wife leave that?" he asked without pause, pointing to the plastic tote sack against the wall.

McGarr nodded.

"Can I ask what's in it?"

"A photocopy of Paddy Power's note cards."

Harney's body rocked; he had guessed right. A puff of fine blue smoke sailed from the cigar. He blinked. "Can I . . . take it with me?"

McGarr shook his head.

Harney considered the sack further. "Why not?"

"Because there are things in those cards that you weren't meant to see."

"Meant by a dead man."

McGarr nodded. "Think if they were your cards."

"But I'd be dead and what would it matter? To me."

McGarr said nothing.

"Tell me now—I wasn't meant to see them, but you were?"

"No, but I did in the course of an investigation."

"And that makes you arbiter of who should and shouldn't see them? You've arrogated that right to yourself and yourself alone."

McGarr cocked his head. "It's not as if I asked or was appointed. Another way to look at it is—Paddy Power never intended *anybody* to see them in their present form. Many of the cards are his most private thoughts, filled with confessions and confidences and the like."

"Which are safe with you?"

"I don't own a newspaper," *or have a son who wishes to be taosieach*, he did not add. "Thanks for the bottle and the smokes, which are much appreciated."

Harney's eyes were fixed on the sack, which, used effectively, could be a potent weapon in his political arsenal. He then glanced at McGarr in the bed in his bandages.

"The door is behind you, sir. Why spoil an otherwise-pleasant visit?" When Harney still did not move, McGarr laboriously pulled back the covers. There, resting on his stomach, was his Walther, which collected Harney's eyes.

"What—you'd shoot me?"

"Think of it this way. We're already in a hospital, and you'll probably not die, though my aim won't be perfect."

"Don't you have the original cards and another copy?" Harney had been speaking to somebody—Frost, McGarr bet.

He said nothing.

"Haven't you understood what we've just been discussing? It's your future, man. These cards will either make you or break you.'' Harney's tone was now stern. "There is no third course.''

McGarr could think of several, including mailing the originals to a rival and uncommitted newspaper, though that would be as wrong as allowing Harney to walk out with the photocopy. "I appreciate the . . . *counseling*, is it?"

Wrinkles furrowed Harney's brow. "You wouldn't shoot me.''

McGarr's hands moved toward the Walther. He worked the slide, then pointed the barrel at the sack. "As I was saying, thank you for the chat, the bottle, and the cigars. They'll warm my afternoon."

The muscle in Harney's jaw tensed, as he bit down on the cigar, which puffed. He turned for the door. "I can hardly believe it! The son of a bitch would have shot me from his *hospital* bed!'' He chuckled. "Now *there*'s a hard man for you. I only hope he can dial my number as easily." At the door Harney stopped and winked. "Still friends?"

"Is it here we sing 'It's All in the Game'?"

Harney began laughing. It was the same rich, deep, contagious laugh that he had entered with.

The moment the door closed, McGarr made a phone call, then began the painful process of easing himself out of bed and into his clothes. At the closet he managed to fit his legs into his trousers and to slip on his shoes if not his socks. Somehow he got shirt, suit coat, and mac slipped over his shoulders, and the last garment buttoned to the chest. His hat, which he needed if only for anonymity, he put on by placing it on the back of a chair, then sitting in the chair and easing the fedora over his brow.

With the Parknasilla sack in hand, he waited until the hallway was nearly empty of nurses, then made his break for the service stairs. A sizable group of reporters had gathered in the lobby of the hospital, but a Garda public-affairs official was speaking to them, and McGarr, walking beside a nurse who was pushing an invalid in a wheelchair, managed to make the street unseen.

There, he found a cab. Rummaging through the Parknasilla sack to make certain it contained the complete photocopy of Power's notes, he also discovered Noreen's voice-activated tape recorder. On it was a note that had been attached by the cord of an earplug. Written in her neat script, it said, "Cued to Frost/Osbourne exchange. Fast-Forward to beep, then Play."

McGarr unwrapped the cord, placed the plug in his ear, and sat back and listened.

Passing Dublin Castle, where his office was located, he glanced up and was struck by how worn and dirty the place looked. Something should be done about it, but when and by whom? With staff and budget cutbacks there was no time and no money, and then nobody, not even he, really, cared for more than the few moments it took to consider some more pressing matter. Like O'Duffy, Sneem, and Gladden. Or Paddy Power and Gretta Osbourne. And the debt and who got what. And Harry Harney and son.

It was institutional plaque, he decided. A kind of governmental arteriosclerosis in which facts and figures just got lost or were vaguely and transiently remembered. Things happened and got lost. Detail piled upon detail, and particular facts, such as those in Paddy Power's note cards and McGarr's own files, really didn't matter.

He studied the statue of Justice that topped the main entrance gate. He hoped the jingle that was known in the last century no longer applied, at least to him. "Statue of Justice, mark well her station/," the lyric went, "Her face to the Castle, her back to the nation."

CHAPTER 26

On History, Which Is Not Life

THE SKY HAD turned leaden again, and wide flakes of wet snow were landing with the delicacy of holy wafers on the windscreen. Outside in the street, however, the slush reminded McGarr that he was not wearing socks, and he shuffled as quickly as his open shoes and strapped arms would allow toward the warm yellow lights of Hogan's, a turn-of-the-century, center-city pub.

In spite of her father's death, Bresnahan was at the bar, a drink in front of her. Wearing some tight wrap of stylish, somber wool, she was staring down at her glass. Even sitting on a tall barstool, her long, shapely legs reached the floor; twined, they had become objects of momentary adoration, whenever a sip permitted eyes to view beyond the lip of a glass.

McGarr placed his plastic sack on the bar and waited for her to raise her head.

"Chief," she said. "I was told you'd be coming."

McGarr's eyes flickered toward the snugs.

"Bernie's already here. He's in back now," she went on bravely. "Hogan gave him the carton with the original note cards and the Nell Power copies." There was a pause, while her gray eyes, which were brimming with tears, met his, then dropped to the sack. "Another copy?"

"My own kind of insurance."

"Did you see the article in the *Cork Examiner*? I didn't think anybody could possibly support anything about Mossie Gladden now, but there they are, saying if the cards had been made public, maybe Gladden wouldn't have been moved to do what he did."

"Busy fingers." He meant that somebody down at the *Cork Examiner* had had some space to fill, but it showed how everything that had happened in Sneem would be played over and over in the media. McGarr waited until she glanced at him again. "You don't have to be here."

"Nor do you, Chief. But you are. And it's only right that I should deliver this in person." Across the top of the desk she slid a typewritten sheet of paper, which McGarr scanned. It was her resignation.

"But don't you want to wait a bit to see how you feel in a couple of days, a week, a month even? I'm no longer in charge, as you know, but I'm sure Liam—"

But Bresnahan was shaking her head. "The funeral's on Tuesday, and I have my mother to look after. I'm just in town to pick up a few things. Sorry about the phone, Chief. When we got cut off, I thought it was just a malfunction. It never occurred to me that—"

"How could you have known? And you had so much else on your mind. I hope that's not what this is all about." He shoved the resignation toward her, as though to have her take it back. When she did not, he went on, "We're all very sorry about your father. If there's anything we can do—"

She shook her head and looked up at the windows, her gray eyes bright with tears. "Even he knew it was coming, and he left the farm and my mother in good shape. She'll not want for much."

"And you plan to do what? *Live* there?"

She nodded, and a single tear rolled down the creamy skin of her face. Somehow McGarr just didn't see her back on a farm in Kerry; she had grown beyond that and would be lost without Dublin.

"Heard from Hughie?"

She nodded. "They'll be letting him out of hospital today. In Limerick. His left leg is in a cast, but otherwise he says he'll be fine."

"Going down to fetch him?"

She shook her head and began digging in the purse for a hankie. Tears were flowing freely now. "I don't know. Rory O'Suilleabhain?" she asked. "He's simply beside himself, asking me to marry him. I know it's just the losses—his mother and my father—and him grieving, but he's the fella from the next farm, and the local T.D. . . . ?'' She glanced up at McGarr, her eyes defiant, as if challenging him to tell her she was wrong. ''He's not much, and Rory plans to stand for the seat. He'll win.'' She sighed. ''I don't know. Maybe I'll be seeing you again.'' She blotted her eyes, then stood and turned, as if she would simply walk away.

''Whoa! Wait a minute. Sit down for a moment.'' McGarr waited until she had and looked up at him. ''Tell me this now, do you love this Rory O'Suilleabhain?''

She shook her head. Tears were running freely now, and she began blowing her nose.

''What about Hughie?''

''I don't *know*,'' she said through honks.

McGarr palmed up her resignation and stuffed it into the pocket of his coat. ''Do me a favor, Rut'ie? I've got to make a phone call. Carry that into the snug. I don't want it hanging about.'' He meant the plastic sack with the photocopies of Power's notes.

''But aren't you going to decide what to do with them?''

McGarr nodded. It was not his way to give advice, especially to friends, but maybe if she understood exactly what she would be missing . . . Power's cards were nothing if not fascinating to somebody such as she, who would know the players by name and reputation.

On the other hand, there was the ambitious Rory O'Suilleabhain to consider. Did McGarr trust her not to tell him? Why not? Without the originals the information contained in them was merely rumor and innuendo, which had been Gladden's dilemma.

And finally, the cards would get her mind off her father and . . . decisions. Hughie Ward was, after all, McGarr's protégé, and anything he could do to advance Ward's interests, he would. ''Care for a peek?''

Like a racehorse, Bresnahan's handsome head came up. ''You're joking.''

''I'm not. You know where the private snug is? The barman will buzz you through.''

An hour passed, then two. And three. From Hogan's office, McGarr kept trying to phone Ward in Limerick, but all lines were continually in use. McGarr was tempted to say it was a police emergency, but—if the operator checked—it might give away both where McGarr was and the fact that he had something for Ward.

When finally McGarr entered the snug, he found Bresnahan with her legs stretched across the tiny room toward a coal fire that was glowing in the hearth. She was looking into the bottom of an empty glass.

McKeon had out his Colt Python, which he appeared to be cleaning.

O'Shaughnessy was still reading a last inch or two of cards, holding them away from his eyes at an odd angle.

McGarr set fresh glasses before each, and they waited for the older man to finish. Beyond the lathed and carved wood of the snug, beyond the leaded-glass window above it that pictured a rose, a shamrock, and a brimming pint of Guinness, McGarr listened to the city—the groan and wheeze of a bus braking, steps on the footpath, bells from the Castle, which was just up the street—and thought how it was just another moment in the lives of perhaps every other Dubliner within hearing of Hogan's, but a crucial time in the lives of the four people gathered in the snug. Five counting Ward, who was not present.

Finally O'Shaughnessy read the last card. He then squared and banded that group and dropped it into the sack with M.J.P. FROST, CHEMIST, SNEEM, CO. KERRY on the side. Looking up, he said, "I don't know exactly when it happened—sometime in the sixties with people like O'Duffy and the debt and all—but a massive—" He paused, as though groping for a word.

"Recrudescence," Bresnahan supplied.

"Exactly, Ruthie. A massive recrudescence set in. The government discovered it could lie to the people and nobody seemed to care. And since it could lie, why not steal too, which they did, if Power can be believed.

"Then everything went haywire. The murder rate, as we know, and drugs, and all the problems in the North. I hate to say this, but in many ways Gladden was right with all his blather about creditors being predators and returning to ancient values that were cherished by our race and forgetting about the rest of the world."

O'Shaughnessy sighed and reached for a fresh drink on the tray on the table that separated them. "Maybe all this should be exposed and made public, but it would make me feel dirty to be Irish. Nobody wants to hear this about their leaders—all the dirty dealing, the graft, and corruption of public trust. Even their personal indiscretions and sordid affairs. Especially not now with the papers making O'Duffy out to be another Kennedy or a De Valera."

He took a sip and added, "But, you know, it *should* be told. All of it. Which is the only way things will ever get any better."

Said McKeon, "Who are we to censor history? What was done was done and should be exposed. Let the guilty be punished."

There was the word again, thought McGarr. Guilt, which loomed so large in Irish life, private and public. But guilty of what? The accusations of a dead man? He wondered how much of what was alleged could actually be proven in court. And what damage any attempt to do so would cause.

No, the allegations contained in Paddy Power's note cards, were they to be mailed, say, to each of Dublin's four newspapers, would then be tried in the court of public opinion, which was the least fair that McGarr knew. Every word of the note cards would be considered truth, and all parties mentioned painted with the same brush. "Rut'ie?" he asked.

She was now looking down into her new drink, turning it this way and that, letting the curtain of amber fluid flow down the bevel of the squat cocktail glass. "In moral terms, it's a genuine dilemma, is it not? As the sergeant has just said—"

"Bernie," McKeon suggested. She was part of them now, and no matter what she decided in regard to her career, her relationship to the three men in the snug had definitely changed. Whatever decision they made there would bind them for life.

"—as Bernie has just said, who are we to censor history? But I suppose the more basic question is, who are we?" She glanced up at McGarr, who nodded to say she should go on. "We're the police, who deal in facts that are provable in a court of law. How many suspects have we brought in whom *we* knew were guilty, but we just didn't have the proof? And how many others have we brought to court *thinking* we had proof, only to have it dismissed or derogated or thrown out for one thing or another?

"If we're now judging the value of the evidence before us, I'd say what we have mainly is smoke and shadow and not much more. Some of the allegations about who got what from the government for which considerations *might* be proven, but we don't even know if laws were broken. Or at least I don't, my brief having been murder during my tenure.

"Power's main contention seems to be that the way the borrowed debt money was divided up and how it will be paid back is unfair. Well—that's what the Dail is for, to dispense fairness. Often it seems to fail, but it's the highest and best court we have, and we have to live with its shortcomings.

"Which still leaves us here with the moral dilemma—who are

we to judge these cards and what should be done with them? Though we must.''

Or, rather, McGarr must. Three pair of eyes turned to him, and he explained the deal that Harney had outlined earlier in his hospital room. "It makes the decision doubly difficult. I wouldn't want Harney to think I truckled and went along with the easy and self-interested choice.''

"Ah, the hell with Harney,'' said McKeon, who was obviously tiring of the chat. "Let him and them think what he will. This country has already made all the martyrs it will ever need. Consider the job they've done on you already. You couldn't resign now, if you chose, with all their allegations flying about. Half the public would think you were a party to O'Duffy's assassination and the other half that you were the author of a cover-up.

"As long as the cards don't fall into Harney's hands, we've done the country a favor, and if you can help yourself into the bargain, all the better.''

Said O'Shaughnessy, "Remember, now—it's not just yourself anymore. You've got a wife and child to think of.''

"Here—gimme the feckin' t'ings, I'll show you what we should do with them.'' McKeon reached into the shadows of the floor, picked up the sack of original note cards, and dumped them on the coal fire.

Bresnahan's head snapped to McGarr. "Is that what you want, Chief? Perhaps we should keep a copy and release it—''

"After the prominent figures are dead?''

She nodded. "For the sake of history.''

McGarr had thought of that, but, he imagined, some one or other of the O'Duffy/Harney inner circle would take care of history in the way that Power had intended. And McGarr did not wish his own death be remembered primarily as the occasion of the destruction of some other persons' reputations. "Did you ever think that releasing the cards at any time would play right into Gladden's hands? In an oblique way it would provide a reason for what he did at the bridge.''

Obviously she had not. She looked away at the fire. "When there can be none.''

Both O'Shaughnessy and McKeon nodded.

A few of the cards had begun burning immediately.

McGarr stood. "While you're about the rest, I've a phone call to make. But, mind—what just happened here is between ourselves alone.''

"*Sinn Fein*,'' McKeon chortled. From between his teeth he

sprayed whisky that showered the smoldering mound of note cards and burst into bright flame. "We need more accelerant here. Tell Hogan, more! Rounds and rounds!" He began laughing, flicking sheet after sheet of the photocopies onto the fire until the hearth was filled with the acrid rainbow flame of photosensitive paper.

When Harry Harney finally rang back, McGarr said, "I'll watch with interest your rehabilitation of my good name. If all goes according to our conversation this morning, you'll get your wish."

"But how will I know you've destroyed them?"

"You'll just have to take my word."

"Which is good."

As was my name before I got involved with the likes of you, thought McGarr. "Some other things—" He now thought of Ward and Bresnahan and Rory O'Suilleabhain, who would soon be a T.D. He did not want to interfere, but at the same time he took care of his own, when he could, and he would not see Ward eclipsed by some culchie farmer with dung on his boots. "I want a special commendation for Hugh Ward."

Harney grunted.

"Also, I'd like him named acting chief superintendent of the Murder Squad. In my absence."

"But aren't there more senior—"

"I'll take care of that. But I also want Bernie McKeon advanced to superintendent. Also I want a writ, back-dated to Tuesday last, allowing me to install a listening device in room two-sixteen at Parknasilla."

"Ah, *McGarr*—who do you think I am? I only own a newspaper. No judges, no courts."

McGarr waited until he heard Harney grunt.

"And finally I want Ward's first official act as acting superintendent backed by you, your son, and all the resources at your command including the paper. No matter what it is."

"You ask too much. I can't be giving you *carte*—" There was a pause and then: "Can't you at least tell me what it'll be?"

"No."

"Why not?"

"Because you won't like it. At first. Ultimately, you'll see, it'll be good for your son, who'll be perceived as his own man."

"Ah, Christ—what *is* this, McGarr? You playing politics now?"

"You do all the time. The difference is, I hold the cards, and not in a manner of speaking." He waited again. "Now—do we have a deal?"

"No! Of course not! I need to know chapter and—"

McGarr rang off.

Seconds later the phone rang again. "Never, *ever*, hang up on me again. Is *that* understood? Nobody hangs up on Harry Harney," he blustered over what sounded like his sempiternal cigar. "McGarr? You there, McGarr?"

"Do we have a deal?" McGarr asked in a mild voice.

"Of course we have a goddamned deal. You just better keep your half of the bargain."

"Ditto." McGarr again laid the receiver in its yoke.

Now he only had Noreen to assuage. Doubtless he would hear how history, of which she was a twice-degreed handmaiden, had been corrupted. Fortunately life was more complicated than history and definitely more forgiving; and she would still love him even though he was wrong.

CHAPTER 27

Death Denial

THE ROMAN CATHOLIC cemetery in Sneem lies to the north of the village, along a road that leads to the mountains. It has been placed on a hill with all graves facing east and the rising sun.

The monument that says BRESNAHAN was erected in the nineteenth century; its limestone obelisk is worn smooth and looks almost translucent at the edges, like mother-of-pearl. Smaller stones that mark the graves of individual members of the family span a wide arc near the crest of the hill.

After the requiem mass to which he arrived late and left early, newly appointed Acting Chief Superintendent of the Serious Crimes Unit Hugh Ward got to the cemetery much in advance of the funeral cortege. Without the aid of his driver he mounted the snowy hill. Walking slowly with cast and cane through the flowered mounds of the several freshly filled graves, Ward wondered how many he might have saved could he have exerted more force on the wheel and crashed Gladden's hurtling truck into a wall or a building. Not his own life, for certain.

Which was guilt, he decided—that he was alive and they were dead. In this churchyard alone there were four new graves that he could see. Five now when he came upon and nearly stumbled into the freshly dug hole for "Thomas Aloysius Bresnahan." And still there was

Power, Ward thought, turning his face into wisps of wind-driven snow toward the very pinnacle of the hill where stood a short, wide woman silhouetted against the dun winter sky.

She was wrapped in a long black fur coat and a stylish Cossack hat to match. Down in the car park was a black chauffeured Rolls, in which, Ward assumed, she had come. With strong, sure steps she approached him. "You're Inspector Ward. Or, rather, newly made Chief Superintendent Ward, who saved all those people at the bridge. I congratulate you on your promotion."

Ward said nothing, only regarded her dark, quick eyes and tanned, leathery complexion that he had seen before. Given her coloring and regular features, she looked not a little like Ward himself, and he imagined that an observer, seeing them standing there, might mistake them for mother and son.

"I'm Nell Power," she went on. A slight smile now bracketed the corners of her mouth, and her eyes glinted as they played over his face. "I was just saying a few prayers for Paddy, who'll need them. Before leaving for Dublin.

"Who's this?" With a toe of her shoe she nudged a little dirt into the grave. "Ah, yes—Tom Bresnahan, a big, strong, sober farmer. A good man and true, if you fancy the type."

"You don't?"

Nell Power made a face. "Not really. Oh, I suppose, he was great for a father. Raised a rare, handsome daughter, he did, though I suspect you know more about her than you'd let on to me."

"Shane Frost is more your type?"

"When he's handy. Actually young, dark, daring fellas, such as yourself, are more my cup of tea."

To be quaffed off at a swallow, Ward thought, remembering how she had taken Frost.

"If I give you my card, will you promise to stop round? I have a wee place in Herbert Park. Call first. I'll make sure we're alone."

"Interview, you mean?"

"Intriguing word, isn't it? But I suppose you have many intriguing interviews."

"A perk of the job." Ward smiled into her black eyes. "Is it the Eire Bank shareholders meeting you're returning for?"

She nodded. "Pity what happened to Gretta when she had so much to live for. Now, I suppose, some foundation will benefit from all her hard work and sacrifice."

"Like with your husband's estate." Frost had announced that the bulk of Power's great fortune would be left to the Paddy Power Fund, which would continue to support Irish charities.

She nodded. "Being in service to Paddy could not have been easy."

Following him into the grave harder still, Ward thought.

She glanced down the road where a hearse and funeral cortege had appeared. She removed a card from a pocket and slipped it into Ward's hand, her long fingernails grazing his palm. "I understand you're an athlete. Perhaps we can golf together." Or swing, her smile said. "I could teach you a thing or two, I'm sure."

Ward raised an eyebrow.

"About life, don't you know. Winners and losers. Your former chief wasn't educable, but now it's your Murder Squad, isn't it? I must be off now."

"Not staying for the ceremony?"

"I think my welcome would be in some doubt. Had Paddy not been—what's your term for his death?"

"Murdered."

"—T. A. Bresnahan might still be alive. There're sure to be some who think I wanted nothing less, absurd as it is. But that's Kerry." She clasped the sable collar to her throat and turned to her car.

And thus Ward was standing alone by the open grave when the funeral procession arrived.

Rory O'Suilleabhain got out first and helped Bresnahan and her mother from the lead car. He then joined McGarr, O'Shaughnessy, McKeon, and two other men, who by their dated funeral suits were obviously from the area.

O'Suilleabhain himself would benefit from Bresnahan's tutelage, Ward thought, thinking of the phone call he had had with McGarr earlier in the morning. O'Suilleabhain's topcoat was also out-of-date. The vent was too long, the hem too short, and the cut too small through the shoulders; he was showing too much wrist, collar, and bum, especially now in bending with three of the other men to lift the coffin from the hearse. McGarr in his bandages merely walked at its side.

Bresnahan approached Ward, careful of the snow and ice and holding the arm of a tall, dark, much older woman who was evidently her mother. "How are yah?" Bresnahan asked. Their eyes met for only a moment before she wrenched hers away.

"I want you to meet my mother. This is Hugh Ward, the Guard who—"

"So sorry," said Ward, taking her bony hand.

"Oh, yes. Your . . . *colleague*." Apparently she and Bresnahan had discussed him, and she did not care for the word. Or him. "You're the young man who, they're saying, saved so many others." Her eyes flickered toward the grave.

"And you, me, and Rory, Ma—if you'll remember. We were right in the path of the thing, before the wheel turned."

Her mother nodded, but her eyes had suddenly filled with tears.

Said Bresnahan to Ward, "Are you coming back to the house afterward? The Chief and Bernie and the Super—"

But O'Suilleabhain was now by their side, all puffed up with himself. "Yes, you must. You're—"

"Hugh Ward."

"That's right. I met you at Parknasilla just before—. And then it was you who—" O'Suilleabhain's voice was too vibrant; his immense mitt came out and engulfed Ward's hand.

Said Ward, "I'm sorry to hear about your mother. And your friend." He turned his head to the open grave.

"Thanks. Thanks so much. I'll see you back at *Nead an Iolair*." And he was off. The priest had arrived; O'Suilleabhain was definitely the man in charge. Ward now noticed that the press was also in attendance. Photos were being taken, and several journalists were approaching him.

"See you there?" asked Bresnahan, as her mother began moving toward the priest.

"If you like." Ward moved toward McGarr, who was adept at handling the press; Ward could take a lesson.

"Hughie—how goes it?" McGarr said, smiling to see Ward back in dapper form and at least his face unmarked from his skirmish.

"I've been better. And yourself?"

McGarr tried to raise his arms. "I'd phone Amnesty International, could I reach the dial."

A flashgun burst in their faces, and O'Shaughnessy stepped forward to have a word with the offending cameraman.

Said McGarr to Ward, "I've a present for you from Noreen and me. To celebrate your promotion." He indicated the pocket of his topcoat. "You'll have to dig it out yourself."

A bottle, Ward thought as he reached down and felt the weight in the pocket. After his experience in the bar at Parknasilla, he didn't think he'd ever drink again. His hand came up with a tape recorder of the sort that were now used to take notes. It was tiny, slim, and black, and could easily slip into a pocket or a purse. Under the earplug cord, which had been wrapped around the body, was a note from Noreen.

"Follow the instructions, then follow your nose," said McGarr cryptically. "You going back to the house?"

Ward nodded, as he studied what he could see of the note.

"Ride with us."

Said McKeon, "Why, for Jesus' sake, when the young dodger has himself a driver?"

Ward turned to McKeon and O'Shaughnessy who, after all, were more senior and should have been offered the Murder Squad command ahead of him.

"Not to worry," said O'Shaughnessy. "It's all part of a grand plan, you'll see."

Before Ward could ask what, the priest raised the cross he was carrying and asked the Three-in-One God to bless His son Thomas and the souls gathered there. Mindful of the snow, which was squalling now, he hurried through the ceremony. A handful of dirt was tossed on the casket, followed by the usual covey of bright, descending flowers, and soon they were back in the cars.

Said McKeon to Ward, "Was that Nell Power you were chatting up when we pulled in?"

Ward was trying to peer through the shaded glass of the first car. It was the seating arrangement in the limousine that concerned him.

"Was it her card she slipped in your pocket?"

Ward nodded again, and McKeon's hand appeared in front of him. "She's more my speed."

"Dead slow," said O'Shaughnessy.

"Play Hughie the tape," said McGarr. And to Ward, he explained, "We had it dubbed and the sound improved, in case anything should happen to the one in the machine. Voice-activated. Noreen placed the thing next to the receiver of the baby monitor you put in Frost's room, and forgot it in all the tumult after the bridge."

"The other lucky part is the phone call," McKeon went on, inserting a tape in the dashboard player of O'Shaughnessy's car. "It identifies both of them. With a voice match, we've been told, it has a good chance of holding up in court. They'll fight it, of course, but I'm thinking we can get one or the other of them to crack."

McKeon adjusted the sound, and through what had become a driving snow storm they listened to the voices of Shane Frost, Gretta Osbourne, and Nell Power in Frost's Parknasilla suite on the night that Osbourne died. It was as much music to their ears as they could hope to hear.

When the tape had finished, McGarr turned to Ward, who offered his hand. "Thanks, Chief."

"Nothing like a fast start."

"Or a slow ending," said McKeon. "Where is this place? I always knew Rut'ie was a hick, but this is re-dick-i-liss."

The line of cars had stopped so the limousine could negotiate the stone walls of the entrance gate. The four men in O'Shaughnessy's car looked up.

Because of the snow and the house, which was painted white, they saw only a great swath of ivory mountain bounded by sea and storm sky. In the middle was a long, welcoming band of yellow-lighted windows with jets of fine blue peat smoke spewing from four separate chimneys. The barns, hayricks, and stables, which lay beyond, had been set off in a pretty semicircle, as if dug into the lee flank of the mountain, and on the windward, ocean side a sentinel copse of towering Norwegian spruce stood as a break. Those too were covered with snow, and looked like they had been composed with artistic care.

Said McKeon, "I always wondered where they got those pretty scenes for Christmas cards. Now I know. Janie—why didn't Rut'ie ever let on the place was heaven."

Janie? McGarr thought. When was the last time McKeon had uttered a euphemism of such delicacy? In the next moment he would be claiming he misspoke himself. "The way Rut'ie explained it to Noreen—all we can see to the left, Rut'ie and the mother now own. All we can see to right nearly back to the village—"

Three heads followed McGarr's hand, which pointed in that direction.

"—is O'Suilleabhain's."

Because of the snow, they could not see that far, but it looked like leagues.

The breath Ward pulled in was nearly audible. The layout explained so much. Sure, O'Suilleabhain was a big, handsome, and undoubtedly capable culchie, thought Ward. And, sure, his prospects were excellent. But what Ward was looking at here was perhaps the most beautiful—how many? five blinking miles, maybe—of Ireland that he had seen in a long time. Especially under the present conditions. And how could anybody (even the woman he loved and who loved him, he suspected) reject out of hand the possibility of uniting both massive parcels in the only kind of perpetuity that meant anything to the people who lived out here? Hadn't she explained so herself?

And there *he* was, a no-longer-exactly-young man who possessed only a bachelor pad, which was mortgaged to the eaves, thousands of pounds of credit-card debt, and the reputation as a amateur pugilist of note, which would get him nothing but a pat on the back and the probability of an aneurysm at sixty-five. Also, there was the superintendency that only made him realize how much McGarr, O'Shaughnessy, and McKeon had done for him.

A few minutes later they found themselves in the warm and commodious farmhouse. Ward enjoyed friendly people. He also liked the sense of community, which, as a Dubliner, he had long since learned to do without and which he felt here. Everybody seemed to know who he and McGarr and McKeon and O'Shaughnessy were. Soon they had drinks and were shown a banquet board that was brimming with roasts and hams, potatoes in a variety of preparations, then fresh and pickled things in a number that he had not seen in some time. As well as breads, cakes, and pies.

Ward also liked understated things that allowed the simple quality of an object to declare its presence. The floor of the kitchen was slate, flagged and solid. Whole inches, Ward thought. Heels fell on it as though landing on the bedrock of the mountain. The woodwork was black walnut. An Aga, such as McGarr had in his own kitchen—but larger, grander, definitely a classic—squatted like a warm, smiling Buddha against an interior wall of the kitchen.

The furnishings of the dining room, which was crowded with people, and a sitting room and parlor, were motley but solid, and everybody seemed anxious to meet and speak to him. Bresnahan's parents had had the sense—to say nothing of the readies—to buy quality. Why had she never told him any of this? He had thought they were . . . peasants, pure and simple. Did it matter that they were more? Of course not. But—

McKeon handed him a drink and said, "Well now, Chief Super—am I looking at new eyes as well as a new leg?"

Ward only set the drink aside; O'Suilleabhain had appeared before them. "So, Hughie—tell us about your career as a pugilist. What was it like? Was it fun or just, you know, the challenge?"

"Not over yet," said McKeon. "Hughie's been known to take shots at yokes bigger than yourself. Last one weighed a couple thousand pounds and was made of steel."

"Threw *roving* punches that traveled at sixty-five miles an hour," O'Suilleabhain joked, tossing back his rich tangle of black curls and laughing at the ceiling. Which was confidence, Ward decided; O'Suilleabhain was acting as if he had already taken title to the property.

Saying he just wanted a word with Bresnahan before having to return to Dublin, Ward excused himself. He found her in the kitchen with an apron on, readying further platters of food.

"Don't we look domestic."

She only glanced at him. "I've done the same for you, if you'll remember. On more than a few occasions."

"Practice for this, the *real* thing."

Well, it wasn't as though you ever told me it *was* the real thing between us, Bresnahan thought. With you it was always fun and games, and no more. "I suppose you're referring to my resignation?"

"Which hasn't been accepted."

"It will be, after a while. Somebody from the Commissioner's Office will come snooping around, wondering why I'm not at work."

Not if the commissioner is Peter McGarr, thought Ward. "Will you tell me *why*?"

Bresnahan straightened up and wiped her hands on the apron. "I will, sure." She was angry at somebody or something, but she didn't exactly know who or what. "There's no future in it. For me."

"I don't know what you mean." Ward could see Bresnahan eventually taking command of some high-visibility administrative post. The superintendency of Public Relations or Community Affairs, where being a big, good-looking, well-spoken woman would be a definite plus.

Her eyes met his, and she blinked, coming at least a little to herself. "I mean, obviously there's a future for you. You're young, a man, well known in men's circles. You're quick, combative and . . . impervious. Everybody knows *you're* tough."

"Me? I'm too sensitive." She shook her head. "To see what you have to go through just to keep yourself from being disgraced." She sighed and looked back at the platter of food.

"You mean the Chief?"

She nodded. "And O'Duffy and the Harneys and the note cards. I think I might have gone back before I read them, but now?" Again she shook the bright waves of her orange hair. "The only civility is what you read in the papers. All the lies about how the government runs. The Dail, the judiciary, and the lot. The rest, the *real* part is . . . mayhem. A kind of jungle and dicey. I wouldn't even know the rules."

"I thought that was part of the crack? You know, Bernie's game. Life as a sudsy, sardonic, upbeat ditty. You play it over enough, you get to know the words."

Bresnahan canted her head. Only a few days past she had thought the same.

"Life under a rock"—Ward looked out through a doorway into the dining room where the other guests were gathered; there, O'Suilleabhain with full smile and laughing eyes was charming a clutch of older women. *Or in the shadow of one*—"is living a lie."

Perhaps it was what had happened at the bridge, she thought. The anger she was feeling. But why should she be angry at Ward? He had done everything he could to save as many people as he could.

"Couldn't you hire in a manager, somebody to run the farm while you're in town? I read they're putting in a new airport somewhere out here. You could pop back and forth. The place would make a splendid weekend retreat." *Without* Rory O'Suilleabhain, he thought; even the self-consciously Irish spelling of O'Suilleabhain's last name was beginning to bother Ward.

It was possible surely, but, "Without a steady hand this place will never be the same. It will go down day by day. I'll run it a while and see how it goes."

"You mean the haying and milking, selling cows and buying calves?" Ward asked. "The barns, the house, the fences."

Their eyes clashed.

Somehow Ward didn't see Bresnahan doing much of that. Not now, not after who she had become in Dublin.

"I've done it before. And well. And I'll do it again."

Ward nodded. "I'm confident you will, but will you enjoy it?"

Bresnahan again looked away. "I'm not sure I want to be discussing this. Not now."

"What about yer mahn?"

Bresnahan said nothing; she had been waiting for that.

"You and he . . . got something going?"

Blood rose to her cheeks, and their eyes clashed again. "Not in the way you mean."

"Please—just look at him. If he isn't the cat that's et the big red canary, I don't know who is."

She shook her head. "That's just Rory. He's full of life, is all."

Among other vital substances, Ward thought. "Is he the fella you once told me about? The one you said you fell for as a little girl and he kept snubbing you time after time, year after year?"

Watching O'Suilleabhain working the room, making sure no potential voter escaped without feeling his winning smile, she said, "Yes," in a small, submissive voice that Ward did not care for at all.

"Why not now?"

Bresnahan paused to consider. "I think because of how I changed."

Or how Dublin has changed you, for which Ward himself was in large part responsible. The irony made Ward smile, but his eyes were bright and hard. "So?"

She hunched her broad, angular shoulders and returned her eyes to his. "I don't know. I'll just have to see."

"You know what I don't understand? I don't understand how everything could have changed so completely between us. Yes, your father has died. Yes, you're bereaved. Yes, his nibs has returned to claim his prize. But whatever happened to *us* in all of that?"

"I don't know myself."

"*Has* everything changed, or do you just need a"—Ward looked wildly around the large kitchen—"break?"

"I don't know that either."

"Then let me tell you this, since I've got to leave. Look at me." Ward reached for her hands, which were still wet from her kitchen work; he looked into her gray eyes that were no different from the storm sky that he could see through the windows beyond the sinks. "Nothing's changed for me. Or will. I should have told you this before, but I will always love you. No matter what you decide. I understand you must do what makes you happy. Nothing else will work in the long run." He thought he should kiss her one last time, but he didn't want to spoil her relationship with O'Suilleabhain, if that's what she should decide.

"No, wait"—Bresnahan tried to hold on to his hand, but the wetness let it slip away—"can't you just stay for a day or two? We can walk and talk and—I'll have some of the women ready a room."

Fitting on his gloves while staring in at O'Suilleabhain, Ward said, "I don't know how much more of the lord of the manor I can take. Isn't there an ounce of sorrow in the son of a—" Ward cleared his throat and tried to calm himself; he couldn't remember when he had felt so . . . total.

"It's different on a farm. Here you see life come and go on a regular basis. It hardens you."

So you think, thought Ward. "Rather like the Murder Squad."

Bresnahan tried to smile but couldn't. "Sure you can't stay?"

"*Can't* is the word. I've a collar to make."

She blinked twice, which gave Ward hope. "Really? In the *case*?"

Ward reached for his cane, then turned toward the door. "I'd love to tell you, really I would. But since you're *resigned*, I'm afraid you'll have to look for it in the papers. Or on the telly."

"Hold on, Hughie," McGarr called from the dining room, "I'll ride along with you." He was then heard to say to Bresnahan's mother, "I've got a colleague who's being released from hospital in the morning. He'll need somebody to drive him home."

"I hope he's well."

McGarr smiled. "Apart from a bullet in the chest."

Horror gripped the old woman's face, and her eyes sought her daughter's.

"Not to worry," McGarr went on. "He's been shot and blown up at least twice that I know of, but—can you believe?—he's not a cat at all but a dog."

In the car on the long drive back to Dublin, McGarr issued only one piece of advice. "Paddy Power was right. Women, they're not like men at all, and there's no explaining why. Just carry on. Things will work out they way they should, you'll see."

"What about Bernie and Liam?"

"There's been some talk of their retiring and setting up a little agency. Insurance work, missing persons, the odd criminal investigation."

"And yourself?"

"I might join them. *After*—" he was exonerated of all charges and named commissioner, he meant. "Get myself a little place down in the country," where he would never again allow himself to become fodder for public chat.

"Take O'Duffy himself," McGarr went on, as they hurtled up the N-7 in a Garda car with its blue dome light spinning. "Would he have believed, had he been told, that he would be assassinated by the likes of a Mossie Gladden? Would it have stopped him?"

A few miles passed.

"Will you be looking up Nell Power?" McGarr asked.

"Directly."

"Good lad. Be sure to give her my best."

Several miles later Ward asked, "Do you think the Eire Bank sale will go through regardless?"

McGarr nodded; there were certain things and people who were larger than life. An institution, like Eire Bank, was one; Harry Harney, who owned 3 percent, and his son, who had just been named taosieach, were two others.

EPILOGUE

Guilt Revealed

SITTING IN HIS Cooper outside the massive Eire Bank Financial Center in Dublin the next morning, McGarr said, "Don't be so impatient," to the young woman who was occupying the passenger seat. "You did me a favor, which I now return."

"But the main story is the funeral. My editor will be beside himself if I come back with nothing."

It was the day of the state funeral for Sean Dermot O'Duffy. A national day-of-mourning had been declared; heads of government from the European Community and other countries had arrived, and security precautions had "never been more complete," the radio had been saying. The American president was flying in. One newspaper even went so far as to claim, "Never in the modern history of Ireland has a man been more mourned than Taosieach O'Duffy, cut down in the prime of his political career as he was leading the nation into the twenty-first century." Harney's pages, of course.

"Ah, drink your coffee," McGarr advised the reporter from the *Times*. "Did I tell you I'll be named commissioner next week?"

Through thick lenses her hazel eyes regarded McGarr. "And *that*'s the story?"

"No, of course not. That's next week's story. You can leak it, if you're brave."

"Who shall I say is making you commissioner?"

"Why, Harry Harney, of course. Who else runs this country?"

Glumly she looked out the window of McGarr's Cooper toward the monumental stone entry of the Eire Bank complex; it looked like something extracted wholly from Mammon or New York.

"Forget about the funeral," McGarr chortled on, feeling very good indeed for the first time in almost a week. "Every"—he rejected Tom, Dick, and Harry—"Moira, Kathleen, and Fionnualla will be covering the funeral, while you'll have the scoop on why ever there was a funeral for the late, lamented taoiseach at all."

"But I *am* Moira, and my name'll be mud without a word to say about O'Duffy's burial."

"Can I ask you something?"

"Why not? I've got nothing but time while my career slips away."

"Why was O'Duffy in Sneem?"

"To attend Paddy Power's funeral."

"And had he not been in Sneem, would he most probably not be dead?"

She nodded.

"Now, we've just mentioned that Paddy Power had been killed *before* O'Duffy. Was there anybody else connected with the whole thing who also died in Sneem *before* O'Duffy?"

"Gretta Osbourne, the Eire Bank executive. But she was a suicide."

McGarr shook his head. Out of the corner of an eye he had seen Ward step out of the building; Ward then held the door for two other people, a man and a woman. McKeon and O'Shaughnessy were behind them, hands deep in topcoat pockets, their eyes scanning the street.

McGarr pointed toward the group on the expanse of the marble atrium. "Your murderers exactly."

"Shane Frost and Nell Power?" she asked incredulously.

"Well, Shane Frost. Nell Power is probably only an accessory."

"Didn't they just sign the papers to sell Eire Bank to some Japanese consortium?"

"I see you're up on current events."

"But—*why*? What reason would Shane Frost have had to have murdered Paddy Power?"

"*And* Gretta Osbourne."

She nodded.

"Four hundred and twenty-three million pounds of reasons, I'd hazard, though Nell's motives might have been more complex. Now''—McGarr reached into his jacket and pulled out a tape cassette—''I'm going to play this once and once only. Since it will be evidence in court, you're not to take notes.'' He plucked the pen from her hands. On her pad he wrote FROST, OSBOURNE, NELL POWER. ''What you hear you can say you learned from a source. It's real.'' And you can launch your career on it, he did not add. And owe one hell of a debt in the Favor Bank for some long time. ''Ready?''

McGarr slipped the tape into the player that hung under the dashboard of his Cooper and depressed the Fast Forward button until they heard the cuing beep. He then punched Play. While the voices spoke, he pointed from one name to another, indicating the speakers.

They heard Frost say, ''Yes? This is Shane Frost. Who's this?'' as though answering a phone. There was a pause, then, ''Ah, yes—'' Frost then tried twice to pronounce some Japanese name. ''. . . Anaki's secretary.'' Another pause. ''Can you speak more slowly, please?'' Yet another. ''Yes, both Gretta Osbourne and Nell Power are here. Yes, they will corroborate what we discussed this afternoon.'' With his hand obviously over the phone, Frost said, ''You first, Nell. These bloody Japs need everything signed in blood in triplicate. They probably won't sleep until they have every certificate back in Kyoto.''

Said Nell Power in her deep, postmenopausal voice, ''Hello—this is Nell Power. Acting as spokesperson for my family, I agree to the terms that you worked out with Shane this afternoon.''

The receiver was evidently then reached to Gretta Osbourne. In speech that was already slurred she said, ''But I tol' you, Shay'—I can't bring myself to divest so soon af'er—I mean, I—'' They heard a crash, like a telephone falling.

''Oh, Jesus,'' said Nell Power. ''She's faded off again.''

Frost took the phone. ''It's late and Ms. Osbourne is tired. Could she call you back in the morning?

''Thank you, and my best to Anaki.''

They then heard Nell Power ask, ''How much has she had?''

''Enough to kill a cow.''

''Overdoing things again, Shane?'' McGarr pointed the nib of the pen to indicate that it was Nell Power's voice. ''Like with Paddy's pills. Perhaps if the overdose hadn't been so much—''

''Enough of that. Jesus—who knows who might be listening? You can hear voices through the door. Put on your clothes now and help me get her back to her room.''

"It won't be easy. She's passed out."

"Has she a pulse?" Frost asked.

"Just, but dead slow. Look at the way she's sweating."

"Right. I'll get her back now. A little stroll, a few shakes, and she'll let me out. What about yourself?"

"I've stayed here enough to know how to get in and out."

"Unseen."

"Count on it."

McGarr switched off the tape. "But, of course, you can't count on human beings. Life is full of improbabilities. A man named Michael, the late-night porter at Parknasilla, happened to feel a draft in a hallway where he had delivered a bag. Checking the door, which was partially opened, he looked out and saw Nell Power—distinctly; he grew up with her—leaving the hotel down an avenue in the willows which surround the place. Hearing him push open the door, she turned, and the light fell across her face. 'Evening, Michael,' she said with aplomb. Michael asked her if she was coming in. No, she said, she was just leaving. "Superintendent Ward also has on record Kieran Coyne, a solicitor in Sneem, saying that when Paddy Power's note cards were dropped off at his office in Sneem, he looked outside the window to see who might have left them. He saw Shane Frost walking away. Later, after Coyne understood how central the cards were in the murder of Power, he approached Frost, who paid him to keep quiet."

"Blackmail," said the reporter.

McGarr nodded. "Superintendent Bernard Q. McKeon—do you know him?"

"By reputation only," she said, widening the large orbs of her eyes.

"McKeon interviewed Solicitor Coyne in Sneem only last night. This is Coyne's signed statement, which, again, I'll only let you read."

Through the thick glasses McGarr watched her eyes move down the page in a kind of long blink. When she looked up, she said, "How can I ever thank you?"

"We'll come to that, one of these days. Now—d'you care to ask Frost a few questions?"

She snatched away her pen and was out the door before McGarr could even reach for the handle. By the time he got to the group of six people, the young reporter was in full spate, asking pointed questions that Frost found distressing.

"*You*," he said to McGarr. "This is your doing, isn't it?"

"Me? How can it be me? Didn't you get me suspended?"

"I'll see you in court for slander, libel, and defamation."

McGarr turned to Nell Power. "I'd slap him, were I you. While you've got the chance."

Evening found McGarr ensconced in a large wing-back chair in the sitting room of his father-in-law's country retreat in Kildare, some thirty miles southwest of the city. In one hand was a snifter of ancient cognac, in the other a Cuban cigar. In front of him was a crackling wood fire. Madeleine was playing on the plush of an Oriental carpet before his feet. Noreen was reading the papers at one end of an expanse of sectional sofa that formed a spacious L in front of the hearth. Her parents were seated in the middle, her mother creweling, her father staring into the fire.

It was a large room with molded ceilings and tall, arched windows that filled the tasteful interior with golden evening light. And it was just the type of setting, McGarr imagined, that every Irishman would covet but few could afford. Out one of the windows he could see rolling emerald fields dotted with thoroughbred horses and a long avenue of beeches, their yellow leaves shimmering in the winter twilight. Out the others loomed the bluish conical peaks of the Wicklow Mountains.

But then Fitzhugh Frenche had gotten in on the explosion of property values that had accompanied the development boom of the seventies. Ground (zero) floor, as it were. While not a politician himself, he was a man of undoubtable taste, who was a pleasant companion and scrupulously avoided judging his peers. Thus his company had been courted by the likes of Paddy Power and Sean Dermot O'Duffy.

Now he sighed and asked, "Do you suppose that Mossie Gladden had planned to murder Sean Dermot all along?"

"Not consciously," said Noreen. "He was a man on the edge. Psychologically. He'd been firing at those *Sean* targets for some time, perhaps in an attempt to relieve his hatred of O'Duffy. And when Peter deprived him of the note cards, he just went to bits."

"A pity not privately," her father remarked into his cup. "He'd been a crank and a mossback all his public life, but who could have expected this."

Who exactly, thought McGarr.

"Are you having another, Peter?" Frenche stood, a tall, thin man dressed in twill and tweed. He wore riding boots on his feet and a cravat in a quiet Paisley pattern around his neck.

McGarr handed him his glass.

Returning it, Frenche said, "But I suppose the madness began with Shane Frost. Did I ever tell you that he approached me about investing in Eire Bank, back when it began? Painted a rosy picture. Said we'd make millions overnight."

Even his wife, Nuala, looked up from her stitching.

"I went to Paddy to make sure that what Shane was telling me was the truth, and when Paddy revealed that Shane would be manager of operations, he called it, whenever he was away, I decided to have none of it. Shane was even then too"—he paused, as though having to think for a moment—"nakedly avaricious for my money, and I let the opportunity pass."

As though to say, What insight but what a loss, Nuala's eyes widened before she returned her attention to her work. The Frenches had made themselves a very nice life on their wits.

"I can see him capable of anything with all those millions in the balance. What was the figure again?"

Said Noreen, "Four-hundred and twenty-three million pounds."

"My God, that's a lot of money," Nuala remarked.

"Not worth a farthing if you lose your good name," Frenche replied almost smugly. Resting an elbow on the mantel, he shook his head once. "Without that, you have nothing. No," he continued, "Paddy and Sean Dermot had the proper touch. When they were together in those early governments, they were an unbeatable combination."

In the quiet theft of billions, not mere millions, McGarr had read in Power's note cards. But he said nothing. Who was he to judge a man such as his father-in-law, who had made his fortune knowing men like Power and O'Duffy and had still preserved his good name, to say nothing of his life.

"Later, Paddy became a bit of a monk, I think, with his blather about two classes and who was to pay back the debt. All well and good with him sitting on his riches." He paused, and then: "Did I mention we received an invitation in the mail this morning?" Frenche waited until McGarr raised his eyes to him. "To a little party Harney's giving on the election eve. It's at the Shelbourne. All the proper *new* people will be there to celebrate his son's triumph."

McGarr blinked. Harney could not invite McGarr, but he could certainly invite his socially prominent in-laws. It was like a signal sent to say he would back the rehabilitation of McGarr's good name. "Are you going?"

"I'm wondering if I should." Fitzhugh Frenche was now a man in his middle seventies, but he was still wily in the ways of the political world. He was asking McGarr's permission.

"Of course we're going," said Nuala. "Somebody has to represent the family, and we wouldn't want anybody to think we're too good to influence such a man. Who knows what sway a quiet word might have with somebody like that? Perhaps all he's been seeking is approbation all along."

McGarr wondered exactly which family she had meant and, after their undoubted triumph at the polls, exactly whose approbation the Harneys would need.

But then it was a world that McGarr knew little about, although he was learning.